PENGUIN BOOKS

THE SEA HOUSE

'Subtle, sophisticated. A graceful novel that will linger in the memory long after you've finished it' *Time Out*

'Radiant, kind-hearted, well-made. As with all the best works of fiction, it lingers' *Guardian*

'There is much to admire in this tender, unorthodox novel' *Sunday Times*

'Evocative, multi-layered' *Red*

'The best that art can be: full of exploration, full of intuition, full of generosity – and full of love' Julie Myerson

'Passionate, moving and beautifully structured' *Daily Telegraph*

'Clever, fascinating. Freud perfectly evokes the atmosphere of a seasonal, seaside village and shows how it is possible to fall in love with a place where the river meets the sea' *Independent on Sunday*

'A beautifully crafted tale of jealousy and betrayal' *Eve*

Esther Freud was born in London in 1963. She trained as an actress before writing her first novel, *Hideous Kinky*, published in 1991. *Hideous Kinky* was shortlisted for the John Llewellyn Rhys Prize and was made into a feature film starring Kate Winslet. Penguin also publish *Peerless Flats* (1993), *Gaglow* (1997), *The Wild* (2000) and *The Sea House* (2003). In 1993, Esther Freud was chosen by *Granta* as one of the Best of Young British Novelists. Her novels have been translated into thirteen languages.

The Sea House

ESTHER FREUD

PENGUIN BOOKS

PENGUIN BOOKS

Published by the Penguin Group
Penguin Books Ltd, 80 Strand, London WC2R 0RL, England
Penguin Putnam Inc., 375 Hudson Street, New York, New York 10014, USA
Penguin Books Australia Ltd, 250 Camberwell Road, Camberwell, Victoria 3124, Australia
Penguin Books Canada Ltd, 10 Alcorn Avenue, Toronto, Ontario, Canada M4V 3B2
Penguin Books India (P) Ltd, 11 Community Centre, Panchsheel Park, New Delhi – 110 017, India
Penguin Books (NZ) Ltd, Cnr Rosedale and Airborne Roads, Albany, Auckland, New Zealand
Penguin Books (South Africa) (Pty) Ltd, 24 Sturdee Avenue, Rosebank 2196, South Africa

Penguin Books Ltd, Registered Offices: 80 Strand, London WC2R 0RL

www.penguin.com

Published in Hamish Hamilton 2003
Published in Penguin Books 2004
1

Grateful acknowledgement is made for permission to quote from the following song:
'Cry Me a River', words and music by Arthur Hamilton © 1953, 1955 Chappell & Co Inc.,
USA, Warner/Chappell Music Ltd, London W6 8BS. Reproduced by permission of
International Music Publications Ltd. All rights reserved.

Typeset by Rowland Phototypesetting Ltd, Bury St Edmunds, Suffolk
Printed in England by Clays Ltd, St Ives plc

For my father Lucian

I

Gertrude's house was pink. That stone-ground Suffolk pink that managed to be manly, and from the front it looked closed in and dark. Max waited for a moment before knocking on the door, wondering who had built on the ugly flat-roofed porch, and then a shadow appeared behind the mottled glass. 'Come in, COME IN.' Gertrude spoke too loudly, unable to accept Max couldn't hear, and he stood quite still in the open doorway and watched the exaggerated movements of her mouth.

Max Meyer was in Steerborough to see if he might do a painting of Marsh End. It was a mercy invitation, a probable last wish from his sister Kaethe, but all the same he was grateful to have been asked, grateful to Gertrude for remembering him and asking him to come. *Dear Max*, she'd written. *I know how much you must be suffering your loss, how much we, all of us, miss Kaethe, but would you consider coming up to do a picture of my house? I shall be here all summer. If you feel you can, please let me know and I'll explain about the trains.* The letter was dated May the 29th, and, to his surprise, within a week he had packed up his paints and brushes, a roll of canvas and some clothes, and set out for Liverpool Street Station to catch the first of three connecting trains.

Gertrude Jilks was a child psychoanalyst, a woman with no children of her own, but standing beside her on the doorstep was a small boy with white blond hair. Gertrude didn't introduce him, and he stood there looking at his feet, shuffling them back and forth inside his shoes. 'COME IN,' Gertrude said again, and Max remembered with a pang that she disliked him.

'Yes, thankyou, of course.' He lowered his head and together they stepped through into the main part of the house, a drawing-room with French windows open to the lawn, dark furniture falling into shadow after the shock of so much sun. Max walked across the wooden floor and out into the garden. The lawn was rich and wide, spreading out in lanes to one tall tree, a spruce pine with sand around its roots, and as Max walked out to it, his bag still in his hand, he imagined that behind the raised ridge of garden hedge the ground was shingle to the sea. 'Yes,' he said, 'I will paint the house, the back of the house certainly.' There was a bench cradled up against one wall and the windows of the upper floor were open to the sky.

'That is the house.' Gertrude had followed him. 'Alf,' she said, turning, 'you may go.' Alf was seven. He was the only child of her cleaning lady and Gertrude was paying for him to learn the piano. He didn't want piano lessons, but it didn't seem right just to give him money, so each Saturday at half past two he went to Miss Cheese for his lesson and then came back to give her his report. No, he wasn't making any progress, she explained to Max, but there was nothing else to do but carry on.

'I see.' Max nodded, although he wasn't at all sure that he did, and Gertrude picked up his bag and showed him to his room.

All his life Max had dreamt of houses. It didn't need a psychoanalyst, not even a children's one, to explain to him why that was so. But even before the move from Germany that was likely to have shaken him, he'd been dreaming of his home. He'd made a map of his house, Heiderose, when he was ten years old – the garden, the park, the big and little woods, the fields, the river and the road. This map had been one of the few things he'd taken with him when he left. The map, and an unwieldy wooden table he'd carved from one of the estate trees himself. Why he'd taken the table he still didn't know, when he'd fully expected to return, but he'd sealed his lifetime's correspondence up into its one deep drawer and had it shipped ahead to England. Max had the table, the letters in their drawer, but not the map, and it occurred to him he might even with his eyes closed, now in 1953, sit down and draw it from memory.

Houses, walls, villages and roads. Since the start of Kaethe's illness his dreams were overrun. He'd be travelling, always at the wheel of some majestic car, when he'd take a turning and find a hidden piece of land. Sometimes it was a cluster of houses, high up, their pathways dropping to the sea. Or he would come round a bend, out into the open, and find white railings, a square in a village that had not been there before. But what he never found was the actual house he dreamt of in the day. It was always just around the corner, out of his view, and sometimes his search was like a tunnel, leading only to one oval patch of sky. Now he dreamt of Gertrude's house, its rich, dense lawn, and the pine tree so straight and feathery, a lookout over the sea. He'd start with that, he thought, it was thin enough to stand right in the foreground of the painting and not obscure the view.

2

Someone was photographing Lily's cottage from the road. The road was so narrow at that corner of the Green that the man had backed on to the grass and was squatting down in an attempt to fit it into the frame. Lily had rented the cottage through an agency and the woman had given her a hand-drawn map with the key. The map was simple – one long, narrow road running along a river to the sea which then turned a corner on to a triangular green.

'Is this Fern Cottage?' she asked, just to be sure, and the photographer looked at his plan of the village, turning it upside down to catch the name. Lily assumed he was taking photographs for the agency so that in future people could see what the cottage looked like from outside.

'Yes,' he called to her, 'that's right,' and then, with the key half in the lock, she heard the whirr of the shutter and turned towards him, startled, as he took three quick pictures of her standing outside the house.

'I know mine could do with a lick of paint . . .' An old lady in a dressing-gown was calling to him from across the lane. 'But I don't want to be left out.'

The photographer smiled. 'Don't worry yourself, Ethel, I'm getting to you next.'

Ethel stood and watched him. She had a round face with dimples in her cheeks and chin, and her hair was white and curling, like a halo round her head. She rested her hands on the slats of the front gate, her face watchful as the camera swept over her house, the walls peeling, the window-frames flecked with splintering wood.

'Will I get a smile?' the photographer asked her, and she tilted her head and beamed into the lens.

Lily's cottage was decorated in every shade of brown. Brown carpet, pale brown walls, a sofa and two chairs in clove and amber stripes. Even the curtains had clusters of hazel and beige flowers. There was a garden, shared between her cottage and the next, where one large tree stretched roundly out over the lawn. Someone's washing flapped on the line. A towel and two pairs of children's leggings, one yellow and one pink. Upstairs there was a large bedroom, with a window that overlooked the Green, and there on the horizon, strangely high like a child's drawing, sat a deep blue stripe of sea. Lily leant there on the window ledge and let her eyes rest on the thin line that separated the sky from the sea. All the tension of the drive seeped from her body and she closed her eyes against the work she had to do. There were twin beds, their ends stretching towards her, their bedspreads thrown over a mound of blankets, and just for a moment Lily lay down, feeling the rough wool as she edged in under the quilt, the feathers of the pillow tickling her ear.

She was woken by a sharp cry, and the shudder of something slammed into a wall. She started up, not knowing where she was.

'Don't!' It was a man's voice, low and threatening. 'Leave it!' And then the wardrobe in the alcove rattled, and she heard the thud of steps stumbling downstairs. Lily rushed to the window expecting to see a fight burst through the front door, but there was no one there except for two lone girls swinging from the parallel bars of the slide.

Lily set out her work on the small, square sitting-room table, covered with its laminated cloth. She let her hands lie against the sticky texture, the cool plastic of its chequered top, wondering what Nick would do if he was in this room. Would he be able to settle down so comfortably, think about architecture when surrounded by so much brown? And then she remembered that she'd promised to call him, to say that she'd arrived in Steerborough safely. First she hauled her computer out of the car, arranged her papers and her books around it, and, scooping her hand into a dusty carrier bag, she prised out a handful of Lehmann's letters and set them on the table in a little time-worn pile. Letters from the architect Klaus Lehmann, written over twenty years, and collected by his wife. Where are *her* letters? Lily thought, and she went outside to find a phone.

In the phone box, which was still red and presumably protected, there was a message under a stone. *Call 999. Wait by the wall . . .* The writing was hurried and sloping, but after the first line the slopes got steeper and the writing turned into a waterfall of waves. She fingered this scrap of paper and waited for Nick to pick up his phone. 'You know what to do,' his message cut in, but instead of speaking she pressed her finger against the connection and with a little satisfying click she cut him off.

Lily stood for a long time in the phone box, her nose pressed against the pane. She knew it was a mistake not to have left a message and now she didn't have any more change. She pushed the heavy door and stepped out on to the Green. The sea was rolling just behind the skyline, calling her, magnetic in its roar. It's my first day, she told herself. I need to get my bearings – And she stumbled off along a pitted lane. Below the border of its brambles lay a flat slow river, crossed by a wooden bridge, and then the path struck upwards through white dunes. Lily walked between sharp grasses, her feet sinking into sand. The closer she got the more it drew her until, as she raced and struggled up the last bank, her heart was knocking at her chest. And there it was. Vast and blue and breathless, stretching to the edges of the world. Wind whipped into her ears, blowing clear air into her eyes and nose. Sand sprayed in gritty showers, scudding along in gusts, and Lily pulled her jacket round her and ran down to the shore. It was calmer here, and she crouched to get out of the wind, fingering the wet sand for stones and tiny transparent shells that slipped on to her fingertips like pads. Lily walked along the beach until she came to the black mouth of

6

an estuary. At what moment does fresh water become salt? she wondered, watching as a sturdy motor boat chugged in, and she followed a path that ran above the river, on and on, until she'd left the village behind.

When she arrived back, it was too late to start work. The house was cold and shadowy and the brown lampshades gave off a dismal glow. She went outside to the small garden to look for the bunker for Fern Cottage coal. It was spitting with the first warnings of rain, and she glanced at the lighted windows of the adjoining house and wondered if they knew their washing was still out. When Lily lifted up the tin slat of the bunker, coal flooded out, surrounding her shoes. She knelt down and shovelled it up into the scuttle, feeling for the black lumps around her in the dark. The cottage was extraordinarily well stocked for such a tiny place. In the cupboard under the stairs – the items listed on a label – there was newspaper for kindling, a small pile of wood, and even a box of matches for the city tenants who might come unprepared. Lily held a sheet of paper over the mouth of the fire and waited for it to catch. It was warmer already, she thought, swaying on her heels, tired from the shock of so much air, and then with a roar the paper caught fire, leaping away from her and dancing into the room. She beat at it with a poker, squashing it back into the grate, but even after it was smothered, tiny blackened twirls of charcoal floated in the air.

Lily curled up on the sofa, eyeing the pile of letters she had so optimistically arranged. Eventually guilt overwhelmed her and she went and lifted the top one off the pile and, bringing it back to her nest by the fire, she prised it out of its envelope. The envelope was thin and dusty but inside it was lined with purple tissue, fine as silk. This splash of colour woke her a little and she sat up and began to read.

Meine Liebe . . . The letters were in German. She'd known they would be, but it still gave her a shock. *My dear, my darling?* She glanced to the end of the letter. *Yours, for ever, L.*

She'd been given these letters by a relative of Klaus Lehmann who lived in North London, in a flat in Belsize Park. She'd had the inspired idea of looking in the telephone directory and had found this man on only the second call. 'Are you sure you don't want me to make copies?' Lily asked, when he offered her the letters, packed in layers into an ancient plastic bag. But the man had simply opened the carrier bag and peered inside. 'No,' he said, 'you look at them. They're probably of no interest to anyone. And if they are . . .'

'Yes?' Lily urged him on.

'You could hand them on to the Architectural Association. That's it.' He began to close the door.

'Thankyou.' She wanted to keep him talking. 'And did you know him? I mean . . .' She was calculating on her fingers, was he old enough, it was impossible to tell, to be Klaus Lehmann's son?

'I assume you can read German?' he asked instead.

'I can. Yes.'

'Good.' And with a nod, he shut the door.

Folded into this first letter, dated 1931, was a map of a rectangular room. *I'm here in Frankfurt waiting for the plans to be approved, and as always there are delays.* Lehmann's writing was fine and fluid, black ink thinning to a scratch as he sped over the loops of Ks and Ls. *Are you aware, my sweetheart, how much of our married life I may have to be away? Although of course as my reputation soars I will be able to demand they accommodate my wife. But there is one benefit. I've seen some quite delightful shoes, and cheaper than you'd ever be likely to find at home. Shall I buy them? I hope you'll say yes as I've already reserved two pairs in your size. Write immediately and tell me that I should.*

Lily found that she was smiling. Lehmann, with his sharp lines and model buildings, with nothing on his mind but shoes. *There is nothing interesting about this room*, he went on. *Except that there is an empty table-top on which your photograph can sit. So, what can you see from your place here? A wooden bed, not so comfortable, an unusually hideous chair, and one wide window with tiny panes of glass.* Lily crept from the sofa to the floor and lay with one side scorched by the fire. *If only you were really here, my angel, but then you would be bored, and I should feel worse than I already do. Your writing is becoming more and more beautiful, did you know?*

Lily sat up with a start. She'd forgotten to call Nick. She felt in her various pockets, hoping to find change, and found instead the scrap of paper from the phone box. *Call 999, wait by the wall.* Lily stared at it hard to see if there was any other sense in it, but once again there was only the disintegration of a line of waves. She pulled the curtain and cupped her hand against the glass. It was black outside, without a single street light, only the glow from the red pillar of the phone box shining out like the north star. I'll wait until the morning, she decided, and she went upstairs to make the bed.

3

'Will you start soon?' Gertrude asked a week later over breakfast when Max had still done nothing but pace and measure the space from the French windows to the tree.

'Yes,' he said, 'yes.' And then, looking up, he asked, 'Is there a hurry?'

He did want to start, but each morning he woke with a restlessness that could only be eased by looking at every other Steerborough house. He couldn't view them openly, but had to pretend to be simply passing on his way. It was the sin of covetousness, he decided, that made him snoop like a spy. So each morning he set off on some errand and, after winding up and down the one long road, he'd veer off after a chimney stack, just glimpsed through the trees. But the truth was he was afraid of starting. It was so long since he'd painted anything at all. And his reputation for being an amateur of promise was based on a period of intensity that had ended almost fifteen years before. There had been one good picture of Kaethe, which hung in their London hallway for everyone to see, and, out of surprise, he felt, more than admiration, visitors stood back to comment on it when they first came in. There had been other pictures, Helga mostly, in the years they'd been engaged, but the more he'd tried to paint her the more elusive the contours of her face had become, so that in his last attempt, he'd ended up with a bench, a branch of lilac, and nothing but a shadowy attempt at her hair.

Max spread paper over Gertrude's oval table and started to jot in all the houses he had seen. He started with his favourite, a long, red-roofed cottage at the top of the Green, and jumped about the village, putting in the houses as they sprang to mind – the church, the village hall – and then he remembered a strange lopsided building, a glass and wood experiment on the corner of Mill Lane. What is that place? he'd wanted to ask Gertrude, but he'd become so used to silence that the words died in his head. Instead he drew a miniature version of the house. An arched front door, double-height windows and a steepled roof with a high flat terrace on one side. There was a white picket fence around the terrace and Max imagined the owners climbing up there at night to listen to the sea.

With his pen still in his hand he wandered outside.

'Were you thinking of using water colour?' Gertrude was lying in a deckchair reading a pamphlet on the phobias of the very young. Max imagined she was longing to analyse him, make a diagnosis on why he was unable to begin.

'No,' he said. 'Oils.'

The whole scene was already a water colour, with no need for him to paint it in. He wondered if this eastern-most coast of England could be painted in oils, and if it was attempted, would it be possible to retain the huge translucence of the sky? Even on a cloudy day, the dome was so immense that somewhere a beam of sun could usually escape the clouds and mark a strip of light across the ground. It turned the grass unearthly green, the puddles Alpine blue, and it made Max think of the studies he had made of Italian church ceilings, the fat cherubs, the fingers of God sparking through.

Max walked away from Gertrude and surveyed the scene – the house, the deckchair, the rug on her knee. And a sudden fear gripped him and he had to lean against the tree.

'Gertrude' – the words, more than usual, made a hollow echo in his head – 'was it Kaethe's idea that you ask me to come?'

Gertrude looked at him for a moment. Of course. Of course it was Kaethe who'd asked her, made her promise right before the end.

'No,' she said, hoping it would help him. She smiled. 'It was all my own plan.'

⋆   ⋆   ⋆

Three days later Max decided to go home. He needed materials, he said, materials he didn't have. It was almost a relief to get on the little train that left from Steerborough, to stop looking and searching, and finally allow himself to relax. The train rumbled across a common, rattled over the river bridge. Sometimes the view was hidden by gorse thickets and sometimes you could see over marshland to the sea. Everywhere there was a smell of sweetness, a cloying honey scent he couldn't trace. He eased the window lower and leant out. There was a head in the next window, bright blond and pushed out dangerously far.

'Hello, Alf,' Max shouted. He saw that the tufts of the boy's hair were pasted down and even the rush of air made by the train had not been able to dislodge them. 'Where are you off to, then?' he called, but just then the train began to slow. There was no sign of a station, but all the same they came to a halt. Alf leaned out as far as he could go and Max, following his gaze along the short length of the train, saw the driver climb down from his cab. He strode over to a thicket of small trees and, after disappearing for some moments, reappeared with a rabbit, grey-brown, dangling from its ears. It gave a desultory kick, as if it knew there was no hope. Soon after, the train started again and, as it chugged evenly along, Max thought of the animal, dying, its eyes milky with fear.

Alf sat across from him now, tapping his toe against the floor. He had a music case in one hand and his knees looked as if they had been scrubbed. Alf didn't move when the train stopped at Great Wraxham, even when the door of their carriage was tugged open, and a tall thin woman reached in to lure Alf out.

'Come along,' she said, 'or we'll be late for our recital.' And with one strong hand she lifted him out.

Max travelled on to Ipswich and changed on to the London train. He drew in a deep breath as they turned inland from the sea, leaving behind the swathes of sailing boats nestled into the curve of the estuary, their sails like white handkerchiefs, a baby armada ready to invade, and he thought of Liverpool Street Station and that first choking smell of London that you grew accustomed to within a minute and a half.

Max stood in his narrow hallway, staring up at the painting of his sister, elongated, superior, hung too high above the curve of the stairs. He'd forgotten what it would be like to come home to a house without her, not a thing touched in the days that he'd been gone. No one to tell him to comb his hair, smooth his unruly eyebrows, buy new laces for his shoes. He sat down on the bottom step and wondered if he had a right to be there, if there was anything in this house that hadn't been arranged by her, and then he remembered his table and he went upstairs to the spare bedroom. The wood was oak, wide-grained and varnished, and when he slid the drawer open, he saw his letters, tied with a broad red band.

He had thirty-seven prized and valuable letters written to him by the artist Cuthbert Henry. He'd had to pay him for them, that was true, but over the years of their correspondence a friendship had developed that went further than the fee. It had been an idea of his father, after visiting an exhibition of Henry's in 1927, that instead of formal art training Max could send his pictures to London, and in return for payment Henry would give his valuable instruction on how each one could be improved. Max dutifully sent off three drawings, pen and ink sketches, views mostly from the windows of his house, and with them went his list of questions. Interminable, he realized now. He'd poured out all his misgivings, his terrors, his absurdly optimistic fears, and waited with unparalleled expectations for the reply.

Henry was a stern teacher. *No*, he remarked often, or, more rarely, *Quite good*. And once, infuriated, *How am I meant to comment on something that is impossible to see?* He enclosed some good quality paper and reprimanded Max for using sub-standard materials for what, as far as anybody knew, might turn out to be worthwhile.

Some deafness? he responded when Max confided in him. What ever made you think you need your ears to paint?

The letters were arranged by order of their date and now he prised open the knot of the old ribbon and lifted the top one out.

Dear Meyer,

You can only get to understand things by drawing them. If you give up drawing something because you don't understand it, then you never will understand it. And if you wait until you can draw perfectly, then you will have to wait until you are dead.

Max smiled at the familiar stern tone of voice. He wished he had his sketches now, so he could see what this particular fault referred to, but they'd been left behind at Heiderose, left in his old nursery cupboard to rot.

There is always something fresh to learn. You must know the saying of one great artist at the age of eighty. 'All I did before thirty was worthless, at the age of sixty I began to understand the forms of plants and animals, now at the age of eighty I'm really beginning to draw and at ninety I shall draw well. If I live to be a hundred, every line and every dot will have a meaning.'

Max sat back stiffly on his heels. He felt old already and he was barely forty-two. He leafed through the remaining letters, feeling their papery advice like braille, fingering one and then another and setting them to one side. Images of his father swam up through his hands, so pleased he'd found a way of keeping his poor deaf son at home. Each letter, each word of praise from Henry, was one more reason why he'd never have to stray. He could be a gentleman painter at Heiderose for the rest of his days. Max opened the drawer further and felt to the back with his hand. He'd had a sudden hope that his childish map might still be lying there. His map, and the Renoir his father had stowed away for him above the rim. But his fingers only tapped at wood, the four perfect corners, grooved and joined together with much careful mathematics, patience and the lessons of his father's skill.

4

Lily slept late the next morning, and when she woke the sun was streaming into the room. As soon as she stretched, she remembered Nick and how anxious he would be she hadn't rung. Quickly she pulled on her clothes and ran straight across to the phone box. The first thing she noticed, even as she dialled, was that the note had been replaced. It was an identical scrap of white lined paper, torn with the same jagged edges around the words. Lily scrutinized it hard, to try and fathom it, but just then Nick answered.

'I'm so sorry,' she babbled, frightened somehow that she was about to be told off, but he was busy, already working at his desk.

'Is it raining there?' he asked, and she imagined him tipping back his chair. 'It's pissing it down here.'

'It's heaven' – Lily felt her excitement bursting up – 'just being in his village. You know, Lehmann, in the village where he –'

But at that moment Nick's other line started ringing and he transferred his attention to it without cutting her off. 'Yes, but you don't understand, those tiles won't last outside. Yes, I know they look pretty, but one hard winter and they'll start to crack . . .'

Lily watched her money slowly trickling down. 'Sorry,' he said when eventually he was back.

'It's beautiful here, full of sky. I wish –'

His assistant was talking to him now, and then Nick started laughing when really, Lily felt, he should be annoyed. 'Tell them to –'

'I'd better go,' she cut in coldly.

Nick tried to keep her, but it was too late. 'Was the motorway all right?'

'What? Oh, yes . . . Look, I'll call another time.' And, although she knew that she was being childish, she put down the phone.

It must have rained right through the night. Everything smelt of earth and, just as she was about to step back into her cottage, Lily found herself veering off along a lane. It was an unmade track that led towards the river with hedges full of raindrops glittering like diamonds on twigs, and spiders' webs as strong as nylon, catching tiny drops of wet.

If I keep walking, she thought, watching the sun glint off puddles, I might even come across Lehmann's house. She didn't have any idea, any directions, but imagined it would be a modern masterpiece, huge slants of glass shooting up into the sky.

The track was mostly mud now, with two ridged lanes of puddles, beaded and looped on either side of a mounded bank of grass. Lily walked on slowly downwards until she saw the estuary, flat and full of sky. There were boats moored up against a row of wooden jetties and all along were signs to warn you to step on only at your own risk. Lily looked out along the river, wondering whether to jump down on to the mud flats or not, and then, half turning, she caught sight of a house, edged into the turning of the lane. It was a brick house, tall and narrow, with one long window on either side of the front door. Before it, like a garden fence, was a row of sand bags piled like piglets three feet high. Lily walked past the house, glancing as she went into its tall bright windows and then, finding the path led nowhere, she turned and walked back. There were no curtains in the windows and her reflection bounced back at her. But she noticed, before politeness forced her to look away, a chalk line between the window and the door. The line was high, just above the handle and there was a date scrawled, 1953.

Just then she heard the low toll of the church clock. She stopped to listen, counting the seagulls sitting on a row of wooden posts, and on the last chime, as if by agreement, they all swooped up and, swirling in formation, arced away. The chimes of the clock reminded her she would have to go back inside. She would have to go in, and sit down at the table. Make a start on her work. If she didn't start soon she'd never finish her assignment by the end of term. She should be making notes on Lehmann's use of light and space. Reading through his letters, finding clues and pointers to the development of his work.

Initially she'd chosen Lehmann because it was a building of his in North London, a dilapidated granite and glass block, that Nick had taken her to admire the first evening that they'd met. She'd been giving him a lift home from a party and he'd made her take a detour, surprising her with his confidence and the way he put his hand on her shoulder as if to steer her to the right. He'd made her pull up for a moment so they could admire the balconies, the curve of the windows, the flash of metal against a panelling of wood. They got out of the car together and stood in a light rain and it seemed as if by Nick's very own order every light in every window flickered on. Yes, she saw then, it was beautiful, a building she'd dismissed until that moment as a huge grey mushroom billowing out above a concrete pond, but for Nick it seemed enough that she had noticed it.

'You'd be surprised,' he said, 'how many people never use their eyes.' As if to thank her for being observant, for noticing the things he loved, he'd drawn her towards him and kissed her very gently on the mouth.

My dear Elsa ... Lily ran her fingers over the paper's surface, untouched, she imagined, since 1931. *Here in Palestine my first place of work is by the beach amongst the ruins of an ancient town. As you have asked about it, I shall explain how we could live here. By the sea, or in the mountains, or in the Jordan valley, hundreds of metres below sea level in a tropical climate. But I believe one day we will be able to live* surrounded by farmers or within a religious community. Servants could be Jewish or Christian or Arabs, the latter being the most likely. Concerning the girlfriends you are planning to bring, does that mean I have to marry them as well? And is that why you asked about polygamy? And who is it, and how many? You know I am for very many children and several wives, but that isn't very common any more, not since the times of the patriarchs. But seriously I do hope that we'll live so simply and hospitably that there will always be room for several guests.

Lily stopped reading for a moment to watch Ethel amble through her gate and out on to the lane. She had her dressing-gown on, wrapped snugly round her, and, nodding sociably to anyone she saw, she set off across the Green.

But, my darling, would you have another look at the parts of my letter that are alien to you and ask me to explain? It would be very painful if we were to always speak two different languages, the one incomprehensible to the other. I can't believe that our languages really are that far apart. Imagine we were married, and we will be SOON, and then, because this is your concern, could you really believe that being married to me would diminish you, and that I would somehow become someone else? There is only one kind of danger, and that is that I might love you too much.

Lily folded the letter back into its square. If only telephones had never been invented. She could have written to Nick as soon as she arrived, keeping the image she preferred of him steady in her mind, and not had it rudely interrupted by his tone of voice. He might have written back to her by return of post, telling her the details of his day, pleading with her not to stay away too long, and she'd never know he'd let himself be interrupted countless times by questions about tiles.

5

'You're back already?' Gertrude was not displeased to see him, only a little surprised. 'You must be tired with so much travelling in one day.' She smiled at Max to show she wasn't cross and went into the kitchen to see if there was still some food that might be heated up. 'Did you get the things you needed?' she called through, swirling the pale circles of a celery soup, but then she remembered he needed her lips to hear her, so she went and stood in the door. Max had a slim leather briefcase that might just possibly contain paints, and as she watched he surreptitiously opened it and peered inside. 'Shall I bring bread?' Gertrude asked instead, and Max jumped, startled, as if by the vibrations of her voice.

'This Saturday' – Gertrude sat opposite him as he ate – 'and I hope you'll still be here, I've invited some people to have supper with us.'

'Oh?' Max felt a coil of dread unfurling in his gut.

'You may even know them?' Gertrude smiled.

Through the soup Max could taste the meaty silver polish of the spoon. 'It's most unlikely, I hardly –'

'Klaus Lehmann, the architect?' Gertrude spoke over him. 'I thought maybe you must have come across him in Hamburg . . . before . . . might have mixed in the same circles.'

'I knew of him, of course . . .'

'Well, they have a house here. He has a rather beautiful wife – well, known to have been a great beauty, although she must be forty by now.' Gertrude waved a finger. 'But no German-speaking, do you promise, or I'll feel horribly left out.'

'Of course.' Max scooped the last thick spoonful, wincing as he attempted to avoid the polish of its shine. 'Thankyou so much.'

Had she not noticed? Not a word of German had escaped his lips since 1941. He took his bowl through to the kitchen and very thoroughly washed it out.

'So, do you have what you need now?' It wasn't that Gertrude minded Max being in the house, but it was a surprise to her, the proximity of this other person, when she was used to spending so much of her time alone.

'Yes.' Max hoped he was being truthful. 'There's nothing I need in London now.'

As soon as Max was in his room he slid his hand into the leather briefcase and drew out the letters, the envelopes discarded, the pages of the text pressed flat.

The fault of the drawing is your old fault. It is too much like a map, and not like a solid chair in a solid room with a solid coal scuttle. There are only two classes of draughtsman. The bad ones who have nothing to say and the good ones who have something to say. Say something and make things exist.

Max fell asleep and immediately dreamt of houses. A whole village with all the living-rooms outside. The tables, the chairs, the coal scuttles, the people peeling their potatoes, washing up. Men and women, without the secret panels of their walls, playing cards, cooking and working, talking to the others as they passed by. And what saddened him most about this village was that it was right across the road. It was in London, opposite his and Kaethe's house, and if only he'd known, if only he'd known about it, he wouldn't have had to live these last six months alone.

Gertrude wanted to surprise her guests with European food. She bicycled to Eastonknoll and left her bike outside the library. She was worried that since the war anything with a mention of the enemy would have been ousted from the library's stock, but there was one book, dark red and tall, that must have been overlooked.

Das Beste aus aller Welt, it was called. She assumed this meant that this food, this German food, was the Best in the World, and then, realizing how strong her prejudice still was, accepted it might very well be a collection of the world's best recipes. She leafed through it, each page as she turned it, letting out a damp and musty smell. During the war, working alongside Kaethe, she'd picked up a little German, but not, it turned out now, enough to make a meal. Potato, she recognized, over again, and chicken, but nothing of the subtleties she hoped lay in between.

Eventually she gave up and slid it back, and as she did so a small green book fell down into her hands. This book was in English, but had recipes from Czechoslovakia, Germany and Poland. The book fell open on a page for goulash, with a recipe on either side, and not for the first time Gertrude told herself how in this small town of Eastonknoll you really could get anything at all. Goulash. Even the word was bound to give the evening an exotic ring. When she'd eaten at the Lehmanns', they'd served eel that Lehmann had smoked in his outhouse himself, and afterwards some rice, which was delicious but had only the faintest hint of a taste. Risotto, Elsa had said it was, but she couldn't tell from Elsa Lehmann's inscrutable mask of beauty whether this savoury rice pudding was for her benefit or not.

Gertrude started cooking early. The first of the two recipes was Polish, with an extensive list of ingredients including sauerkraut and vodka, and the second was Hungarian with nothing more unusual than paprika sprinkled on the meat. But even so, the search for paprika had taken most of a day, and, having found it in the kitchen of an army widow, she knew she'd better just begin. As she browned the meat, she read the asterisked note at the bottom of the page. 'The word goulash means herdsman, and his method of cooking is ideally suited to preparing food while looking after cattle or sheep.'

'Hmm.' Gertrude smiled. 'For cattle I shall substitute pudding.'

And not wanting to be seen to patronize her guests by serving them with only foreign food, she made an apple upside-down cake, which might be eaten with milk instead of cream.

Max spread a sheet of paper over the table, and closed his eyes to see if he could conjure up from memory all the houses running down Steerborough's one street. There was the old crooked house, the beams slanting to one side, and the thatched cottage with its moss-green roof tucked in beside a terrace of flint and brick houses, the arched doorways of which led through to gardens at the back. Max made a sketch of the Tea Room, the low red roof draped over a row of dormer windows like a currant-coloured cake, and the tiny window of the maid's room poking out from under the eaves. Something startled him, knocking at his leg, and Alf appeared from under the table, sliding his small body up on to a chair.

'Where do you live, Alf?'

The boy peered over the table at his map. He trailed his finger down The Street, along the edge of the Green, round to the mouth of the estuary and back along the marshes. Max remembered a little collection of wooden houses, white-painted and on stilts. Alf's thumb tacked back to the river, stopping by the bank from which the ferry sailed. He knew from Gertrude that before the war there had been a pontoon ferry that could take anything across. There was a sign still there with the prices written on it, just legible if you peered close. *For each sheep, lamb, goat, pig – 2d.* But the residents of Steerborough, and those at Eastonknoll, were convinced the ferry might be useful to the Germans, and so it was taken down and dismantled in the first weeks of the war, and now just like in all the years of the last century, and the ones before it, a ferry man in a small wooden boat waited to row you across. He pushed out fast into the current to a point midway between each bank, and then with a guiding oar he let the river bring the boat back in. Alf licked his finger and trailed it once more over the page, to show, Max imagined, how the family had moved.

'First you were on the riverbank?' he suggested, and Alf nodded. 'And then?'

In the dip of a hollow, in the last stretch of green before the sea, Alf made a tiny dot.

Max screwed up his eyes to see it. 'You moved down here?' The new family home was conveniently placed below the pub. If you wanted, you could stagger through the door and roll from there into your own house.

The door swung open and Alf's mother came in with a stack of linen.

Guilty at his thoughts, Max turned to her. 'Alf has just been showing me where you live.'

Mrs Wynwell looked surprised. 'Yes,' she said. 'My Harry said we'd better move if we didn't want to be washed away to sea, so we moved the house, bricks, beams and all, but then, well, he was taken anyway.' The corners of her mouth turned down, and she pushed her chin up as if to tilt her tears back in. 'A wave tipped up his boat.' There was a silence in which they all stared through the walls. 'And now' – Mrs Wynwell shook her head – 'Alf's learning the piano.'

'Yes.' Max placed a hand on the boy's head, and they stood like that until, with a sudden rush of energy, Mrs Wynwell began beating the curtains with a broom.

Gertrude put the cake into the oven. The goulash had been simmering for over an hour and the liquid was starting to turn a thick and syrupy brown. The onion had melted into the stew and even the paprika, though rather old, was giving off a quite distinctive smell. Mrs Wynwell came in, wrinkling her nose. 'So what are you stirring up for them, Mrs J?' she asked, and when Gertrude described the cubed beef and the onion, the tablespoon of paprika stirred into the sauce, Mrs Wynwell's face widened in alarm and her eyes seemed to swim out to the sides. 'But they're all Jews, they're not going to want to eat meat!'

'Why ever not?' Gertrude felt herself flush with indignation. She went to the French windows and looked out. Max had set up a rough workbench with two chairs and a length of plywood, and he was stretching a canvas over a pale wood frame. He'd been cutting and banging and measuring all afternoon. So finally, she thought, he'll be ready to begin.

'Well . . .' Mrs Wynwell sounded sure. 'They're not allowed to kill a living thing, not even a fly. It's why they put no fight up . . . you know, in the war.'

'No!' Gertrude spun round. 'That's not it at all. Hindus, you're thinking of, or Jains.' She found that she was shouting. 'And what could they have done? You went to the cinema. You saw the newsreel. Rows and rows of them, just skin and bone.'

'Oh, Mrs J, I'm sorry. I thought I was being a help.' And with a small affronted nod she went off to polish the glass in the front door.

Gertrude was trembling, the image of those striped figures etched in her mind, and she wondered if Hitler had consulted a psychologist, or if he had simply known that if you put a person in pyjamas you turned them into children and had them doubly in your power.

6

Dear Nick, Lily wrote, *I'm afraid the only phone box in the village is broken.* She bit her lip guiltily and turned the postcard over to gaze into the gaudy scene. Sunset on the Suffolk coast. The picture must have been taken from a boat. The sea, the shore, the sky, all turned to molten gold. She hoped to make him smile with it, but even more, to galvanize him into driving up. *Working hard, making good progress*, she wrote. *Very quiet and peaceful. Average age here – 82. Average colour – beige.* She didn't know why she was telling him this if she wanted him to come. Nick was allergic to anything dreary. It made him feel his life was running out. She imagined him in the Steerborough tea shop where the old women outnumbered the men by three to one. *We could hire bikes* – she felt optimistic suddenly – *and do an architectural Lehmann tour. Write to me? Please. Love, Lily, XX*

Lily looked towards the window, unsure whether to risk Eastonknoll without her jacket or not, when she saw two heads bobbing about below the sill. She tiptoed nearer and glanced out. The two girls from next door were squatting in her front garden.

'Hello.' She tapped on the glass. They didn't look up. They were lining up a row of pebbles, setting them up like sentries on the low wall. As she watched, the elder girl took a large stone and tried to spin it through the barricades. Lily looked down on their bent heads, the sandy partings of their hair, the dusty plaits tied with elastic bands. 'Hello,' she said, opening a window, and two sets of pale blue eyes turned up towards her. 'Would either of you like a biscuit?' Lily was intending to pass the biscuits out through the open window, but as she rummaged in the bread bin the door behind her opened and the girls trooped in. They stood behind her quietly, waiting, and when she brought out her half-eaten packet of chocolate digestives, they took one each, seriously, and without a word went into the sitting-room and sat down.

Lily glanced at her watch. It was nearly twelve now and if she was going to go to Eastonknoll the last ferry before lunch would be about to push out into the tide. She took a biscuit herself and stood in the doorway, watching them eat.

'Do you like living here?' she asked and, still munching, both girls nodded their heads.

'Yes,' they mumbled, their mouths full, and then in the ensuing silence all three watched as a fine film of crumbs rained down on to the floor.

Lily tried again. 'How old are you two, then?'

The oldest one gulped down the last of her biscuit. 'I'm seven. I'm Em' – she pointed to herself – 'and Arrie's five.' Arrie looked straight at Lily and quite unexpectedly smiled. She had a heart-shaped face and a soft layer of plumpness that made you want to hoist her up into your arms. But even then she stayed still as a donkey, her legs dangling resolutely from her chair.

'I was just going down to get the ferry,' Lily said when they'd all stared at each other for a few minutes more. She picked up her jacket and the one large cottage key and, seeing her waiting there, they filed out of the room. Carefully Lily locked the door and then smiling she walked away towards the river mouth. But the girls were following. Lily turned and smiled, more definitely this time, with a parting nod, but when she walked on, she could still hear their steps behind her, and so instead she slowed a little to accept them, and they all three walked on side by side. It was ten past twelve and from the jetty they could just see the ferry girl tying up her boat on the other side. Lily waved at her, just in case she thought it worth making one last crossing for the sake of thirty pence, but she only waved back, straddled her bicycle and headed away for lunch. Lily stood looking across at Eastonknoll, its light-house as white and bright as an illustration, its houses dotted unevenly over the slope of the hill. Of course you could get there by road, and Lily had driven in on her second day to buy provisions, but the estuary forced you inland for at least four miles before the land was solid enough to take a road across. It seemed wrong to get into her car and do a noisy forty-minute trip, when there it was, just a step away across the water.

'There's a bridge.' Em was pulling at her jacket, pointing her up the river.

Lily shielded her eyes against the sun. There was nothing before her except smooth flat water, bending at the skyline, to the right. 'Well, I'll see you later I expect,' and she set off along the river path, skirting the rotted jetty stumps. When she looked back, she found they hadn't followed. Instead they were bent over the harbour mouth, dragging up seaweed with long sticks.

All along the river, boats were moored, some dilapidated, some shiny and new, and all with their halyards caught up in the breeze. It was like walking through a world of wind chimes, each one very slightly tinnier than the last. Light cascaded down the river, turning it bright blue, picking up the puddles in the marshland on the other side, dazzling the grazing cows. Lily walked with her eyes half closed, feeling over the uneven ground until the river curved and the promised bridge came into view. It stood out black against the skyline and when Lily climbed up to it she tried to imagine a time when steam trains would shudder regularly over its rails. The whole bridge rattled as she walked, and with each step a spray of seagulls spiralled into the air. Just above her on the Common loomed the water tower, sinister in its top-heavy form. It had long granite legs like a primordial beast, and a high circular belly where the water was held. There was a small door in the foot of one leg and Lily, as she passed, wondered if you opened it, the water would come rushing out.

Saturday was market day in Eastonknoll. Stalls had been set up around the war memorial, their backs to one another, their feet on cobbles. For sale were dishcloths, rubber gloves, and trolleys full of strangely unattractive plants. Busy Lizzies with fat rubbery leaves, dwarf marigolds, and fuchsias with bursting, purple buds. Lily circled the stalls several times and eventually bought some washing-up liquid for half the recommended price. Clutching her brown paper bag, she peered into the tea shops, all serving lunch, the people inside all old, all silent. It alarmed her to think she would be one more silent person ordering her food alone, so instead she wandered down on to the beach. There was a kiosk there that served tea and sandwiches with all the finery of a grand hotel. Tea in a china pot with a jug of milk and another for hot water. Sandwiches cut into triangles and sprinkled with cress. There was even a little vase on her white plastic table, from which sprang a tiny cluster of wild flowers. Lily sat huddled in her jacket as the waves crashed in, watching the sun fight out from behind a cloud. She was the only person eating on the sea front, although the hardier pensioners still strolled up and down.

Dear Nick . . . She took out her postcard and read over it again. She had thought she might buy an envelope to conceal its contents, but there was nothing private here. *Average age here – 82. Average colour – beige.* She wrote the address, added a kiss and pasted on a stamp.

Lily was careful to get to the ferry before it stopped at four. She climbed in and took her place and waited while a Scandinavian couple, with two bicycles and a child, arranged themselves beside her. The ferry girl began to row. Her hands and arms were strong and wiry, but her face under a hat was smooth and young. She rowed against the tide, out into the middle of the water and then, with a practised eye for the right angle, she pulled in her oars and let the boat steer itself in. It arrived with a small thud against the Steerborough jetty, flipping the book shut on her lap, and the couple, clutching their bicycles, gave up a nervous cheer.

Home, Lily thought, as she unlocked her cottage door; and, throwing herself down on the brown sofa, she laughed to think how quickly she'd settled in.

7

Max's frame was finished. He wondered, as he'd often done before, if making up the frame wasn't his favourite part of the job. The one thing he knew he could do well. But then the very fact of having made a frame, expertly tacking the canvas to its back, forced him to embark on the next part of the journey, the sketching, the first stroke of the paint. He'd kept the measurements of Gertrude's mantelpiece in mind as he'd sawn the lengths of wood. He knew this was absolutely the wrong way round, that paintings were not furnishings, that Henry would be outraged, but all the same it was Gertrude who was providing his room and board, had helped him to get away from the last dying memories of Kaethe, and he wanted, if he possibly could, to show that he was grateful. He carried the frame carefully inside, and turned it to face the wall.

Gertrude was before him as he straightened up. 'Max,' she said, and he noticed only then that the house was heady with the smell of food, the table cleared of sketches, laid with an embroidered cloth. There were napkins fanning out from wooden rings, and on each ring was a white label. Elsa, Max, Gertrude, Klaus.

'Did you remember the Lehmanns will be here at seven?' Gertrude asked.

Slowly Max backed out.

'I'll find you some flowers,' he called, and he hurried into the garden and slipped through the side gate.

Max walked fast, taking the road towards the church, dreading the possibility of small talk turning the past into a piece of news. He could feel his feet pounding, batting away the questions they might ask, and he tried to remember what he knew of the

Lehmanns, how they'd left, when, and which members of the family got out. Why here, of all places? But then he came across his view. It was a space between two houses, entirely made up of shades of green and blue. He hadn't noticed it at first, so intently had he been concentrating on buildings, but then one day he'd happened to glance sideways and there it lay, a long thin alleyway of light. Sometimes Max just snatched a look at it, taking a bite, using the colours to chew on along the way. But today he stopped at the mouth of the lane. The ground was muddy, the fields shimmering with rain. Max looked at the soft leather of his shoes and, knowing it was ludicrous, he stepped in. The path was narrow, edged by private land, a sumptuous garden and a tennis court, the wire interwoven, the court swept clean. There were dark shadows from the hedgerows, but always, opening up before him, the overlapping stripes of blue and green.

It was late when he arrived back. 'I'm so sorry.' Max stood in the doorway, his trousers sodden, his shoes abandoned in the hall. He looked at the table, his empty place, the other guests already seated round. 'I became delayed.'

'It's quite all right.' Gertrude was holding a dishcloth, attempting to manoeuvre a casserole on to a tile. 'This is Klaus Lehmann, his wife, Elsa. This is Max. Max Meyer.'

Klaus Lehmann nodded to him, a small, neat, handsome man, but Elsa rose up to greet him.

'Hello.' She took his hand, and then, looking at his trousers, darkened to the knee, 'Did you enjoy your walk?'

Her hand was light as paper and one strand of hair had curled across her cheek. Max blushed. Her beauty was so dizzying it stopped him where he stood. He stared at her, he couldn't help it, and for a moment he thought he'd forgotten how to speak. He could feel the others watching him, see Elsa's lips parting as she smiled, and then a distant cog shifted in his brain.

30

'I should change,' he said, relieved, forming the words as clearly as he could, and, stepping like a wade bird, he made his way to the stairs. Would Gertrude tell them, Max wondered as he peeled off his wet clothes, would she tell them he was . . . crippled, or would she let them find out for themselves?

Max took his seat at the end of the table. He was opposite Elsa, but lengthways so that, although facing him, she was the furthest away. Even if he stretched his fingers out to her, and she to him, they would never touch. These thoughts were so unfamiliar it took him moments before he realized they must be slapped away.

Gertrude served out the goulash, and, as Max spooned in each mouthful, he attempted to hold Elsa in his view, tried to watch for her lips moving, in case she was addressing anything to him. But just the sight of her, the light in her long eyes, the blue, like irises blooming, made him incapable of speech.

'So Max, Max . . .' Gertrude was talking to him, trying to shift his eyes to her. 'I was just explaining to Klaus here about the painting, how much thought you've put into it, and how . . .' – she was urging him to take her on – 'how you are ready to begin.'

Lehmann smiled understandingly. One artist to another, although of course he must know that Max was not a professional like him.

'Yes,' Max nodded finally, over-emphasizing this one word. 'At least I hope I am.'

But he was saved much further talk by Klaus who began to outline the details of a new library for which he'd just completed plans. If he could gain this contract, he'd have a chance to prove himself again, remake the reputation that he'd left behind.

'When I first met my husband,' Elsa told them, 'he was already well known. A dazzling star, to me certainly.' She smiled at Klaus. 'I was, of course, seventeen.'

'And now, not so?' Klaus didn't blink.

'Still so.' She squeezed his hand. 'After twenty-two years.'

Max watched Klaus as he talked, watched the words form on his lips, distorted as he chewed, twisted by his accent, and those missed as Max bent to fork up his own food. By the end of the meal he had pieced together an unlikely image of a swimming-pool, suspended below chandeliers, with tiers of tottering bookshelves revolving in mid-air. It made him smile, just the thought of it, and Gertrude, noticing his usually black eyes, lit up, told herself she should have invited guests before.

After supper they sat by the open window, a fire lit in the grate and watched the midges swarm out of the dark. 'So, your paths never crossed before?' Gertrude couldn't resist trying, although Max had told her already that they'd never met.

'Yes.' Elsa leant towards him. 'I think your family had a summer house not far from ours. You wouldn't remember me.' She looked at him, her luminous eyes ringed round with black. 'But I remember you.'

'Hiddensee?' It was almost a whisper. It was Hiddensee that he'd been thinking of on his walk.

'I was there every summer since the age of three, and I remember you particularly . . .' There was a hush as if this were a private conversation and the others were caught up in it against their will. 'Because you were always alone.'

'Elsa . . .' Klaus tried to interject.

'And then one summer, you were with a girl, a girl in a green dress, and I saw you . . .' Elsa laughed. 'I saw you kiss her in one of those little booths on the beach.'

'Elsa . . .' Klaus was stretching, standing up. 'I really think it may be time to go.'

'It was the first time' – she looked at her husband – 'that I was introduced to love.'

'I don't know what to say.' Klaus folded his arms. 'I'd hoped that the first time had been reserved for me.'

Everyone laughed, but Max felt the coldness behind the other man's quick look.

'Yes.' Max became aware of the formality of their language, speaking in this foreign tongue as if it were a kind of code. 'It was the summer I became engaged.'

'And now . . .' Elsa was leaning towards him. 'Your wife? She's . . . ?'

'We never married.' He wanted to add something softer, to hold her disappointment, but there was nothing else to say.

'I'm sorry.' Elsa looked at him. 'You're not offended?' she was bending towards his chair, touching his fingers with the soft tips of her own.

'No.'

Helga. He spoke the word to himself. 'No. I'm not offended at all.'

Of course a shadow has no shape alone. I don't mean a cast shadow on a flat surface, but the shadow which explains where a solid object turns from the light. Max read feverishly. If only, he thought, he could write to Henry now. *Remember,* he had said, *the whole object has a shape to be drawn, not the shadow by itself.*

That night Max wandered through the rooms of Heiderose. He drifted through walls, following the notes of the piano, into the blue room with its oval table, the long windows opening out on to the terrace where his mother liked to sit. Up, he was going up the stairs, past the bathroom with the great juddering boiler which toiled and bleated and woke him in the night, past Kaethe's room, so neat and tidy, the high bed smoothed, the white sheet tucked tightly in. Light filtered through the window, dappling across her desk, and he took out his sketchbook and held it open to show her what he'd done. Kaethe, he called, and then still in his dream he remembered it was Kaethe who had made him stop. 'It pains you too much,' she'd said, and as soon as he'd arrived in England she'd

33

organized a job for him as a book-keeper. He'd been good at figures, his fingers clever on the page, and just as with painting, she'd told him, you didn't need your ears to multiply and subtract.

8

Lily was woken by the smash and shattering of glass. She lay quite still, her eyes open, her blood pounding, and tried to remember if she'd locked the door. There was silence now. Only her own breathing, and she waited, paralysed, for someone to leap out at her from the corner of the room. She didn't dare sit up or turn her head, and then, just when the waiting was more than she could bear, there was the scramble of raised voices and a scream rang out. Lily leapt out of bed. She spun around, unsure what to do, and then the thud of something heavy hit the wall.

'I don't want to hear it!' It was the woman's shrill voice, and underneath it, the man's, a growl of rage. 'I've told you! I've warned you . . .'

Instinctively Lily shielded her face and, as she did so, there was that scream again, another crash, and then the sickening roll of someone tumbling downstairs. Lily ran down her own steep staircase and stood in the darkened kitchen, where in a flash of white a figure rushed past the window, head bent into the night. The gate clanged open and then shut, and she heard the choking of a car.

Lily stood, her feet slowly freezing, unable to think what she should do. Those little girls were still inside there, and she imagined them lying, eyes wide open, too frightened to speak.

Very slowly Lily opened her own door. The night was radiant with stars, thick dazzling clusters, dripping from the sky. A gust of wind swept by her and then she realized that she was surrounded by sound. From behind the house, across the Green and up and above the sand dunes came the crashing of the sea. Lily forgot what she'd come out for. She opened the side gate and stepped round

35

into the lane. The noise was louder now. Wave after wave of sound. Was this noise always there, and was she simply too busy to notice it during the day? If you didn't know, you might think it was a motorway, the lorries hurtling by, but as she listened she could imagine the water drawing back to crash on to the shore. Lily glanced back towards her cottage and saw a figure lit up in the window of the house next door. It was the man, leaning against the glass, and then in an instant the light flicked off and he was gone. Shivering, she turned and hurried back inside. She closed the door with an unexpected slam and listened for a moment. No. There was nothing. Silence. No calls or whimpers, and then she wondered if it was possible the children had slept right through the fight.

The next morning she saw him. He was standing in the yard, sawing a length of wood between two chairs. Until now Lily had only seen the children, and once or twice the shoulder of the woman, hanging clothes out on the line. But here was the father standing side on to her, dressed in an old jumper and a woollen hat. She leant forward to see, and, just as she pressed her face to the window, the wood snapped apart and he turned to catch at the short end before it fell. Lily stepped back. She took her tea and went through to the table where she'd laid out her work. She picked up a letter, and began busily to read, turning the words, as she understood them, from German into English, drifting as she did so into a foreign rhythm of speech.

On the cold, dark train, Klaus wrote to Elsa in 1932, *I began to fear that I haven't shown you enough love. But what can I do since you became the loving one, and I simply had to open my arms to you and accept? At 1.30 this morning I was still horizontal in my carriage, thinking of you, and attempting to sleep. Weren't the days at Hiddensee as beautiful as the memories? And how many there are going to be till we grow old?*

Lily could still hear the man sawing. If she glanced behind her and out of the kitchen window she could just see his shoulder, working back and forth.

Darling, I am so glad that the small feather that I sent you made you happy. For years it has been my favourite kind of feather, and I took it as a good sign when it simply floated down on to my page. Will you think me ridiculous if I tempt you with another pair of shoes? Black. Rounded, very pretty and well made. In size 37 there is just one pair left. Similar high boots! I can hear you laughing. Is my urge to buy you shoes so funny? But I really do believe we might not be able to get anything so nice for many years to come. My darling, until my return let there be nothing beside you but empty space.

Just then Lily saw the postman walk past her window and, her heart leaping, she jumped up and ran round to the side door. If Nick didn't write to her soon, she'd have to call him, tell him the phone box had been mended, but still she might last out one more day. The postman hesitated for a moment and then stopped. Lily watched as he drew an envelope out of his bag, but instead of turning towards her he pushed open the gate to the house across the lane. In a flash the door was opened, and Ethel appeared. She took the envelope and, smiling broadly, she sliced it apart with her thumb. Lily stood, watching her face frowning and brightening as she read the words.

'Morning.' Ethel had seen her, and blushing, Lily nodded 'morning' and slipped back inside.

Lehmann's next letter was from Dahlem.

I never dared to hope that I'd receive a letter from you even on a Sunday. But there can't be any doubt about who the loving one is now. And who is planning to give us both a child? While I am here working I hear the sound of the bells ringing out at 7.30 each morning, and in my semi-sleep it sounds like Elle, Elle. Ellie, Elle. So I wake up thinking of you, and longing for you my El.

L, xx

Lily put down her pen and walked outside. She'd started to treat the Green as her front garden, standing in its centre looking up at the sky. She glanced irritably at the phone box, as if it really was broken, and then feeling the warm sun on her face she lay down in the grass. There were five white clouds, fine as carded wool, fraying and stretching, pulling back together in the breeze. Lily pressed herself into the earth, her head, her legs, the heels of her feet, and then she closed her eyes and listened for the sea. It wasn't roaring now. She could hear it, gently murmuring, smooth and lapping, like the long drone of a bee.

'Are you all right there?' Someone was standing over her, casting a cool shadow half across her face. Lily opened her eyes and started. It was the man from next door, looking down at her, the sandy ends of his hair sticking out below his hat. 'Right,' he nodded, as Lily scrambled up, 'just thought I'd check,' and he was moving away across the Green, followed by a black and white cat. 'Psst,' he turned for it, and it hurried after, its tail held high, its footsteps dainty as if it were treading over tar.

Lily turned away, embarrassed, hoping he hadn't seen the fear in her face, and in the distance, stepping on to the bridge she saw a white-gowned figure heading for the sea. Lily set off after her, relieved to have a purpose. Down the lane, along the river, over the wooden bridge and up the sandbanks, wading, climbing, up to the plain of beach before the sea. And there was Ethel standing by the water, on the treacle line where the wet sand meets the dry. She was slipping off her sandals, placing them neatly out of danger, dropping her white towelling dressing-gown to reveal a bolstered bathing costume, exploding orange petals from hip to hip. Lily walked nearer and sat on the sand. There was a cool breeze that swept over the beach, and the waves, though small, were capped with spray. Ethel stood for a minute with both ankles in the surf, and then she strode out until the water reached her thighs. This was the hardest moment, the point where your body shivered most, begging to be saved from pain, but Ethel lowered herself into the water and swam, ladylike and strong. She swam towards the skyline until she was nothing but a round white ruffled speck, and then, having reached her mark, she turned. She turned around into the sun and waved. Lily sprang up and waved back. And then she stood there watching, as Ethel began to drift back in. The swimming was less purposeful now, as if the hard work had been done. She let the waves billow her about, flecking up and wetting the edges of her hair. Soon she was rising up out of the shallow water. 'Good morning,' she called, as sand and shells and pearly drops scattered from her arms.

'Do you swim every day?' Lily asked as Ethel tugged on her gown.

'If I can. I've been swimming most days since we moved here. It's that that keeps me young. Are you going in?'

'I haven't got a costume.' They both looked along the deserted beach and grinned.

'Well, I'd better get back.' Ethel turned and, holding her gown around herself, she shambled back up the sand slope of the beach and down the other side.

She would go in, of course she would. She might even slip in without any clothes at all. But as she pulled off her top, she thought of the row of fishermen she'd once seen. Green macs, green wellingtons, a small army of circular tents. What if they appeared over the hill the moment that her back was turned, and then when she was ready to rise naked out of the water, they would be there like a green-tented firing squad to greet her as she came out. Slowly she peeled off her jeans, grateful for her vaguely matching bra and pants, and then, with the tip of one toe, she tested the sea. It was so cold it scalded. She tried the other foot. 'For God's sake!' The water clasped her foot and froze it, stabbing knives into the bone. Quickly she stepped back. If only she could plunge right in, get it over in one go, but the water was too shallow. She would have to walk out half a mile to even submerge her waist. She tried again, testing for pockets of warm sea, and then, knowing there was nothing else for it, she waded in. 'God, God, God, God, God,' she mumbled to take her mind off screaming, and she reminded herself that if this arctic water had failed to kill a woman in her eighties, then the chances were she would survive. The water was up to her knees now. She took a deep breath and looked around. There was no one and nothing for as far as she could see. 'Right.' And she turned and raced back out. Her legs were alive from the knees down, bright red and tingling. I should have just plunged in, she told herself, as she pulled on her clothes. Tomorrow, she promised, or the day after, and she walked the long way round, past the sea wall, and the one stilted house in a flat deserted scrub of shingle, up the ridge and down past the pub. Ethel would know from just one look at her how cowardly she had been, and she imagined how she would feel if her whole body was lit up like her legs. She walked faster as she approached the corner of the lane and quickly, using the side door, slipped inside.

9

'Am I in your way?' Gertrude asked him, when to her delight she found Max at his easel sketching in the outlines of her house.

'Yes,' Max said, and then he saw that, of course, he had offended her.

'It's quite all right.' Gertrude had her book in one hand and was tugging at the deckchair, pulling it with her to the back of the lawn. 'I'll move.'

Max wanted to explain his unease over the human form, how if she was there, even on the edge of his eye line, he would feel compelled to paint her in.

'Really, it's perfectly all right,' she said, when, between them with great awkwardness, they had succeeded in moving the one flimsy chair.

'I suppose I could have worked around you.' Max was able to breathe again now she was out of his view, but Gertrude looked up sharply.

'I said it was all right.'

Max sketched roughly with a soft thick pencil. The beauty of Marsh End, he realized, was not in its actual features but the way it rested on the ground. The texture of the lawn, the old, old earth, and the way the bench belonged there, tucked into the wall. The house was almost square, and he began inching sideways to feel its corner, to get at the side view.

Gertrude's head jolted up from her book. Where was he going? She could see him, his canvas abandoned, sidling away. She exhaled deeply and let her shoulders drop. They had the rest of the summer. What difference did it make? If he wanted to ease his grief by wandering, then who was she to fail to understand.

Max was examining the grained glass of the porch. It was clear to him now. Lehmann must have built it. Ruined the old line of the house with his vision and his lines. Well, Max would make a sketch of it, show him in a picture how ludicrous it looked. He went inside for paper. He'd used up the loose sheets he'd brought with him, used them all up on making Steerborough maps. He looked around the living-room. Surely Gertrude must have some paper hidden somewhere, and, not wanting to disturb her, he opened the walnut bureau, peered into its cupboards and drawers, but found nothing but a sewing basket and some supplies of sugar and salt. The compartments of her roll-top desk held only stationery, too small and dainty to be of any use, and even the larder, which he opened in desperation, had nothing but jars of chutneys and stewed fruit. Unable to stop looking, he tugged at a small door under the stairs, and as if it had been waiting there, a roll of paper fell out and unravelled at his feet. It was lining paper, dusty round the edges, the outer layer mottled yellow with disuse, but it was strong and plain and perfect. He took a board to rest it on, and hurried back outside. But without a knife or scissors to cut the paper, he simply chose the first clean section and let the rest flow over the edge of the board, cascading down his legs and out along the ground. Quickly he sketched in the old front of the house. He did it easily, like a boy released from school, taking pleasure in each stroke. Say something. He thought of Henry, and he smiled to think that for once he did have something to say.

Max was so pleased with his drawing that he crept round to the back garden, purposefully not looking at Gertrude, who was still intent on her book. Very gently he picked up his box of paints. He took a sheaf of brushes, his palette and a flask, and, leaving only the canvas on its easel and his bag of oils, he tip-toed back to the front. Each brick, or the impression of each brick, each reddened tile, each leaf of ivy clinging to the wall, he would put them in. He worked on through lunchtime, through the afternoon, until there was nothing to be added but the flimsy flat-roofed porch. He attached it, just as incongruously as it had been built on in real life, and, aware suddenly of the thinning light, he carried his picture, the roll still attached, into the house and up the stairs, and laid it on the floor beside his bed.

This is too much like the task of a tired and weary man. He had Henry's letters off by heart. *You say you had four hours? It would have been better to have done four smaller drawings, and not to have taxed yourself so much.* But there was nothing weary about the front of Gertrude's house. He lay down on the bed from where he could see it perfectly, spread out on the floor, still glittering with light, and, amazed by his own stamina, he fell into a dreamless sleep.

Gertrude was preparing supper when the clouds broke over the sea. She moved to shut the windows, and then she noticed Max's easel still set up, the canvas optimistically turned to face the house. 'Max!' she called, knowing he wouldn't hear, and so instead she ran out into the sleeting rain to bring the picture in.

Yawning, Max came downstairs, just as lightning cracked across the sky, lighting up the garden, the high branch of the tree, and the sight of Gertrude, fighting through the rain. 'Let me, please.' Max rushed out through the French windows, and together they released the canvas. There was a roll of thunder, and then more lightning came forking down. Gertrude gasped and for a moment they looked into the eerie whiteness of each other's eyes.

'Go in!' Gertrude shouted and Max turned the canvas against him and stumbled with it into the house. Gertrude was struggling with the doors, wrenching them out of the storm, bolting them fast. Max took a quick look at his sketch, embarrassed by the smudges and soft lines for which they'd risked their lives. Quickly he set its face against the wall.

'It's quite a storm, and right above us.' Gertrude moved to the window as another wave of thunder rolled. And sensing how disappointed she was in him, he moved with her, and they stood there, looking out at the waving branches, starting each time the lightning cracked. But the storm was moving away now, the seconds lengthening between each lightning flash and, as they watched, the black clouds were blown out to sea. Gertrude turned from the window with a sigh, and when she suggested supper, Max nodded, ravenous, taking the tea towel from her, insisting on helping so that they knocked against each other in the galley of the room.

There were flowers on the table in a little local vase. Max stretched his hand out to them, cradling the ceramic belly of the pot.

'Mrs Lehmann' – Gertrude nodded towards them – 'she brought them over this afternoon.'

Max drew away his hand. How could he have failed to see her? He'd been sitting by the front door all day. To hide his confusion he examined the flowers. A bright red poppy, its petals trembling, its stalk sinewy and thin. It was resting among a spray of corn. Max thought how he used to pull off the unripened ears, peel back the pale green husks and suck the kernels, the juice inside like beech nut, sweet as milk.

'Yes, I was reading about the power of soiling, how some children use it as a tool,' Gertrude was saying, 'and then I looked up and there was Elsa Lehmann gliding through the hedge. She'd been walking in the salt marsh, she said, and thought she'd just come by.'

'I didn't think you could pick poppies without breaking them.' Max put out a finger to touch the soft fur of the stalk, and just then, as if in obedience, one damp papery petal fluttered off into his hand.

They ate in silence. From time to time Max glanced at Gertrude, wondering if, like him, she was worrying that Elsa might have been caught out in that storm. She might even now be stranded, shivering, too stung by rain to get back to her home.

But Gertrude was thinking about Alf. Would it be more beneficial, she was wondering, if instead of piano lessons, she were to offer help of a more analytical kind?

★   ★   ★

The first thing Max saw when he woke the next morning was his picture spread out below him on the floor. It wasn't as good as he'd remembered it, the glisten was all gone, and without warning he was overwhelmed by an image of his father. His spirits fell with such force that he had to ease himself down to the floor. He must keep moving, or he'd sink, and he wasn't sure he would ever rise back up. Slowly, slowly, he crawled across the room. Henry's letters, in their case, were propped against the wall. He reached for them and held the leather close, breathing it in, nuzzling it against his face, chewing the soft edges between his teeth.

Yes, he read, when finally he'd roused himself enough to slip a letter from the case. *Much, much improved. Go on like this and nothing will hold you back.* Where, he wondered, was that picture now. Meyer . . . Henry had turned stern. *It is all nonsense to take tips from people as to how things should be done. How does the ground model itself? And in what direction does the grass grow? It is YOUR solution to these problems that I want to see.*

To lie still, Max thought, and never get up, but he forced himself to the window, and clinging to the ledge he pushed open the casement and leant out. The day was soft. A primrose-yellow morning lined with blue. The storm had taken something with it, and just for a moment he felt lighter, purer, more able to forget. Quickly, before his spirits slumped again, Max pulled on his clothes. He rolled up his painting and, without waiting for a cup of Gertrude's brown brewed tea, he took up his water colours and set off along the lane.

He walked purposefully towards the church, past the crooked house, the old farm and the postbox with its royal red seal. He walked until he was outside the village's last house. It had a trellised porch, white-painted, with three steepled windows in the roof. Its small square garden was fenced in, and beyond it there was nothing but heath land as far as you could see. Max sat down on the stump of the old gatepost, the iron of which had been torn out, patriotically, for the war. He unrolled his scroll of paper, revealing

Gertrude's house, and just beside it, white and ready, a waiting, empty space. Heath View. The house reminded him of apples, the wood painted in the palest green, its windows, pips, its bricks laced through with pink. Max was just peering closer to gauge the exact shade of the wood when a woman stepped out. She hovered on the path, staring at him, suspicious, and then, turning back, she locked her front door.

Lily took a triumphant bite of her toast and, folding Nick's letter into her pocket, she sped across the Green. She'd done it. She'd forced him into writing, and not just a letter, but a love letter.

For God's sake, Lily, it started. *Surely there must be another phone box somewhere? Or give me the number, why don't you, and I'll ring up and complain. Sorry to go on* – his writing was smaller and less legible with each line – *but why are you the only person in the world without a mobile? I miss you, that's all . . . It's hellishly busy at work, but I'm not going to say another word until you get on your bike, or your mule, or whatever it is you travel about on up there, and get to a phone box. I want to hear your voice.*

As she dialled, Lily scooped coins out of her purse. Tenpences, twenties, two fifties and a pound. She stacked them up in little piles beside the pebble and the ever-present note. *Call 999. Wait by the wall . . .* Lily stared at the faded paper, its texture already grained with sun and damp, and she was just leaning over it, peering into its jagged face, when Nick's message cut in. 'You know what to do.'

The abruptness of it always fazed her, as if the last thing in the world he wanted was another call.

'It's me.' The sound of her own voice made her tentative, and she realized it was some days since she'd uttered a word. 'Listen, thanks for the letter. Oh Christ, I'll try you at work.'

But Nick wasn't at work.

'He's off . . . Is that Lily?'

'Yes.'

'Oh, he's . . . Hang on.' She could hear his assistant, Tim, filling up the kettle, hear the water pounding into the metal drum. 'Yes, he's gone to Paris to check on . . .' Another phone started ringing and Tim must have splashed water up his arm. 'Oh fuck!'

'It's all right,' Lily shouted over the noise, 'I've left a message on his mobile,' and, deflated, she put down the phone.

Lily piled her change back into her purse. She picked up the pebble. It was round and worn, stripes of ivory and gold, the rings of colour grazed and faded at the edges as if it were a million years old. Lily rolled it in the palm of her hand, and without knowing why she slipped it into her pocket, leaving in its place a twopence coin.

Lily walked the long way round to the shop. She took deep strides, sucking in the air, the soft grass smells, the honey scent from a bedding of white flowers, and then on the corner of a lane, a sharp blast of currant stopped her in her tracks. It made her think of London, the incongruous smell of nature on a city street. Dust and damp and cat's piss and the sharp sap of the stalks. Lily snapped off a dark green leaf and pressed it between her finger and her thumb. The veins were red like rhubarb, the juice bitter with the tang of fruit. There had been a plant like this on the corner of the street where she grew up. She had often stopped by it to finish up her sweets, breathing in the acrid smell that came to her in bursts as she waited for her mother to come home from work. Lily uncrumpled the leaf and, folding it carefully around her pebble, she pushed it into the pocket of her jeans.

Stoffer's, the village shop, was stocked with everything you might ever need. As well as fruit, vegetables and cheeses, bread and tins, and packets of dried food, there were beach balls, fishing nets, buckets and spades. There was a whole shelf of biscuits and just opposite the till, at eye level to a toddler, a hoard of penny sweets. Two children were crouched over, holding plastic tongs, and as the door rattled shut behind her she recognized Em and Arrie, clutching miniature paper bags. Mrs Stoffer was leaning over the counter watching them, and when Lily caught her eye, she gave her a look full of misgiving.

Lily concentrated on the postcards. There were photographic

highlights of at least five local villages and towns. Harbours, castles, sunsets, the ruins of a church. And then on a stand all of their own, a rack of 'local artists'. Lily examined each pale and faded scene. The beach deserted, the beach with paddlers at low tide. There were watercolours of the ferry, with and without a queue, and one picture of the wooden house, up on its stilts, cornered on three sides by water as the estuary swooped round to meet the sea. Each picture was four-fifths full of sky. It made the land look insignificant, as if it were unable to keep up. If she were to paint this scene she would only paint the sky, and she smiled at a sudden image of herself, sensible clothing, sandwiches, and an easel dug into the sand. Instead of watercolours she chose a photograph of the Eastonknoll lighthouse, its lookout a lattice of white icing, its dome a blob of cream.

'Twelve pence . . .' the lady was counting the sweets out by the till, peering and poking at Arrie's paper bag. 'Fifteen, that's twenty-seven pence.'

Em dug her hand deep into her pocket. Her face was a mask of worry as she picked out the coins. Mrs Stoffer held the bags as if they might have to be returned, as if she'd been in this particularly tiresome situation before.

'Twelve, thirteen, sixteen . . .' Em laboriously counted pennies while Arrie stood beside her, wistful and concerned. 'Twenty-two?' she offered hopefully and Lily looked up just in time to see Mrs Stoffer shake her head.

'It's all right. I'll make it up.' Lily pushed her postcards forward, and she slapped a two-pound coin down on the counter as if she were a millionaire with a chauffeured car idling outside.

Together they walked back down towards the Green. 'No school today?' she asked them, and they explained about their mum taking the car. 'There's no bus, you see, and . . . well, some days it's too far to walk.'

'Where is the school?'

'It's over at Thressingfield,' and, spinning round in the direction of the main road, they pointed vaguely at the horizon. 'Sometimes we get a lift with Mr Blane, but he wasn't going in today.'

'Oh,' Lily said as they strolled back down through the village. 'I expect she'll be back soon.'

Em hung her head and Arrie, with grubby fingers, slid a flat green octopus into her mouth.

'I didn't mean . . .' Lily bit her lip. 'I mean, I'm sure . . .'

'Anyway,' Em said quickly, 'Dad's getting a new car.'

'Not new new,' Arrie corrected. 'But new for us.'

Em offered Lily one of her sweets. They were like jelly babies, but much harder to chew. Strange flattened shapes, rubbery and thick. For some time it was impossible to speak.

There was no one on the Green and Lily sat on one of the two swings, watching while Em kicked higher and higher into the blue sky. Arrie was polishing the slide. She was using her bottom as a duster, walking up backwards, rubbing at each section until the stainless steel shone. Finally, she said, the slide was ready, and with a small bow she sped down at great speed and shot off the end. She landed in a dusty dip of wood chips, and Lily noticed, when she struggled up, that the seat of her leggings was worn thin.

'Does she do this often?' she asked Em, and Em said it was her job. 'I pick up the litter, and Arrie polishes the slide. We asked Alf if we could, and he said yes.'

'Who's Alf?'

'Alf??' Em looked at Lily as if it was impossible not to know. 'Oh, he's . . . he . . .' She turned almost upside down. 'He's on the . . . he's at the . . . he's sort of the boss.'

Arrie had finished sliding and now she hovered in front of Lily. 'Do you want to see something' – she stepped up close – 'secret?'

'I'd love to,' Lily said.

'Arrie!' Em jolted her swing upright, her eyes furious, warning her to stop.

'What?'

There followed a moment's silence in which they communicated with glares.

'Oh, come on, then, if you really want to,' and, screwing up her eyes at Arrie, Em took Lily by the hand.

They walked down the lane towards the sea, but instead of crossing the bridge they veered off along a smaller path, banked with long grasses, ducking to avoid the brambles that looped out and caught them on their way. The path wound and dipped, the river on one side, marshes and hillocks of thick grass on the other. Eventually they came out on the salt marsh. There were bright patches of water glittering between sedge, and tiny hardened paths, wide enough for one. The sedge was head-high, bleached white by last year's sun, waving very gently in the breeze. Occasionally they came across a shorn patch, mowed down like a boy's hair, taken away for making thatch. Then it was flat and silent as far as the sea, although living in these marshes were birds and voles and coypus, water rats and bitterns, even if Lily had still not heard a single sound. Every few yards they crossed over water, back and forth on planks embedded in the bank.

'Where are we going?' she asked, wondering how anyone could know their way so well, and just then Em doubled back over another bridge.

'There it is,' Arrie said, and on the horizon were the ruins of a mill. It looked like an abandoned sandcastle, its roof missing, one corner crumbling in. 'Shhh, it's haunted.'

Em turned, and at her hiss a pair of great black birds rose out of the long grass. They flew fast, straight ahead, their legs tucked up, landing on the river on two posts. Luxuriously they spread their wings and held them out, bat-shaped, as if to dry. Lily watched them, felt them watching her.

'Come on,' Em and Arrie called, and she turned and ran after them towards the mill.

'You don't come out here alone, do you?' she shouted, but they didn't look round.

From the doorway of the mill, a short flight of steps disappeared into a stagnant pool of water, and there floating on the surface were some sticks and a red, high-heeled shoe.

They all peered in. 'Hello, lo, lo, lo.' Em let her voice echo between the walls, and they all looked up at the cone of sloping brickwork, the circle of pale sky.

'Who says it's haunted?' Lily asked, and just then a shadow fell on them, chilling the air. Arrie clutched her arm.

'It's all right,' Em said, 'it's just a cloud,' but she took Lily's other arm.

They moved round the side of the mill and sat on a block of granite implanted with shells. They sat there in silence, waiting for the sun to come back out. Both the girls kept their faces turned upwards as if their lives depended on it, while Lily looked along the coast. There was a huddle of houses on the first curve and a mass of boats beached up on the shore, and just beyond it, shimmering silver, was a huge dome.

'What is that place?' she asked Em, but Em was still watching the sky.

'It's Daddy's job,' Arrie told her.

'It used to be.' Em wrenched her eyes away. 'Not any more. It's a nuclear power station. They make power.'

'No.' Arrie was perturbed. 'They make bacon rolls.'

'Oh, yes,' Em nodded, serious. 'And bacon rolls.'

It was after midday when they finally returned to the Green, and the first person they saw, standing by the foot of the slide, was Em and Arrie's father. The two girls shot each other a quick look, and Arrie put her hand up to her mouth. 'We never even showed you the secret!'

But Lily was hurrying forward. 'I'm sorry,' she called. 'It's my fault. They've been with me.'

His eyes looked strained, tired with searching. 'It's all right,' he said. 'I thought they'd be all right.'

Arrie sidled up against him, twisting her small body for a stroke and Em stood with her head against his arm.

'I'm Lily, we haven't really met . . . I'm renting next door . . .' She trailed off with the implications of this. The thin walls, the thud on the stairs.

'Grae,' he said, his head nodding forward, his eyes half closing in the faintest hint of a smile, and he put his hand down and ruffled Arrie's hair.

II

'So how was your lesson?' Gertrude asked Alf. 'How was Miss Cheese?' Alf stood before her. 'Still no progress?' she prompted, and then to her surprise he raised his hands and began fluttering his fingers, trilling them over a set of imaginary keys. He sped over the ivory, up and down and back again in a rolling crescendo of sound. She could almost hear the high notes, tinkling on a hairline creak, and then the ricochet of thunder as he boomed down to the far end. Gertrude was so taken aback that she leant too far over on her lounger, upending it so that her books slid on to the grass.

'Well, I . . . that's wonderful.' She started clapping. It was the first sign of life she'd seen in him since the storm. 'Come and sit down.' She patted the space vacated by her books. 'So you're enjoying your lessons now?' Tentatively he perched beside her. 'I'm very pleased.' She looked at him, his hair as white as butter, so bright it shone, and she thought of the small boy she had cared for in the war nursery, the boy whose mother had said she wouldn't ever visit if he cried.

'Mustn't cry, mustn't cry,' he'd muttered, clinging to a shred of blanket, 'mustn't cry,' until slowly, over the weeks and months, this instruction fixed itself so tightly inside him that there was nothing left of it but a little nervous smile.

'Alf?' She touched his arm, but he was restless, tensed to be away. 'Go on, then.'

Alf sprang up. He skidded to the edge of the garden, slipped through the hedge and was gone.

Gertrude went back to her book. She was reading about children's nightmares, their fear of the dark, and how one boy had been told the bogeyman would get him if he touched himself in bed. But what no one seemed to understand about the boy, and why he was still afraid, was that the bogeyman was already there in his imagination, so he might as well go on.

It was hot. Too hot for early June. Gertrude forced herself up and into the house, shivering in that moment of near blindness as she stepped in out of the sun. She felt her way into the kitchen and, running the tap for coldness, she glanced sideways at Max's canvas still turned against the wall. It had been a week since the picture had been started, and just as long since work on it had stopped. Now her guest slipped out before breakfast, and did not come home again until late. If she wanted to talk to him, she had to wander through the village, peer round corners, traipse down lanes until she found him, perched on an old milking stool, wrapped in a paint-splattered smock. He'd taken to wearing a felt hat, old and brown and dented on the top, and he sat, oblivious to opinion, surrounded by his roll of lining paper, his paints and brushes, his palettes and his pots. He'd painted five houses now, and he was on to the sixth. They were intricately done, the bricks in all their shades of reddened clay, the pantile roofs, the thatches, the gardens and the trees. How many buildings were there in the village? she wondered, and as she started to calculate she realized he'd be here until next spring.

'When I die,' Kaethe had said to her, trying to smile as if it were hypothetical, a meandering conversation between friends, 'I worry that Max will be . . .' – she tried to breathe, but the breath came only as a rasp – 'that he'll be lost.'

Gertrude had squeezed her hand. 'I'm sure . . .' But Gertrude had no idea what would happen to Max. In all the years of her and Kaethe's friendship he'd always held himself aloof. From her. From everyone. He'd used his deafness, she was sure of it, to keep himself apart.

'Max likes to do things for people,' Kaethe went on. 'He painted all day and half the night because it pleased our father, and then when he came to England he stopped, really just for me. If no one asks him to do anything, I worry that he'll . . .' Kaethe's voice cracked and she turned her face away.

'I'll invite him to the country.' Gertrude smiled. 'Ask him to do a painting of my house.'

'Yes.' Kaethe nodded, releasing her hand, exhausted. 'That's it. Then he can do something for you.'

But Kaethe had been wrong about her brother. No one had asked Max to paint the whole of Steerborough. No one understood why he was even there, muddling up the traffic on the village's one street, peering through windows, examining borders, choosing which house or cottage would be next. He'd painted Molly Cross's cat, enticing it with scraps, throwing crumbs of cake to keep it still, and then at the last minute he'd turned it from black to ginger just so it would stand out to more effect against the hedge. He'd painted the wasteland behind the Woollards, the village's one disgrace, hens and bedsprings and old bicycles rusting away in nettles three feet high. There was even Mrs Stoffer's poster for her production of *Twelfth Night*, pinned up outside the shop, and in tiny letters he had painted the time, the date and the fact that Mrs Stoffer had taken on the unsuitable role of Olivia herself.

Gertrude trickled water down over her face. Was it that her guest had overstayed his welcome? Or was it actually that he was never there? She stood still, testing her responses, listening to her breathing and her pulse. She looked at herself in the mirror and her face softened as she smiled. Yes, it was much as she suspected. She didn't mind him staying, it was simply galling to be in the company of someone who needed so little of her help.

That night Max dreamt that he was measuring. He was measuring the grounds at Heiderose, scribbling the results on a piece of paper that continually blew away, and then, just when he had finished, had pocketed his notes, he'd found himself surrounded by a family pushing their way through his front door. A mother, large and ruffled, and four children with tow-coloured hair. Their father stood beside a car, unloading boxes. 'I was just measuring,' Max informed them, but no one saw him, no one noticed he was there.

Max sat late over his breakfast. He felt wound through with weariness, unable to control the page of Henry's letter trembling in his hand.

'Is it your day off?' Gertrude asked him, and she sat down and poured herself some tea.

'Yes,' Max said, as if the thought had just occurred to him, 'I think it may be.' He laid his letter down beside his plate.

'Important news?' she asked, and Max very solemnly scooped the first page up and pressed it on her.

It seems scarcely worth doing, the letter started, *as the discussion must have been set out more than a hundred times, but in my opinion the definition of Art is simply the way impressions are received and assimilated from the world outside.* Gertrude looked up to catch Max's eye, but he had turned away. *Of course it is interesting to consider whether certain artists choose the right art in which to express themselves. Or by what peculiar gift, or train of events, anybody came to choose a particular form of art. But in my opinion the important thing is that you keep on. I expect if you left off swimming for long enough you would find your muscles were stiff. And if you left off drawing, the head, the hand, the eye would get rusty. If you left off long enough, you might find you couldn't start again. But having said that, I know a man who drew, not very well, but in an interesting way, and then he went out to a farm in South America for six or seven years, and when he came back he started drawing again. I suppose he couldn't help it.*

Cuthbert Henry, she read. 'Yes, I saw a show of his once. Is he still . . . ?'

But Max was pointing to the date. *May 15th 1938.*

'I see . . .' 1938 was on the other side of history. A time when you could assume men, grown silent, were at least still alive. 'So how are your muscles? Are they very rusty?'

'Yes.' He smoothed the letter with such tenderness it gave his face a kind of glow. 'I've been in South America for very many years.'

The invitation was looped around with violets, the words formed in such elegant calligraphy they resembled lace.

'I know it's rather short notice.' Klaus Lehmann stood at the front door. 'But if you have nothing else planned?'

'No,' Gertrude said. 'We'd be delighted.'

'In that case, we can expect you tomorrow?' And he nodded to her and walked back down the lane.

Gertrude examined the card. A woman with not enough to do, she thought, and she put the card in pride of place beside the clock.

Gertrude waited to see if Max would notice it. He came in at seven, just as the light began to change, sweeping long shadows across the ermine lawn. 'Have you had a good day?' she asked him, and, not seeming to hear her, he set down his scroll, his leather case, his bag of paints, and walked over to the mantelpiece like a man pulled by a rope. *Mrs Elsa Lehmann requests the pleasure of Max and Gertrude at a lunch to be eaten in the garden.*

Max turned. His face was still and questioning and it occurred to her he was about to ask permission to go.

'I've already accepted,' she said. 'I hope you don't mind.'

'Yes.' Max shook his head. 'I mean no.' He laughed at the confusion. No. He didn't mind.

The Lehmanns lived in the lopsided house on the corner of Mill Lane. It was the glass and wooden building Max had marvelled at on his first day, with one steep side, dark wood and frosted glass. Below the slope, like a garden plateau, was the terrace with its picket fence, and there on the terrace, looking out, was Elsa, a hat held to her head. When she saw them, she took her hat off and waved, and then almost as suddenly she disappeared from view.

She reappeared to open the side gate and, taking Max's hand, she led him triumphantly into the garden, where under a triangle of trees the table was laid for lunch. There were flowers twisted round each place mat, petals floating in the centre on a plate, and, as Max turned to her, he could see just from the shape her mouth made that it was German she was about to speak.

'Hello, welcome.' Klaus was striding out of the house, and Elsa's face closed up again, her mouth swallowing the words. 'Come and look around, will you?' Klaus put a hand on Max's arm, and Elsa nodded to him. 'Bitte,' she said just under her breath as Klaus ushered him away.

The house didn't smell of Heiderose, exactly, but it smelt familiar just the same. The same oil that they used to polish the furniture, could that be it, that made this house smell like every other German home? He stood there for a moment, until he realized Klaus was waiting for him to speak. 'Yes, yes, most unusual,' he said, waking from a sort of dream, and he followed his host across to the open staircase, light rippling between each laddered step. Upstairs, he glanced into a bedroom, a white rug spread on golden hardwood tiles, and then out they went on to the terrace, where, just as he'd suspected, there was a high blue stripe of sea.

'Hiddensee.' Gertrude leant in towards Max. 'Was it an island? This place where you and Elsa . . . never met?'

Max nodded, and to draw the place towards him he closed his eyes. Hiddensee. His sea-horse of an island, its narrow tail and ridged rock of a head.

'Vitte.' Elsa formed the word, and he realized he'd had his eyes closed for too long. 'I'm almost sure I know which house.' They all turned to watch Elsa as she bit into her lip. Her face was like a mirror, her eyes a map, and Max sat suspended as he waited for her to travel the length of the longest street and come upon his house. 'Was it near the bakery?' she said then, and, stretching her hands out like a psychic, 'There was a pear tree, a huge pear tree, growing outside.'

Max closed his eyes again as the house swam into his view and he could feel her across the table from him, like the secret member of a club.

'Is she right? Was there a pear tree?' Gertrude was impatient. 'Outside Vitte?'

'No, no,' Klaus joined in. 'Vitte was the village. The houses there didn't have names. Isn't that so, my El?'

'Just marks,' Max spoke up. 'Each fisherman had a mark, which they scored into the wall.' With his finger Max drew an X on the tablecloth. He traced a line across the top of it, and added a tiny squiggle to one toe. It dented for a second and was gone. Klaus took a pen and a notebook from his pocket and slid them across to Max.

'Go on,' he said, 'you're the artist.'

The pen was smooth to hold, the black ink soft as wine. The signs rolled out. X's and Z's with forks and tongues and roofs, A's and R's with twists and swirls. There was one sign like a flash of lightning and another like a horse. He'd made a study once of all the Vitte house signs, and now to his surprise they came crowding back.

'You'd think' – Gertrude examined them – 'that it would be easier to learn to read and write.'

Very carefully Max drew a flat-headed A, with what looked like a hangman's arm. 'This was our house. It belonged to a fisher family called Gau.' Helga, he thought, but he didn't say her name. 'And yes,' he looked at Elsa, 'we were beside the bakery.' He had a vision of his governess balancing a towering box of cake. 'We shared the house. The Gaus, they had one half, and we lived in the sunnier side of it, behind a dividing door.'

'Didn't you wonder,' Elsa asked, 'if they moved into your rooms once you were gone?'

'Elsa!' Klaus looked at her. And Gertrude laughed.

'The strange thing is' – Max shook his head – 'I never once thought of it till now.'

'Well,' Gertrude suggested, 'maybe that was the agreement. They just rented out those rooms for the summer.'

'We always thought of it as ours . . .' But Max had never dreamt about it. And his parents hadn't sacrificed themselves to keep it for his return.

'And how about you, Elsa?' Gertrude was asking. 'Was your house near by?'

'There were Nazis in the hills at Kloster,' Klaus answered for her. 'And nudists in the south. Vitte was the only place for a nice artistic family like Elsa's.'

'Nudists?' Gertrude was amazed.

'We were discouraged from going,' Max cut in. 'But all the same . . .'

'Well . . .' Gertrude shook her head. 'It must make Steerborough seem rather dull.'

'No. Not at all.'

Max wondered if Elsa had seen the carriage of drunken men, their insignia blazing as they rattled through Vitte in their cart. His mother was playing Boccia with two friends and he was sketching, shading the heavy balls as they thudded to the ground. He was rubbing with his pencil to create the sprays of dust. And then the cart had stopped and the men were leaning out. 'That boy' – they seemed to be falling half out of their cart as they pointed at him, sitting on his step – 'that is a rather Jewish-looking boy.' Max turned to his mother just in time to see her face flush red.

'It was a sort of idyll,' Klaus was telling Gertrude. 'With no cars. Just horses, bicycles and boats.'

'Do you remember the people always searching for amber on the beach.' Elsa was laughing now. 'And then the poet Ringelnatz put up a sign, "Amber. Lost on beach. Please return to Ringelnatz."'

'Yes,' Max smiled. 'Yes.'

'And twice a day the steamer came.' She was talking just to him.

'There was *Swanti*, and there was *Caprivi*.' Elsa said their names so tenderly, like long-lost friends.

'*Swanti* and *Caprivi*,' Max repeated, remembering how he'd waited at the harbour to see which one it would be.

'We were going to build a house there when we were first married,' Klaus said. 'We even chose a spot for it and drew up plans.' There was a silence while the four of them looked at their plates. 'But who needs Hiddensee when we can be here? For that one thing, we can be grateful. Thankyou, Adolf, for forcing us to Steerborough, where the sea is infinitely more refreshing, the summers full of . . . shall I say suspense?' Klaus raised his glass. 'Herr Hitler, I thank you again.'

Max stared at him.

'How about some coffee?' Gertrude stood up, although it wasn't her place to provide help.

But Elsa was collecting dishes. 'No, no, I'll bring it.' And she disappeared into the house.

12

Everywhere Lily looked now she saw Grae. Without the car, she supposed, he was bringing his work home. The back garden had turned into a workshop. A workbench was permanently set up and lengths of wood and half-finished constructions were propped against the shed. He wore the same checked jacket and the same hat through sun and rain, and one evening when she went out to fill the coal scuttle he offered her a box of kindling for the fire. Soft white ends of wood that needed to be burned. The rain was falling, it was starting to get dark, but he carried on sawing and measuring, never breaking his stride even when Em and Arrie called to him, hungry, from the back door.

It was May bank holiday and Nick was driving up. 'Right,' he said, 'I've got a pen. How do I get out of London?' Lily stood in the phone box and weighed the pebble in her palm. It was brown and unexceptional, probably to stop anyone replacing it, like she had, with a twopence coin. 'Christ,' she heard Nick sigh, 'I can't believe you're doing this to me . . .'

'Well,' Lily said. 'You head for the M25 . . . and go east . . . you know . . . the opposite direction from Heathrow?'

'East . . . Not . . . to . . . Heathrow,' Nick murmured as he copied her instructions down.

'And Nick . . .' she warned him as gently as she could, 'bring some warm clothes . . . and no . . . no white trousers.'

'No white trousers.' He paused to make a note of it and they both began to laugh. The year before they'd spent a week in Cornwall, during which Nick had almost immediately run out of clothes. He'd packed two T-shirts, no jumper, and one pair of oatmeal-coloured jeans. 'How was I to know?' Nick had protested.

'I'm a city boy. I've lived my whole life in Shepherd's Bush. Yes, yes.' He'd looked at her. 'You're from West London too, but you've got some kind of hiking, rambling blood, I'll swear to it. It must be in your genes.'

'So . . .' Lily could hardly believe that he was really coming. 'I'll see you tonight, then. About nine?'

Nick had been unusually attentive since his return from Paris. He'd even sent her a postcard. Notre Dame, the Louvre, the Pompidou Centre and the Seine. *You see*, he'd written, *we could do an architectural tour here. We could go by taxi. Just think of the money saved on hiring bikes!*

'Yes, I'll ring you from the car . . . Oh, bollocks . . . I forgot, you don't have a phone.'

'Sorry to deprive you of that call to say you're nearly there.'

'Cheek.'

'See you later, then. Drive carefully.' Her money was running out.

'Lily . . .'

'Yes?' But the last coin made a hollow echo as it dropped into the box.

Lily stood in Stoffer's wondering what she could possibly give Nick to eat. Everything that had seemed tempting to her before now seemed inedible. Crumpets, bacon, vacuum-pressed salami and ham. There was shortcake and treacle tart in silver-foil cases, one over-ripe tomato, a cluster of cauliflowers, a sack of onions and three leeks. Instead she hired a bike from the rack outside the shop and set off for Eastonknoll, taking the back lane that cut across the river. It ran through fields of cows penned in by ditches and was edged in places by huge flowering bushes of bright yellow gorse. Lily rattled over the Bailey bridge and set off across the corner of the golf course, glancing up at the shadow of the water tower, careful to avoid being hit by flying balls. She came out on the Common and swooped down towards the sea. The wind was fierce on the promenade, rippling the beige macs of the pensioners, ruffling their dogs, forcing them to clasp each other hard against the rails. Lily wheeled her bike along the sea front and bought tea at the kiosk, where the chairs were stacked three deep to weigh them down. She sat, as if in a high chair, her legs dangling inches from the ground, and watched the woman shutter up the hut. Above her, at the top of a steep flight of steps, she could see a ship's figurehead arching out from the wall of a large house.

'I might as well close up.' The woman stood before her, her apron flying, her sleeves flapping as she rolled the tables in.

Lily carried her bike up the steps towards the figurehead. It was not, as she'd imagined it, a mermaid or a queen, but a neat girl with a hat on, an umbrella at her side. Was she the captain's daughter, or the ship owner's young wife? and Lily saw that she had lost one of her arms, leaving a clean white plaster stump. Beside the building a mast was planted in the ground. Arrows fluttered from it, pointing the way towards Ramsgate, Zeebrugge, Holland. *The Sailors' Reading Room*. The words were moulded on to a plaque and Lily realized the house was a museum, open to the public, with arched white doors, and a well-worn copper catch. There was no one inside the reading room, and nothing very much to read. Just three copies of the *East Anglian Times* and two brown chairs. Around the walls in high glass cases were models of ships. Punts and schooners, battleships and yawls. Each plank of wood, each tiny rope and sail, minutely replicated, washed down, painted and oiled. Above the glass cases were photographs of fishermen and sailors, notebooks held open at the records of each voyage. There were lists of names, Harper, Seal, Child. Harry, Bertie, Mabbs and Mops. And beside each name the dates their lives spanned. There was another door at the back of the room, marked private, covered in green baize. There was a round window halfway up, not much bigger than an orange, and Lily pressed her face against it. To her surprise she saw two men playing billiards, a third reading a newspaper, a fourth doing nothing at all. She squeezed closer, peering to the side, catching sight of a ship's wheel balanced on a bench, and then someone tapped her on the arm.

'We're closing up now.' The man had a peaked hat, braided with blue cord, and he was wearing rubber wellingtons turned over at the knee. The clock behind him chimed as it reached five, a rich deep gong that warmed the room. 'Thankyou.'

Lily glanced around her at the photographs of men, the tools and scrolls and telescopes, the doomed faces of Seal, Harry, Child, all drowned in 1951. 'I'll come back when there's more time.' The man watched her until she was out of the room and then she heard him locking himself in.

There was a delicatessen in the market square that sold fresh parmesan, black pasta, Greek yoghurt and organic crisps. Lily filled two bags and topped them up with lamb's lettuce and fruit. She glanced into the window of the Regency Hotel, where an old man was dozing in a room of chintz, and noticed an advert for a waitress. *Urgently needed. Please apply within.*

Slowly she cycled home, her shopping hanging from each handle like the saddlebags of a mule. The wind had dipped, the sun hung low and warm, and in each hollow hovered the thick, sweet coconut smell of gorse. Lily meandered up and over a tiny ridge of hills, stretching her legs as she reached the top and letting the bike coast down. She was a child again. Warm and safe and happy, skittering and playing, bathed in breeze and birdsong and the Ambre Solaire smell of a beach. And then a man stepped out of the hedge. Lily's heart jolted so violently it strained against her ribs. Her blood spiralled, and as if it were a horse shying, her bike lurched over to one side. The man stood in the narrow path, so squarely that she couldn't pass. She was caught halfway down a slope, too weighted to pedal backwards, too frightened to go on. A tin of tomato purée rolled into the hedge and she heard the crunch of the spaghetti as the strands began to snap. The man took two steps towards her. He was wrapped in strips of plastic bag, his feet, his body, the top half of his head wound round with black. There was a sound, like hissing, rising from his legs, and his face was grizzled, camouflaged by beard. Lily glanced behind her. There was no one, nothing, as far as she could see. The scream that had been rising in her died. Keep calm, she told herself, keep calm. The man had picked up speed. He was lumbering towards her, his body squat, his eyes rimmed round with red, and then just as he was almost upon her, he keeled away through a thicket of tall grass. Lily gasped. It was possible he hadn't even seen her. His eyes, as he passed, were fixed on something else. Lily hauled up her bike and watched him go. He was walking through a field of heifers, following a path ridged up out of the ground. Ahead of him on the horizon was a clump of trees, a white wooden signpost where the path split into three, and beyond that, just visible, a cottage, the roof of which was bare.

Lily scrabbled the lost shopping back into her bag. Her legs felt weak, her arms stiff and painful, but as she cycled on she found that she was laughing with relief.

At eight o'clock Lily moved her car. She hadn't used it for almost two weeks and it took her hands and feet a moment to find their way around the gears. She backed it out and then parked it again, right over by the wall, so that when Nick arrived he'd be able to glide in beside her, and wouldn't block the lane. She made a fire, and found an old checked blanket to throw over the sofa, softening at least some of the brown. From time to time she went to the door and looked out, in case – just in case – Nick might be planning to surprise her and arrive early. She could, she thought, go to the phone box and find out how far he was on his way, but she had an image of him racing over the Orwell bridge, the wind tugging at his car, forcing him to swerve into a line of trucks as he reached out for the phone.

My sweet El, she read instead. She had become an expert on Lehmann's handwriting, the curls of it, the widened lines of his pen as it swept down. It amused her to think of the agonies of her school German, the endless repetitions of the grammar, the feminine, the masculine, the neuter, and how finally they had proved to be of use. *Today*, Lehmann wrote, *your first letter to arrive here was brought to me as I ate breakfast and all the tears that would have rolled down my cheeks because of your being alone were swiftly dried up by the sun. It sounds like you have been working very hard, my El, and you've told me about it all so beautifully, apart from the meals, which hopefully you haven't forgotten to have? Last night I couldn't sleep and I thought of all the things I wanted to tell you. Are you shopping properly for yourself? And when the doorbell rings, do you always look through the spyhole before you fling open the door and welcome whoever is there? Won't you get a chain put on? Write it down now so that you don't forget. And please don't get up too early, and don't race around after any trains. I could fill up this whole page writing to you with cautions and good pieces of advice. Don't forget, my El, love, my sweet body El, I want this child as much as you.*

PS. You've forgotten to tell me about your evenings. AND what you had to eat!

Lily was woken by a pounding on the door. The fire had died down, and when she jolted up, letters and deep purple flashes of the undersides of envelopes scattered to the floor. 'I'm coming,' she called, and then, remembering where she was, 'Come in, come in. It's open.' She turned, running her fingers through her hair, straightening her clothes. 'How was it?' she called out and then she gave a little yelp. Grae was standing in the hall. 'Oh.' She caught sight of the kitchen clock, and her face in the mirror below it, creased and red on one side where she'd been lying on a seam. It was ten-thirty. 'I'm sorry. I was expecting somebody else.'

Grae looked uncomfortable, his broad shoulders hunched a little

in the narrow hall. 'I'm sorry to disturb you, so late . . . it's just . . .
your car . . . it's parked too close to the gate and I've got to bring
some wood through, not now, but first thing in the morning. I saw
your light on . . . and . . . well . . . I thought it would be better than
knocking at six.'

Lily stared at him. She was only now starting to wake up. Pins
and needles were tingling in one leg and her pulse was racketing.
Where's Nick? she thought. He can't still be on the road?

'Of course. I'll move it now.' Like a sleepwalker she backed the
car away from the side gate. 'Is that enough, it's just I'm expecting
someone.' Lily peered at the black mass of the Green. 'My boyfriend.' She didn't want him to think she was alone. 'I'd better call.'
But more than any fear of Grae was her terror of stepping into
darkness, of being inside the phone box, sealed into its tower of
light, the only object visible while all around was night. 'Excuse me
. . . Would it . . . could I use your phone?'

The back door of Grae's cottage opened straight into the house.
A tiny kitchen, neat and tidy, and a sitting-room with a patterned
bedspread thrown over the sofa.

'It's on the windowsill,' Grae said, and she sat on the arm of a
chair and dialled. What if no one answered? She imagined Nick's
phone flung away from him, his car a shattered wreck, the ringing
the only sound on the black road.

'Yup.' Nick's voice was confident and gruff. Lily felt so angry
tears sprang into her eyes.

'Where are you?'

'In London.' Nick sounded as if he was entirely in the right.
'Sitting here, waiting for you to ring!'

'You said that you'd be here by nine.'

'Listen, five minutes after I spoke to you something came up.'
He lowered his voice as if to lure her. 'An unbelievably exciting
project. I even tried ringing you back in that bloody phone box, but
. . . well, I . . . with the exception of sending a carrier pigeon . . .
Lily, I'm sorry. You've got to get a mobile phone.'

Lily sat in silence in Grae's sitting-room. In the corner was an orange-crate full of the girls' toys. Teddies and stripped naked dolls, and a thread of cotton reels strung in a long line. 'So, when are you coming?'

There was a pause at the other end, and the unmistakable buzz and chatter of a bar. 'I don't see how I'm going to make it now. It's a huge project. If we start straight away, work on it all weekend and every second of next week, maybe there's a chance of winning the account.'

'Right . . .'

'And you'll be back next week, anyway. Won't you? Lily? Come on, don't be like that.'

Lily felt Grae watching her, leaning into the frame of the door. He was waiting for her to finish so that he could go to bed.

'Let's talk about it tomorrow.' She tried to sound breezy, as if she didn't care. 'It's just I'm . . . using someone's phone.'

'Oh.' Nick's voice was deflated as if he'd been looking forward to a row. 'Right, then. Speak to you, then.'

'Goodnight,' she said cheerfully, and she turned into the room. 'Thanks so much. Can I give you something towards . . .'

'No, no, it's fine.'

Grae went to the back door, and without another word held it open for her as she slipped out. She stood in the dark, the stars clustered above her, hard and glinting, crackling with light. 'Bastard.' She let herself say it out loud, and warm tears of disappointment rose up into her throat.

There followed three days of unseasonably hot weather. Lily took her towel and a bag of books and straight after breakfast she walked down to the beach. She lay there, soaking up the sun, leafing through photographic studies of the buildings that had been built in Europe between the first and second wars. Long, low houses, great sheets of glass, and she looked at these structures and thought that despite their Modernist predictions most people still lived in tall narrow terraces, row after row of them, stretching interminably through city streets. She read the short biographies of each of Lehmann's colleagues, Austrian and German, for the most part Jews. She traced their migration to Britain or America, the influence they had had there, or the inevitable dates of their deaths if they stayed on. But hard as she tried to concentrate, she soon became distracted by the beach. She had to sit up to watch Ethel, her shoulders sloped and freckled, her dressing-gown a warm white puddle on the sand. There was something magisterial about the way she strode into the sea and the moment when the orange flowers of her costume disappeared from view. Shortly afterwards a man came to exercise his horse. He thundered it along the sand, pulling it back time and again from its natural desire to swim. The horse was wild, its front legs rearing as it tried to escape the harness of its reins. By eleven, women with small children were starting to arrive, dragging push-chairs, windbreaks, bags packed with bottles, blankets and spare clothes. Lily watched these women caught between laughter and despair as one child dashed towards the sea, while another, wailing, lay face down on the ground. They stood there, unable to move forwards or back with the pack horse of a pushchair stranded wheel-deep in sand. By mid-morning Em and Arrie had appeared. Lily watched them as they scouted round the beach. They liked to surprise her, to jump out at her from behind a dune, and they'd wait until she least expected it before creeping up and digging a moat around her towel.

'What do they say at school?' she asked eventually when the day-trippers had receded, and they had the beach back to them-selves. 'Don't they mind about you never going in?' She was stretched out, still and patient, while they buried her with sand. The grains were damp below the surface, dry and ticklish on top.

'It's half-term.' They shook their heads, staggered by her ignor-ance. 'And anyway,' Em said, 'we saw you sunbathing. You said you were only renting Fern Cottage so that you could do your work.' She picked up one of Lily's books. 'Which house would you like best?' And the girls hovered over it, gasping, sighing, muttering, as they flicked through for their dream home.

13

Max was almost at the Lehmann house. His scroll, when he unfurled it, spread right across the living-room floor. A length of green and brick and window, birds and cats and sky. He was tempted to pin it like a border round the room, but more than anything he liked the secret knowledge of it, rolled up under his arm. As an experiment he took a sharp black pen and made a tiny sign. A miniature fisherman's squiggle on the front door of Marsh End. He hid another under the eaves of Heron House, and the strange lopsided K that stood for the family Gottschalk, he slid into the porch of Sole Bay View.

Max walked up and down the lane. Passing and re-passing the Lehmann house. He'd become acclimatized to thatches, pantiles, pebbled walls and bays, and now he could not think how to begin. He remembered an article from the early 1930s about a house Lehmann had designed. It was in a suburb of Hamburg, had been commissioned by the director of the Deutsche Bank, and Max remembered his father marvelling at it, predicting that this young architect was destined to be Germany's next star. Slowly the sun curved around the corner of the house. It crept over the picket fence and washed the glass with colour, Max sat on his painting stool and noticed the dark wood softening, saw how the panelling turned from rust to gold to grey, so that the whole garden was reflected in its windows, the leaves of the beech tree opposite dancing in the open panes of glass. Max closed his eyes. All day he had been haunted by the smell of gherkins, the smell of the barrel in the grocer's shop in Vitte that stood just inside the door. He used to sniff them, lean into the pickling water and breathe in, and now as he let his face hover, he could hear the shopkeeper talking to his mother, telling her there was no more wool in the colour she desired. She could, he told her, order it from Stralsund, and then it might come in on the steamer by the end of the week. 'Yes,' she said. 'Maybe I'll do that.' And then Kaethe's strong hand came up behind him and pushed his head down into the barrel. His nose brushed against the gherkins, his mouth filled up with brine, and there was the cold sharp pain of vinegar water seeping into his ear. Choking and spluttering, he came up. Before him was his mother, furious and alarmed. 'Max!' she scolded, and then he saw his sister, her hands folded innocently behind her back. 'Max,' Kaethe reproached him softly, and she took a handkerchief from her pocket and began to mop his neck.

Max realized he was moaning, still sitting on his stool. He staggered up, embarrassed, staring round, and as he moved, his ear shot through with pain. He put one hand to it, and found that it was seeping, a thin translucent liquid trickling from the drum.

'Gertrude,' he whispered as he stumbled into the house, and, not finding her at home, he soaked a tea towel with cold water and pressed it to his head. It seemed ridiculous that his ears should still be capable of giving him such pain. They should feel nothing, should be removed, the drums pulled out, but just then he heard a little pop, and after it a strange clear gust of air. His heart leapt. It was there, a tunnel of sound, but then everything closed up again, like a screen door easing shut, and he was left with the familiar low whirr and echo all trammelled through with pain.

'You should have fetched me,' Gertrude said when she came in. 'I was only at the vicarage, helping with preparations for the fête.'

'There's nothing that can be done.' Max was slumped over in his chair, shivering, longing for a blanket to wrap around his back.

Undeterred, Gertrude lit a candle and, pouring a pale oval of oil into a spoon, she began to warm it over the flame. 'You forget,' she told him, pressing his head to one side, 'I've looked after children all my life,' and she eased the liquid into his ear.

'Thankyou,' he mouthed, and she nodded brusquely and laid her hand across his forehead. It was comforting, the cool, broad strength of it, the calluses on the curve of her palm.

'You've got a fever?' And when he nodded she went through to run him a cold bath. 'Go on, then, get in,' she told him, holding open the bathroom door, and when he resisted, whimpering, she threatened to take off his sweat-soaked clothes herself. To his surprise the first chill of the water helped him. It seemed to bring him down into himself, and he took the metal cup from the side of the bath and began emptying it over his head. Soon, his teeth stopped chattering, and his face began to cool. Now there was nothing left except the pulsing of his ear, a sick and heavy agony that tasted, when he thought of it, of tin.

Gertrude helped him up the stairs, turning to the window as he settled into bed. 'Can I bring you anything?' she asked, but Max's eyes were closing, and with his hand pressed between the pillow and his ear he sank down into sleep.

Gertrude had been careful not to use the word 'analysis', but had explained her idea to Mrs Wynwell more as a kind of cosy chat. 'It's been over a year since your husband . . .' – she didn't believe in letting sentences trail off – 'since Harry died. A year, Mrs Wynwell, that's a long time in a child's life.'

'He's always been quiet,' Mrs Wynwell said, 'and I thought what with the piano . . .' She looked up at Gertrude to show that she was grateful, but would rather not. It was true, Alf had always been a quiet child, playing in a corner while his mother worked, and Gertrude had admired the way they moved around each other, attached invisibly, but with no great fuss. But after Harry's boat went down, Alf's voice turned to a whisper, and then stopped.

'After his tea, then?' Gertrude persisted, smiling, her eyebrows raised, and they agreed he might come to her on Wednesdays at half past six.

Gertrude rearranged the furniture, shifting the sofa out into the room, and moving her chair a little nearer so that she could stare out at the lawn. She had a toy for Alf, a bag she'd sewn herself, and in it she'd put a rubber ball and seven jacks. She knew it was unethical to trade gifts for trust, but from her own experience with children in the war nursery knitting clothes for dolls had often done more to console them than any amount of wise words.

Alf arrived just after six, slipping as usual into the hall. 'Come and sit down,' Gertrude called, and he sidled into the room. Alf kept his eyes fixed on his shoes, his face mournful but shiny as if it had just been washed. He sat as directed on the sofa. 'So,' Gertrude said eventually, 'how are you today?'

Alf looked at her, clear-eyed, as if he were running over everything in his life, and then – maybe it seemed to him that he had told her – his face closed in and he stared down at his feet.

'Well.' Gertrude smiled. 'I've been very busy, helping sort through the raffle prizes for the summer fête.' There was nothing really there to interest him. A watercolour of the estuary, a bottle of whisky, another of rum. 'We might,' she said instead, 'have a "Guess the currants in the cake" competition. Or we could hoodwink them, what do you think, and just put in one?'

Alf was staring into the garden, chewing his lip, watching two magpies pecking at the grass. One for sorrow, two for joy, Gertrude thought, but all the same she felt a quiver of misgiving when one of the birds flew off over the hedge. Gertrude waited fifteen minutes, and then, leaning towards him, she gave Alf the jacks. She'd made the bag out of a scrap of curtain, and plaited green ribbon to make a string. Alf drew it open.

'Shall we play?' Gertrude offered, and Alf slipped down off the sofa and tipped the jacks on to the parquet floor. He caught the ball which was skittering away from him, and waited while Gertrude pushed away her chair. Her knees cracked as she knelt down beside him, her heel stinging as it dented into wood. Alf flashed her a smile. His two front teeth were missing, and she hadn't known. He bounced the ball and picked up the first jack. He bounced it higher and scooped up two. Three, he had to scrabble now and the ball hit the side of his knuckle. 'Bad luck.' It was Gertrude's turn. She bounced the ball, not too high, not at an angle, but expertly giving herself time. Two, she swept them up and turned her wrist to catch it. Three, but the ball was thrown too high and it hit the link chain of her watch. 'Ahhhh,' she let out a sigh of frustration, but Alf had already started his turn. This time he was more careful. Measuring the bounces, not taking his eye from the ball. He scooped up three and let it fall neatly into his palm. Four. He'd done it. 'Five,' Gertrude whispered, and they smiled as the tension mounted, as slowly, carefully he aimed the ball. It bounced high. He scooped and swept the floor, but he had to take his eye away for one flick of a second to find that last fifth jack. Down the ball fell, skimming his palm. 'Bad luck,' Gertrude exhaled, and Alf laid his jacks down.

Gertrude was determined to do at least as well as him. Not all children appreciated it if you let them win. She arranged the jacks carefully, a bright cluster of kisses, with just the right amount of space in between. She stared at them, holding their formation, determined not to look down. But no, she misjudged it, picked three jacks instead of four, and, although she caught the ball, she had to relinquish her go. She could hear Alf's breathing, feel his heat as he squatted on the floor. With quick flicks of his wrist he scooped and turned his hand. Six, Gertrude's heart was beating, she wanted him to win, and then he was scooping up the seventh jack, cramming it into his hand. 'Yes,' the word escaped him, and he caught the ball.

'Well done,' she said, and Alf got up and very carefully stowed his treasure back into its bag.

Gertrude stood up and stretched her legs. One shoulder had locked as she'd pressed herself into the floor. 'That wasn't so bad?'

she said. 'Run home now, and I'll see you next week at the same time.' Alf looked her over warily as if she might be mad, and then, tucking the bag into his pocket, he slipped through the door and sped off down the lane.

14

Folded into the next letter was a plan of Lehmann's room. He had his own notepaper now with his name and title – Architekt – printed large across the top. *Under the window is a table, and on the right of this table are my drawing things. In the middle is my writing case, and on my left my inkpot and the silver box with your lock of hair. I shall have to make do with their company until I can come home to you. Don't be sad, don't cry. I hesitate to say I told you to be careful, not to rush around, and I shan't say it. Or even think it. But rest now, and wait, and I'll be home soon to look after you. I know a child is the one thing you most want, but don't forget that you've got me.*

Lily searched hungrily for the next letter, examining the post-marks for 1932, for June.

Next to the picture of you on my table, a dark red carnation is standing in a narrow vase. Just as you love them, it is admiring you. But you look sad, and I'm trying everything to make your lovely eyes a little happier. Last night I lay awake, thinking about our plans for Palestine, and all the difficulties involved in settlement and travel. You must bear the possibility of this in mind, my love, because the time is coming when we will have to find somewhere else to go.

Lily folded the letter, the cream of the paper, the grains watery as silk, and as she slid it into its envelope she pressed it to her nose. There was the sweet, sour smell of tobacco, the dry dustiness that threatened to make her sneeze, and she wondered if this was Lehmann's smell, sealed in a capsule, or more likely the smell of a cupboard in North London where the other Lehmann had stored them in their carrier bag through all these years.

*   *   *

Dear Nick,

I'm still here. I just thought, as you were working so hard . . . Lily chewed the end of the pen. She hadn't told him she was taking Fern Cottage on for another month. *I just don't know if I'm cut out to be an architect.* She hadn't meant to write that, but since she'd been here she didn't know if she was the right person to redesign a kitchen, organize a team of builders while they refurbished a house. Was she ambitious enough, she didn't know, to create her own buildings, to do what Lehmann had done, to invent himself, not once, but twice. 'So? What then. . . ?' She could see Nick's face. 'Go back to waitressing?' She felt a wave of anguish that after three years of training she still didn't know what she wanted to do. *I'd like to make a house,* she was doodling now, *not just design it.* It would be surrounded by larches, looking out to sea, it would be sustainable, adaptable, in tune with its environment. *Maybe I'll go on one of those self-build courses . . .* and she remembered that there were packs you could order from Sweden. Wooden houses with verandas running round two sides.

When she'd first met Nick she'd been a waitress at a restaurant in Covent Garden. She'd started working there part-time to supplement her art school grant. But gradually her hours had lengthened, doubled, until, almost without realizing it, the restaurant was at the centre of her life. It was like a family, the small evening world of it, the hierarchy, the bonuses and rules. It gave her pleasure, slipping into her uniform, the black and white of such a limited choice. She loved arriving, walking against traffic, when everyone else was finishing for the day, and now she thought of it, she could almost feel the linen skirts of the tables, smell the cane baskets and bread sticks, hear the crunch of the tiny Hoover as it rolled over the tablecloth for crumbs.

But when she met Nick she'd felt ashamed. 'Is this what you really want to do?' He'd cupped her face in his hands, looked at her so intently she felt she must be worth much more.

'Not necessarily,' she faltered. 'Not for ever . . .'

Lily's paintings were ranged around her walls. They snaked in and out of her bedroom, were lined two deep along the hall.

'Can I?' Nick was heading for the largest of them, while Lily lurched forward in alarm.

'No,' she said, 'please don't.'

But Nick ignored her, turning a whole row round to face the room. 'They're lovely.' He was staring into a pale and chalky landscape, a light-filled space of calm. 'But . . . Unless you show them, have an exhibition, you'll be working as a waitress when you're ninety-three.'

Lily turned each painting back to face the wall. She didn't want anyone to see them. Dreaded the thought they might be spirited away. Once, her landlord, who lived downstairs, had arranged an exhibition. He'd knocked on her door, beaming, to tell her a friend of his who had a café in Highbury would be happy to let her hang them on his walls. 'You might even sell some, you never know.'

Lily had stared at him. Shocked to hear herself shout, 'No, I don't want that!' People flicking spaghetti, discussing their love lives. Her face, she was sure of it, must be bright red. 'Tell him he can't.'

Her landlord had backed away. 'I just thought you'd be glad of the exposure, not to mention the extra cash.' He looked rueful. 'If they sold.' She guessed he'd been thinking how much he'd like to raise the rent.

'Come with me.' Nick had seized his car keys. 'Come on, let's go for a drive.'

It was late, and London was slick and black and empty. They drove towards Victoria, lit up by the lights along the palace garden wall, over the bridge at Vauxhall, and along beside the river. 'My favourite view of London,' Nick told her as they crossed the river again, at Waterloo, and hungrily they twisted their heads from side to side to try and take it in. The strings of lights across the water, the arches and tunnels of the bridges, the boats, the buildings, their every shape of window, the green and gold of their roofs. 'Drive more slowly,' she begged, but there was a car behind them, and they were forced into the tunnel of the Holborn Viaduct and up towards Bloomsbury. Nick parked outside the British Museum and they got out and clung to its railings. It was lit up to glow like Egypt, the orange light trickling warm over its steps. 'How would you feel?' he asked her, 'if you had any part in something as beautiful as that?' They gazed at the great heads of the lions, the beauty of the pillars and the new glazed dome. 'You're mad,' she told him, and he said that it helped when submitting plans for someone's toilet if you were thinking on the most dazzling scale. He picked her up and spun her round and they fell against each other, laughing, staggering as if they were drunk.

More slowly, they drove into the City, along the narrow gorges that ran between old buildings and new. 'When,' he asked her as they came out into the clearing of St Paul's Cathedral, 'did you last climb up?'

'With school?' She could only dimly remember the flurry of bodies, the coats and bags as her whole class wheeled to the top. 'And, anyway, I didn't think you were allowed to admire St Paul's. I read somewhere that Wren wasn't a true architect, although I can't see how . . .'

'You're right.' Nick leant across and kissed her ear. 'But it's the buildings you can see from there that should force you up. And, anyway,' he grinned at her, 'if we want to admire St Paul's Cathedral at two in the morning, then who's to know?'

'I'll go up tomorrow.' She kissed him back. 'Or today.' And inspired by his passion, and his faith in her, she applied to his old college to study architecture on a three-year course.

There was a cupboard at Fern Cottage filled with maps. *Maps*, it said helpfully on a sticker pasted indelibly to the outside. There were maps of East Anglia, local footpath maps, Ordnance Survey maps dating back over seventy years. With all this information it seemed ridiculous that she still hadn't found the Lehmanns' house. Each day she imagined she would come across it, see it somewhere on the corner of a lane, but there was nothing in the village that wasn't thatched or gabled, pebbled, terraced, beamed. Lily pulled out a map of Steerborough and spread it over the floor. The houses were drawn in little blocks, sitting for the most part along the village's main street. There were some she already recognized. The old Dutch house that leant to one side, the double-fronted cottage that had once been the pub. It had been moved by wheelbarrow, brick by brick to its new site beside the shop. 'Was that a common practice?' she'd asked Ethel. And Ethel had told her about a converted barn behind Kiln Lane that had travelled eight miles. Maybe, Lily thought, the Lehmann house had moved. Had been taken off to another village by wheelbarrow, had even been discovered and submitted by a more imaginative student as the winning project of their term. She should ask Ethel. Ethel would know. Ethel may even have remembered Lehmann. Might have known Elsa, known what had happened to her in 1953 after Lehmann died.

Lily folded the map. There was one road, Mill Lane, down which she'd never ventured, on the corner of which foundations for a house were being laid. 'Hidden House' the map had said, but there was nothing there but mud and rubble now. Mill Lane ran behind the garage, curved round towards the sea, and she'd avoided it because it looked so recent, had a pale, suburban gravel drive. But the gravel was misleading. The houses on each side were ancient, elaborate, huge lawns behind wrought iron gates, the only sound the twitter of small birds. No, Lily told herself, there is nothing useful here, but she walked on anyway, lulled by the silence and the curve. Almost at the end of the road, nestled to one side, she could just make out the corner of a house. It was old and low, a rhubarb shade of pink, and as she drew nearer she saw that welded into the crook of its two halves was a 1950s porch.

Lily leant against the gate. The house looked abandoned, its curtains open, its porch empty and chilled. She pushed the gate, but the grass around it had grown up solidly and it would not move. Lily glanced around and, seeing no one, she jammed her feet against the wooden slats, and, climbing on to the gatepost, she jumped down from the top. Quickly she knocked on the door. She waited, watching for a shadow behind the watery glass, and then, when no one answered, she edged round to the back. Her heart was thumping, her ears magnifying every sound, but she had to keep on. The garden was round, a green bowl tipped up to the sky, with a lawn so dense and springy it might have been nibbled flat by sheep. In the centre stood a tall thin tree, with one branch, high up, just asking for a swing. Lily breathed, a little calmer now, and turned to look at the house. A bench, French windows, eaves and arches all looking out to sea. The windows were dark, the wood and glass doors bolted shut. Lily tiptoed closer and pressed her face against the glass. Inside, everything was neglected. Tattered furniture and threadbare rugs, dishevelled somehow, and suffering, she could smell it through the wood, from damp.

Lily walked to the back of the garden. If she could slip through the hedge, she might come out on the marshes, on the flat waterlogged heathland that led up to the sea. She climbed into the scrub of the hedge and felt her way along, looking for a weakness, feeling with her hands and feet for a gap. But the branches were matted, prickling with hawthorn, and Lily was forced to walk back through the garden and climb over the gate. It was then she saw the car. An old grey Morris parked right up by the fence. Lily stopped and stared at it. Surely she would have noticed if it had been there before, its fawn and blue interior, its roof as round as a bald head. She put out a hand to touch it, to see if it was warm, but was halted by the sensation that she was being watched. She swallowed, glancing at the house, but there was no light, no shadow. All the same she turned away, and, as quickly as she could, she crunched back along the drive.

*   *   *

Working like crazy. Going well. Should know soon if we've won. It was Friday again and Nick had scrawled his message on an official envelope from college which he'd forwarded on. She should call him. It was stubborn and stupid not to have called before, but then if he really was working so hard there wasn't much point in interrupting him, unless to wish him luck. Yes, she thought, she should call, but when she went to the phone box she found that it actually was broken. Broken or full up. 999 calls only, the message flashed. *Call 999. Wait by the wall . . .* The note was still there. It was held down by the same grey pebble, the edge jagged and torn. Lily pulled a pen out of her pocket and made a tiny mark, a little zigzag in the corner, and then, self-conscious, she looked round to check if she'd been seen. Stop it, she told herself, there's no one there! And shaking her head, wondering if she really had now spent too much time alone, she walked back across the Green.

'Sorry' – Grae was hovering by her door, pacing up and down – 'but I was wondering, could I . . . it's just Em's cut her foot. I've tried calling a taxi but I can't find one even as far as Waveney that's free.'

Lily looked at him. He didn't seem like a man capable of throwing someone down the stairs. He smiled at her, anxious, and his face was Arrie's, heart-shaped, golden brown. 'I've wrapped it up, but it's still bleeding and I think maybe she needs stitches, or a shot of tetanus.'

'Of course. Wait one minute.' Lily rushed into the house to find her keys, and by the time she came out again Grae had brought out both the girls. He was holding Em by the hand, leading her towards the car. One foot was wrapped in a tea towel and her face was streaked with tears.

'I didn't mean to,' Arrie was whimpering, and Grae put an arm out to her. 'It's all right, I've told you already, it's not your fault.'

Lily opened the door and waited while they manoeuvred them-selves into the back. 'What happened?' she asked as she reversed.

'They were playing up by that old mill, and . . . What happened, Emerald?'

'Arrie pushed me in.'

'I didn't mean to!' Arrie wailed, and Grae sighed as if he was too tired to say anything more. 'There must have been something sharp in there, that's all.'

They drove silently up the long straight road, through acres of corn, pale green and swaying, turning right by a mud-brown field of pigs. The field was dotted with small tin houses, and the pigs, like campers, smiling, stretched out beside them on their sides. Lily curved inland around the swamp mouth of the estuary, slanting back towards Eastonknoll, over the hump-backed bridge. Once they reached the outskirts of the town, Grae directed her past the tea shops and the scouts' hut and the town hall with a poster advertising a meeting of the WI, and on towards the sea front, zigzagging through back streets, until they pulled up in front of the surgery. 'Right,' he said with evident relief, and without asking if she was needed Lily followed them in.

The waiting-room was empty and Grae and Emerald were ushered away through white swing doors.

Christ, Lily thought, next time I'm in London and I need Accident and Emergency, I must remember it'll be quicker to drive here.

Arrie had crouched down on the floor and was building a tower of bricks, pressing so hard on each plastic block that the raised circles were pockmarking her palms.

Lily knelt beside her. 'Can I help?'

'I didn't push her.' Arrie's whole face had fattened up with tears. 'I grabbed her, that's all, and she tripped in.'

'It's all right.' Lily began passing her the coloured blocks. 'But how did you get back?'

Arrie looked at her suspiciously. 'She hopped, and then . . .' She glanced round quickly. 'Bob the Bog gave her a ride.'

'A ride?'

'He carried her.'

They both glanced at the receptionist, clean and smooth, her head bent over the desk.

'Who is Bog the Bod, I mean . . . Bob the . . .'

Arrie started to giggle. 'He's . . . He's our friend, and Alf's,' and then the swing doors swished open and Grae reappeared holding Em by the hand. Her foot was bound round with a thick cream bandage and, compared to the other, looked startlingly clean.

'Did she need stitches?' Lily struggled up.

'Superglue.' Grae said, disbelieving. 'I could have done the job at home. They squeezed it in and held the cut together, just like . . . I don't know. A chair.'

'Ice-cream,' Em whispered. 'You promised.'

'Yes, it's true.'

Grae let her climb up on to his back and they walked out on to the front. There were people sprawled inside their beach huts, others building castles on the sand, and children in huge black rubber rings floated about in the sea. They walked until they reached the tea hut, and both girls, taking advantage of the drama, chose huge double-flaked 99s.

'I think we'll have four of those,' Grae ordered, casting a glance at Lily, his eyes bright slits of blue. And so they sat on the sea wall, the four of them, licking, turning their ice-creams slowly round to catch the drips. The sea was empty, flat and shimmering, the tide pulling out, drawing with it sand and stones and seaweed, a thin layer with each wave. Em, seemingly recovered, hopped off along the beach, and Arrie scurried behind her, head bent, looking for treasure. They found a hag stone, meant to bring you luck, although Lily thought they looked sinister, eye sockets with the centre eaten out. 'Keep that for me,' Em said, pressing it into Lily's hand and Arrie found a worn green piece of glass. It could have been jade, so fine and milky, and Lily slipped off the wall and began searching too. There was amber on this beach apparently, but instead she found a one-pound coin, a pale pink pebble, transparent when wet, and a flint, cracked open, with the tiny fossil of a sea horse embossed into its side. She glanced back at Grae. He was quite still, his face set, watching them, and she wondered if he was thinking about Em slipping down into the swampy water of the mill.

The girls made a castle, with towers and turrets and a drawbridge over a moat, and Em's white bandage was forgotten, camouflaged with sand. Grae called them. He'd brought a tray down to the beach, loaded with toasted sandwiches, apple juice and a huge brown pot of tea.

'Dad!' His children leant against him, amazed, but he just shook them off and poured.

'Milk and sugar?' he asked Lily as he stirred.

They sat against the sea wall and basked in the low rays of the sun.

'It looks cloudy in Steerborough,' Lily said, shading her eyes as she stared out along the coast, and Grae told her how the horizon was so huge it was possible to choose your weather and drive.

'Once,' Arrie told them, 'when we had a car, we drove all the way to Lowestoft so we could have a picnic in the sun. 'Didn't we, Dad?' Arrie persisted. 'When we had a car, didn't we chase the sun?'

Grae touched her head, absentmindedly, but he didn't reply. Lily shivered. The sun was sinking red behind the lighthouse, its warmth stopping just short of the shore. The beach was striped in shadow, the bright stones turning dull, and as if they had all agreed it, they got up and walked back to the car.

There was sand in Lily's hair, and her legs and arms were covered in a sheen of salt. Her hands were dry, her fingers smooth as dust, slipping as she gripped the wheel. When she got home, she thought, she'd lie in a hot bath, tease the wind out of her hair, but as they turned on to the Green, there was a car parked in her space.

'Cheek,' Lily said, relishing the idea she owned this patch of ground. 'What's going on?' And it was only then that she recognized the car.

'Thankyou.' Grae turned to her as the children scrambled out. 'Really thankyou. If you ever need anything . . .' He gave her a wide smile. 'More kindling?' And just at that moment Nick opened her cottage door.

15

Max stopped halfway down the lane and listened. Almost always, after an infection, his ears were worse. They whirred and popped and crackled, and once for three long days and nights he'd heard the robust singing of a male voice choir. But today his ears were cloaked in a warm blanket of quiet. It was like looking through a window – the trees gently swaying, a dog with its mouth open, the slap of a gate swinging shut. He walked past the Lehmanns' house – Hidden House, it was called, he hadn't noticed that before – and set his stool up in front of the thatched cottage on the other side. The walls were weathered brick, pink-seamed and darkened by the wind. The thatch was steep and grey, netted in with string like an old lady's bun.

'What are you doing?' It was Elsa, leaning over him, scrutinizing the place where her husband's house should be. Max looked up into her face. Rose and quartz and chestnut, her eyes, a fractured splintering of blue. 'You're leaving us out?'

'I'm sorry.' He shook his head. He'd tried, he wanted to tell her, but it was impossible to fit it in. Elsa turned away. He could feel her back just to the left of him, her ankles, her calves showing below a cotton skirt. He knew she was looking at their house, examining it, and then, without a word she walked away.

There are artists, Henry wrote, *who make the mistake of setting up for themselves a standard of beauty. They choose to paint only those things which can be made to conform to that idea. This is the attitude of the critic and not the artist. Now if you compare this attitude with that of Degas, Manet, Monet or Pissarro, who all went to nature like children to*

find new beauty, and whose work points to the fact that beauty exists
everywhere, then you will find that the critic leads nowhere, whereas these
others are like a river carrying you to wherever you want to go.

Max thought of Helga, and the pictures of her he no longer had. They were the first things he'd done that he was proud of, the first pictures that were actually his own. Helga Gau. His friend and playmate. The daughter of the fishing family that lived next door. She was a straight, thin girl with hair cut square as a box, her face the colour of sand. They'd ridden their bicycles together, scooped eels up with their nets, and then one summer he'd arrived and found her changed. There was a new-milk look in her eyes, and her hair was long. When she walked, her hips, still narrow, swayed in little jolts from side to side. Helga was the one person who never seemed to notice he'd gone deaf. She'd call to him, curse him when he didn't come, and slap him on the arm. Now she wheeled her bike round to face him, tilting her head as if to slide the words out on a spoon. 'Come.' Max wasn't sure he liked this new slippery girl, but he pulled his own bike out of the shed and vigorously pumped up the tyres. Helga stood and watched him, her pale hair blowing in the wind, and when he was ready she swung her leg over the cross-bar and sped off along the lane. Max flew along behind her, watching her straight back, the way her shoulders seemed to be pressed down, lengthening her neck. They cycled fast along the lane that led away from the harbour, and when it petered out they jumped their bikes like horses over the ridged land until they were on the track that led to Neuendorf.

Max had been told so often not to go to Neuendorf, to where the naturists had taken over the beach, that he found himself looking over his shoulder. But Helga cycled on. She pedalled fast, never looking round, and so Max leant into the wind and gained on her, bit by bit, until they were riding side by side. Her shirt was pushed flat against her chest, the wind pressing into her, and there, as if they had sprung up overnight, were two small breasts. Max looked down, surprised that she would change without him, and, self-conscious, he began to follow the arc of his front wheel. A second later he was lying on the ground.

'You silly fool.' Helga skidded round to help him. 'Keep your eyes on the road.' And as he hobbled up, he found he'd grazed the length of his arm. 'Come on,' she said, examining him, 'we'll wash it.'

They splayed their bikes against a sand dune and ran down to the sea. Max squatted in the shallows and laid his arm against the surf. The salt water lapped in and stung his graze, but when he withdrew it it hurt more. He kicked off his boots, pulled his shirt off over his head and waded in. His shorts darkened with each step, the small hairs on his belly electrified with cold, and, although he was sure Helga was calling to him, he didn't look round. He could feel her following him, the current of her body pushing out into the shallow sea, and his heart beat faster the further he strode out. Her fingers, he imagined, must be moments from the hollow of his back, and he plunged, kicking to escape her, and only when he emerged did he allow himself to turn his head.

Helga was still standing on the beach. Her hand was up, shading her eyes, and just beyond her, a naked couple were playing a game of ball. They looked married, even without their clothes, their bodies worn and solid, matching as they stretched and threw. They seemed joined together, throwing, catching, throwing the ball again, while their feet stayed rooted in the sand. Max lay back into the waves, resting his head on water. He did a little flip and pushed himself under and when he looked up again Helga had taken off her skirt. She was standing in her white underwear, unbuttoning her shirt. Max began frantically to tread water. He mustn't swim towards her, but neither could he bring himself to turn away. Under her white shirt, she had a white vest, and under her vest – she was pulling it off over her head – there was nothing but her newly moulded chest.

A small ripple broke out in the easy rhythm of the naturists' game, as the ball spun out of the man's hand and rolled towards the sea. Max laughed and floated for a moment and when he looked back the woman was retrieving it, her body softening for a moment as she bent to scoop it up. Helga stepped out of her underwear, laying it with her clothes in a pile, and then she was wading out to join him, throwing herself down and skimming out along the knee-high surf. Max felt his body grow rigid in the water, an energy pulsing through him as if he were being pumped full of iron ore. Helga was swimming towards him, and with every stroke he felt himself grow hard. He wanted to push his hand into his shorts and release himself into the sea, the brushing of the cotton, the restriction was almost more than he could bear, but she was closing in on him and he was so paralysed it was all he could do to remember how to float.

'Hello.' She was flitting round him like a dolphin, her snub-nosed, freckled face lit up with drops, her hair still gleaming, dry, the ends like rags. She looked at him for a moment, and then she put her hands on his shoulders, and without warning, pushed him down. He'd had no time to breathe, and he was gasping, his eyes open, looking up at her naked body, as white as roots below the sea. He lashed and struggled, choking, kicking at her knees, until her hands weakened, and laughing she flung herself away. Max had to fight to hold his tears. His body was weak, his erection gone, and, instead of shouting, he turned and crawled away in long sad strokes. When he stopped, he lay back on the sea, staring up into the sky, calming himself, stretching his arms and legs as straight as they would go. He lay like that for a long time, glancing round occasionally to get his bearings from the beach, until there was nothing to be done but swim back to the shore. He found his shirt and boots lying where he'd left them, but Helga's pile of clothes was gone.

'You were too young, of course' – Klaus leant in towards Max – 'to fight in the first war?' They were at Gertrude's, drinking sherry, braving the garden and the evening gnats.

'Yes . . .'

'I was fourteen when the war started.' Klaus was leaning back, pulling on his cigar. 'If I had been younger I might have escaped it. "Thank god," my mother said each birthday, "I had my girl children first," and it's true, my life was probably saved by being the youngest of four.'

'My father fought . . .' Max said, but Klaus was still talking, remembering the day that he was seventeen, the day his mother's prayers ran out. The day he marched off to the Front, quite sure it was just his effort that was needed to give that final push. 'But within six months I was at home again, helpless as a child, thin and wretched, my whole body . . . – you'll appreciate this, Max – a shade of palest green.'

'Were you wounded?' Gertrude asked. The word sent a tiny shiver through her – *wounded*, as if she'd just that minute been pricked by a pin.

'Not wounded,' Elsa told her. 'But Klaus lay all night beside a man, dead from tuberculosis, and after that . . .'

'I didn't realize . . .' Klaus talked as if to himself. 'I was so exhausted I didn't realize he was dead.'

Gertrude narrowed her eyes at the brown roll of his cigar. She had urged him to light it to keep the midges off.

'After the war ended, I went up into the Alps, to Aroza, to take a cure. I lay on a terrace, eating, sleeping, reading, letting the sun beat down on my bare chest. But at night . . . See what you make of this' – he turned to Gertrude – 'I dreamt only of the war. Horses blown open, young men sliding into graves of mud. My screams threatened to wake the sanatorium, and so my doctor moved me to a little room at the back of the building, a room originally intended for storing furniture when it rained. And there, instead of my feather bed, I slept quite peacefully on a wooden board.'

He looked at Gertrude, one eyebrow raised. 'So' – he sighed when she offered nothing – 'I slept on my board, tramped through the woods to tire myself out, and every day they weighed me and fed me milk and cream until I was so fat and brown and handsome that they declared me cured.'

Max looked at him. He *was* handsome. A small man, his face brown, his dark hair, although he must be fifty, only just beginning to grey.

'But you've always taken care.' Elsa laid one hand on his arm.

'Yes,' he said, as if to reassure her. 'Although never could I drink a glass of milk again.'

'And the cigars?' Gertrude asked him. 'Are they prescribed?'

'Gertrude' – Klaus fixed her with a sombre eye – 'there is a psychological interpretation, is there not, for the need to be always chewing on cigars?'

'Perhaps your mother didn't breast-feed you?' Gertrude challenged. 'Or breast-fed you for too long?' She waited to see how he would rise to this, but all the same she was glad her house was overlooked only by the sea. She did not want the inhabitants of Steerborough to gain more ground in their suspicion that psycho-analysis was in fact simply pornography in another form. It would pain her if she was no longer asked for her advice on fund-raising, taken off the list of village residents who could be relied on for cakes and chutney to sell at the fêtes.

'Max' – Elsa turned to him – 'was your father wounded? In the first war?' For a moment he thought she might be referring to the other war. Too recent to ever be discussed.

'Yes,' he said. 'He fought at Loos and his feet were pierced by splinters from a large grenade.'

Pierced, Gertrude repeated to herself, but there was not the same hot feeling in her gut.

'He had an operation to remove them, the splinters and frag-ments of bone, but there was no serum in the hospital, and my mother had to sit beside his bed to check he did not contract tetanus. If he had trouble swallowing, it was a sign. "Help. Help!" my mother shouted when some hours later he tried to speak, and, although he never did contract tetanus, she did get him moved to a private room.'

It was an anecdote his father always told when people asked about his orthopaedic shoes. They were heavy and thick-soled, built up with stacks of black, and the government provided a new pair every year, even in 1938, even after his arrest.

But Max didn't tell them his own story. The story of how his ears had failed. First one and then the other, when he was thirteen years old. His mother sent to Rissen for the doctor, but the doctor was away. 'He has an ear infection,' she called his father, who promised to find someone who would come. All through that night Max lay with a pain like hot metal pinning him to the bed. 'Are you all right?' His mother laid a hand on him, but he could hear nothing, just the whirring and rushing of his blood. He'd had infections before, but this one was different, this one reached from ear to ear.

In the early hours of that morning they were disturbed by a loud knocking on the door. 'Who are you?' His mother was alarmed to see a man dressed as a huntsman with a bow strung across his back.

'I'm the doctor,' and he explained how he'd been at a fancy dress party to celebrate the fiftieth wedding anniversary of his great-uncle and -aunt. He looked at Max. Peered into his ears, his eyes, his throat, but, just like the doctors who came after, there was nothing he could do to help.

Helga was waiting for him in the shed, her hair still damp, her eyes liquid in the dark. Max pushed his bike in and leant it against hers, and just as he was turning, she reached out.

'Come here,' she said and, although he didn't remember either of them moving, in an instant she was pressed against him, her fingers examining his skin, sliding along his arms, around his neck, and up inside his shirt. She found the three fine hairs that had sprung up during that winter, as if in a vain attempt to keep him warm, and then she was circling his chest, stroking and tweaking,

96

her nails pressing in. Max stood still, terrified to move in case she stopped, in case she remembered it was him, and then her hand was reaching down, pushing past the waistband of his trousers; feeling over the cold smooth dampness of his skin, the jut of his hip bone, the goose bumps on his thigh. He almost fell against her, and then her other hand was there, warm against his belly, sliding down towards the private centre of him, bone-hard inside his shorts.

'Helga . . .' He didn't know if he was shouting or whispering, so he pressed his face into her hair, straining against her as she stroked him, once, twice . . . and he was bursting through the walls, rearing up to take a jump and just as quickly arcing down again. He crumpled at both knees, and as he slumped, he looked at her and saw that she was far away, gazing out beyond him, at the knots and waves of the shed walls.

Max was sitting on the floor, squeezed into the corner, where spiders hung on ropes of air. He could feel his stickiness all around him, congealing as it cooled. Helga reached into the basket of her mother's bicycle and brought out a towel. She smiled shyly as she handed it to him, and he felt himself blush hotly as he took it, mopping at himself, thanking her as he handed it back. She rolled it up again, and replaced it in the basket. 'Thankyou, so much,' he'd said, but it was only later as he lay in bed, trying to recreate the feeling of her hand, that he realized how he hadn't touched her, hadn't lain a finger on her body, hadn't kissed or even stroked her hair.

Max woke early the next morning. He chose a book and lay down in the shared garden beside the path that ran straight to the sea. He looked up for her after every line, and when by eleven she hadn't appeared, he knocked on the kitchen door to ask for her.

'She's gone to Stralsund,' her aunt told him, 'taken the steamer, won't be back until tomorrow night.'

'Thankyou,' he said, and he felt himself prickle all over with mortification as he backed away.

Max cycled up to Kloster, the rough track rising, lifting away from the flat land until you could see the whole island spread out below. There was yellow broom growing on the hillside and the scent of it uncurled as he laboured up the last slope of the hill. He abandoned his bicycle and ran panting to the top. There was a bench, positioned for visitors, but he walked on past it, until he was almost reeling over the cliffs at the far end. From here, instead of looking out over the island, he stretched his eyes to the horizon, searching for Denmark, Sweden, or the coast of Russia, a day away by boat.

16

Nick looked out of place in the tiny palace of Fern Cottage kitchen, the cups and saucers laid out in a row, the mugs all facing the same way.

'Where were you?' he asked. 'I've been here for ages.'

'I'm sorry . . .' Lily shook her head. 'I had no idea . . . I thought you were too busy . . .' She noticed his trousers, not white but almost, the colour of clotted cream.

'And I can't believe you didn't lock your door.'

'Oh Nick!' She had that sinking feeling of a misunderstood child.

'Come here.' He pulled her against him, and she felt the wall of his ribs, his chest so warm it heated through the cotton of his shirt. 'I've missed you.' He was kissing her, too deeply, so that she had to pull away, and as she did so she saw him reach out to draw down the flowered blind.

'Not here,' she whispered, pretending to be scandalized, and so he half picked her up and hustled her upstairs. The staircase was so narrow that they almost slipped on the old carpet as he kept hold of her, both hands on her hips, half lifting, half pushing her along. Lily wavered on the landing. It's too soon, she thought, and she found she had to shut her mind off to the party wall, the thought of Em and Arrie, Grae.

There was a silent moment of formality as she drew the curtains and Nick took off his shoes.

'We could push the beds together?'

She was losing it, the thin trickle of desire, but Nick began undressing her, turning her round as he did so to face the dressing-table mirror.

'Look at yourself,' he said, and there she was, lint-white in the gloom, her breasts rounder, the nipples pinker than they ever were when she was alone. Did she change for him, she wondered, and she looked at the tiny, pleasing curve at the top of her legs that waxed and waned depending on her weight. 'Aren't you beautiful? See?' She looked at her face. Her nose was sunburnt, her hair tied back, the straggly ends looping round her ears. The two parts of her body didn't seem to fit, the smooth pale curves, good for nothing, it seemed, except for sex, and then there was the ruddy intentness of her face. She closed her eyes and let herself sink into her body, take on her voluptuousness, reach down for the hot well of desire waiting there inside.

'Open your eyes,' Nick urged, 'look at us,' and although their bodies did look beautiful, welded together like two waves, she couldn't ignore the familiarity of her face. It was comical, ridiculous, like someone peering through the cut-out cardboard at a fair, and so she closed her eyes again, and let herself sink into pure sensation, with the first hot thrill of him like shards of sunlight flying up into the night.

Afterwards they lay under the sheets and blankets of the single bed, watching the light against the curtain fade until eventually the room was dark. 'Did you get the contract?' she asked. 'Have you heard?'

Nick flicked on the lamp. 'No, they still haven't decided. It's possible they might keep us waiting for another week.'

Lily started to get dressed. 'Would you like tea? Or . . . We could go out for a drink?'

'Yes.' Nick glanced around him. 'Yes, let's get out.'

The cloud that had been gathering must have thickened, because now when they stepped out into the lane the night was black. 'Christ,' – Nick grasped her arm – 'I can't see a thing.' They stood still, waiting for the darkness to separate and let them through.

'Shhh,' she said, although the sound was all around them. 'Can you hear it? Can you hear the sea?'

Nick had one arm outstretched and he was edging forwards. 'Come on or we'll never get there. They'll be ringing out last orders while we're still searching for the pub.'

'OK.' She led him by the arm, and as they turned the corner their path was lit up by the window of the house next door. The curtains were still open and she could see Grae and the children sitting at the table, slapping cards down by the light of a lamp. Quickly she glanced away. 'When I first arrived,' she whispered, as much as anything to remind herself, 'there were the most terrible rows . . . I don't know what was going on, but one night . . . There was such a fight . . . Well, I haven't seen the wife since.'

Nick jerked round to peer in. 'That's what happens in the country. There's fuck all to do, so just for entertainment people come home and beat up their wives.'

'Well . . .' She felt a stab of guilt. 'Unless it was her, beating him up?' And Nick began to laugh.

There were two huge dogs asleep on the floor of The Ship. They lay outstretched between the fire and the door, and Nick and Lily had to step over their haunches to find a seat. 'Just look at this place!' Nick said, and the five men, seated along the bar, dark pints of bitter waiting to be drained, all glanced towards them.

'Shh.' Lily frowned, but it was true, the pub was unbelievably decrepit. There were strings and nets and animal traps trailing from the ceiling. The publican was only just visible in the cave of his bar.

'What's he wearing?' Nick talked out of the side of his mouth, as if this would turn his words to a whisper. 'It looks like a corset!'

'I'll get the drinks,' Lily insisted. She didn't trust Nick not to stare, but while she waited she found herself transfixed by the barman, his beetroot face, the lank hair scraped across his scalp. Laced tightly over his patterned jumper, once white but now grey with grime, was what she could only imagine to be a surgical support.

'Yes?' He startled her. 'What will you have?' Lily looked up into his swimming eyes and realized it was his corset, and only this, that was keeping him up.

'A pint of bitter and . . . and . . .' Almost as a warning against the danger of alcohol, the barman took another swallow of his pint. 'And an apple juice please.'

The pub was stifling, the fire heaped with ash-white logs of wood. Nick and Lily sat in the window seat, lapping at the draught, batting away the wood smoke that coiled and circled the room. 'It's June,' Nick protested, and Lily, feeling she must defend this village, Lehmann's village, where until now she had felt entirely at home, said more irritably than she intended, 'He's ill for God's sake. Maybe he feels the cold.'

Nick raised his eyebrows at her, and they sat in silence staring at the dogs, their great hot bodies overlapping as they slept, their paws like brass casters, their pink tongues lolling out. They were dreaming most likely of basking on a desert plateau, of watching birds of prey go wheeling round. Or maybe they were chasing rabbits over sand dunes, dribbling and snapping as they sprang away.

Beside them on the wall was a small gallery of photos and each time Nick went to the bar, Lily stared into the faces of fishermen. Harry, Kitner, Seal, Dibs and Mabbs and Mops, all in their corded hats. There was one photograph of the old chain ferry taking an elephant across, while another elephant stood on the riverbank, its trunk raised, its mouth open, as if unable to accept that the only other creature of its kind in the whole of Suffolk was leaving it behind.

Nick drained the last of his drink as the barman called time, and the same row of five men watched them as they got up to go.

'There's another pub we can try tomorrow. Further up the village.' She took his arm to guide him as he stepped out into the dark, but he stopped and peered around as if sniffing for the sea.

'I'm not sure I can stay *all* weekend,' he said.

'What do you mean?'

'Shh, I can hear it.' They listened. 'It sounds rough,' and Lily looked up at the thick dome of the sky, without a star or a hint of moonlight and hoped that there was going to be a storm.

'What's so important, anyway,' she asked once they'd started forward again, 'that you have to go home as soon as you've arrived?'

'Lily.' She couldn't even see him, only feel the pressure on her arm. 'I'm working, it's a very busy time. This' – he added after a moment – 'is a retirement village, and I'm *not* retired.'

Grae's cottage was dark now, and all around the Green, as if to prove his point, the houses were shut up for the night.

'Don't you ever lock your door?' Nick asked as she pressed down on the handle, but without answering she left him to follow her in.

Nick's work was laid out on the table, his fine graph paper spread over the laminated cloth, his Rotring pens, his ruler, the elastic bands he flicked when he got stuck.

'Listen,' she said, flooded with sadness, 'please listen to this.' And she reached up to Lehmann's letters in their cream and purple envelopes, and lifted one down.

My beloved El,

You've ordered a love letter and this is exactly what you shall have; you should never think that I was cross with you because of your decision. I was merely a little tired of how many times you changed your mind. But it shall never happen again. I shall never again doubt your love, even in the slightest. From your short hair to your even shorter fingernails and down to your little toes, from one end to the other and to your middle soul, you are very dear to me, with courage or without, with a lot or only a little sense in your decisions, none of this shall matter.

Lily looked over at Nick, who was listening, his head bent, his forehead ruffled in a frown.

My El,

A telegram from you has just arrived. At 9 p.m. So three and a half hours after it was sent. It is a wonderful feeling for me to know that you are lying down now at the same time as me, and that your morning will also be the same as mine.

'Look,' Lily said, handing him the map, 'he made a plan for her of every room that he stayed in.'

There was a silence while Nick scrutinized it. 'How on earth,' he said slowly, 'do you think all this is going to help you with your work? At this rate you'll fail on your thesis' – he looked quite shaken – 'and after all the work that you've put in.' He began to clear his things, packing them away neatly into his bag, and when he finished he went upstairs to the bathroom and Lily listened as he brushed his teeth.

She reached up for another letter.

My sweet Elsa,

Here I lie many hundreds of miles away from you, in such a fury you can hardly imagine, waiting for those tender letters which should be hurrying towards me. How can I imagine your life when you've stopped sharing it with me, and I know nothing of your days except the rooms in which they are played out. You only have two duties during this in-between time. The first, and most important, is to look after yourself. The second is to write to ME. Everything else. Lunch with the Mendels, afternoon tea, visiting Eva, these all come far down the list. It must not be allowed that in more than a week I only receive three or four postcards, and a telegram in apology. Until the next long letter. Angrily, but still yours, L.

Nick was reading, not in her bed but in its twin. He was naked, the pink sheet under its cream blanket rucked across his chest. She stood in the doorway and watched him, incongruous against the pastel shades of the bedding, like the wolf from 'Red Riding Hood' dressed up and pretending to be Granny.

'What?' He looked up.

'Nothing.' She shook her head and, slipping out of her clothes, she climbed into her own bed.

'Right,' he said then, switching off the light between them. 'Goodnight.'

'Goodnight.' Lily felt so lonely that she had to turn away and, muttering half-remembered verses, she forced herself to sleep.

17

Max arrived home with one and a half new houses on his scroll. He'd added a bungalow, simple in its construction, its roof identical to a house he'd already painted in Church Lane. He'd moved on then to a cottage, windows like eyebrows poking from the thatch, but he'd been interrupted by the rain, a drizzle to begin with, and then, like an umbrella collapsing, it had come sheeting down. Max waited under a tree, his jacket wrapped around his precious scroll, the sleeves outstretched, his back bent into the rain, and then he'd given up and run. He didn't mind being wet. It was trying to avoid it that was tiresome, and he was out of breath and steaming when he arrived in Gertrude's porch.

Anxiously he unwrapped his scroll. It was undamaged, only a small welt across one edge that could be transformed into a shrub, but as he uncoiled the paper he noticed that he had almost run out of space. There was room for two, maybe three more houses, and as he looked back through the stippled glass he caught the shaky outlines of a cluster of unpainted roofs. Max hung up his jacket, dabbed at his trousers, and walked in. The house was silent, but busy somehow, as if a horde of people were working diligently upstairs. He tiptoed into the dining-room. The table was newly polished, the smell edging at his nose, and on a flat linen-and-lace doily was a vase of formal flowers. Max had bent his nose to them, sucking up their bitter scent, when he saw Gertrude, squatting by the garden doors. The grey bun of her hair was slipping sideways, loosely spiked through with a wooden clasp, and on her face, turned half towards him, was a look of such concentration that he was unable to move. As he watched, she raised her hand and with great precision bounced a rubber ball. The ball flew up, and with its release there followed a flurry of activity as Gertrude scrabbled wildly, and then, in triumph, half sliding her body across the floor, she caught the ball as it came down.

'Better!' she exclaimed, and she bounced the ball again. It sped up at an angle, and even Max could see she would never have time to rush over to the fireplace and catch it before it fell. 'Well . . .' She'd seen Max now, and he admired her for flushing only slightly. 'Alf's bound to have been practising.' She held up a handful of dull metal and, taking a bag from the table, she tipped the jacks back in.

Unless you make yourself invisible, you are bound to be observed. What's the good of bothering about it? The most important thing is to get yourself into the best position for drawing what you want to draw. Listen, I can tell you again and again to lighten this sketch, to darken another, but a discovery you make yourself is worth twenty thousand things that you are taught, even if it is a discovery that everyone else has made. But having said that, a school is the best place to have your drawings pulled apart, to get over the monotony of technique, just like a pianist practising perpetual scales. Couldn't you just go and get it over with?

Max's father did not believe in schools. He'd wanted his children to develop their own skills. There had been lessons in the nursery with his mother, and au pairs from Switzerland, England, France and Scandinavia had taught him all they could. Mary had explained the rudiments of English before he was five years old, and the year he was twelve, Mique, a plump girl from Avignon, had given him a French novel to read. They had sat together over it in the blue drawing-room as they read each page in turn.

There was a school in the village, not more than two kilometres away. It was a small school run by a Herr Reeder, where everything, he informed Max's mother, 'was done by the book'. Max went there for a week each summer to see whether he was making suitable progress or not, and when he arrived, in the last hot days of June, his fellow pupils greeted him with surprise. Few of them remembered him from one year to the next, and each time they would prod and jostle him, testing him out yet again to see where he would fit in. 'I want to know,' his mother said when he came home, 'if the exercises are easy?' They were easy, boring too, so that once, finishing early, Max had looked up to see Herr Reeder slipping off one of his socks. He had it pulled over his fist, and he was sitting there, head bent, darning, while the whole class scratched laboriously away.

Max hadn't told Klaus Lehmann that his father was an officer. Lehmann would know, and Gertrude wouldn't, that to become an officer his father had had to convert. It was impossible to rise through the ranks of the army if you had any kind of mark against your character, and being Jewish was the blackest mark. Max had had these arguments enacted for him by his father as they worked together in the basement workshop, making the cabinet to hold his sketches, the wide deep drawers that interlocked with fretted teeth.

'Why suffer the indignities inflicted on Jews, when Christianity is a natural continuation of your faith? It is wrong,' his father's mother had scolded him, 'to remain a Jew simply out of pride.' Later she had spoken gently. 'If you are going to convert, then why wait until after your military service? Then it will be too late.' So Max's father had been christened, and along with the other young officers he'd been presented with a horse. He'd called it Applesnout and shared with it his roast beef sandwiches. He'd loved his horse, and enjoyed his privileges, but Max suspected he'd always regretted his decision to convert.

Gertrude was waiting for him at the bottom of the stairs. 'Will you eat?' she asked, and together, just as he and Kaethe used to do, they worked side by side, cutting and mixing, spooning and stirring, knocking their shoulders against each other companionably as they prepared their evening meal.

18

Lily had promised herself she wouldn't wave, but as Nick's car turned the last corner of the Green, her hand shot up and like an idiot she shouted, 'Bye.' Nick hooted, startling an old man who was standing by his hedge, and with a revving of his engine he accelerated and was gone.

Lily went back inside. She sat down at the table and made rough slashes with her pen. It was obvious, he'd driven a hundred miles for a fuck, and now, well, he was on his way home again. Lily took a new sheet of paper and more calmly, with softer strokes, she drew a map of the room. There was the window with its eight small panes, the fireplace, its mantel made from tiles. She sketched in the dimensions of the sofa, remembering how when Nick had sat on it, the blanket had fallen over his body in a woollen shroud. He'd looked up at her, his eyebrows raised, as if to say, 'You want me to stay here?' Lily drew the table, the three heavy chairs, the bookshelves in the alcove where the wall was at its thinnest between her cottage and next door.

'What are you doing?' It was Em, standing in the doorway.

'Hello.' She hadn't heard them come in.

'Come and see.' Arrie shuffled forward. 'We've got our new car.'

Lily got up and followed them to the open door, where a black Renault 5 was parked, identical to her own. 'It's like a fleet,' she said, and she could imagine the two cars travelling in tandem, dignitaries, fallen on hard times.

'Ours has got a dent though,' Arrie pointed out, 'and this window won't quite shut.'

'Well, look at mine.' Lily showed them the blemishes on her

own car, the scratch that had appeared mysteriously one night, the missing passenger wing mirror.

'It's better than our old one, though.' Arrie stroked the bonnet, and Em gave her an offended look.

Grae appeared, swinging through the gate, the car keys spinning from one finger. 'Right, who's coming for a drive?'

'I am, I am.' The girls climbed in, and just for a second Grae looked at Lily. The girls wound down their window and looked at her too, their eyes as clear as pebbles. 'Please come, please.'

'I should be working' – Lily smiled – 'but thanks.'

'It's Saturday?' Em tried.

Grae was standing, waiting, the ring of the keys still looped around his finger. 'Well?' he said, as if it wasn't obvious she had decided no, and for a moment the three of them stared at her, half smiling, half paralysed with hope.

'OK, I will, then.' Lily ran into the house to get her purse. What am I doing? What's going on? But it didn't stop her rushing.

The new car took a moment to start, coughing and dying before it fired. Lily's heart, which was skipping, began tumbling over until it hurt, and she had to stare out of the window to calm herself down. No one talked as they left the village, driving along the one straight road, slowing by the top field to inspect the new-born piglets, at least ten to each sow.

'Left or right?' Grae asked when they reached the crossroads.

'Right,' the girls called, but they didn't seem to notice when he drove straight on. He followed the road inland until they could see the spire of the cathedral, oversized, the huge body of it turreted like a castle, rising up above the land.

'Anyone want to go inside?' Grae offered, but the girls, lying across the back seat, the sun playing over the sand stripes of their skin, said 'nah'.

Grae drove on through an avenue of oaks, their boughs knobbled, their arms arched over to form the roof of a cave.

'Wooo,' the girls sighed as they chugged under the green canopy, and 'Waaaah' when they burst back out into the light. There were cornfields now on either side, pale gold and swaying, bordered with poppies, red and orange, their black centres beautiful as eyes. The cathedral was on their left, and they began to curve, speeding along lanes high with hedgerows, the girls now sitting upright, on the lookout for a deer or a fox. 'We saw an owl on this road once,' Em told her.

'Yes,' warned Grae, 'but that was at night.'

'And a rabbit,' Arrie added. 'This is rabbit lane.' They entered a little wood, so thick they could see only the undersides of branches, the ground a den of curving tree roots, moulding leaves and small flashes of green grass. 'There's one, and there.' Everywhere was a scurry of white haunches, dove-brown backs, hind legs bobbing, as a whole colony of rabbits lifted up their heads. Arrie counted frantically, but before she could get to twenty they were out of the wood and crossing back over the main road. 'The sea, the sea.' The girls craned forward, and Lily thought how odd it was, to have this chorus, where everything was rounded up into a theme. It was soothing somehow, and took away the need to talk. She glanced at Grae – the dusty side of his face, his one hand on the steering-wheel, the white neck of the T-shirt he wore under his shirt – and felt relieved not to have to make any comment of her own.

They were driving very gradually downhill, along narrow lanes banked high with hedges, straining to catch a glimpse between the gateposts of the marshland that spread out to the sea. 'There it is!' But the road forced them round into a village, past a church like that at Steerborough nestled in amongst the ruins of a larger church. There was a shop the size of a garden shed, a pub with latticed windows and, as they turned off down a lane on to the beach, a huge barn spilling out with people. *Fish and Chips*, it said and its doors were open to the sea. There were tables and chairs outside crowded with people, and each table was heaped with overflowing plates of food.

'I hope you're hungry,' Grae said, and at that moment a red-faced girl wearing an overall came out with a tray.

'Molletts!!' she shouted, and a family of six all waved their arms.

Lily, Grae, Em and Arrie queued up to order food. Cod and chips, haddock and chips, bread and butter, peas. Peas were the token greenery to brighten up your plate. 'I'll get this,' Lily offered, knowing as she said it that her attempt was doomed.

'No,' Grae shook his head, 'we invited you.'

Lily was pulling a note out of her purse. 'At least let me get mine.' She pressed it on him and their hands met in a kind of tussle as Grae tried to push her money away. His fingers were rough and splintery, as if they were part wood, but they were warm and full of feeling, and sent a shock along her arm. 'If you're sure,' she said, her blood stilling, and at the same moment they both saw that the girl at the till was watching them, without impatience, a little swell of laughter at the corners of her mouth. 'Thankyou,' Lily said, and she put her money away.

When their food was ready they carried it out of the restaurant, away from the car park, the waitresses, with their perspiring faces, shouting out an endless list of names, and walked with it up a steep bank and on to the beach. The beach was deep and sloped down harshly to a rough brown sea. Along the curve of the coast she could see Steerborough, ash-blonde, flattened, and beyond it, Easton-knoll, its lighthouse, the outline of the Regency Hotel. She didn't want to see the nuclear power station, its unearthly dome flashing in the sun, but turned instead towards the sea, her tray of drinks, tea and hot water chiming in her hands.

'Over here.' The others had huddled into the low cliff wall, were laying their lunch out on a strip of sand. The cliff behind them was curved over at the top, striped in seams of rust red, umber, paprika and mace. There were tufts of grass growing from the overhanging ridges, with slides and gulleys where the sand came drifting down. Grae had placed his tray under a precarious looking overhang.

'It will fall down,' he said, noticing Lily glancing up, 'but probably not today.'

Em and Arrie tore through the white flakes of their fish, the golden batter, the molten chips, and as soon as they'd finished, hardly pausing to catch their breath, they began to climb the cliff. They made a sideways shoot out of the slope, scudding down on their backs, each slide bringing with it a fine layer of ground. Lily sat back against a little dune, her feet nudged and warmed by flat grey stones.

'This used to be the biggest town on the east coast.' Grae glanced at her. 'People used to come here to trade from all over the world.'

Lily looked along the beach. There were three small boats pulled up on to the shingle, and nothing beyond but the one village street.

'There was a walled city here, with gates, and a king's palace, fifty-two churches, chapels, hospitals, even a forest. Up there' – he pointed to the cliff behind him – 'you can see the last fragments of the outer wall.'

Lily laughed. 'How do you know all this?' She turned towards him. 'I didn't take you for the local history type.' As soon as she'd said this, she regretted it. It was a London comment somehow, and it didn't fit at all.

'It's Em.' The colour in his face had risen. 'She did a project for school, there's a little museum . . .'

They sat and looked at the great mass of water.

'I suppose the ruins are all under there.' She tried to make amends. 'The farms and church spires.'

'Yes. There are some people who say if you come to this beach at midnight you can hear the church bells tolling out the hour.'

Lily felt a shiver run through her. 'Stop it,' she laughed. The sea had calmed as they'd been sitting there. It was so beautiful she felt a pull inside her, as if the tide were drawing out her heart.

'I suppose it happened slowly?' Lily had an image of the tall house by the river with its sand bags piled up to form a front wall. It had the date scrawled along what must have been a water line. There must have been floods then, too. In 1953.

'Yes.' Grae stretched out, closing his eyes against the sun. 'Little by little over the last thousand years. And then, every so often, whoosh.'

'Whoosh.' Lily echoed him and just then a clod of earth fell down and landed on his head. Lily covered her mouth. She could feel the laughter bursting up out of her, felt it burning, out of her control, and then to her relief she saw Grae's shoulders rising. He scrambled up and looked at her and, shaking their heads, they began to choke and rock and cry with laughter as they crawled to get out from the overhang of cliff.

'My God,' Lily said, when she could speak.

Grae wiped tears from the corners of his eyes. 'Christ,' he said, and he crawled back for a last gulp of cold tea.

'So' – Lily was shivery with laughing, the walls of her stomach vinegary and weak – 'are you from here, then? Originally?'

'No.' Grae looked away from her. 'From about twenty miles inland. We used to come to the coast on day trips as children. Sue . . .' He paused, and the air grew very still. 'My . . . umm . . .' He coughed. 'My wife . . . She saw an advert for the cottage in the paper. Everywhere else we'd looked at was plain miserable . . . for the price. You know what it's like if you rent. And we had to move . . . needed to get away, have a change.' He rolled over and lay face down, his arms and legs spreadeagled as if he'd been marooned. 'Christ,' he said, and then said nothing more.

Lily got up and went down to the shore. Em and Arrie, their skirts tucked into their knickers, were running in and out of the surf, chasing the tide as it pulled out and then racing to beat each wave as it crashed in. The hems of their skirts were soaking where they'd fallen free, and the narrow lengths of their feet had turned the palest blue. 'You're turning into mermaids,' she told them, but they carried on.

'Cox!' The shout of a waitress breezed towards her on the wind, and then a moment later, exasperated, hot and tired and greasy. 'COXS!!'

19

Gertrude was on the committee for the local history exhibition. It was to be held in the Gannon Room to celebrate the half century, although the half century was already three years old. The idea had come from the Reverend Leweth, who, the previous autumn, while digging in his garden, had unearthed the neck and handle of an ancient pot. It had a grotesque face, like that of a demon, and had been thought by an expert in Lowestoft to date from 1410. The excitement of this find had propelled him into pinning up a notice by the village green urging anyone with relics from Steerborough's past to enter them for a local history exhibition. Many useless and uninteresting things had been submitted, but among them – and it was Gertrude's job to sort them out – were some items worthy of display. There was a collection of fossilized bones, some of them elephant, found thrown up on to the beach, and also a piece of granite, although no granite existed nearer than Aberdeen. There was a bronze cannonball from the Battle of Soul Bay, a written account of the barque *Nina* wrecked in Darwich Bight in 1894. Gertrude ran her finger down the names of the men lost and was shaken to see Wynwell, twice. Bert and Alfred Junior, drowned within three miles of their own home. One of these must have been Alf's great-grandfather, knowing as she did from a plaque on the church wall that his grandfather was one of the fourteen men from the village who lost their lives in the Great War. There was a clockwork spit, a poulterer's grapple, and a large collection of domestic and farm implements dating back over hundreds of years. There were coins, many of them discovered in the river mud at low tide, and among them were three shillings from the reign of Elizabeth I. There was also the christening gown worn by the retired ferry man, whose grandson now rowed the boat, and both the gown and the ferry man had just turned ninety-six.

The exhibition was set for the middle of July, and it was to be held over a long weekend. The Reverend wanted it to run for a week, but the badminton club, who played in the Gannon Room on Tuesday and Thursday evenings, had protested. Gertrude was enraged, not seeing the point of badminton herself, but the Reverend pointed out that it was membership money from this club that paid for newspapers, milk and tea, and for the cleaning lady, Betty Wynwell, to sweep and tidy for the fishermen who used it during the day.

Gertrude sat in the wide window of the vicarage and wrote out labels giving information on each piece. What was a poulterer's grapple? she wondered, but she continued just the same. Beeting needles. Braiding needles. A fid for splicing rope. There was a mysterious flat-edged object, rusted green and red. It was either a kiddle, or something else entirely, and had been donated by a person of that name.

As Gertrude worked, she wondered about Alf. For three weeks now they had played jacks. The boy was making startling progress, throwing and catching with remarkable skill, but it began to worry her that this might not be enough. This week she would introduce a pack of cards. She'd teach him Racing Demons, and hoped this game, with its tension and the frenzied slapping of hands, might draw from him another word.

Max examined his new scroll. The lining paper was slick and firm, bought from the building suppliers in Eastonknoll and transported by bicycle to what he had privately begun to think of as his home. Today, he thought, he would start with Alf's. He remembered the boy's finger trailing along the river, past the ferry man's hut, and so he set off, his scroll under his arm, his paints in a bag across his back. As he walked, he stared in at the fishermen's huts – their nets all meshed and tangled, the planks of their front doors, some painted blue, some stained in salt-proof black. The names of the fishermen were there above the lintels – Blucher, Kitner, Child, Seal, Sloper, Mop and Mabbs. And then he remembered Mrs Wynwell telling him how they'd moved their house inland, put it bit by bit into a wheelbarrow and heaved it away. He turned back towards the river mouth, intending to meander over to the dip of land below The Ship, when he was distracted by the figure of a woman, her head heavy with a bun, her arms wrapped around herself against the wind. She was dressed in dark clothes, her legs in black stockings as narrow as a bird's, comical almost below a pleated skirt, and then she turned a little and he saw that it was Elsa.

'Elsa!' he called, his voice thrown unimaginably into the void, and to his surprise, as if by magic, Elsa turned to face him. He waved and, after a moment's hesitation, she lifted her hand and waved too. They stood there looking over at each other, the gulls between them shrieking and skittering, and then, as if with one thought, they both turned towards the river mouth and began to walk. Occasionally they glanced across at each other, their faces slowly coming into focus as the river narrowed, until they stood each one on the wooden jetties between which the ferry sailed.

At first Max couldn't see the boat, and he felt his throat tighten with alarm, but it was there, tucked into the Eastonknoll bank of the river, and there was the ferry man rising up out of it to help Elsa in. Elsa sat in the middle of the boat facing him, engulfed by the man's broad back as he rowed against the current to a midway point and then let the water ease the boat back in. Max walked along his jetty, feeling the structure shiver with his weight, shift a little and then quake as the ferry bumped against it. The ferry man leant forward to hand Elsa out. He didn't see Max, hovering behind him, stretching out his own hand, so that for a moment as Max bent forward, both of Elsa's hands were gripped, making it harder and not easier for her to climb out of the boat.

'Thankyou.' Elsa freed herself, taking out her purse to pay, and shyly, now that they were face to face, Max led her along the jetty and on to dry land. In silence they walked along the harbour wall, up to the tip of the estuary where there was a cluster of white houses built out of the marsh. The houses were like storks, with legs of stilts, their underbellies brick and muddy, their wings fluted with windows and slim boards. Until now it had not occurred to Max to paint them. They did not seem to belong to the village, but as they walked to the tip of the estuary where the rough ground, seeded with fennel and cowparsley, turned to mud, then swamp, then sand, he imagined his scroll, billowing with whiteness, unfurling gently into the brown and green of solid land.

'I'll show you my favourite,' Elsa said, as if they'd been talking about houses for the last half-hour, and brushing against his sleeve she walked with him past the Tea Room, past the most recently painted house, its front porch set with a table and chairs, past the boatyard, the salt store and the herring curing shed. They passed Little Haven, where, she told him, the vicar took a holiday each year, packing up the rectory on the corner of Church Lane and moving with his family a quarter of a mile down the road. Elsa stopped by the most easterly house. Once white, and almost square, its stilts were higher than the others, its front door looking out to sea. *The Sea House*, Max read, and below the sign another smaller sign: *To Let*. It had steps up to a wooden porch, the rails of which were peeling paint, and above it was a terrace.

Elsa put one foot on the step and, when Max glanced at her, she smiled at him and walked up to the front door. Max watched her as she pressed her face against the glass, and then with some alarm he saw her turn the handle. 'Come,' she motioned to him, and Max followed her in. Inside was a long wooden table, a dresser hung with cups, and just behind, a ladder that led up vertically to a trap door of light.

'Hello?' Elsa called to the room above, although they both knew there was no one there, and so she began to climb the ladder, her legs, the shin bones long and narrow, easing up in front of Max's eyes. 'Quick,' she mouthed to him from the top. 'It's wonderful.'

Max, one-handed, still clutching his scroll of paper, reeled himself up. Elsa was standing by a round table covered with a cloth. Just behind her was a bed, a cover pulled up over it, pillows curved in towards one another in two mounds. It looked so soft that if you laid one arm across the quilt, you would sink down into it and be lost. Quickly Max went out on to the balcony. He closed his eyes to linger one more moment on that hint of shadow between the pillows' curves, and when he opened them again he found himself at sea. There was nothing between him and the horizon, only water, shimmering in stripes of blue and grey. Max took a breath of it, sucking it in, and then Elsa came and stood beside him. Her arm, narrow like her leg, hung so close that he felt his whole chest quake with the desire to touch her. It was like a sickness, like the ache, he realized, of his dreams, and he saw himself for an instant at the wheel of that car, searching the lanes and turnings for his perfect home. Max fixed his eye on the fine line where the sea ended and the sky began, a razor's edge of shading, just thickening a fraction before the two blues parted, and the sea rolled away from them to the next great mass of land. On a day like this it was clear the earth was round. There was the rim of it, curving away, and then, just as he'd hoped she might, just as he'd dreamed it, Elsa pressed her hand against his arm. He turned to her.

'The door!' she said. 'Someone's coming in.' She looked back into the room as if she were searching out a place where they could hide, the bed, the wardrobe, and then she recovered herself and let go of his arm. 'I suppose I'd better go down.' She shook her head, amused at her own terror, and quickly, feet first, she disappeared from view. Max stood at the top of the trap door. He didn't want to trample on her hands, so he waited until he could no longer see her, and began descending the ladder rung by rung, turning expectantly, when he reached the ground. But there was only Elsa, standing by the front door. 'It was just the wind,' she said, and she put out her hand and drew him outside.

Max could still feel the touch of Elsa's hand. It hurt him when he thought of it, created a quick spasm of pain, but even so, he wouldn't let it go. He played it over, his insides quickening, the air around him fizzing as her fingers melted into his. Her hand was light, the bones right near the surface, but in her palm it seemed that there was hope. Max sat opposite the Sea House, drawing in its outline, his mind so full of thoughts he felt half blind. Twice he sketched in the tin funnel of the chimney and twice he rubbed it out. In irritation he pressed so hard down on the paper his pencil snapped its lead. Seagulls wheeled above him, their necks out-stretched, their feet skidding out to land. What must it be like, he wondered, to have permission to touch that shoulder whenever you felt the need. Klaus, he thought, and he pushed the image of the man away. He'd be in London, Elsa had said, until the end of the week, and Max made a sudden flurry of bold strokes, sketching in the steps, the railing and the front door.

20

Lily avoided Grae over the next few days. She turned away as he passed the window, as if utterly absorbed by her work, and then spent the next hour distracted, wondering if he might have looked in and smiled at her, only to be met by the cold side of her face. With a huge effort she forced herself back to her letters.

My El,

This morning I woke up suddenly and worried about you. But then I calmed myself. It was much too early for anything to have happened. It's been snowing here, and heavy, fantastical shapes are lying on the branches outside my window. Please, please don't let yourself be talked out of coming to visit. As far as the doctor's advice is concerned, and I have tried hard to suppress this, I think he is completely WRONG. It is over a month now since you lost the baby . . . and you are young and healthy, and as far as catching a lung infection up here in the mountains, that is ridiculous too. You would have caught a lung infection from me if you were going to catch one. Really! I keep wondering if your mother had a word with the doctor, and turned him round to her point of view. Of course I understand, she wants to keep you in Hamburg, but I need you here. I've been working hard, and the preliminary plans for the sanatorium are almost finished. You can look everything over when you're here, as my companion. Today I had a look at the room in which we'll stay. I enclose a sketch of it for you so you'll feel doubly at home when you arrive. As you can see, if you sit up in bed, it will be possible to look out at the mountains, where the snow may even be melting a little by then. Now, will you promise to preserve all your strength for the trip? I'd prefer it if you didn't go to Gerda's party, but if you do feel you have to, then don't dance. That could be dangerous.

Please could you bring me a bottle of fixative and a blowpipe, and also Einstein's book on the Theory of Relativity? Be well for me, your L.

Lily unfolded the map. The room was large, with an adjoining annexe with tall windows on three sides. There was a desk there, and Klaus had sketched in Elsa's portrait, royally waiting, on top. The bed, as promised, faced the window, and on it, like two pipe-cleaner figures, were Klaus and Elsa, entwined.

Lily reached for the next letter.

Thankyou for the fixative and the blowpipe, but where is the Einstein book, and more importantly where are YOU? I shall write to your mother, and insist she let you come, and also you must begin to warn her that one day we will be leaving for good. You know that I am right when I say this, don't you? Am I the only one who has actually taken the trouble to read Mein Kampf, apart from the Semmels and Liebnitzes, of course, who have already left. But you should talk to your mother about leaving too. She could come to us once we are settled, and help with the busy household we will have. I found myself at lunch yesterday with a woman who talked of nothing but her patriotism for the Fatherland, and I sat there, choking on my food, as she looked towards me for a sign of my sympathy! I had the beginnings of a migraine and this made me more than usually sensitive, but then later, as if sent to me as a reward for biting my tongue, I met an architect by the name of Hermann who has already made plans to move to London. He may be able to give us some good advice, and will be a good contact if we decide to go there. Also, and you don't have to tell the photographer this, but I'm not at all happy with the pictures he sent of the apartment. First of all, he's moved everything around, and just as you have to make a portrait of a person without changing his looks, one also shouldn't rearrange a room. The pictures lack everything made so beautiful in reality by light. Well, at least he didn't photograph you and miss out all the important bits. And once again I beg you to be reasonable, and NOT to dance when you go to a ball. Also don't go out to the cinema or for a walk. I'm sure you could get a cold that way. I would really prefer it if you slept long on Sunday. Just wait to see all the things I've planned to do with you . . . the most terrible things! Stay well, my love, and do not be apart from me. Your L.

Elsa must have visited because there were no more letters for some months, and then when they started up again it was the summer of 1933, and Klaus was in London. Lily thought of writing to Nick, begging him not to work too hard, to attend, or not attend the cinema, but instead she doodled with her pen, building a miniature pattern of bricks. What did she want from him, anyway? Or he from her? She felt a stab of envy for the entangled lives of Elsa and Klaus. The men she knew didn't seem to feel the need to so utterly possess their women. They didn't want to marry them, or even necessarily to have children, so it was left to the women to want everything, to keep yearning and longing and pushing forward from the past.

When she'd first met Nick she'd framed him with the future. Planes and boats and travel, the limbs of babies, the roof of a house, but he had forbidden it, would not discuss more than a month ahead, and now, four years later, she saw that maybe he was right. The mirage of her hope was clearing, and for the first time, she was looking at his actual face.

Dear Nick, she wrote in a swirl of anguish, as if at that very moment she had lost her faith. *I miss you. I'm sorry . . .* She had to scrub the 'sorry' out or admit that she'd not really missed him before. *I don't think I've been very happy in London*, she tried to explain. There she was, walking obediently up and down the steps of her college, collecting information, spilling it back out, surrounded by pillars, glass and courtyards, railway stations, monuments, and vents. *I don't mean ever . . .* She'd been born in London, had hardly left it in twenty-seven years, and she saw herself sitting on the flaking plaster gatepost of the house in West London where she had grown up. She used to sit there, after school, watching the people come wearily off the main road, and then she'd see her, the most weary of them all, her mother, carrying shopping, her tights always with a hole. When she thought of London she thought of that warm crumbling seat, the taste of sherbet as she sucked the liquorice dipper, the way it fizzed when she dipped it again.

The wide steps of that house narrowed as they curved down to the basement, another land among the pipes and drains, and as she followed her mother down to their side door, she'd catch the drift of currant, intoxicating on the breeze. The flat was dark and damp, and smelt ever so slightly of gas – a grass and urine smell that could never be quite traced. But behind it, stretching down to the railway, was a jungle of a garden. Lily loved the garden, the great lion of the train, and was proud of the waist-high rhubarb, itching you with furry stalks if you attempted to get by. Below its leaves long arms of nasturtiums struggled to find light, trailing and clinging with tiny elbows until a sudden clutch of orange flowers burst out.

Lily knew every inch of her street, belonged there, owned the pavement, felt the corner shop was hers. She sniffed, and tried to summon up the smell of dust and chilli, could feel even now the soft squelch of the rubber matting as you pushed open the door. But her mother had moved away from there as soon as Lily had left to go to college. She had found a bright and sunny top-floor flat in Kilburn, with no damp, no garden, nothing that smelt to Lily of home. It shocked her, this move, more than she could say. She had always assumed they'd lived there, in that gloomy basement, because there was nowhere else to go.

'Lily, LILY!' A fist was banging on the window, and when she looked up, she saw Emerald, with Arrie squeezed in beside her. Lily went to open the door.

'Our mum's back,' Em said, her face one smile, and Lily saw pushed in against Grae's car, half blocking the lane, the long dusty Volvo she'd seen parked there when she'd first arrived.

'That's great.'

She turned to go back in, but the girls followed close behind her, creeping on to the sofa when she sat down. It was just the right size for them, and they sat there, upright, like two old men. After a minute Arrie went and switched the television on.

'Won't your mum . . . ? Shouldn't you be . . . ?' Lily tried. But the girls had their eyes fixed on the screen, a fearsome crackling cartoon, and she knew she would have to go and stand in front of them if she wanted to interrupt the beam.

My dear El, she read over the jets of noise, surprised to find this letter had been typed. The typing was dense and clumsy, its thick grey letters denting out through the back of the page, and rather than official the words felt intimate, full of effort, the actual impression of Lehmann's finger and thumb. *Let me tell you about my days here. Each morning I have my English lesson and then I'm off, rushing across London meeting anyone I can. Yesterday I had a proper working day. I visited the Architectural Review, which was a success, and I urgently need you to send photos of the children's rooms that I designed for the Bermanns. Here there is an exhibition in which there is a quite miserable children's parlour, so I'm sure people would be interested to see a better one. And please, my El, please don't take everything I write to you as a reproach. I'm just trying to remind you of things which are important. This afternoon two English ladies came to visit me about plans for another sanatorium, about which we have to be discreet, and in answer to your question about the ladies here, since you ask so jealously, I have to admit their complete lack of interest in me is quite alarming. I sometimes see quite beautiful apparitions dressed in the most splendid clothes, but they seem to me to lack a soul. So none have presented even the slightest danger, and you can be quite calmed. Please don't miss me too much, I'll soon be with you, and don't worry so much if my letters don't reach you every day. It pains me that they mean so much to you. With all my heart, your L.*

From now on the letters were all typed, and Lily found she missed the grandeur of the writing, the swirls and loops of the black ink. She was used to straining for the meaning of a too hurriedly drawn word, missed the satisfaction that came to her when she'd deciphered something she'd first thought impossibly unclear.

Dear Elsa,

I'm so glad you have decided against going to Hiddensee. If you want adventure, just wait, and soon you will have it. I wrote a letter to you in Vitte when I thought you were on your way there, but there was nothing important in it, just a menu, pork chops, roast potatoes, rice pudding and bread and butter, to show how well I am eating. Last night I dreamt I was steering the Stralsund ferry across the strait to Hiddensee. The boatman, old Kolwitz, let me take the wheel, and I was so happy, the wind on my face, the spray of that cold sea, and then I woke up and found that my bedspread had slipped off and I was in fact in an un-heated English room. I can't yet think about my return, and must stay as long as things continue to be busy here. In the meantime, be extremely well, and try to make for yourself the most pleasurable and active life. Your L.

The children had pushed forward the sofa and were using the space behind it as a shop. Lily watched them, wondering why they were here, when their mother was next door, and then through the wall, above the roar of the adverts she heard the woman's voice. 'NO, I will NOT!!' Lily froze, her eyes fixed on Em, who was looking out at her from the blanket canopy of the camp. 'Get off!' There was a scream, followed by the crash and ring of what sounded like the phone.

Em dipped out of sight. 'Arrie,' she asked, persevering with the game, 'do you sell frozen peas?' There was a pause and then Arrie solemnly replied, 'That'll be twenty pounds.'

Lily stood up and switched the television off. Immediately she regretted it. She could hear the low growl of Grae's voice now, and above it his wife's shouts. 'I won't! I won't.' A scuffle rose up above the drag of what sounded like a chair and, just as she was about to press the button back on, Em peered over the parapet of the sofa. She looked at Lily, a quiver in her lip, and then, behind her, out of sight, Arrie began to cry.

'Arrie . . .' Lily was on her hands and knees, crawling in to her, relieved to have something to do. 'Come on out. Come on.' It was like coaxing out a cat, and eventually the two girls crept into her lap.

Lily helped them with their shoes, buckling and lacing them, although she knew they could do this themselves. Arrie kept her head down, wiping her nose occasionally on her sleeve, and Em looked at her in that curious and distant way in which children regard another in distress. Lily held the door for them and they trooped out. It was spitting very lightly with warm rain, but Ethel was there, in her dressing-gown, standing by her gate. Her hair was wet around the edges and her face shone.

'Beautiful day for a swim,' she called to Lily, but Em and Arrie had turned away and were heading off across the Green. Lily followed. Down the lane, beside the river, and out into the reed beds. They walked in single file along the whitened planks, the sedge rustling, the rain rippling the water where it lay in filmy pools. Before them was the sea. A high grey bank of water, so wide and spacious it rolled round on three sides to meet the sky. She had to stop and marvel at it, acknowledge the effect it had on the muscles of her eyes, and she wondered if you would ever get used to seeing to the horizon, after spending a lifetime of having your vision cut short.

'Come on,' Em called. She'd stepped off the path and was trudging up a wide green track. Arrie ran after her, struggling to keep up, but Lily was loathe to turn inland from the sea. Mist was rolling in over the sand dunes and above it the grey was turning white. When Lily glanced back towards the track the girls had disappeared.

'Em?' She started after them. 'Arrie?' The land on either side was high with gorse, caves and mounds of darkening green. She walked slowly, looking to each side, expecting them to jump out at her, holding herself ready for the pretence of shock. But they were nowhere and she found herself peering into lanes of water falling away into still black pools where whole trees grew quite happily submerged. Where were they? She spun around, and then between the bushes there was the opening of a path. She followed it, and found herself at the top of a flight of steps. They were the steps to an old bunker, its concrete shell half hidden, its corners crumbling, eaten away as if by mice. Lily put her foot on the first step and called, and her voice seemed flattened by the walls.

'One minute,' Em shouted back, 'we're coming.' There was no hint of invitation in her voice, so Lily walked off round the bunker, stooping to peer through the rectangular openings, arrow slits towards the sea. Down below her were the huddled shapes of Em and Arrie bent low over some kind of shrine. She moved as quietly as she could to get a sideways view and saw that they were laying out biscuits, taken from a packet she'd last seen in her own home.

'Coming,' Em called, turning towards the stairway, and as they moved away Lily saw they'd been attending to a bed of plastic bags, black crinkled sacks laid out in lengths, with a black sack bolster at its end. The bolster was stuffed with clothes, spilling out on to the damp grey floor, and on its top were four flaked almond biscuits.

'Lily?' The girls were skipping round to find her. 'Where shall we go now?' But before she could ask what they'd been doing, ask whether it was safe, they were racing off along a straight grass path that led towards the mill. Lily ran after them, the rain falling faster now, slanting into her face so that she could hardly see. When she caught up, they were standing, their tongues out, catching enough drops to make a drink.

Lily tilted her face too and just then there was a crack like the buckling of metal and the rain came crashing down. The noise of it, the sheer grey volume, huge drops the size of pendants, splashing and pounding, so that it seemed pointless to attempt any kind of cover, and they rushed, their legs and arms gleaming, out from the shelter of the mill.

They shouted like small warriors as they hurled themselves about, and Lily followed, half blind, deliriously happy although she couldn't imagine why. But then as suddenly as it had started the rain fell away. Small patches of blue appeared, and a streak of sun blazed out across the grey. They stopped in the curve of the dunes and shook themselves, wringing out their hair, flicking the water from their faces with the backs of their hands.

'There'll be a rainbow,' Arrie said, and they all looked towards Eastonknoll, where, as if they'd wished it, an arc of colour formed itself before their eyes, strengthening, widening, until it spanned the estuary, one foot planted by the ferry hut, the other striping down into the sea.

They took their shoes off and walked towards home, their eyes fixed on the rainbow, drawing them towards it for their pot of gold. They stopped when they got to the car park, and stood in front of the one wooden house, watching as the colours finally began to fade. Their clothes were steaming now, heavy and wet, and so they turned up the last stretch to home. Even from the Green Lily could see that the Volvo was gone. The lane was empty, just the two flat backs of the Renaults, parked side by side. Em and Arrie began to run. Lily watched them, waiting until they were through their front door, and then, head down, she walked on. She hadn't meant to look through the window, but at the last minute she'd given in, and then immediately, shocked, she'd jolted her head away. The room had been destroyed. The table lay sideways, books and toys were scattered across the floor, and in that moment she'd seen Grae, bleeding from a gash across his face.

Lily locked her door and stood with her back pressed hard against it. She'd caught Grae's eye just as he'd looked up to greet the children, to smile and show it was nothing but a scratch, and in that instant he'd seen her looking, and he'd warned her with a savagery that was chilling, under no circumstance should she go in.

21

Max began to dream about the Sea House. Sometimes he climbed that steep ladder alone, stood looking out surrounded by water, but more often he was there not as he wished to be with Elsa, but with Gertrude, her hand in his, the hot pulse of desire flooding up his arm. He wandered through the rooms with her, pressed her strong palm as they admired the view, and then sank on to that downy bed, her arms outspanning his, her grey bun releasing, the coils of her hair like Brillo streaming to her waist. Sometimes he woke, his nightshirt cold with sweat, and tried again, tried to find Elsa through his sleep.

Tonight, instead of searching for her, he began building a cupboard out of shells. It had tiny compartments lined with samphire, hangers of seaweed and mother of pearl drawers. Look, he called, stepping back in admiration, but it was Helga who took him by the hand. Helga, in her green dress, the day of their engagement. They'd had a party to celebrate on the twenty-first of June, a midsummer party out of doors, and his mother and Helga's had each made a tureen of eel. Eel cooked with onion, flour and water so that the chunks of grey flesh sat in a transparent stew. He could see the little lengths of skeleton, the knuckled backbone and the spray of fins, and feel the downturn of his mouth as he pushed each forkful in. There was a salmon too, caught and smoked by Helga's father, sweet and orange as jelly, and small round sunflower Brötchen, crisp with seeds, the soft dough warm on the inside. There were bowls of pickled vegetables, cabbage, carrot and green vinegary beans, and they drank beer, and afterwards small glasses of yellow cream liqueur. They'd carried the feast into their shared back garden, and on along the lane, across the path, and down on to the soft sand of the beach. Helga's brother had run about collecting wicker beach chairs, wide enough for two, and after they'd eaten Helga had turned his face towards her, and told him that she loved him, the slippery smell of the burnt onion still hovering on her skin.

Sometimes Max climbed the ladder all night long, his hands folding over each rung, his head almost level with the ceiling, but somehow never reaching the next floor. 'Love, I love, Ich liebe liebe love . . .' He could hear the words as feathery as splinters, and it was Elsa who was whispering them, who was waiting for him to appear.

Elsa he now saw every day. She came and sat near him as he painted – first the Sea House, then the little fleet of huts that stretched back over the marsh. She didn't mention Klaus, but he knew from Gertrude that there were problems with the library – another architect's drawings were favoured above his – and in the meantime he was designing a terrace for a lady in Pimlico so that her dogs would not have to go down two flights of steps to the street. 'It's a disgrace,' she said. 'A man of his talent.'

Elsa watched Max as he filled his scroll with white. White wood, white cloud, and the white sand of the dunes that sloped up in between. He'd finished the tea shop, painting in the heads of the people, the waves of the sign, the geraniums on the ledges. He was considering climbing the steps towards the pub, starting on the cabin where Mrs Wynwell lived with Alf, when a car drove slowly past, threading its way through silt and pebbles until it stopped by the Sea House steps.

A woman climbed out, holding a baby, hauling a toddler by one arm, and then a man rose up out of the driver's seat and stretched. There was another woman, older, and she was opening the porch door, while out of the back of the car children uncoiled like springs. Max began to walk towards them. One child was shouting in excitement over the discovery of an eel net slung between the stilts, and another, he could see through the glass front door, was shooting up the ladder, no doubt leaping with its boots on to the quilted bed.

The woman moved inside and began unpacking baskets of food, picking cups up from the dresser, using one finger to test if they were clean. Above him on the terrace the younger woman appeared, the baby pressed against one shoulder, stopping as her eyes stretched out to sea.

'No,' he wanted to call up to her. 'This is my house.' It WAS his house. He hadn't known it until then. 'Elsa,' he called, desperate, forgetting that she had gone. 'Elsa!' and it was only then he saw the faces of the visitors, peering at him, concerned.

That night he lay awake in the quiet of his room and thought of Kaethe. Not the dying Kaethe, he tried not to think of her, but the sister she had been to him through all the years before. Fierce and haughty, clever, strong, saving him, making a home for him, writing to him weekly when he was interned. But hard as he tried to hold her she began to wither in his arms. Shrunken, yellow, wincing from her own thin smell, it had taken her eleven months to die. Her face became a silver mesh of lines, her hair was coarse, her wrist a knot of bone. Once Max caught her, staring at herself in an oval mirror she then hid quickly in her sheet, and he knew that, just like him, she was thinking of their mother, following her last days in a dormitory at Buchenwald, feverish and stinking, with no one to nurse or hold her, no one who even cared to know her name.

'We should not have allowed it,' Kaethe wept to him. 'Eating, and laughing, forgetting for whole minutes at a time.' She'd stretched her hand out and clutched his arm with force. 'Don't believe that. Promise me you won't?'

Max switched on the light. There was a mirror hanging on the wall and he looked into it. No, he did not have his father's face. His father was darker, broader, more handsome than his son, although they shared the same unruly eyebrows, the same brown eyes and pale skin. And of course his father's shoes, stacked up with solid strips of leather, had given him an awkward height.

Jos Meyer wore these shoes, provided by the government, a new pair each year, whether he needed a new pair or not. *For injuries sustained at the battle of Loos. One pair of shoes, black, size 42.* Jos Meyer, war veteran, decorated for bravery, baptized into the Christian faith. At first there had been preferential treatment for heroes of the war. Jos was allowed to continue his practice as a lawyer when so many others had their licences revoked, and the Meyers lived on at Heiderose undisturbed. 'Why emigrate?' They had discussed it. 'When our life here is not so very bad. To leave with nothing, with no promise of work. With no prospects . . .' They'd looked at Max, already twenty-four, and he knew that they were wondering how he'd manage, their invalid of a son. Kaethe had moved to England, had a flat in London, shared with a young woman, Gertrude Jilks, a nurse, and she wrote regularly, telling them about her teaching and her passion for her work.

And then one night Jos disappeared. He was working late in Hamburg, had promised to be home early the next day, but when Max's mother called him to say goodnight there was no reply. She called again at midnight, at three in the morning, at dawn, and then her cousin Marie telephoned to say that her own husband, who worked for the bank, had been taken away.

'What can we do? Is there nothing we can do?'

His mother despaired. Other wives and relatives rang to report the arrest of their own men, and after each call she became more frantic, running over and over the arguments they had made for staying, cursing the trick played on them, making their lives just bearable enough so they would not leave. That night, all over Hamburg, Jewish shops were smashed and looted, synagogues were burned, and no one knew when those arrested would be seen again.

But on the evening of the second day Jos reappeared. 'It's all right.' He was labouring slightly on the ridges of his shoes, his face and neck dark grey with stubble. 'Everything is all right.' He slept a little, ate, but would not say a word. 'No.' He shook his head, but even as he said it, he looked round anxiously and placed a large cushion over the telephone as if the mouthpiece had ears. Later he went down into the basement and Max watched him as he chose the boards to make a box. He sawed and planed and chiselled, fretting the teeth and sanding smooth the grooves until he had a crate.

'You will go first,' he said to Max, and into the box they placed the feet, the legs, the two smooth leaves of Max's table. 'Wait.' Jos put a hand on his son's arm, and he returned with the Renoir that hung above the drawing-room fire. He pressed it out of its frame, carefully releasing the tacks that held it to the wood, and when it was flat, its corners curling, he slid it between the table's top and its one drawer. It clung there, a perfect fit, just above Henry's letters. 'Kaethe will take care of you till we come.'

Two years later, in an internment camp on the Isle of Man, Max met a man, a Mr Guttfeld, who asked him if he was related to the lawyer Joseph Meyer.

'Yes.' Max felt his blood lie still. 'I am his son.'

'We were arrested together,' the man went on, 'in November 1938,' and he told him the story of that night. How he'd been at home in bed in his apartment on the Esplanaden when he was startled by a knocking on the door. 'Open up!' There was one moment of civility as the soldiers asked to see his papers, watching as he folded them away, and then, when that was done, they took hold of him and dragged him down the stairs. He was thrown into a truck. It was dark, but he could make out others, lying where they'd fallen on the floor. He managed to stagger up and push himself to the back, before twenty, maybe forty more were forced in. Some of these stumbled on the metal lip, tripping themselves and those behind, so that when the truck finally pulled out of the city, it was full of moaning, injured people, too densely packed in to stand up. It was almost one o'clock in the morning when the truck came to a halt.

'OUT.' Everyone began to stir. 'OUT! NOW!' the soldiers screamed, and they began hurrying them, pulling them out by limbs or hair, beating them where they had fallen until they struggled up. Guttfeld had been standing at the back, and it was then that he saw Joseph Meyer, and recognized him as the lawyer who had won for his cousin's textile company an important case. He took his arm and jumped with him and they landed together, still upright, on the ground. Now they were forced to march, on and on through the forest, for ten kilometres at least. 'I lost sight of your father then,' Guttfeld said, 'but when eventually we were allowed to stop, he was standing beside me in the line.'

They were in a clearing in the forest, surrounded by pine trees, tall and widely spaced. Fallen needles lay mouldering on the ground and all around was the smell of damp, thick, woody sweetness, and nothing but the silence of the night. Beyond they could see the wire mesh of a camp. And then a car roared out through its gates and an SS officer jumped out.

'He walked very slowly up and down before us, inspecting us, looking into each exhausted face. First, he told us, we were never to discuss a single detail of this night unless we wanted those we loved to suffer, and second, we should do everything in our power to disappear. "Disappear from Germany."

'He clicked his fingers, and then a man, a prisoner, whispered something to his neighbour, just one word out of the corner of his mouth, and before the curl of his breath had faded, the order was given and he was pulled from the line. A soldier kicked him hard so that he fell, and then another stepped forward and stamped on his face. You could hear the splintering of bone, the crack of his nose and cheek, and then the first man, greedy for more, kicked him in the side. His ribs crunched, he let out a moan, and when I looked again the man was dead. Now everyone was standing, chins in the air, chests pushed forward, eyes straight ahead. We stood, hardly breathing, into the dawn. Birds began to sing, the branches of the trees rustled in the wind, and then finally, as the sun came up, two carts arrived and served out soup. I felt grateful for that soup, so grateful . . .'

Guttfeld turned away in self-disgust. And then, remembering, 'Your father. Is he here?'

'No.' Max shook his head. He could see the cushion squashed over the telephone, as if its bulk would save their lives. 'No.' His father had not disappeared from Germany, and in that moment he knew he would not see him again.

22

Lily left while the girls were at school. She listened for the splutter of Grae's car, and then watched it wind its way around the corner of the Green. Quickly she piled her work into a folder, her notes and books and letters, the sketches Klaus had made of every room. She scooped up her own drawings, her plan for an extension to Lehmann's Heath Height Flats. She'd designed a sun terrace walkway with areas for playing cards, a maze with animals carved from box hedge, and at its centre a fountain that ran into a bright blue pool. There was a jungle of bamboo, and a small grove of oleander, and at each level of the building she'd attached wide wooden terraces with steps leading down.

All week Lily had avoided Grae, and the girls, unusually, had kept away. Now she threw a bag of clothes into the car and, taking one last look at the sea, the high straight line of it hardening where it touched the sky, she backed out of the lane.

The nearest station was no more than a level crossing, with two platforms and a white wooden gate that dropped across the road. Lily parked in the small commuters' car park and walked across the track, treading quickly as she stepped between the rails. There was no one else waiting, and she thought for a moment hopefully that she might have missed her train, but then a high song, like a mermaid calling, rang out and with a flash of orange lights the barriers closed over the road. The cars in both directions stopped, waiting patient as ponies at a fence, and then the train whistled into view. Lily slipped in next to a window. There were only three carriages, and hers she had entirely to herself. Quickly, before she drifted into a daze of fields and trees and flatness, she opened her folder and pulled out some work. With it came Nick's letter.

Dear Lily . . . She'd already read the letter, more than once, but found it impossible not to start with it again. *We've got the contract! We have nine months of solid work! I'm thrilled, Tim is thrilled. Could you be just a tiny bit pleased? Pleased enough to come home and start making the tea? But seriously we can't hire anyone who isn't qualified. So are you planning to come and do your Pin Up, or have you applied for a job as barmaid at the Ship? They need you, that's certain, but there are others who need you more. I'll expect you this weekend, unless the wife-beater is holding you hostage, in which case, good luck. See you then. Love, N.*

Lily read the letter again. The more she read it, the more she needed to keep reading it, hoping to get at something underneath. *There are others who need you more.* Presumably that meant Nick, or was he referring to the restaurant in Covent Garden where she'd worked as a waitress all those years? Eventually she pushed the letter away. Pin Up was in the morning. She opened her file, and began to study her drawings, imagining how she would arrange them over the college walls, how they might look, her vision unfolding, a sympathetic, sustainable extension to Lehmann's world. She flicked through her notes, the names and dates and theories, circled and ticked and underlined. Lists and boxes, capitals and exclamations, arrows pointing on to where she'd made a find. The train was steaming past an estuary hamlet, white sails fluttering on the wind, the water rippling with such definition it looked solid as sand. Lily pressed her face to the window. Soon they would arrive at Ipswich, and she would change on to a long, sleek inter-city train. It made her nervous, the thought of re-entering London, descending those metal stairs into the tube, pushing against the heavy doors of her building, hearing the click of the lock as they snapped shut. For comfort she reached for Lehmann's letters. He was back in Hamburg, writing to Elsa from their dismantled home, and Elsa, it seemed, was living alone in London, in a room near Goodge Street, waiting for him to come.

My little London El,

It's not easy to report on my progress as there's so little of it. The man at the Office for Emigration told me that he'd approve my application, but first he'd have to get it back from the higher authority to which he sent it himself, three weeks ago! I nearly fell to pieces with the impatience of it. I went for lunch with your Mama who read out the letter she'd just received from you. She was so pleased to get it, but I was shocked at the way you describe your situation. Can't you remember that these weeks will soon be over? Also your note to me of today contains a misunderstanding. You asked recently whether I hadn't half forgotten you, and I replied, joking, 'at most, the smaller half'. And you take that as a statement of fact. Oh, Elsa L, what will it take to make you happy? Well, of course I know, and you mustn't lose hope. In the meantime, have you been studying your English? There is a new method, Basic English, I think you should try. I want to see you again, all of you, very soon, and in good spirits. I Love You, so remember that. Your L.

Have you ever said, 'I love you', and not meant it? This was a question asked in a newspaper questionnaire Lily sometimes read. 'No. Never,' came the most common reply, laced, she always felt, with a certain self-regard. It reminded Lily how often she'd misused the words. She'd wanted to say them to see how they'd affect her if she ever was in love, but she'd been shocked the first time, when the boy for whom she felt a strange powerful blankness turned to her, amazed. 'Yes,' he said, 'I love you too,' and Lily felt the first flicker of a disbelieving smile. Dominic, he was called. Dominic Barton, and it had taken her two months, right into the week of her fifteenth birthday, to prise herself away. She wouldn't do it. She swore she wouldn't use those words again, but she found they were impossible to resist. 'I love you,' she'd said, looking down on the smooth white chest of a boy doing ceramics in his final year at Camberwell, and even as she spoke, she thought, Wouldn't it be wonderful if I did?

But when she met Nick everything was different, and she realized it was only when you actually did love someone the words were difficult to say. She would wait for him. He couldn't be afraid. It was Nick, after all, who'd steered her round North London, ordered her to stop outside the Lehmann building, had kissed her as the lights flashed on. Any moment now he would tell her that he loved her, and released, her own declaration would come reeling out. For the whole first year Lily waited. She imagined, sometimes daily, that he was about to tell her, whisper the words across the pillow, scatter them through drops of water as they stood together in the rain. She thought she heard them on an autumn walk, whistling down Kite Hill, and then, on their anniversary, a year to the day after they'd kissed, Lily took courage and sighed the words into his ear. Nick squeezed her shoulder, smiled, and then, startled by its sudden ring, fumbled to answer his phone.

Lily moved in with Nick the following month. There was no request, no whoop of acceptance when she said she would, just the assumption, when her landlord raised her rent, that it would be more convenient if she brought her things to his. They had talked about where they'd store her paintings, her clothes, her washbag, even her bag of cotton wool, and somewhere in between their plans to extend the wardrobe right into the corner of the room she forgot there was something that had not been said.

My El,

Today, once again, I am frustrated and horrified by my application. My papers have been handed back to the higher authority! An immediate phone call from me has resulted in another meeting for tomorrow at noon, which will probably only slow the process further. So my visit to the Ministry can only happen on Friday at the very earliest. If all goes well, I'll send you a telegram. It's really not that easy any more to remain even-tempered. For two days now the weather has been awful, with such downpours you would think that Mama and Papa were visiting from

Berlin! It's better today, but I've sent my winter coat off to be cleaned and repaired at Zirkov's. So at least someone is benefiting from my being here.

Yours, always, L.

Lily rang the doorbell, just a short warning ring, as she fumbled for her keys. 'Nick?' she called into the hall, but there was no one there. Lily stood and looked around her. 'Nick?' she said again just to be sure, and it almost made her blush to see how much their home resembled him. Long and lean with sleek pale floorboards, white walls, and a kitchen as streamlined as a ship. There were oil-blue doors hiding everything from view, so that if you went hunting for a teaspoon, or the fridge, there was nothing to give even the smallest clue.

Lily took her shoes off, and put her bag down on the floor. She felt dusty suddenly and hot. There was sand between her toes, and spores of bright gold pollen clinging to her shins. Her shoes, on the bare floorboards, looked like a Van Gogh. She poured herself a glass of water and marvelled at the power with which the water rushed out of the tap, the weight of the smooth glass, the immaculate steel of the worktop, as if she'd never seen it before.

There was no room in the flat for a bath, just a shower in a tower of glass in one corner of the bedroom. At Fern Cottage she'd become accustomed to lying in a pool of rusted water, drifting and dreaming and thinking about nothing at all, but here, in the funnel of Nick's shower, she felt her body blazing into life. Her shoulders, striped in every shade of tan, seemed to creak and sigh under the jets, and she smiled at the sight of her legs, so pale at the thigh, darkening and darkening until they reached her feet. Her face, reflected back at her in the bathroom mirror, was freckled gold with sun, and she realized that she hadn't been able to gauge her appearance in all the weeks she'd been away. This was the mirror by which she judged herself, the mirror she believed in, imagined to be the only true one, as if everyone in the world who saw her was looking through this glass.

She wrapped herself in a thick white towel and lay down on the bed. The cleaner must have been that day, everything was so well folded, sleek and smart, with only her old beaded lampshade, a ladder in its frill, to show that one side of the bed was hers. She closed her eyes and let the sounds drift up to her from the road below, the purr of engines at the lights and the birdsong outside the window in the street's one tree. Nick must be at work, she thought, yawning, glancing at the clock, as a tube train on the track behind the houses opposite rocked the room as it roared past. She should get up, slide open the wardrobe, discover her lost clothes, get dressed. Nick would be at work till late, he would always be at work. Nine months, he had said in his letter, and she knew that meant a year. Lily closed her eyes. Motorbikes, bikes, cars, the quick clipping of heels, the rushing of flat sandals, the squeal of tyres. A door thudded on the floor below, and then, in the dip of silence that followed, Lily fell asleep.

'Where shall I put them?' a woman's voice rang out, and then another lower voice, not Nick's, not Tim's: 'You can put them over here.'

Lily sat up. The towel was damp around her, and on the grey squares of the quilt, like a shadow where she'd lain, was the imprint of her body.

'Righto.' There was the high-pitched voice again, followed by the familiar metal clunk of the flat's front door. Lily glanced at the clock. It was six, just after, and she was cold. Quickly she slipped out of her towel, pulled on Nick's dark robe and very slowly, quietly, inched open the door. At first she could hear nothing, but then, when she'd stepped into the hall, she could hear someone in the kitchen, the shuffle of feet over the tiles, the click and shudder of the cupboard doors. She was stretching forward, straining to see, when the footsteps turned and moved decisively towards her. Quickly she retreated to the bedroom. Her clothes were lying in a puddle on the floor, limp and worn, and with unnecessary force she picked them up and flung them out of sight. The panelled wardrobe door slid smoothly open, and there inside were skirts and dresses, a winter coat that skimmed the tops of shoes. Beside them in a stack of shelves were Nick's shirts. They were sealed each one in plastic, their chests thrust forward, all buttoned up, and like waiters, exaggeratedly bowing, their arms were tucked out of sight. Lily picked one up, the cellophane so new it sparkled, and, as she looked at it, she thought of the orange-crate of toys in the corner of Grae's room, the dolls and ragged teddies, the clumps of Lego thrown in.

Lily stood on tiptoe to swing her clothes along the rail, remembering as she did so why each item of clothing remained unworn. Too tight, or short, or long. Too flimsy, too low cut at the neck, but none of them were quite hopeless enough to part with, so she kept them, as she had done now for years. Eventually she chose a pair of trousers, black linen that creased as soon as you sat down, and a shirt that tied in at the waist. It was a shirt she'd tried on many times. It looked so pretty on the hanger, its polka dots and sleeveless arms, but even now as she fastened it, she was raking through for something else. She caught a glimpse of white and was just stretching to unhook it when the telephone rang.

'Holly. It's Nick.'

Who on earth was Holly? 'Nick, it's me.' Or had he forgotten her name?

'Lily! What are you . . . ?' He was gasping, literally, as if the last news he'd had of her she'd been lost at sea. 'I'm sorry, I mean, it's just . . .' He began to laugh. 'You're back. Great. Welcome home.'

'Where are you?' Lily asked. 'I was going to come and meet you.'

'Oh . . . Don't do that.' Nick sounded distracted. 'Listen, is there someone there called Holly? I need to have a word.'

'There might be.' Lily put her head out of the door and called.

'OK. Just coming,' a voice floated back, and Lily waited while the tap was turned off in the kitchen, a cupboard door clicked shut, and then, swishing slightly, a girl, with long, pale hair appeared in the hall. She smiled as she took the phone. 'A hundred glasses, yes,' she said, standing perfectly still. 'No, Pauline's waiting downstairs for them. Sure, and I'm just doing the bagels.' Nick must have said something then, because the girl's face broke into a smile. She smiled with all of her, her body swaying, her hip floating to the side. Lily stared – the strands of treacle in her hair, the little smoothness of her stomach as it rounded out of the waistband of her jeans. 'All right, then, anything else?' Lily put out her hand expectantly. 'All right. See you later, bye.' Holly pressed the button and, still smiling, handed back the silent phone. 'Thanks,' she said, and she turned on her sandalled heel and walked away.

Quickly, furiously, Lily dialled. 'Nick?' But it was Tim. 'Hi there, Lil,' he said. 'Where are you?'

'I'm . . . in London, at home. Is Nick there?'

'No, let's see. He left . . . half an hour ago. Listen, do you want to hear a joke?'

'Well . . . ?'

'A woman goes to a hospital in Suffolk. Straight away she's whisked off for an X-ray. She's examined, tested, put to bed. At the end of the day she calls out to the doctor, "I thought I should mention it, but I just came in this morning to tell you that my friend couldn't come."'

'Ha, ha.'

'What does the East Anglian doctor put in his notes after seeing a patient who's never learnt to read or write?'

'I don't know.'

'NFS.' Tim began to laugh. '"Normal for Suffolk." It's true. It's an actual medical term.'

'I'll try his mobile.'

'See you later, then,' and still chuckling Tim put down the phone.

'Nick?' Lily had caught him. He sounded out of breath. 'Where are you?'

'Here.'

'What do you mean?'

'Right here,' he said, and just then she heard the rattle of the lock.

Lily walked along the hall, the phone pressed to her ear. 'How are you?' she said, as shoulder-first he eased through the door.

'I'm fine.'

She could see his smile now, his mouth moving as he spoke, and there in the crook of his left arm was a huge parcel of flowers. Roses, dark red, the whorls of their buds, a kaleidoscope of spirals, at least a hundred of them, packed together in one solid mass.

'Hello,' she said, cutting off her phone, and just as she was moving to embrace him, his elbow, the creased paper of the flowers, Holly stepped smoothly out of the kitchen, and rolled the package into her arms. 'I'll start arranging these,' she said and she left Nick and Lily alone.

Nick looked at her. 'Hello,' he said, and then he glanced down at her bag, abandoned, dusty, cluttering up the hall. He raised one eyebrow. And you are leaving this where?

Lily stretched up to kiss him, smiling. 'Nice to see you,' she said, but her kiss was cold. She took the bag, scooped up her shoes and, running with them into the bedroom, pulled open the wardrobe and threw them viciously in. One shoe landed among his shirts, the other upside down. She stepped back guiltily and glanced around, but he was in the kitchen, she could hear him talking to Holly, hear the scrape of a chair as he stretched up above the cupboards to lift the vases down.

'Can I help?' she asked from the doorway, checking the buttons of her shirt. Holly had unlooped the paper and the green wet stems of the roses were rolling out along the worktop.

'Lily,' Nick urged her in. 'Yes. Christ. People will be arriving in half an hour.'

'People?' she nodded towards Holly. 'Hi, we haven't really met.'

'We thought we'd have a bit of a party, to celebrate the contract, just a few people . . .'

Holly was clipping the end off each stem, stripping the stalks of leaves, placing them in water. 'Hello,' she said.

'Nick, I've got a big day tomorrow.'

Nick looked at her, unfazed. 'Well,' he said. 'It's too late now.'

Lily felt her insides quake. 'What do you mean?'

But he had already turned back to Holly, and together they were running through the list of things still to be achieved. 'Right, Pauline's bringing the wine up. Flowers, food, napkins, ashtrays? I suppose we'd better open all the windows. Lily?' But she was already unlatching the panes.

Half an hour later the room was full of noise. There were plates of smoked salmon bagels and bowls of vegetable crisps, pistachio nuts and small dried Hunza apricots sprinkled round the room. The flowers had been arranged on every available surface. They looked festive, Christmassy even, with their red and green.

Tim was already drunk. 'You're looking gorgeous,' he told Lily, eyes bright, mouth loose. 'It must be NFS.'

'It's all right,' Nick said at half past nine, 'they'll go off soon, they'll have to eat.' But at ten-thirty Holly began making cheese on toast. She tipped up the breadbin and emptied the fridge, and everyone cooed around her and held out their plates for more.

Lily went into the bedroom and retrieved her bag. She peered mournfully into it, at the file of drawings, at the notes and books and pens. It was too late anyway, Nick was right, but in a last hopeful effort she arranged them on the bedside table, as close as they would go to the bed. There was a small chance that the contents might drift through to her, and inspire her during the night.

Eventually there were just the four of them. She and Nick, Holly and Tim. 'To us.' Tim raised a glass. 'To me!' And then, still laughing, his eyes sank shut.

'I'd better go,' Holly said. 'I'll take him with me.'

'You're a gem.' Nick rose up out of the sofa. 'How did we manage without you?'

'How did you?' she said and, nodding for a moment in Lily's direction, she eased Tim's arm around her shoulder, and manoeuvred him out.

'So, how long has she been . . . ? I didn't know you'd hired anyone.'

'Just this week.' Nick took her hand. 'We couldn't wait, we needed someone, you understand that?'

'Yes,' Lily said. 'You did need someone.' She lay against him, thinking, waiting, listening to the music Holly had chosen, a long pure flute of jazz. Eventually her arm started to go numb. 'Nick?' she said, but when she twisted round to look at him she saw he was asleep.

23

Max stood at Hamburg central station with a small green suitcase at his side. Inside his coat, thrust deep into the pocket, was a wallet which contained the ten marks he was allowed. 'Start looking for a place for us,' his father said. 'We will come soon.' Everywhere people were whispering the same. Soon. The word seemed to slip along the rails, up and over the rim of the grey platform. 'Soon, soon.' Max looked around him, at the couriers holding out their clipboards, ticking the people off their lists.

'The crooks of the stock exchange, slave-drivers of the nation . . .' The Nazi youth song rose up in his brain, as the pale, over-padded children boarded the train. 'When the blood of the Jews spurts from the knife' – Max had seen those words swell in their marching mouths – 'then everything will be better.'

'We'll only come if we can find no other way.' No. Max shook his head. But he knew his mother was thinking of their garden, the wood behind the pond. The staircase and the landing, the attic windows that looked out over fields. 'We'll keep it safe for you.' He saw the tears she was holding make a film over her eyes.

Max stepped on to the train. He was packed in with them now, the crooks and slave-drivers, and he imagined Helga watching him, her snub face pressed against the glass, relieved. He reached a window and stretched out to touch his mother's cheek, and just as he did so, the hand of the clock that hung from the roof of the station shuddered into place.

'Give our best love to Kaethe.' They were both reaching up to him, and then a whistle must have blown. Max felt it shrilling through him, and with it, like a sea of birds, the mouths of all those on the platform opened in alarm. Max saw the noise, the stretched throats and the fingers, and then the train began to move. The faces fell back, white framed against the black of hats, and the children inside the carriage looked around as if they never expected, really, that the train would leave.

Max stumbled to his seat. There was a boy beside him with a violin, his fingers white against the canvas case. He was small, no more than twelve years old, but as Max caught his eye he saw a flicker of excitement. 'I've never been to Great Britain,' he said as Max sat down, and he took a deep breath.

Max sipped his tea and wondered what had become of that boy. His name was Walter Lampl, and he'd been on his way to Kent. There was a school there, set up especially for refugees. 'My parents,' Walter had told him, 'will be coming soon. And if they can't . . .' – there was one fleeting moment of doubt – 'take me home, I mean, then they can work at the school. My mother teaches piano and my father . . .' What could Walter's father do? 'My father could work as a cook.' Walter Lampl had been a good companion on that train, talking occasionally, smiling often, and crying only once when they reached the Hook of Holland and saw a large white sign: *Help the Jews of Germany*, it said. And Max had to hold his arm as they walked up the gangplank and on to the boat.

'Good morning. I've just come back to change.' It was the morning of the local history exhibition, and Gertrude had been up since six.

'Tea?' Max half rose to find a second cup, but Gertrude was heading towards the stairs. 'No, I won't have time.'

When she reappeared, she was wearing a printed summer dress, fitted and flowery and quite different from her usual large buttoned suits. She stood in front of the hall mirror. 'Well . . .' She had hairpins in her mouth, and her head was tilted to one side. Her words came out lopsided, impossible for him to grasp. 'We have seventeen Victoria sponges, three dozen butterfly cakes, and a tray of cheese scones, another tray of tea cakes, and more food is on its way!' She could see as she swerved her eyes towards him that his face looked strained, but the excitement was bubbling up inside her, making it impossible to stop. 'To think we've been worrying about a shortage of food! Anyway, Mavis and Peter are doing sandwiches, there's no stopping them, and when I get back I'll start up the urn. Look, it's almost ten now.' She turned to Max. 'Will you walk back with me?'

Max gestured helplessly to his unfinished tea.

'Oh, please do. If I'm on my own I'm bound to start running. What if I twist an ankle?' She felt a surge of pleasure in the power of her body. 'I don't want to be hobbling around for the next three days.'

Max and Gertrude walked towards the Gannon Room. Max seemed diminished somehow with nothing in his hands, no bag strapped to his back, no scroll. 'Are you all right?' Gertrude smiled, hoping to pass on some of her good cheer, but Max only bent his head. The day was overcast, the sky a thick pale grey, and as they reached the Green the rain began. Thin drops like spears, widely spaced and warm. Not enough to keep them in their houses, Gertrude hoped, but enough to drive the stragglers into the hall.

There was quite a crowd outside the Gannon Room, milling and chatting and waiting for half past ten.

'You can come in with me if you like,' Gertrude whispered. 'No one will mind.' Why was she treating him like a child, holding out small scraps of favour, just as Kaethe had always done?

'No,' Max said. 'I'll wait.' He patted his pocket to show that he had change.

Elsa and Klaus were sheltering beneath a tree. Max walked over to them. 'How is London?' Max forced himself to speak.

'Impossible.' Klaus shook his head. 'A foreman who is a fool, workmen who stop two hours for lunch. How can we make progress?' Elsa looked at the ground. She had a cardigan draped over her shoulders, oatmeal with an embroidered trim, and beneath the soft folds of the wool her arm hung cool and close. 'Impossible, impossible.' And then Klaus began to laugh. 'That's enough. You will not hear another word about it. I have promised. Isn't that right, my El?' Elsa put her arm through his and held it close.

'But as for you . . .' He was talking to Max. 'You have done the sensible thing. You have chosen a working holiday. Elsa tells me you're making a painting of the village. I should like to see it when it's done.'

Just then the doors to the Gannon Room opened and everyone fumbled for the twopence that was needed to get in. 'Yes, of course,' he said as they moved forward. He imagined Elsa must have forgotten to mention that he'd failed to include their house.

The hall had been transformed. A snake of tables wound through the room and on each available surface, labelled and arranged, were the exhibits. Scattered among these were tiny sprays of flowers. Harebells, broom, milkwort, and bell heather, tormentil, wild rose and gorse. They stood, each individual stalk, in tiny glass containers, medicine bottles, sherry glasses, pots.

Max stretched his fingers towards a collection of coins. Some were perfect, without a chip or dent, while others were battered, green and crusted white. *Please do not touch*. A sign stood in the centre, and Max shrank back, needing the weight of each object in his hand to see.

On the next table were a pair of Dutch clogs. Pale wood, decorated with red, but one was a little larger than the other. Max imagined them bobbing over the water, small masts rising out of their soles, but it was just as likely that they had been abandoned by some visiting family, and found the next day in the surf.

Max moved along a little and found himself beside Elsa. She was reading a copy of the 1577 agreement that allowed the ferry to work the river on a lease. Max peered at the words. He could see they were in English, but with so many extra flourishes, shortenings and curls, that he continued on to where Gertrude was presiding over a table displaying a mole trap and a clockwork spit. Behind her at a hatch morning tea was being served. The sponge cakes had been sliced and laid on chalk-green plates, and the scones and tea cakes buttered. Four card tables were draped with linen cloths and Mrs Wrenwright from the pottery was already manoeuvring herself towards one, an egg and cress sandwich in one hand, a tea cup in the other.

Klaus was looking at a copy of the Doomsday Book. He was staring into it, while people swelled round him and moved on. Max stood before a screen of photographs and then – almost as if he'd willed her to him – Elsa was at his side again. Together they looked at a print of the old ferry man standing by his hut, and beside him, his grandson, taut and wiry, who worked the ferry now. Down at the harbour the fishermen were grouped together in their peaked wool caps, the ropes of braid glistening with detail, their profiles beautiful in black and white.

Max sat at a table while Elsa brought tea, and as he waited he pushed away the images of Heiderose, the face of the gardener with his heavy moustache, the girls who worked on the farm, their hair in plaits above their heads. What, he wondered, had become of Georg, the boy who bicycled from Rissen with their post, and the small son of the carpenter who stuffed the bread and jam they gave him into the bib of his shorts? 'I chose a tea cake for you.' Elsa was setting down the cups, and Max, as he framed each picture, reminded himself that even a child in lederhosen was now a symbol of rottenness and hate.

24

On Sunday Nick suggested going to Hyde Park. Lily was lying reading on their bed, trying to turn her mind away from thoughts of college. The scramble for space to pin her drawings up, the crush of people, the pained look of her tutor as he caught her on the stairs. Why, he'd asked, had she not responded to his emails?

'Nick.' Lily sat up. 'Are you all right?'

'Yes.' He sounded cross.

'I mean . . .' She put on a smile. 'It's just in all the years I've known you, you've never, ever suggested going to a park.'

Nick looked at her. 'And that's because . . .' – he spoke slowly, as if he'd given the subject furious thought – 'usually before I get a chance, you suggest it first.'

They stared at each other, coldly.

'All right,' she said, 'let's go.'

Hyde Park was dry and arid. There were patches of bare earth, hard ovals of baldness where too many people had hovered, playing rounders, at first base.

'I'm thinking,' Lily said, as her feet crunched and snapped the brittle stalks of grass, 'of keeping the cottage on. It just seems a shame to give it up, when I've almost finished my work. We could spend August there, or you could visit when you have time off?'

Nick kept on walking, his eyes fixed on the lake. 'How can you afford it?'

'Yes, I know.' Lily didn't want to tell him. But she'd written to her bank, a month ago, and taken out a loan.

'I don't understand.' He was frowning, straining for something Lily couldn't see. 'You need to get your work experience, we'd even pay you. It's true, not very much.'

'Yes.' Lily felt sad. They were almost at the Serpentine, and she could still hear the traffic, roaring down Park Lane. 'Maybe I'll get a summer job in Steerborough. They might need someone in the shop, or I could waitress, serve cream teas. They need people in Eastonknoll.'

'I was joking, you know, when I wrote to you about The Ship. What is it about you and –'

'Waitressing?' Her voice was sharp.

They walked on in silence, pushing past the people who were drifting, idling, shredding bread for ducks. At the tip of the lake, where it swept under the bridge, there was a café where once, when they'd first met, they'd stopped and had a drink. They'd had a fruit juice each, gritty and warm, in glasses without ice, and when the bill had come they'd gasped together at the price. Nick had put his arm around her and whispered into her ear, 'I'll bring you here for your birthday if you don't behave.' It had been a joke between them, an unlikely pavilion of their love, but now, heads down, they walked fast past it and up on to the road.

'Now what? Lily stopped on the bridge, looking across the road at Kensington Gardens. 'Shall we go back, or on?' But neither of them seemed able to decide.

Lily had a huge bag full of summer clothes; towels and books and sandals, a straw hat buckling slightly at the rim. Nick watched as she piled more and more in.

'But you'll come next weekend?' She tried to make it sound as if she were packing this multitude of things for him.

'Yes,' he agreed irritably. 'Yes, I will.'

Lily's car was waiting in the station car park. It was all alone, its bonnet dusty and its windscreen streaked with one long seagull's dropping, hardened to a splash of green. All the same, she felt inordinately pleased to see it, and she wrapped her arms fondly round the steering-wheel as she drove over the slats of the level crossing and on along the road. Already she recognized the hedge-rows, the field of pigs just by the turn, and there on the horizon the outsized cathedral and the legs of the water tower bearing down. Lily stopped at the village shop for milk and bread, and irresistible, on the counter, a Kinder egg, one each for Arrie and Em. Outside she scanned the shop window for anything that might resemble a job. There were cottages to let, a bike, a washing machine for sale, and on the door a handwritten notice.

Money found in Palmers Lane.
If the money is yours,
PLEASE
contact Mrs Townsend at Old Farm.

Lily read this notice twice, her hand over her mouth, looking round for someone to tell, but there was no one except a frail old lady who might for all she knew be Mrs Townsend herself. Running the message over in her mind, and laughing each time she came to the word 'please' she drove the car very slowly down the street.

Fern Cottage smelt unpleasant. Musty, mouldy even, as if all that brown furniture was never intended to withstand so much heat. She switched the kettle on and went into the sitting-room. The blanket had slipped down off the sofa and the curtains were half drawn. Lily ran her eyes over the bookshelf. *Knitting for Fun*, *Ornamental Sea Shells*, and her favourite, *Wines, Syrups and Cordials*, a book of recipes collected by the WI. The original price showed five shillings, but at some point, at some long ago summer fête, it had been marked down to two-and-six. Lily unlatched the windows and stared out on to the Green. There was no one there she knew. Two women stretched out beside a pushchair and a man following a toddler up the slide. Quickly she rearranged the blanket, tucking it in, plumping the cushions and gathering up the jug of flowers, the water evaporated, the stalks turned half to slime.

In the kitchen the kettle had forgotten how to switch itself off, and white clouds of steam were billowing against the window-panes, rolling in a thick mist around the room. Lily made herself tea with the last scorched inch of water and took it into the garden, leaving the door and windows open to give the house some air. The garden was uncharacteristically neat. No washing on the line, no bikes, the shed empty and latched shut. Lily sat against the wall. She felt deflated. She could hardly admit it, but she'd been hoping to be welcomed home. The arms of the children round her, the chatter of their news, and behind them, Grae's quiet smile.

She sat with her legs in the sun, her face in shadow, the sweet scent of a rose drifting from the climbers on the wall. From time to time she glanced up at Grae's house. It was clear there was nobody at home, but it looked worse than empty. Closed. Abandoned even. Where could they be? Her heart looped over with the loss. And then it struck her. It was a mistake to have come back. She was lonely here, this wasn't her home, and to steady and distract herself she reached into her bag and drew out her envelope of letters.

My dearest El,

I'm sitting here in our empty apartment, in our empty bedroom, for the last time. Tomorrow I shall sleep at Greenberg's. The packing is done. All the furniture and boxes have been organized and wrapped in their red paper, and as I wait here with nothing but my case I am tired but relieved. The shipment of the furniture will happen any day now, and I do want to be there in London when everything arrives, so that I can pull out your cases and mine, before they're put into a warehouse. You cannot be amazed that I have written so little. The packing was an enormous task. I had to stand over it, otherwise everything would have been mixed up. Your beautiful material from the linen cupboard I just managed to save, but the key to your writing desk was nowhere to be found. Now, something that I want from you. I want you to write to me about your life. How are you getting on with the new people that you know? What do you speak about with them, and in what language? Have they all fallen under the spell of your loveliness? Your nut-brown hair and the downy little dent at the nape of your neck which luckily you can't see or your head would swell to the size of a house. I want to know. Tell me by return of post.

Love, (sincerely,) L.

My El,

Today, on the most peaceful Sunday since your departure, nothing has come from you. Mr Field came to talk English with me, and our conversation became so very interesting that I'm sure he forgot to correct me. Yesterday I went to the Office of Emigration again, and I hardly dare weary you with the outcome, but next week I must go to the Department of Trade. It can't go on for much longer now. But soon I know we will realize how little we have left behind here, and once I am with you, and as time goes on we won't have to see people, who, as you so politely put it, 'we are less fond of'. Here it is the most beautiful weather.

With all love, your L.

Lily spent the afternoon in the garden, reading, thinking, occasionally walking up the lane to the shop. She bought an apple, and some spaghetti sauce, and just before closing time a thick vanilla ice-cream dipped in white chocolate. Slowly, very slowly, she walked back to the Green, and each time she rounded the bend she was doubly disappointed not to see Grae's car.

My El,

Have you been reading English newspapers? You need to understand the wording of the different advertisements for flats. We have the choice between hotels with bed and breakfast, £6 per week, £9 per week full board, or a furnished flat where we'd have to cook for ourselves or go to a restaurant, about £5 per week. Eventually, when we know where my office is going to be, we can get an unfurnished flat, and make a proper home. Perhaps you could get someone to explain London to you, which is *what I wanted to do with you, and will do, one day soon. You need to know about the good and bad, the beautiful and ugly areas, the parks, the City, and where one should live. I think, I can see the end to things here. Another ten days at most. Be strong, have courage.*

Your L.

Later Lily walked out to the mill. She followed the soft plank paths, catching sight of the occasional figure to the left of her, up on the high ridge of shingle, standing above the level of the sea. But there was no one on the marshes, and she had the path to herself. She walked slowly, lulled by the swish and rustle of the sedge, past a hollow hill of hawthorn, its flowers scattered into the pool below it, leaving white petal bubbles on the surface like a witch's stew. She sat on the pebble-chip wall beside the mill and watched the sun as it began to sink over the fields to her right, lighting up the undersides of clouds, turning them bright pink. She lay back as the sky changed around her, the pink fluffing out to pastel, merging with the last blue sweep of day. And then with a shock it occurred to her she didn't feel afraid. Is this sensible? Am I being a fool? And she clambered up and stood on top of the wall. There wasn't anyone or anything for miles and miles around. How strange. It was a new sensation. To feel completely safe, and it occurred to her that for years now, every time she'd stepped out on to a London street, into a city park, she'd been bracing herself for an attack. She looked behind her and almost cried out. The sky had turned to gold. Streaks and swirls and watermarks, so burnished and fiery that if you saw it on a postcard you'd laugh. It was reflected in the puddles, in the river, even in the sea, the waves of which were capped with copper as they rolled in.

The air between her fingers had changed. It was grainy, thickening with dark, and she could feel it, soft against her skin. Regretfully she eased herself off the wall, and walked back the way she'd come. She turned left at a signpost with a yellow arrow on its arm and walked up a springy path. Soon the path widened and she came out in a glade of green. There was a wood ahead, an island of shadow, and, as she turned to avoid it, she caught sight of the back of the bunker, its grey walls growing out of the ground. She stopped and listened, but there was nothing but the rustle of sedge. Very slowly she moved nearer, and bending her eye to a narrow window she peered in. She started back, and immediately bent to look again.

At the centre of the bunker a figure knelt over a candle. His face was closed off by a beard, his shoulders draped in shreds of black, and his fingers which fumbled for another match were greased and thick. She knew him. It was the man who'd stepped out of the gorse. The man who'd startled her. Lily breathed in deeply and peered around his room. His black plastic bed was still set up, and all around him were rolls of long black bags tied with elastic bands, as if the dustman had simply tossed them in. Bob the Bog. Em and Arrie knew him. It was possible the whole village knew that he lived here. There were bowls and cups and half-eaten packets of biscuits. Just then the man looked up. Lily stepped back. He'd seen her, she was sure of it, but there was nothing she could do. Slowly, so as not to abandon him too harshly, she walked towards the sea.

She climbed the shingle of the ridge and stepped along its top. In the distance there was the beginning of a fire and as she looked back over the salt marsh she thought she heard a bittern, its song like the echo of a gun. Eventually the Steerborough beach huts came into view, half submerged by sand, and she cut inland over the wooden bridge, back up to the village, where lights had been switched on in almost every window, orange in their glow. She opened the dark door of Fern Cottage and flicked on her own light and as she pulled the curtains she imagined her window shining out like a beacon in the dark.

25

'I've rented it.' Max felt the touch of Elsa's fingers. 'It's mine!'

They were standing on the furthest point of land, up at the top of the estuary, looking back. The tide was low, the acres of sand separated into islands where children ran from pool to pool. Max looked inland towards the Sea House, its windows open, figures, sitting, happy on its steps.

'The Vicar rents Little Haven every year for a two-week holiday.' Elsa's eyes were bright. 'Little Heaven, the locals call it. So, I shall follow his good example and take the Sea House from the first of next month. I would have taken it before, but it was booked until then.'

There was a pause as they stood side by side.

'May I visit you?' Max asked.

'If Gertrude can spare you.'

'I meant for the day.' Max bowed his head. His heart was racing. Had she rented the Sea House for him? And to hide himself he bent to pick up a stone.

'Let's walk,' Elsa said and, slipping off her sandals, she let her toes sink into the sand. It was like a pudding, the uncooked dough of a cake, and shyly Max unlaced his boots and let his feet sink too. They walked south over the moving ground, skimming on before the sand encased them, looking back to see their footprints wobble out of sight.

Will your husband not mind? Max wanted to ask, when you move from his perfect house into a wooden hut? But with Elsa he was beginning to find that if he stayed quiet for long enough she would come round eventually to what was in his mind.

'The Sea House belongs to a Mrs Bugg,' Elsa told him as they splashed through an inlet, ankle-deep. 'Usually she is here, but her husband is ill this summer and they must stay in London to be near the hospital.' The sand had risen up into a long narrow island, and there were three boys from the village playing cricket in bare feet. 'She used to be a war correspondent but now she writes about the countryside. More than anything, she does not want this village to be lost. Homes and jobs for the people of the land, that's what she campaigns for. Last summer she wrote a play about the village, and we all came to watch it, weekenders and locals, and laughed at ourselves whether we wanted to or not.' Elsa was walking out to sea, testing the depth, holding up her skirt. Max had to follow to catch at what she said. 'I wrote to her and she said yes, do take the house. She hates the thought of it empty and unloved.'

Max was aware of people watching them. Modestly dressed ladies taking a stroll and a man throwing sticks for a dog. Elsa's skirt was splashed with wet and her bun was beginning to unstrand. She stopped and looked up at the sky. 'I can never get enough of it,' she said and, as her back arched over and her head fell back, Max had to turn away to stop himself from slipping his arm around her waist.

Elsa, Elsa. Max pressed against the mattress, the pain of his desire for her uncoiling in his gut. He closed his eyes and, just as he was drifting into sleep, he realized he'd forgotten his house. He'd stopped searching, straining, fighting through each night. He'd look for it, he promised wildly and he sank into a determined sleep.

'Gertrude,' he ventured the next morning. 'Do you know of a house that I could rent?'

'Rent?' Gertrude turned to him. Her eyes were wide, her mouth affronted. 'Why would you want to do that?'

'Well . . .' Max was unsure. 'I'd like to stay in Steerborough and I thought . . . if I was in your way.'

'But you still haven't done my painting!' Gertrude's neck seemed extravagantly long, her head as fierce as a bird's. 'Finish my painting, that was the agreement, and then' – she smiled to show she was capable of a joke – 'you will be free to leave.'

'I'm so sorry. Of course.' Max had forgotten the canvas, leaning against the skirting, gathering dust. 'I shall start on it right now.'

'Don't be ridiculous. When you are ready, when you've finished your scroll.' She stood up and he saw that her hands were trembling. 'I promised Kaethe that I'd ask you to stay. I promised her, and I intend to keep my word.'

'Yes . . . I only thought –'

'No,' Gertrude said firmly and she walked out of the room.

Gertrude was shocked to find that she was shaking. She stood over the kettle, letting the whistle scream, sickened to think she'd twisted Kaethe's wish. But Max had taken her off guard. She'd been following the progress of his scroll and could see from the lengths of unfinished whiteness, and the tally of houses in her mind, that he had weeks to go. 'I'm sorry,' she whispered into the steam, and she remembered, when Max first came to London, had sat all day in the tiny partitioned flat she and Kaethe shared, how much she'd disliked him then. Kaethe had fussed around him, used up her time and love settling him in, and it was only when Max had been interned, and Kaethe came to work with her at the war nursery, that her friend had time for her again. Maybe, she wondered, it was a mistake to have taken a sabbatical this year, to have left behind the distracting troubles of her charges, but after Kaethe's death it seemed wrong to go on as if everything was the same. Gertrude tipped water into the pot, carelessly, letting one long splash scald red across her foot, telling herself all the while in a smooth practised voice that it was natural to want to cherish people, whether they were there to be cherished or not. It was natural but not necessarily in their best interests, and she took the pot and moved through to the next room.

'Mrs Wynwell?' she called, walking to the bottom of the stairs. 'Mrs Wynwell, are you there?'

There was the thwack of a mattress and Mrs Wynwell's voice came travelling down. 'I'm just doing the beds,' she said, and a moment later, red-faced, she appeared.

'Will you tell Alf he needn't come today?' Gertrude smiled to show it was all right, she wasn't angry, but all the same Mrs Wynwell looked at her, alarmed.

'It's quite all right,' she urged her. 'Just tell him he needn't come.'

Mrs Wynwell's face closed in. 'As you think best,' she said and, stamping harder than was necessary, she climbed back up the stairs.

Gertrude sat down in her chair. Now what would she do? She felt utterly bereft, and she wished the blackberries were ready so that she could force herself against the brambles, prick her fingers as she picked, enough to fill a basket, all smeared with juice and blood until she'd had enough. A book of recipes lay on the table. *Wines, Syrups and Cordials.* Gertrude flicked through them angrily. Gooseberry wine, hawthorn-berry wine, spinach, parsnip, pea-pod wine. Pussyfoot . . . Nettle beer . . . Dandelion – thought to be a tonic. *Collect a gallon of dandelion heads . . .* This very order made her smile, and she pulled down a large basket and stepped out into the lane.

Gertrude picked dandelions all morning. She scoured the village for them, plucking them up in clusters, the older ones snapping easily, the younger ones all oiled with milk, slipping through her hands. She roamed along Mill Lane, up and down The Street, pushing along the bridle way and up on to the Common. It was a perfect Steerborough blue and yellow day, impossible to be sad in. You could try, clamp down your jaw, shut up your mind, but then a breeze of birdsong would come whistling through, the lift of a horse's hooves. There was a sweet salt smell in the air and Gertrude had to admit it was hard work being cross.

She arrived home at lunchtime and poured the flowers into her largest pot, the great soft fluff of yellow like a tub of chicks. 'A gallon,' she murmured, and she went out again.

This time she walked towards the Green, scouring the allotments behind the tennis courts, stepping out on to the marshland almost to the dunes, where she found dandelions by the dozen, small starry versions, clinging to the riverbanks, winding through the mounds of grasses in the lane below Hoist Wood. This time she was sure she had enough. She emptied her flowers into the pot and when she turned to find her apron, she caught sight of Alf.

'Hello.' She was ridiculously pleased to see him, sitting in his usual place. 'I'm so sorry. I'm late.'

Very slowly Alf pulled something from the pocket of his shorts. Gertrude held out her hand, and Alf stepped over and laid a flower on her palm.

'Thankyou.' The dandelion was wilting, its petals closed in, its stalk shredded and wet. 'Thankyou so much.' And not wanting him to see how much it meant to her, she very carefully put it with the others in the pot.

They sat together for ten minutes, Alf examining his feet, Gertrude thinking, for once, about nothing at all, and then she roused herself. 'Shall we make the wine?' Alf stood up and Gertrude found the page of the recipe. *Boil one gallon of water* . . . She put two kettles on, and filled a saucepan, hoping the three would add up to enough, and while they waited they worked together to pare down the stalks. *Pour the boiling water over the flower heads*, the next instruction read, and very carefully she slooshed in the first kettle. A ripe green smell rose up, of heat and summer, and the bitter sap of stalks. The next pan sent the mixture to a soup. Gertrude poured more carefully now, sinking the flowers with a wooden spoon. She found a spatula for Alf and together they began to churn and mash. They were like two alchemists, making gold, plunging and stirring the tiny fins of fire. Gertrude leant sideways to study the page. *Leave for three days* . . . Three days! They had only just begun, and as if some kindly member of the WI were trying to console her, . . . *with an occasional stir.*

'In three days' time,' she said to Alf – it occurred to her she was only pretending to be an adult – 'will you come back and help me? We will have to strain it through muslin, add sugar, the rind of a lemon, and . . .' – she checked the recipe – 'bruised ginger'. How had she failed to read these instructions before? Her eyes skimmed down the page and she saw she would need corks, wax, bottles and the coolness of a cellar she did not have. 'Well,' she said aloud, 'what's the hurry? Saturday afternoon, we'll do it then.' Alf looked up at her and smiled and she saw that his first big teeth were cutting through. They were large and square, and Gertrude felt a pang to think that by the time the dandelion wine was ready his face would be quite changed.

Elsa and Max stood on the bridge like two poachers eyeing up their prey. There were new people renting the Sea House now. A group of watercolourists, two men and two women, who sat together every day painting the same view. Max wondered if they judged each other, comparing techniques, offering up criticisms of each other's work, or if one was the teacher and the others, pupils, following a lead. Elsa inched forward. Come on, she said with her eyes, but Max hung back. The four were facing Eastonknoll, the outcrop of the town. He didn't need, he told himself, to see four replicas of the lighthouse. Soon Elsa was leaning over, examining each picture, asking questions, listening to unimaginable replies. Max thought about his scroll. There was a green screen door on Palmers Lane that he wanted to paint. If you went close and pressed your face against it, the mesh cleared and you could see a perfectly tended vegetable patch, cabbages and brussels sprouts in neat, raked rows. He'd been sitting before it this morning, mixing up his colours for the day, wondering how he could create the solid mesh of it and still give an inkling of what was on the other side, and then Elsa had appeared. 'Please,' she'd said. 'I'm lonely.'

'Of course.' Max got to his feet. 'Of course.' And he began packing his things away.

26

Friday came and Nick did not appear. Lily felt angry, then relieved, so preoccupied with whether or not to call him that she didn't notice until it was almost five o'clock that the postman had left something for her by the door. It was a large padded envelope that must have come while she was out, shielded from view by a straggly arm of ragwort that had grown up by the drain. The envelope was worn and brown, and on the back Nick had scrawled a message: *This came for you, I thought it looked important.* Lily turned it over, noticing with surprise that it had originally been sent to her from Suffolk. There's no one here I know, and her throat tightened, and she thought of Grae. *Sorry, sorry,* Nick's writing snaked round the paper rim. *I won't make it this weekend. Usual reasons. Maybe next? RING ME. Love, N.*

Lily stood in her kitchen and slipped her finger inside the paper seal. The package felt soft and hollow, but when she tipped it up small bundles of cream envelopes fell out on to the fridge. Small and worn with the addresses typed. Mrs Elsa Lehmann. There were twelve of them, and a note for Lily on a sheet of lined paper, the ring binder leaving torn circles along one side.

Dear Miss Brannan,

I found these letters tucked away and thought you might like to see them. Hope they are of use.

Yours, A. Lehmann

Lily released the letters, easing out their ruffled sides. The first was postmarked 1953, September, and the rest spanned the autumn of that year. 'Mrs Elsa Lehmann. The Sea House, Steerborough.' Lily traced the words of the address, said them to herself out loud. Steerborough. It gave her such a twist of pleasure to see it written down, although of course she'd known the Lehmanns had lived here. It was why she'd come. Tentatively she pulled the first letter out. It was headed 'Architect', in English now, and there was a London address in NW3. But first she had to find the house, she could not wait a moment more, and putting the package on a shelf, preserving it for later, she pulled on her shoes and ran out of the door.

The Sea House. She'd seen it. Saw the sign now in her mind. She ran into the middle of the Green and twisted round. Where was it? Signs and gates and porches flashed before her, and then, there it was, the white hut that stood on stilts. The last house in the village. Lily ran towards it. Past the Ship, down the hill that led towards the harbour, and then up again, over the sea wall. Below her was the car park. A flat land of puddle dips and stones, separated from the marshes by a river, slick with the dark mud of low tide. There was an ice-cream van, and a scattering of children fishing for crabs, and for a moment she thought she saw Em and Arrie hanging off the end of the bridge.

The river wound round and doubled back to join the estuary, and standing white and solid in its bend was the house. It looked ugly from here, its weathered bulk, its thick legs moulded green. There was a boat tied up under its belly, and a bicycle lay rusting on its side. Lily picked her way along beside the river. Wooden steps rose up to a porch, and there in the window was a sign: *To Let*. The porch was glass and so was the front door and she could see through into a kitchen with a long table and a dresser full of plates. Beyond her, straight ahead, was a steep ladder that led to a trap door. Lily pressed her face against the glass, peering in, up, craning to the side, and then the door swung open, and she tripped and stumbled in. She jumped up and swung around, but there was no one there. 'Hello?' she called, as if she'd been intending to visit, and with her heart beating she walked across the room. 'Hello?' She stood below the trap door, and, biting her lip, she began to climb.

The room above her was spectacular, a round table, pictures of flowers on every boarded wall. Lily stood, her legs still on the ladder, and twisting round, she found that she was in a boat. Wooden to the ceiling, water stretching away on every side. There was a bed, a wardrobe, and it occurred to her that she'd been living in a small brown world, when she might have been here, sailing the high sea. She caught hold of herself then, remembered she was trespassing, and quickly she climbed down. She skidded across the room, slid through the front door, and only stopped for breath when she was outside. Very slowly she walked across the car park. She stopped at the bridge and stared at the children, too neat and tidy to be the ones she knew. 'Em?' she called, 'Arrie?' But rather than look up at her they swung their long lines out into the river, trailing their bait of bacon, hauling up the same grey crabs.

My dear Elsa, Lily read, the sun striking in as it sank to the level of her window. *I thought you'd be back with me in London by now or I'd never have made such arrangements for building work with Kett. But if we don't have the work done now, then we'll only have to do it next summer, and next summer I have reserved for us. So, my sweet one, how do you like living in a hut? I wish I could be there with you, but as always, I must get these plans approved, must start on the project for Bermanns, and the chairs I promised to design for Jones. Keep well, write to me about ALL moments of your day. I want to know that you are getting everything that can be had from this one precious life.*

Next summer, Lily thought, next summer Lehmann had reserved for them, and in a sudden rush of energy she leapt up and ran across the Green. She tugged open the phone box door and slammed her change into the slot. 'Nick,' she said, almost before he answered, 'I do miss you, you know.'

There was a small pause on the other end. 'Good.' He sounded pleased.

'Come and spend a few days here.' It occurred to her she'd spent months trying to reel him in. It was so much easier just to ask him to come. 'Reserve it. Book it in if you have to. Think of it as work.'

'It's booked,' he said. 'Thankyou, I'll try and be there next Friday . . . for six.'

'Try.' Lily spoke soft into the low cup of the phone. 'It's the most beautiful evening . . . If you were here, we could walk along the beach . . .'

'Lily,' he said, 'I'm actually in a meeting.'

'Oh. So I'll see you next weekend?'

'Ring me before then.'

Why? Lily thought. So you can tell me what's just happened that makes it impossible to come? 'Bye, then.' Her unused coins rattled down into the slot. She scooped them up. *Call 999. Wait by the wall* . . . The note was still there, and in one corner the tiny mark she'd made. She felt for a pen and added another, a little L right in the middle of the page. She eased open the phone box door and as she did so she had the uneasy sensation that she was being watched. Was the note checked? Did someone come nightly to see that it was there? And then she stopped. The paper. It was the same. Lined and ripped from a ring binder of the exact same size as the note she'd received from A. L. Lehmann that day. Lily looked towards the marsh. Her hair, she could feel it, was crawling on her head. There must be a thousand pads of paper the same size, every newsagent stocked one, and to prove she was not afraid, she pushed her way out of the phone box and walked down towards the sea.

Its beauty caught her every time. The unexpected flatness of it as you came over that last hill. It stretched your eyes, relaxed the muscles of your heart, forced you every time to stop. The beach was almost deserted. It had been cooler that day, the first after a long, hot week of sun and, as if glutted with pleasure, the holiday-makers had seemed relieved to stay away.

Lily sat on the sand. The tide was coming in, shortening the shore, lapping high and calm at a thread of shingle on the sand. She collected pebbles in a salty pile and thought how never in her life had she spent so much time alone. As a child she'd been almost constantly with her mother, huge swathes of time set aside for them to share. Her mother, possibly to make up for the absence of any other family, seemed intent on filling her whole world.

'I,' she had once said, when Lily asked about her father, 'do promise to love, cherish and support you,' and she'd handed her a spaghetti ring on the tip of her fork. When Lily thought of this she imagined herself in a high chair, shrouded by the rhubarb that pressed against the panes, but she knew she must have been older, sitting on one of those yellow-bottomed chairs that clustered round the table. Her mother *had* cherished her, *had* devoted every minute of her time to her, so that they had grown towards one another, sometimes spending an entire weekend drawing and shading and reading library books to each other in the damp nest of their front room. In the long summer holidays they had roamed through Portobello Market, scooping scraps of material off stalls, digging their hands into a mound of jackets to draw out a lining of pink silk. They made outfits for Lily's dolls, sheets and blankets, knitted scarves, and then, when she was older, they bought suits, dresses, outsized jeans, and rushed home to rip and alter them, using each other's bodies as models, spending whole evenings stitching and unpicking, searching for the scissors, while jokes and rippled laughter fell from the TV. Lily had thought she might apply to fashion college, create a line made exclusively from other people's cast-off clothes, but she ended up at art school, on the other side of London, and when she was offered a room in a flat on the estate behind the college she decided to move in with three friends.

'It'll be all right.' Her mother's face was swollen up with crying. 'Of course it's the right thing.' And she began, quite unnecessarily, to divide up the knives and forks. Lily couldn't imagine how her mother would survive, and at first she'd call her several times a day, promising to visit each weekend, sending her short notes, but soon, it became clear, this attention was unnecessary. Rather than destroy her, Lily's absence had rejuvenated her mother. She sold the basement and bought the top-floor flat, painted it yellow, and within weeks, although it may well have been a year, she'd met and married Clive. Now they rarely spoke. Lily's mother had vowed to love and cherish her, not until death, it seemed, but until she was eighteen. It embarrassed Lily, made her sad, as if it were she, through all those years, who had held her mother down. Now her mother had gone travelling, set off to India with Clive.

'I had other considerations when I was young,' Lily heard her state matter-of-factly at a party they'd held to say goodbye, and the last news she'd had of her was a postcard, signed from both of them, with a picture of the holy sea temple at Chivanundra, faded on the front.

Lily stood up and stretched. It was getting dark, the light gone from the sea, and the faint smell of cooking was drifting towards her on the breeze. Purposefully she'd not bought any supplies, hoping that by being unprepared, it would hoax Nick into coming, and now as she walked into the wind, she thought of her bare cupboard, the half-empty egg box in the fridge, the wilting carrots. She could make an omelette with some sort of salad, and then as she rounded the dunes she saw the drift of smoke from a fire.

It was coming from the row of beach huts, unused mostly as sand blew down and blocked shut their front doors. Some had sunk so far below the level of the beach that men spent half their summers digging just so they could get in to make a cup of tea. There it was again, the smell of sausage, rich with meat and herbs, and like an animal, sniffing, she followed the scent of it. She walked fast, stopping only to shake out her shoes, and then ahead of her was a small figure, running with a bundle of wood. Lily followed, silent in the sand, and rounded a ridge of scrub to see a wide flat clearing and a fire. The girl dropped her wood, turned, and Lily saw that it was Arrie. She ducked out of sight, and then the door of a beach hut opened and Grae stood in an oblong of light. The inside of the door was blue, and behind him she could see the corner of a bed.

'Em,' he shouted, 'Arrie,' and, not knowing what else to do, Lily walked towards the fire.

Grae stepped forward, squinting into the dark, and then as if from nowhere the girls were on her, their arms around her, their heads butting her waist. 'You came back,' they said. 'You came back.'

Lily laughed. 'I was hardly gone.'

'Will you have supper with us?' Em hung from her arm. 'We're toasting marshmallows.'

'Oh.' she looked towards Grae, bent over the fire. 'If there's enough.'

Grae walked back towards the hut. She could see him, bending down, opening boxes, taking out a cup. There was something languid in the way he moved, and she remembered his shoulders, shaking silently before he laughed. Untangling herself from the girls she followed him. The hut was tiny, twelve foot square, two sets of bunk beds built in against the walls. There was a table, a one-ring cooker, a kettle, bookshelves, even a jug of flowers.

Lily stood in the door. 'Is this where you're living?' She swallowed, not wanting to show that she was shocked.

Grae straightened up, a string of sausages dangling from one hand. 'No. We're not living here. Law of the parish council. It's not allowed.'

'But people must know?' The black and white cat jumped down from a bunk, stroking itself as it swept against her leg.

'As long as no one complains.' Grae shrugged. 'We'll see how long we last.' He looked at her, and she saw the thin line of the scar where his cut had healed. 'It'll be fun in the winter.'

'You're not serious?' She'd spoken before she'd had time to think.

'Yes,' he said and he handed her a cup.

They walked back to the fire and Grae gave Lily, Em and Arrie a sausage each on a pointed stick. 'Hold it out over the heat,' he said, 'and keep turning.' They waited while their supper blackened and burned. They ate the rest of the sausages wrapped in folds of bread, with apples, and marshmallows melted into ghostly shapes.

'It's wonderful out here,' Lily said, as Grae poked at the fire, and, copying the girls, she took up a blunt knife and began whittling sticks, stripping the thin bark, shredding the heads to form a pointed spike. Do you like living in a beach hut? she wanted to ask. Is it an adventure? But what if the girls said no, they didn't. They missed their bedroom, their garden and their mum. So they sat in silence, watching the crystal-dripping stars until eventually Em and Arrie wrapped themselves in blankets and curled up in the sand.

'I'll carry them in.' Grae stood up and he bundled Em up in his arms. Lily followed with Arrie, her cheek so silken-smooth against her own. They slid the girls into their bunks and stood for a moment, squeezed into the narrow room, their arms, childless, unsure what to do. Lily walked back and stood looking up the dune, listening to the sea, high on the other side.

'It's calm tonight,' she said, and then Grae reached out and touched her. A spark shot through her, hurting, exquisite as his hand rested for a moment and was gone. 'I thought you'd left the village,' she said.

'And you' – Grae hung his head – 'you did leave.'

'Only for a few days.' She laughed and her laugh came out as a quiver.

'But . . .' they both began at the same time, and not knowing what she was about to do she stretched out her hand. Grae reached forward and took it. The touch of him fizzed along her arm, and he was drawing her towards him, folding her up, cradling her head in his hands, his fingers sweeping her cheek, her neck, her ears.

'Why didn't you find me?' he asked, but before she could answer his mouth was on hers, his breath as sweet as air, his stubble warm and rough, prickling her chin. He was pushing her down into the tall soft grass, his hands sending sparks over her body as they slipped under her clothes. He was easing her, kneading, whispering in her ear, and she thought nothing ever in the world felt so good as this. Who invented it? she thought. Who invented sex? The sheer, pure smell of him, heat and salt and wood smoke all mingled with desire. And then he stopped. He straightened his arms and leant above her. 'Are you all right?'

'Yes,' she laughed. 'Yes.'

He let his elbows bend and lay beside her. She slowed her breathing, imagining the stars spinning and falling as they began to land.

'Go easy,' he said, as if to himself.

They lay side by side, staring into each other's faces, as if, before then, to look at each other had been banned, and then for hours and hours they kissed and sighed and murmured until their lips were frayed.

'I suppose I'd better go,' Lily said, when light began to seep into the sky.

'Crawl in with me.' He held her tight, but she imagined Em and Arrie, peering at her, furious, in a few hours' time. 'Sleep in the top bunk, then.' He'd guessed her mind, and so they stamped out the fire, still smouldering, and trailed inside. Grae fastened the door and, stopping in the galley between beds for one last kiss, Lily climbed on to the narrow bunk and fell into an ashen sleep.

When Lily woke she couldn't think where she was. Sun was streaming through an open door, and the wall beside her bed was wood. She turned and almost fell on to the floor and then she remembered, she was in a hut. She lay back down. There was the sound of a radio and the clatter of someone washing plates. She recognized Grae's whistle from listening to him work and the cat jumped up and looked at her with yellow eyes. She reached for it, but it rounded its back, haughtily, and leapt on to the ground. Lily lay and looked up at the ceiling. How could they have spent so many hours together and leave so much unsaid?

27

You can only understand things by constantly drawing them, Henry had written at the very start of their correspondence, and Max wondered if, after more than half a village, he should put some people in. *If you feel certain of destruction, go to destruction cheerfully and often,* Henry advised. *Give up any conventional ideas as to what a head is like. If it looks like a potato with two eyes in it, make it so. You might try and treat the chair and figure as one object. I think of your reverence for the human figure as a kind of stage fright. This is the figure. Look at it as if it were a lump of clay. But, and I'm talking now about your sketch of 'Helga', why draw her so faintly, and why leave off her hair?* But Max had had no choice. Her hair had looked like marble, had sat on Helga's forehead like a hat. He'd scrubbed at it until it was a shadow, and then, later, when he'd appealed to her to let him try again, she'd made him too uneasy to go on. 'Your father . . .' she wanted to know. 'Is it really true he was an officer?'

'Yes. He fought at Loos, and then after that, when he recovered . . . He risked his life to be a scout.'

'But he was made an officer?' Her hair was plaited. It hung down one side of his picture like a rope. Max knew what she was asking him, and, disloyal, to whom he wasn't sure, he explained about his father's conversion, his military service, Applesnout the horse. 'He was awarded a medal for bravery.'

'That I knew.' She looked at him as if he were an idiot. 'We all know that. Everyone on the island. It was the other part I wasn't sure of . . .' And absentmindedly she twisted her plait on to the top of her head. 'The mother,' she said more slowly, 'if your mother is . . .' – she shivered at the word – 'then you must be too.'

Max felt himself grow heavy. He put his pencil down and sat

beside her, reaching for her hand. 'My parents are liberal, tolerant, they won't mind. Our children . . .'

Helga withdrew her hand. 'Yes,' she said. 'Yes.'

After some moments Max stood up and continued to draw, but it was hopeless, her hair was like a curtain cord, and eventually he accepted there was no point going on.

What kind of day was it? How was the sky? Henry demanded. *Show me, was the grass fresh and green? Or all burnt up and yellow?*

A week later Helga cycled past his window. Just behind her was the son of a fisherman, Gottschalk, a fisherman himself now, with a share in a new boat. He was gaining on her, steering with nothing but his knees, and Max could see from the way Helga's head was thrown out sideways, that she was urging him to hurry on. Max leapt up and threw open the front door, dodging past the pear tree, and out into the lane. But Helga and her fisherman were skidding round the corner, the spokes of their wheels like sun dials, their tyres a flash of black. He pounded after them, up to the corner, round the side of the bakery, but they had gone.

Max gulped down the last of his egg sandwich, packed for him by Gertrude and slipped into his bag. He was almost at the end of Palmers Lane now, outside Teal House, its huge windows like a chapel, looking out over a field. He had almost reached the end of his second scroll. Slowly, he thought, sizing up the chimney stack, if he didn't go more slowly he'd have to go home. The walls of Teal House were a deep red, its roof rounded like a bowler hat. It reminded him of the boss of his old firm where, ever since the end of the war, he'd worked on the accounts. He'd been given a week's leave after Kaethe died, and although he'd intended it he'd never written to say why he had not gone back. He could manage, if he was careful, on what he and Kaethe had saved, and then maybe he'd do what Kaethe ordered him not to, find his way back to Heiderose and see what was left.

*   *   *

On the first of September it started to rain. It started early, just as Max was dressing. He stood at his window and thought of the Sea House key. It was kept for safety by a Mrs Cobbe at number 17 Church Lane. She would go over the property in the morning and give it a good clean, and then at midday Elsa could officially begin her lease. Of course Mrs Cobbe could leave the key for her at the house, but she insisted Elsa walk up and collect it, she was adamant that things should be done right.

'Well,' Gertrude told Max, 'Elsa Lehmann has packed up the most tremendous amount of things. Books and plates, and two huge suitcases of clothes. I shall have to take the car out and help her move. She says she'll manage, will take one thing at a time, and I suppose when Kett comes in to start the work he could always put the boxes on a cart.'

Max looked at her blankly.

'Kett. The local builder. He's working on the Lehmann house. Redoing the slope of the staircase, some idea of Klaus's, to give a more luxurious feel to the steps.' Gertrude laughed and shook her head. 'Why else did you think they should have to move into a hut?'

'I hadn't thought.' He frowned, and he turned away.

By mid-morning the rain had not let up and Max, unable to bear the suspense of waiting, pulled his hat down over his ears and went out. He didn't take his scroll for fear it would be ruined, so instead he wandered up and down the village, collecting information, choosing summer colours for the last house in Palmers Lane. It was his village now, he thought, and it was true, the few people that he passed nodded to him and waved as they hurried to keep dry. Max closed his eyes. He wanted to test himself, prove he knew each inch of lane and hedgerow, each bend and over-hanging tree. Slowly he moved forward, relying on his remaining senses, the feel of the lane beneath his feet, the smell of each front garden, until the smoothing of the ground told him he had reached his view.

He turned into it and opened his eyes. The grass was shorn, the wheat field stubble, the sedge razed to the ground. Brambles clung to the wire of the tennis court, scattered with blackberries, and everywhere there was the smell of wood smoke, curling through the rain.

Max began to edge along the track. The sea was right ahead of him, a sheet of silver, beaten into flatness by a sudden streak of sun. Max skirted the edge of a field until he reached the wood where the track doubled back, taking him inland, ploughing through hillocks and over green mounds until he came out on the salt marsh directly above the mill. There were three men working there, repairing the roof. Max ducked along a narrower path and found himself by the opening of a lookout shelter, its granite greyness uneasy in the ancient ground. Max wound himself into it like a snail re-entering its shell and, as he stood by one of the narrow windows, he wondered which of the village men had taken their turns here, on guard for the enemy, night and day. Not a single house in Steerborough had been bombed, and maybe it was thanks to this small bunker that the Germans had been too fearful to come. Max leant against one wall. Today he had no energy for anything but Elsa and he checked his watch again to see if it must surely be one. Eventually he rose back above ground, and, keeping his eyes turned away from the workmen, he walked along the swollen gulleys and on to the thick slick of a path that ran parallel to the sea.

Three swans were sitting on the water, huge and white, the third still flecked with brown. As he approached, they began to beat their wings, and, with the maximum amount of effort, they lifted off above the water and flew. Max picked a cane of sedge and used it to beat his way along the river, through mud and reeds, emerging on the bridge, a cattle gate barred over its middle, the only manmade object between the Sea House and the sea.

The glass of the front door shivered as he knocked. It was past one, but there was no one in. He tried the handle, but the door was locked. Max retreated to the dunes. The sun was gaining strength, the rain had stopped, and he lay back against coarse grass, watching the mud on his shoes crust over into hardness, the hems of his trousers drying in dark rings.

'My Good Lord.' Gertrude was afraid she'd come across a body, the legs of which were half buried by sand.

Max uncrumpled himself. 'Good day.' He glanced at the sun, shocked to see it far out over the village, hanging above the spire of the church. He scrambled up and stood beside her, tiny stars of fennel holding resolutely to his clothes.

'Well, she's in,' Gertrude sighed. 'All settled with her things.'

Max turned towards the Sea House, but Gertrude looped her arm through his. 'It's been days,' she said, 'since I've seen the beach.' Was it a shadow or Elsa herself who was standing at her window, straining towards him as she waved? 'Let's walk.' And unable to resist, Gertrude began brushing the husks of flowers from his sleeves.

Max let himself be led. Along the beach, around the small curved bays. 'There's one old man, lives up on the Green,' Gertrude told him. 'Fifteen years since he's been to the sea. "Don't have the time," he said.' Max nodded although it was almost impossible to watch her mouth and walk. 'It's only us Londoners who think we have to worship nature night and day,' she went on. 'Who daren't pass a lilac or a crab apple tree without stopping to admire its scent. We've been starved, that's the truth of it, and when people retire here from the city, they spend the rest of their lives trying to catch up. My aunt, you know who left me the house, she went out walking every day until she was ninety-one.'

Max almost lost his footing as they climbed the narrow path, past the jetty where the ferry was moored. Gertrude tugged at him, heaving him up, and their hips bumped against each other hard. 'I'm sorry,' she said as she unclasped his arm.

Surreptitiously Max glanced behind him. The Sea House had disappeared from view. There was nothing to his left but a great waterlogged meadow, and no way forward but to carry on. Max saw the hours drift on without him. The thinning light, the midges thickening to a swarm, and he imagined Elsa accepting he was never going to come.

Eventually they reached the bridge and turned inland beside the railway. The path ran over a rise of hills until it joined the village. Gertrude stopped occasionally to tug at a blackberry, smiling at him with blackened teeth. They did not talk, and slowly, as they walked into the sunset, Max began to breathe more easily. He was resigned to Gertrude now, and the fact that when eventually they arrived back in the village it would be too late to pay his call. But Gertrude did not stop at the turning to Marsh End. 'My car,' she said, 'I left it at the harbour,' and so they walked down towards the sea.

It felt strange to slip on to the leather of the seat, to rest back against a cushion, and feel the rain and salt and sunshine of the day dissolve as they drove up the lane. Together they made supper, mashing potatoes, grilling chops, picking parsley and small sweet tomatoes from a vine by the back door. Max laid the table and Gertrude carried the plates through and at the same moment they looked up and nodded to each other, content. After supper they played cards, one game and then another, and Gertrude, flushed from her string of wins, insisted on reading to him from an anthology of Suffolk verse. She read him a poem, not a single word of which he understood.

> 'Ye four bright wires, so slender and so smooth,
> How many wakeful nights y've helped to soothe!'

It was, she explained, a poem about knitting.

'Nor have you fail'd, through many a darksome day,
To keep the potent fiend, Ennui at bay:
Affording occupation mute and kind,
Taxing no powers of body or of mind,
Leaving them free their higher due to pay
Fresh air to breathe – to meditate or pray.'

It was after ten by now and Max looked out at the black night. 'I shall go up and read,' he said, standing, stretching, and Gertrude stood up too. 'Yes you're right,' and in single file they climbed the stairs to bed.

Max sat up in a cloud of light. He'd forgotten to draw the curtains and the first rays of sun were dappling the glass. 'Will you visit me?' Elsa's words were in his ears, and he could hardly believe that he'd squandered his first chance.

Quickly he pulled on his clothes, the clock showed half past five, and, as delicately as he could, he crept downstairs. Exhilaration hit him with the first sweet air. The morning was blue, just rising out of black, and the sky was flecked with the dark formation of migrating birds. He ran along the lane, up to the corner where the Lehmann house stood empty, and on across the Green. It was still night on the Green, but the river was alive. Small boats worked back and forth, unloading nets of fish, with gulls, hysterical, wheeling above.

Max took cover in the shadow of the huts, flitting from stilt to stilt, his eyes fixed on the Sea House window where there was a light. The light, he was sure of it, was on for him. He hurried towards it, dragging the air into his body, only stopping to catch his breath when he was on the wooden steps. He climbed up to the porch and knocked, and waited, and then he turned the handle and stepped in. The downstairs room was empty. 'Elsa?' There was a square of lamplight at the top of the stairs, and just possibly she was calling down. One hand, one foot, following the other, he was in his dream. Climbing, each rung of the ladder warm under his hand, until, blinking, he came up.

There was the wardrobe, the round table and the chairs, the bed, the quilt thrown back. But Elsa wasn't there. A book lay on the bed. He walked over to it and sat down. It was new, unread, its cover smooth.

Anne Frank
The Diary of a Young Girl
An Extraordinary Document of Adolescence.

Max looked into the girl's face. Dark hair parted far over to one side, round eyes in pools of white, and her mouth, the top lip wide and hopeful and somehow reminding him of a duck. Max opened the book. On the inside flap there was a photograph of a house, four storeys, with hardly room for a brick between the glass, and beside it another picture of a landing and a shelf of files.

And then Elsa rose up out of the trap door. He saw her scream, cover her mouth, all in the second before she realized it was him.

'I'm so sorry.' He sprang up. 'I couldn't come before and I wanted to wish you . . .'

She was wearing a nightdress, ruched around her shoulders, and her hair was unpinned. She came towards him. 'What time is it?'

'I'm sorry . . .' he started again.

'It's all right.' She put out her hand to him. 'I couldn't sleep.'

Max was too close to her now, and, not knowing how else to get away, he sat down. Elsa sat beside him. The bed sighed and rocked, threatening to throw them together, and with every muscle in his body Max held himself apart. Elsa reached for the book and they both looked down into the girl's bright face.

'Maybe it is better to have had no children.' She shivered in the thin cloth of her nightdress and Max said, 'I should go.'

'Yes. Thankyou.' Her hand was on his arm. 'Be happy,' she

whispered, and then, as if she'd had some sudden thought, she leant forward and kissed him. Max stood quite still, the flutter of her lips on his cheek, and then he was drawing her towards him. He kissed the top of her hair, her eyebrows, so straight and serious, and the wide lids of her eyes. She didn't struggle, so he kissed her nose, her chin, her neck. He knelt before her and pressed his head against her stomach, felt the warmth of her through the folds of cloth. And then she was kissing him too. She kissed his forehead, the stubble of his chin, his neck, his shoulders, his arm, his ears. He took her then and pressed her down, and frantically he began to pull off his clothes. He kicked away his boots, ripping at the laces, terrified, pleading with God, with anyone, to allow him to go on. He felt tears welling in his eyes, unable to look at her, afraid she was drawing away from him in the muddle of tearing off his clothes. But when he turned back, she was kneeling before him, naked, her body narrow as a girl's, her breasts so full, the undersides a perfect curve. 'You see,' she said, glancing down, 'I never did have children,' and Max reached for her and with one sock still trailing, his shirt half-buttoned, he steered her to the bed. They fell on to it just as he had dreamed they might, and he opened his mouth and laughed with happiness as the great quilt folded them in.

28

The Sea House, Steerborough, Suffolk. Lily spread the letters out over the table, stroking them, her fingers sensuous, her skin still papery from lack of sleep. She felt light-headed, the thought of Grae, his hands on her, the sweet tip of his tongue against her teeth.

My sweet wife Elsa, Lehmann wrote in 1953. *Last night I dreamt I was parachuting into Germany just as we did in the last months of the war. We were crowding round the door, ready for the drop, when the green light appeared inside the plane. I fell into the darkness, my parachute opening above me, my rucksack hanging below me on its line, and in my dream, just as it happened then, I floated, drifting, weightless, not knowing where I was going to land. There I was, dangling above Germany, a place I'd taken so much trouble to leave. And then a most peculiar sensation took hold of me. My mind separated itself from my body. It seemed to float above me as if it were asking, Who is that madman? What can he be doing? Never have I had that sensation since, until last night when I jolted awake with such a feeling. Is everything all right? I think of you now, as I thought of you then, and, more than anything, I hope you are finally learning to be happy, just as you are, living in your hut above the beach.*

My sweet,

I am so glad that you are managing without me and that the mosquitoes are able to resist your left ankle at least. Here the work is busy, especially when I think back to Before when I thought I would never find anyone to commission me at all. So now I must remember to be grateful. Sammel, Liebnitz, Koenig, are all long gone to America, but I could not start again in a third place. And, I know, nor could you. I hope the mood in your letters is quite genuine. Don't hesitate to come here if you are lonely, but

it is hard to be lonely in Steerborough, I know. This receiving of letters is
a wonderful thing, and now they're arriving so swiftly. Do you remember
when I used to have to reprimand you for leaving too much space between
one letter and the last, or order you to write shorter, more frequent letters
so that after one huge monster letter you did not need to rest. I'm sorry to
have been so harsh with you, my El, but from the first I couldn't bear to
think of you living your life without me, and now after twenty years of
marriage I can tolerate it just for a few days at a time. If I can I will take
the train to you on Saturday. Will you meet the fishing boats and buy me
flounders to poach. I have a sudden craving for them, and for those
salty-brown prawns they sell at the harbour. Just like the mosquitoes I
also am particularly fond of your right ankle. And of course your calves,
your elbows and your wrists. Keep them safe and covered up for me.
　Your L.

As Lily reached for the next letter, she caught sight of Ethel on
the corner of the Green. She was swaying, the belt ends of her
dressing-gown flapping as she fought for balance with one arm.
Lily pushed open the window. 'Are you all right?'

Ethel straightened up, steadied by her voice. She took a few stiff
steps towards her. 'There's nothing to recommend it,' she told her.
'Nothing to recommend getting old.'

'No,' Lily said, although she hoped there might be, something,
anything at all. 'Are you going for a swim?'

'I was.' Ethel frowned. 'I'm all right once I'm in the water, it's
just getting in and out . . . There's no warning, you see, and then I
lose my bloody balance.'

'Wait there . . .' Lily ran upstairs and snatched up her swimming
costume. Sand in sugary sprays flew out from the elasticated seams.
She rolled it into a towel and slammed out of the side door.

Together they walked across the Green. Ethel bobbed along
beside her, her body stiff, her legs straight. She reminded Lily of a
chick with her white fluff of hair, and the soft oval of her dressing-
gown crossed in the middle like an egg. As they neared the beach

Lily glanced round nervously for Grae. The huts were to the right of her, shielded from view by the ridge of the dunes.

'We'll see you later?' Grae had looked at her, his fingers just moments from her hand, and they'd both known he meant this afternoon, or evening, not in half an hour, before either of them had had time to change their clothes.

'So you're coming in?' Ethel asked, letting her gown drop on to the sand.

Lily pulled off her jeans. Her shirt was creased, half buttoned, raw with the smell of wood smoke and fresh air. Her fingers brushed against her skin as she peeled away the last of her clothes, closing her eyes for a split-second as if her touch were his.

'Ready?' Ethel coughed, and Lily, blushing, pulled her costume on. Shyly they reached for each other's hands and walked down to the shore. The water was freezing. The tide was high, and soon, too soon, they were wading, sinking, spreading out their arms. Lily felt the water burn as it crept in under her costume, a cold well at her navel, ice in the tips of her bra. 'I'll be all right now,' Ethel shouted, unclasping her hand, and happily she struck out for the horizon. Lily was knocked under by a wave. She fought and choked and wrestled and when she came up she was warm. She tipped on to her back, her arms and legs stretched out like a starfish, her face in the sun, and then, from nowhere, a streak of pure gold happiness spread through her. The feeling was so powerful it sent a tremor down her spine, tingling in the bones of her toes and fingers, leaving her afraid. She turned, straining for the white seal head of Ethel. She could see her, on the froth of a wave, and she struck out in a ragged crawl, mouth closed, eyes squinted into the sun. Eventually she caught up with her. She was treading water at some invisible boundary, arms spread wide, resting on a wave. It took Lily a moment to realize she was naked. Her orange costume was floating beside her on a string, and just below the water her body, white and happy, was overlapping with relief.

'My salt bath,' Ethel smiled, 'there's nothing like it,' and Lily, feeling over-dressed, slipped off the black straps of her own costume and pulled it off. Water gushed around her, making her want to leap and spin, and it seemed then that the thin case of nylon she'd been wearing was in fact chain mail weighing her down.

'It's this that keeps me young,' Ethel told her, and she lay back on the cushion of a wave.

'So how long have you lived here?' Lily asked.

'How long? We moved . . . Let's see, I'm eighty-four, must be twenty years now. When my husband retired.'

'And . . . Is he . . . ?'

'Oh no. He died, not long after. But to be honest we never got on. I've got a lovely boyfriend. Lives in Stowminster. He'll be coming up this weekend.'

Eventually they swam in, towing their water-logged costumes behind them, idling in the shallows to pull them on. Lily put her arm out as they scrambled up and together they stepped on to dry land.

My El,

I know you will be furious. I can't come, and I am sorry. Lily sat in a rust-red bath eating toast, straining to see the grey type of Lehmann's letter propped between the taps. *Please don't take my absence as a Sign. I had an urgent call to look at workmen's cottages in Sussex, and from there to Hambledon to check on a wall that was in fact being built in the wrong place. Once I am finished I shall get the first possible train. Have you looked in at our house? Has Kett begun? Is everything covered and protected? How is that strange creature Meyer with his scroll? I do think it very kind of you still to talk to him after he missed out our house. Please forgive me. I allow you five minutes to be angry and then I want you to write to me and say it is all in the past.*

Lily lay back in her bath. Thoughts of Nick crowded in on her. 'Bastard,' she muttered as if it were he who had been unfaithful, and cursing she tried to push his face away. But her mind was chattering on with all the ways in which he'd slighted her, denied her, kept her guessing and hoping, refusing to say what surely it must be obvious she most wanted to hear. She caught sight of her face in the strip of mirrored tiles, cut up into pinched and miserable squares, and to purge herself she poured shampoo on to her hair and began to cuff her ears. Later, feeling punished and worn almost to the bone, she climbed the stairs and with her letters got into the twin bed.

My dear El, she read. *I seem to be reliving all the great moments of my life. Last night I dreamt that I was at a huge round table with a group of Army Mandarins. I was there as a member of the British Army, come to demand they hand over their aerodrome to me, and as they talked on and on, unable to make a decision, someone tapped me on the shoulder. 'Lieutenant Lehmann . . .' It was a high-ranking Nazi, asking if I would come outside for a private word. 'Lieutenant Lehmann,' he said, 'I love the Jews. I had a second cousin who was Jewish who I protected during the whole war. Please, can this be taken into account when everything is over?' 'Yes,' I told him, 'all things will be taken into account.' And I went back to my seat. Five minutes later I was tapped on the shoulder again. 'Can I have a word in private?' It was another Nazi and he also took me outside. 'The sister of my best friend's wife was married to a Jew,' he said. 'I did all I could for her.' So it went on. 'Yes,' I said to them, 'all you have done will be taken into account.' They knew, these men, that the War Crimes trials were coming, and it gave me an unearthly pleasure to see the fear on each face. I looked at them in their fancy uniforms, with braids and decorations, trying to smile, doing their best to be civilized, when civilization to them had meant the enslavement and extermination of a man like me. If they had any courage –* the words were swimming now before Lily's tired eyes – *they would have had me shot.*

'Lily. Lily!'

Had someone called her? It felt like minutes since she'd gone to sleep, but it was already late afternoon. *If they had any courage they would have had me shot.* The words lay beside her on the pillow, the letter still in her hand. She listened but there was nothing. Just the low hoot of wood pigeons chortling in the trees. 'Lily?' There was someone calling her from just inside the back door. Her heart leapt and then lay still. Nick? She hardly dared breathe and then the door slammed shut and whoever it was had gone. Very slowly she got out of bed and crept towards the window. Three small children with buckets and spades were piling wood chips on to the end of the slide. She ran into the back and stared down at the garden. But there was no one there. Who was it? She had to know. She pulled jeans and a T-shirt on and ran downstairs. There was no car parked beside hers. *Lily?* She tried to recreate the voice. Grae? Maybe it was Grae, and she ached for him to have taken courage, to have climbed the stairs and found her in her bed. She ran back into the kitchen and caught sight of herself in the mirror. Her hair was flattened on one side, tufted like a koala on the other. The sight stopped her, made her laugh, reminded her that she was starving, and, instead of rushing out on to the Green, she put the kettle on and began preparing food. Those children playing on the slide, one of them, or more than one, might have been called Lily. She sat with her omelette and her salad in the garden, trying to eat slowly, allowing herself only one glance towards the gate each minute, less hopeful with each mouthful that Grae was about to return. How would they greet each other? She wondered, would they have to wait through the whole evening before they could touch? Her stomach hurt, her throat constricted, and all the while the sweet hot sun, the distant humming of the waves, forced her into a daze.

At seven o'clock she took a jacket and a bottle of wine and just as if she were going out officially for the evening she locked the door. Slowly she walked along beside the river, over the wooden bridge and down the path towards the huts. Grae's door was open, the slice of bright blue startling against the worn grey of the wood. There was a small table set up outside with three chairs, and, although there was a mug of half-drunk tea and a plate of crumbs, there was no one there. Lily stood in the doorway of his hut looking in. A shelf of books, mostly children's, a car maintenance manual, and a history of the East Anglian coast. Below each bed there were suitcases of clothes and the orange-crate of toys Lily imagined the girls had pleaded must not be left behind. On the floor, as if it had been delivered, was a copy of the *Village News*. Lily picked it up. There was to be a Millennium exhibition – photographs of Steerborough. It would be open to the public, admission 20p, for three days over the August bank holiday weekend. 'Any help or suggestions willingly accepted. Contact Alf and Cassie Wynwell.' Underneath in bold black letters:

Surprise Exhibit.
Raffle. Teas.

A hand clamped down on Lily's shoulder. She started, dropping the *Village News*, although, even as she did so, she knew it was Grae. She turned and stared into his face. He was so close she could hardly see him.

'Where are they?' she whispered, and, knowing what she meant, he grinned and pulled her down on to the bottom bunk.

'They're out.' His eyes were sparkling. 'They're with their mother. They won't be back tonight.'

'But . . .' Lily was wrestling between curiosity and desire. 'I thought . . .'

But Grae was kissing her, peeling off her clothes, only leaping up for an instant to shut the door. Lily watched him unbutton his shirt, tug the T-shirt off over his head, and there he was, half naked against her, squeezed on to the ridiculously narrow bed. His body was tawny, the same colour as his hair, and he smiled at her as he kicked off his boots.

'Yes,' she said, before he could stop and question what was right or wrong, and she kept her eyes open, beaming at him, delirious.

Afterwards they lay in silence, admiring the overlapping colours of their limbs, marking each other with their fingertips, shining white and luminous against their skin.

It was dark when they re-emerged from the hut. 'We could go for a drink,' Lily suggested, as Grae looked around him for the site of his fire.

'I've no money.'

'I . . .'

'No,' he said firmly and then, 'I'll make a fire.' They sat in silence while he cradled the flame, stooping and blowing to get a spark. He stacked it up with drift wood so that soon they were enveloped by a bright circle of light.

'Look, I don't belong to the village,' he said. 'I'm not welcome in the pub.'

'Surely . . . you . . .'

'In Steerborough' – he sounded angry – 'you're either from one of the old families, or you come in with money, enough to buy a second home. I know to you it all seems idyllic. But not to real people. Not to people who need to work.'

'I need to work.' Lily pictured the loan she was living off, like a small mountain, narrowing to a precipice as she reached the top.

'Well, you know they banned Guinness from the craft shop.'

'Guinness?'

'Our cat . . .' Grae shook his head. 'He followed me in and knocked over a jug.'

Lily rustled her thumb against her fingers, calling for the cat. 'Guinness.' A dark shadow slunk towards her, topped by a flash of white. 'Have you been banned you dangerous thing?' She coaxed the animal on to her lap, feeling the wet tip of its nose, its spray of whiskers as it pressed its head into the palm of her hand. 'So' – she coughed rather than swallowed – 'what happened to your cottage? Did you have to move out?'

'We're in our holiday home.' She could feel Grae bristle. 'Everyone else has one, why shouldn't we?'

Lily leant against his side. It's me, she wanted to say, but of course he didn't really know who she was.

'We couldn't afford the rent,' he said eventually. 'Once Sue went, and I had to get another car. I could have had my job back at the power station, but . . . It's shift work there, and then who would look after the girls?'

'I'm sorry.' Christ, why did she always ask so many questions, when they'd been so happy, lying, murmuring about nothing in the dark? Not trusting herself to stop, she got up and went to fetch the wine.

'So how come you speak German?' Grae asked. For want of a corkscrew she was pushing the cork in with her thumb. 'Translating letters? That's what Emerald said you were doing all day long in your room?'

'Well . . .' So he had been watching her. 'We did German at school, and it was something I was good at. My father was from Germany, originally . . .' She hadn't expected to be telling him this. 'He came over when he was twelve. His parents sent him ahead . . . So I expect it's in my genes.' Grae was quiet beside her. Waiting for her to go on. 'He was a violinist. Walter Lampl.'

Walter Lampl. She used to repeat that name to strangers to see if anyone might have heard him play, but instead they laughed and told her she was lucky she'd got her mother's name.

'He was in an orchestra, and when my mother . . . When they started seeing each other . . . he was already married.' He'd been married since he was eighteen to a girl he'd known at school. He couldn't leave her, that was out of the question. She was his only family, and he was hers.

'So did you . . . spend much time with him?'

Lily tried to make it cheerful. 'No. We never met.'

'Right.' Grae nodded. 'Right.'

'He travelled . . . All over the world.'

'And were you never tempted to track him down?'

She shook her head. 'I don't know why.' They sat watching the fire. 'Although I did go to Germany once. On an exchange for a whole term. I went to a place called Ulm. I think my father came from Hamburg, so it was all quite pointless, and in Ulm, I hadn't realized, they spoke a kind of dialect. Schwäbisch. It was like trying to learn English in . . . I don't know . . . Newcastle.'

The family she'd gone to had had eight children, seven girls and finally a boy, and the father had the most enormous stomach, hard as a football, as if he were trying for one more. They'd collected Lily in a car with three rows of seats, everyone except the mother who was ill, and, while the children talked and argued, she kept thinking of Sabine, her exchange, going home alone with her mother on the tube.

'I was twelve. I was so lonely. Even with all those children. Even after I became fluent in Schwäbisch. I wrote to my mother every day. I wrote to everyone I'd ever met.' Grae stretched out beside the fire. 'I'd have written to you too if I'd met you even once. And then a girl at school, Astrid, invited me to her house to stay the night. We'd been on a school trip, gone into the countryside by train, and when we arrived back at the station her mother was going to pick us up. I remember walking out on to the station steps, seeing my class jumping into their parents' cars, watching the crowd thinning out, expecting any second that Astrid would tap me on the back. And then suddenly everyone had gone. I waited. She was bound to remember and come back. So I waited. And waited. My family weren't expecting me. Not until the following day. But she would have to remember. Or her mother would ask why I hadn't come. I must have waited there for hours. There was a bus station opposite, and occasionally I ran over to it, but not one of the names or numbers looked familiar. My family lived in a suburb, on a red-brick estate, and I knew the name of it, you know how it is, when you can recognize something, but can't actually bring the words to mind? I'd got the bus home from school virtually every

194

day, but always with the other children, and I'd read the direction on the front of the bus, but never said the words aloud. It started to get dark. There were people looking at me, watching me, so I began to walk. I didn't know if I was walking the right way or not, and then I found myself on an autobahn. There was no pavement and cars were rushing by. Suddenly I was sure that Astrid *must* have remembered, so I turned round and tried to find my way back to the station, but now I was completely lost. And then a miracle happened. I saw my bus. Donaurieden. Of course that's what it was. I caught it up and jumped on just as the doors were closing. But I didn't have enough money.

'"Please, could someone help me?" Six pfennigs was all I needed. But no one would help. There were lots of people on the bus and they all just stared at the floor. It was like being in a dream when you want to scream, charge at someone with a knife, but instead you stand quite still. And then I remembered I was half. "A half fare," I said, "bitte," and the bus driver shrugged and stamped out a ticket, and I was on.

'My family were getting ready for bed when I walked in. At first no one noticed. I opened the hall door and sat on a chair and then the father saw me. "What happened?" He knelt in front of me. "Was macht's, mein Liebchen?" He put his arms around me, and I couldn't help it, I started to cry. I cried and cried. I couldn't stop. His stomach was pressing into me and I could feel the damp skin of his cheek, and then I started laughing because he was the nicest man I'd ever met. "Meine kleine Mädi . . ." He brought me a glass of milk, and then he asked if I was Jewish.

'"I don't know." I was laughing, and crying at the same time. "My father was."

'He nodded as if it was what he'd thought, and after that they were so nice to me. My little maid, they called me, all of them, even the woman who came in to cook when the mother became too sick. They kissed me and cuddled me and gave me all kinds of presents, and on the day before I was due to go back home they took me shopping and bought me a whole set of clothes.'

Grae's eyes were closed, but he reached out a hand. Lily lay down beside him.

'Sorry. I haven't talked so much, ever. Well, not for months.'

Grae slipped his arm around her. 'If you say another word, I'll send you back to Germany with six pfennigs in your purse.'

'OK.' She pressed herself close. 'But I just have to say one more thing.'

'Christ.' He rolled his eyes. 'What?'

'I still feel bad about it, but I never wore the clothes.'

They slept outside. Grae dragged out all three duvets and they made a soft swamp of a bed. They could hear the sea behind them, rolling in above their heads, and on the other side of the river the lights of the village flickered in the dark. The stars cascaded down above them, a hundred more breaking through each time they looked, so that eventually Lily had to force herself to turn on to her side, folding her arms around Grae's back in order to sleep.

There was a note pinned to Fern Cottage door. *Where the FUCK were you?* It was Nick's writing, the capitals bulging with rage. *I called for you in the afternoon. You weren't there. I came back in the evening. YOU WEREN'T THERE. I waited all night! It's 9.30 AM and I'm GIVING UP.* Lily looked at her watch. It was ten past ten, and she'd almost persuaded Grae to come back for a bath. She went inside and sat on the sofa. She should call Nick but then what if he stopped and turned round? She'd call him in an hour. He'd be almost home by then. She put her head in her hands to think what a deceitful person she'd become. She sat there, unable to move, the thought surfacing every so often that Grae, who was preparing breakfast, would be wondering how it could take this long to brush her teeth. Eventually she walked across to the phone box. There was someone else inside it, a woman complaining loudly about a leaking roof, and when she looked out apologetically Lily shook her head and mouthed it was all right. 'There's no hurry,' she said, and she shivered as she sifted through her pockets for change.

29

Max pushed down on the smooth metal of the handle, and pressed with all his weight, three times, before he could accept Gertrude's front door was locked. She must have risen in the dawn and checked it, unless she had purposefully shut him out? Anxious, he ran round to the back. The garden was scattered with drops of dew, held like gems in every blade of grass, and in each border the last of the summer flowers were closed against the cold. He tried the French windows and the small side door and then, finding the kitchen latch unfastened, he began to ease himself through. He had almost done it, his toes were reaching for the floor, when the edge of his jacket caught a poaching pan. The three tin sections came apart and fell, scattering and spinning on the tiles. He froze, the minute hand of the kitchen clock moving from seven-twenty-two to -twenty-three, when the pans were finally still.

Max took courage and crept up the stairs. He sat on his bed and took off his trousers, the sand spilling out of the creased tops of each leg. He unbuttoned his shirt and found one button lost, and then the passion in which his button had gone missing flared inside him. He crumpled up, the pain and pleasure of it forcing small whimpers from his throat. Elsa was there, crouching above him. What was it she was asking him? He couldn't tell. 'Shh, now.' He shook his head, and he started to make love to her again. It was as if a lifetime's knowledge had been stored till it was needed, and he began to kiss her and caress her until she was leaping and laughing in his arms.

★   ★   ★

Gertrude felt unsettled. Autumn. It often took her this way. There was a sharpness in the air that had not been there even the day before and it made her feel the need to start at something new. She turned her thoughts from London, where the busiest time of the year was about to begin, putting a harsh stop to the doubts that were liable to track her. Had she or had she not been wise to take herself away? And where was Max? Surely he couldn't still be sleeping, it was almost ten, and, in a sudden expectation of finding him unwell, she marched upstairs and with the briefest of knocks she threw open his door.

Max's clothes were strewn across the floor. His sheet was crumpled, the counterpane rolled into a ball, and there in the midst of a fury of blankets, he lay, exposed, on the bed. Gertrude closed the door. Her face felt tight and grey. She would ask him to leave as soon as he awoke, and then she remembered her reputation as a psychoanalyst of the broadest and most open mind. For years she had traded in fearless banter – masturbation, penis envy, anal, oral sex. But she had not expected to find a man naked in her own home. Max's penis danced before her. The head of it, the dent of its oval eye.

She took down her wicker basket and set off for the shops where, almost blind with the surprise of hair and testicles, she stared at the noticeboard in the shop window rather than go inside. Three kittens needed a good home. A bicycle was for sale, an almost perfect Silver Cross pram. For anyone who might be interested, there was a half-finished lady's jumper that needed three skeins of matching turquoise wool. There was an advertisement for watercolour painting. *Beginners welcome*, it said and, underneath, a sketch of a young woman staring in great concentration at the stump of a tree. The array of penises faded for the first time in half an hour. She peered more closely at the sign. *Limited places available. Contact T. Everson. Fern Cottage, The Green.*

Had she needed shopping? She couldn't remember now. Instead

she set off down the street. At first she couldn't see Fern Cottage, but then she found it, a tiny house on the corner of the lane. She knocked on the side door and waited, wondering if, when it said no experience necessary, it really meant none at all.

'Yes?' It was a young man, dishevelled, with a large hole in the ribbing of one sleeve.

'I've come about the watercolour lessons . . . If . . . there's still room.' Gertrude felt shy standing there in the street. 'I really am a beginner.' She looked round as she said this, hoping he might ask her in.

'Oh yes.' He fumbled in his pocket and brought out an elaborately creased form. He leant it up against the door jamb and then, realizing he didn't have a pen, he disappeared inside. Gertrude waited, glancing away from the vicar on his bicycle as he sped by, hoping she had not been seen.

'Right.' The young man was back. 'Can I ask your name?'

'Miss Jilks,' she told him. 'Will there be room?'

He flicked through his notebook, scattering scraps of paper and small sketches in smudged forms of black and grey. 'I think there should be.' He told her to meet him on the bridge the following morning at ten.

'Should I pay you in advance. . . ?' Gertrude asked, hoping for more information, but he looked so ruffled by this that she quickly put her purse away. 'Do I need to bring anything? Equipment of any kind?'

'No,' he said, as if that was something he was sure of, and he made a quick scribbled note in his book.

Max had given himself a goal. He was not allowed to visit Elsa until he had finished Old Farm. Old Farm and Old Farm Cottage would take him to the centre of his scroll. He was on his third roll of paper and if he pasted them together they would lap his room four times. Max worked fast. All fear of finishing forgotten. A sudden free style in the middle of so much painstaking work. His bricks were pink and red and brown, the Crittal windows sharp lines of metal in their new rectangular frames. Beside it, the farm labourer's cottage was a worn heap of a building. Its roof low, its front door squeezed round to the side. *When painting a comedian,* he reminded himself of Henry, *do not try and make the picture funny.* And keeping his mind on the weight of the thatch, he carried on. It was after six when he finished, and he sat there a little longer, waiting for the colour to dry. There was a chill in the air and he pulled his jacket round him, wondering if tonight would be the night when Gertrude lit the fire. And then he remembered, Elsa was expecting him. He would not be there.

'Elsa Lehmann,' he told Gertrude, 'is interested to see Henry's letters. She thinks that maybe I should have them published.'

'I see.'

Max was washed and dressed in clean, pressed clothes. His hair was combed and flattened, his eyebrows smoothed down. ' "Is it better," ' he pulled out a letter, ' "to think of yourself as a genius although you may not be one at all?" '

Gertrude did not entirely trust herself to reply. 'Possibly,' she nodded. 'It depends on whether you are delusional, or simply in need of a bit of cheering up.'

'Tonight,' he said, 'I won't be here for supper.'

'Yes, I see.' He was waiting for her blessing. 'Well, I won't wait up. But Max' – he was about to leave – 'are they your letters to publish? I mean aren't letters the property of the sender?'

Max frowned. 'Even if they're dead?'

' "Promising subjects are always liable to turn out badly because you get tired of them while you are carrying them out." ' Max felt impelled to read at least one of Henry's letters to Elsa or the lie would be complete. '"If you have too great an admiration for a certain person, then it is hard to make a decent drawing of them. Forget that your subject interests you at all."'

'Then why would you want to draw them in the beginning?' Elsa frowned. 'And who was this subject that was so promising?' She came round to his side of the table and stood close against his arm. 'When were you at your happiest?' She planted small soft kisses on his neck.

Max pressed his fingers against the bones of her face, along her jaw line, around the socket of her eye. 'Last night. This morning. Now.'

'No.' Elsa laughed. He ran one finger along the inside of her gum, skimming it across her teeth. 'Tell me.'

'All right.' He drew a sheet of paper towards him. He'd make his map for her. He'd show her around his house. 'Look.' He pulled her down on to the edge of his chair. 'Take the forest road from Rissen, the one that runs between the vegetable garden and the woods.'

'What are you saying?'

'Cross the stream, there is a wooden bridge, and there in the shade of three huge trees you will find the house. Heiderose. It was built by a German poetess and above the door it read:

'"One cries or one laughs, That is our destiny.
Life is too short, Death is too long."'

Elsa slipped an arm around his waist. 'You're not allowed to miss it,' she said. She shook her head.

'There are two balconies on either side of the front door, for sunbathing, for looking out towards the stream, and a terrace where the cook peels vegetables when the weather is warm. Beyond lie fields, and beyond them, "the great forest". If you walk into it, on almost any path you'll come to a clearing where there is a pond.' Max could feel the dark water cool between his toes, and hear with perfect ears the sounds of the farm hens. 'But if you take any path to get home, you'll almost never come out where you intend.'

Max led Elsa through the inside of the house. He took her through the green room with its fragile furniture, the card table, the Renoir still in its frame above the fire. He seized new paper for the dining-room, which was blue and almost filled by a round table. There was a swallow's nest in the wall above the long windows, and while you ate you could watch birds swoop down with food for their young. The library was panelled, and beyond it was the schoolroom. It was from the window of this room that he'd first seen Father Christmas. A great knock on the window had alerted him, and then a gruff voice asking if he'd been good. Father Christmas talked of goodness, and of whipping, but happily he left then, as quickly as he had come.

Max ran upstairs, past his mother's linen cupboard, a place of order and great beauty, where every sheet and pillowcase was bound round with pink cord, past her bedroom, also impeccably tidy, and beyond it, his father's, a mire of clothes and books and papers. There in the walls of this room his father had made a hiding place. He'd shown it to Max once when he was young, but when, some months later, he'd crept in again to find it, he could never discover where it was.

'Max?' Elsa had her hand on his shoulder. She was peering anxiously into his face. 'Are you all right?'

'Yes, but . . .' He couldn't tell whether he'd been dreaming, or talking to her out loud.

'And you,' he said, shaking himself, 'when were you happiest?'

'Me?' He could see her eyes travelling backwards. 'When I was first married, I suppose. In 1931 there was a house that Klaus designed for the director of the Deutsche Bank, and it was the most beautiful building that anyone had ever seen. I was newly married, I was eighteen, and I had no doubts whatsoever that we were destined for great things.'

'But here, he has made himself a success? You left in time. You did everything you could.'

'Yes, you're right. I have nothing to feel sorry for.' Elsa looked out at the horizon and then, turning, she led him to the bed.

30

Nick was on the M25 when Lily got through. 'What the fuck!' he said. 'I thought you were dead.'

'Sorry, no. I'm not.'

'You could have been anywhere, fallen into the river, down a well, Christ . . . I even started thinking the wife-beater might have got you, I actually knocked on his door.' Nick laughed, furious, and Lily felt goose bumps spring up along her arm.

'I decided to go camping.' She had to say something. 'There's a little campsite, on the beach, and I thought, for a change . . .'

'The beach? But I looked on the beach!'

'Well, it's further along, in a hollow. You wouldn't know, really, unless you knew . . .'

There was silence then. Just the shooting hiss of cars. 'I'm really sorry . . .' she pleaded. 'Nick? I wasn't expecting you . . . We said next Friday . . . If I'd known' – guilt seeped into her voice, forcing it up high – 'obviously, I would have stayed in.'

'I wanted to surprise you.' He sounded sad. 'Well, I suppose I did.'

'You surprised the postman anyway,' she said, 'with your note.' For a moment they both laughed. 'So . . . next weekend . . . if it hasn't put you off . . . ?'

'We'll see.' He gave a great, tired sigh. 'Actually the drive isn't too bad, now I'm getting used to it, and you know . . . last night as I was walking round, looking for you in ditches, I did see . . . There is something about it . . . the village, maybe it's just the darkness, being without street lights . . . hearing the waves, there is something . . .'

Lily was shivering. 'Yes.'

'Maybe you're right. Maybe I should take more time off. Maybe . . . Ahhh, BOLLOCKS.' There was a pause and a compression of air. 'Shit, I've just been photographed by a speed camera. That's another six points on my licence.'

'I'm sorry.'

'It's not your fault.'

'Next Friday?' she said gently, 'and I'll ring you before?'

'All right. But Lily . . .' He was struggling, she could hear it in his voice. 'I didn't know you had a tent.'

'I bought one. There was a fête in the village hall, to raise money for missionaries, of all things, and I . . . it only cost three pounds.'

'Bloody hell, what's it like?'

'Well . . .' Lily looked out of the window and rolled her eyes, although there was no one there. 'It's . . . You know those green canvas boy scout tents that you have to lace up to close the door? The ground sheet isn't even attached, so in the morning my clothes were all scattered around outside.' God, what was she talking about? 'But Nick' – she caught sight of the flashing row of O's – 'I'm sorry, my money's about to . . .' She started scrabbling. 'It's about to –' The line went dead.

The phone call had cost more than the imaginary tent. She wandered up to the shop and looked into the window. But there were no adverts for tents. Only a row of holiday houses, all sweetly porched, climbing with vines, to let.

Lily added to her basket as she waited in the narrow aisle. Biscuits and tea-bags and a newspaper with a photograph of a young Palestinian, tranquil and dark-eyed, and another of the carnage in a Jerusalem street after she'd killed herself and seven passers-by. *IS THERE ANY HOPE FOR PEACE?* the headline read, and underneath in smaller, greyer type a description of what the Israeli army were planning in order to exact revenge. What was she going to do about Nick? she wondered, but instead of deciding she leafed through the thin sheets. Home News and International. Enough disease and drought and violence to wipe out most of a continent, even without a world war.

Grae had set his workbench up outside the hut and was building a set of steps. He'd made the structure, free-standing, triangular sides to hold it in, and now he was sanding it down.

'Sorry,' Lily said. 'I got delayed.' She spread her newspaper over the table and set out lunch. Bread, ham, olives, cheese. Red and yellow tomatoes steaming up the inside of their plastic box.

Grae stopped sawing. 'Thankyou.' He looked at her as if no one had ever done a kind thing for him before.

Lily smiled. She wouldn't mention Nick. 'When are the girls back?' she asked instead, and he tore off a piece of bread.

'Teatime, Sue's going to have them every other weekend from now on.'

Instinctively Lily looked at her watch. It was only one.

'She's got a job. Assistant to the pig man over at Uggleswade.' Grae gave a snort. 'It means she's up at five and can't take them to school.' He twisted his mouth into a smile, as though this in itself were good.

'Is she from round there?'

'Yes, grew up on a farm, gone now of course. Sold off.'

Lily made herself a sandwich. She was so hungry the insides of her stomach contracted with the promise of food. Wouldn't it be wonderful if no questions needed to be answered, nothing ever asked? They ate in silence. Breaking the crusts with their fingers, tearing at the ham and cheese.

'Is there a campsite round here?' She wiped pips away with her arm.

'Yes, there's one just over the river. Why, is all this comfort getting to be too much?'

'No, it's just . . . I wondered.' There was water on the table and she took a long warm gulp.

Grae looked at her. 'The old lady who runs it, Dolly, she's . . . Well . . . Since she turned eighty it's not so easy to get a pitch. She's switched currency, gone back to old money. If you're lucky, you can stay a week for two-and-six.' He got up and carried on working, knocking nails in with small clean taps. Lily closed her eyes. She could see his outline through the red glow of her lids. 'Sometimes she just takes against you.' He was talking to himself. 'Sue once offered her ten shillings, but no, she said, the campsite was full.'

When Grae had given the wood a coat of bright blue paint, they walked along the beach towards the power station. It shimmered at them from the curve of the coast, its dome white and thin as pearl.

'What's it like there?' she asked. 'Do you wear masks and protective suits?'

'No.' He hesitated, 'But I'm sworn to secrecy. I had to sign a pledge before I was allowed in.'

'Really?' She looked at him, alarmed.

'No. Don't be ridiculous. Anyway, I only worked in the canteen.'

They wrapped their arms round each other and walked on, trudging through soft sand and moving pebbles, climbing up the sheer wall of shingle, up to where the ground was hard. It was windy here and they kept their heads down, forced to walk in single file, the grasslands below them, the sea rushing in on their other side. 'Here.' Grae reached for her hand, and they ran down towards the river and crossed over the bridge to the mill. The mill water was low. The path around it spliced with little cracks. White butterflies skittered just above the bracken, so close it seemed you could reach out and catch one in your fist. Lily stretched out on the granite wall. Question after question rose up in her mind and each time she caught herself, just in time, and pushed it down. Grae came and sat beside her. He eased out the salt strands of her hair.

'We should get back,' he said, 'if I'm going to drive out to the farm.'

'Oh, I thought she was bringing them here.'

'No.' He stood up. 'That's why I got myself a car.'

'Right . . .' There was a small hard grit of silence as they walked back the way they'd come.

Lily picked a frond of grass and swiped at the stalks along the path. 'Sorry.' Grae reached back for her. 'Sorry,' he said, 'it's still . . . It's . . . difficult.' He kissed her, his eyes softening into hers. 'Here,' he was nodding sideways, 'what do you think?' and there beside the path was a clearing, a den under the low-hanging branches of a tree.

Lily looked around. 'No,' she said, but she didn't know quite why. Grae slid a hand under her shirt, denting the crevice of each rib, smoothing his thumb along her side, up and over the smooth curve of her breast.

'Come on,' he said and, bending low, he led her under the canopy of branches, the gnarled arms of the tree, the hardening leaves. It was dark inside and cool. They kissed again, and this time she let herself breathe in the hotness of his breath, keeping her own eyes open while his eyelids closed, his face furrowing in concentration as he pressed her hard against him, holding her steady, unbuckling his belt.

Dear Cathy and Clare . . . The problem page letter came to her as she rearranged her clothes. Her legs were trembling, one buttock indented with shards of bark, one arm grazed and numb. *Is it possible to get pregnant if you do it standing up?*

'*YES IT IS,*' the magazine replied and she'd wondered even then, aged fourteen, at the unique force of gravity of sperm.

'Are you all right?' Grae was calling to her. He had backed out of the cave and was dusting himself down.

'Yes.' She clambered out to join him. He took her arm and they walked on, their limbs loose and carefree, the syrup of their closeness welding them together at the hip. They reached another bridge and hesitated – whether to go down to the sea, or take the path that led inland, where the grass grew so tall it closed over their heads. They stooped and ran along the white bed of the tunnel, tumbling out on to a bridle path, where mud had hardened into dust-brown mountains, crumbling at the top. They stumbled over it, slipping occasionally into horseshoe craters, laughing and pulling each other out.

'You can hear nightingales in these woods, just for a week or so at the end of May,' Grae told her as they walked into a copse of trees, stopping to admire the great gnarled trunks, the huge horizontal branches, the deep colour of the leaves that blocked out the light. 'Shh.' They listened, although it was months too late for nightingales, and there somewhere beyond them was the unhappy roaring of a car. Grae looked at her. 'Someone's stuck,' he said, and running towards the start of the track he leapt over a gate. Lily followed. The car was stuttering now, catching, then shrieking like an animal in pain. Lily jumped down from the gate and there ahead of her was an old grey Morris.

'Are you all right, mate?' Grae was calling, and Lily reached him just as he began to push. 'Turn it, to the right,' Grae called, and the driver, only his legs visible, twisted the wheel. They put all their weight behind the car and then with one great sudden jolt it jumped out on to the lane.

'Thankyou.' The man unbent himself from the car. He was middle-aged, fifty, with thick grey hair and eyebrows that needed to be smoothed.

'My God,' Lily started, 'it's him.'

'Who?' Grae turned to her, but the man was walking towards them. 'Mr Lehmann?' she said. 'I didn't know that you were here. Sorry, you don't remember me.' She put out her hand, 'Lily Brannan. I'm doing the thesis . . . You sent me the letters?'

Mr Lehmann looked at her, nodding his head. 'You're being most unusually thorough coming here.'

'Yes, well . . .' She laughed, not wanting him to know the opposite was true. 'I wanted to see the house that . . . Lehmann . . . The house that he designed. And then, well' – she cast a glance at Grae

– 'I got distracted.' She stopped, hopeful he might offer something more, but he said nothing, just looked back at his car. 'Thankyou so much for sending those last letters,' she went on. 'It helped so much. The house. It's beautiful. I even looked inside.'

Lehmann sighed. 'I have a photograph, taken just after it was built.'

Grae was shifting from foot to foot. 'I should go,' he said. 'If I'm going to be on time.'

'I'll see you later?' Lily touched his arm. 'Tomorrow?'

Grae turned away. 'OK.'

'I mean . . . If the girls . . .' But he was striding fast up through the allotments, towards the village hall.

Mr Lehmann was holding open the door of his car. 'If you'd like to see?'

'Yes,' she said, 'the photo,' and she climbed in.

Lehmann drove with extreme caution along the rutted lane. No one, she told herself, could be a danger to women who drives at five miles an hour. Eventually they turned into The Street and then, as Lily knew he would, into the gravel drive. The new building on the corner had made considerable progress since she'd last really looked. Its walls had raced up to the second floor and the wooden beams of the roof were being laid. A man in a hard hat, weatherworn and strong, nodded to their car. 'Alf.' A. L. Lehmann braked. 'How are you?' He leant out through the window and his whole face changed.

'I'm all right.' Alf put his head on one side, and the two men looked at the building, almost sorrowfully. 'Really, my friend' – Alf spoke slowly – 'it's not going to look so bad. You did the right thing, selling the land.' His face broke into a smile. 'But you're never going to guess what the blasted fellow wants us to put in now? Listen to this, Bert. A heating system that can be operated from London. When he sets off for the weekend, he'll just flick a switch and by the time he gets here the whole place will be toasty warm.' The two men looked at each other in disgust, and Lily thought of Nick and how much he would approve.

Bert! Lily thought, Albert Lehmann, and they drove in silence down the lane, curving at the end and turning on to the small grass bank beside Marsh End. 'How long,' she asked him, 'have you lived here?'

'I was born here, and then, well, it was my good fortune to be left this house.'

'Yes,' she agreed. 'How wonderful. And do you drive up and down from London in this car?'

He turned to her, seeming to study her question for offence.

'No,' he said, 'I take the train.'

'Right.' Lily got out, and as if by accident she let her fingers rest on the warm grey bonnet of the car.

'Miss Brannan?' He was holding open the door.

'Lily, please.' And she followed him in.

The porch smelt damp. So did the house, and for a moment Albert Lehmann stood lost in the middle of the room. Where was he going, anyway? Lily thought suddenly. Taking his car into the marsh?

'The photograph,' he said. 'Ah yes.' Slowly he turned around. There was a sideboard full of shelves and drawers. Lily stood behind him as he opened it. Biscuit boxes, napkins, folded and old, table mats and ribbons and some cocktail sticks and ancient straws. The man bent down and peered into a cupboard and then, randomly it seemed to her, he walked through to the kitchen and opened the larder. One pot of jam stood on a shelf and two corked bottles, their contents flecked and brown. Lily looked back at the room. Above the fireplace was a painting of a man, young and thin, his clothes loose around him, the outlines filled in with watery paint. Below the painting, on the mantelpiece, was a box. Lehmann must have seen it as she did, because with sudden eagerness he moved forward and lifted it down. He set it on the oval table, and began to finger through, lifting out photographs in small creased piles. Lily caught snatched glimpses – women, hatted, leaning into the wind, and figures in army uniform, too quick to see which side.

There was a man, handsome in shades of sepia grey, an eel dangling proudly from one hand, and a dark-haired woman with two babies, her face stricken, a bundle lying helpless in each arm. 'Here it is,' he said and Lily, eager, reached out her hand. But the photograph wasn't of the Sea House. This house had a fence around the roof, and the steep glass wall beside the door was shadowed with reflected leaves.

'Where is this house?'

Lehmann was at the French windows as if he needed air, and she could see him from behind, struggling with the bolt. 'How could I have missed it?' The bolt came up and he jolted open the doors. 'It's gone,' he said. 'The house was destroyed, five years ago.'

'No!' Lily felt close to tears. 'How?'

'There was . . . a crisis. My brother and I . . .'

Lily interrupted him. 'But are there plans?'

'The plans are lost.'

'How can they be?' She realized that she was shouting. She turned the photo over and saw in that familiar blue-black hand, 1950. *Hidden House*. 'But how was it destroyed?'

A. L Lehmann shook his head. 'I'm sorry,' he said. 'I should never have asked you here.'

'But so little is known about him. At the Architectural Association, at RIBA, when I went to look in the archives there were only photographs of chairs and bookcases. Some plans for loft conversions and the Heath Height Flats. Nothing else. I wrote to Germany, to Hamburg, to the Historical Archive, and the Lands Archive, and apart from details of one spectacular house that had already been demolished, there was not even a mention of his name.'

'All Jewish architects were removed from the files,' and then, almost in spite of himself, he said, 'Shall I make a copy for you?' He reached across the table for a pen and paper and very carefully he began to draw. He kept the photo in his sight but mostly he drew blind, sketching in the turret, the staircase, the steps like a ripple through the glass. 'There,' he said, when he had finished. 'I hope this will help.'

Lily held the paper carefully before her as he showed her to the door. 'You inherited your father's skill,' she said, looking down at the fluid lines of Hidden House.

'Yes, Yes.' But he sounded almost angry as he cranked open the door.

'I might see you again?'

Albert Lehmann shrugged, and it was only then that Lily thought of the letters and remembered the Lehmanns had never had a child.

31

It was raining the next morning but Gertrude was undeterred. She had slept badly, waiting for Max, but then she must have drifted off because all of a sudden it was dawn and Max's hat was on the table in the porch. The first drops of rain were falling, pattering against the roof, and as she stood there in her nightdress she felt a strange hot anguish that her lesson was about to be called off. By a quarter to ten she had hardened her resolve. She put on her plastic raincoat with its matching scarf, and took a huge umbrella that was intended for the sun. The umbrella made it difficult to see, casting shadows for several feet around, so that at first she didn't notice Alf, leaning over the rails of the bridge.

'What are you doing?' she asked, moving closer to draw him in out of the wet, but instead of answering he reeled in his line of string to show a family of crabs. The crabs were clinging to a fish head, its flesh ragged and grey, and she felt her stomach turn as with great care he shook the crabs into a pot. She watched them for a moment as they clawed the sides. Alf dropped his bait again. This time one giant crab came up, its legs hairy, its back red. Carefully he eased it to the level of the bridge but this crab was old and clever, and, taking one last bite, it dropped back to its bed.

'I didn't think you'd come.' The young man startled her. He had no umbrella and his hat and coat were already dark with rain.

'Good morning,' Gertrude said brightly and into her dry circle came his arm.

'Thomas . . . Thomas Everson.'

'Well . . .' He looked towards the sea, but he must have caught defiance in her face, because he added quickly, 'We'd better make a start.'

Everywhere was greyness. Flattened grass, the wet sludge of sand. Gertrude tried to shelter him with the umbrella, but he was taller than she was and soon her arm began to ache. They walked back and forth, holding their bodies stiff to avoid touching. 'Possibly,' Thomas suggested, 'we could choose an interior. I could set up a still life and we could have some tea.'

'Yes,' Gertrude agreed and, with the umbrella rammed before them, they hurried up the hill.

Fern Cottage was remarkably untidy. All around were plates of paints, cups, mouldering sticks of flowers, half-eaten toast.

'I'm so sorry,' he said. 'Mrs Wynwell came, but I couldn't let her in.'

Gertrude looked for somewhere to sit. There was an old cane chair scattered with paper, and one moth-eaten stool. She began moving books on to the floor, unearthing an old ripped letter and a tobacco pouch.

'That's where it is.' Thomas looked amazed.

And then Gertrude almost sat down on a small fine Stanley knife embedded in the folds of the seat.

'You're sopping wet,' she told him, noticing the worn ends of his jersey, the wet footprints of his socks, and for the next fifteen minutes she listened while he roamed around the room above her, opening drawers, banging cupboards, cursing occasionally. Then she heard the roll of wheels as he moved the bed.

Eventually he came down. 'Just one sock,' he said, apologetic, 'and I've just thought, I don't have any milk.'

Gertrude looked at the fine bones of his foot, the high arch, the toes, long knots of white. 'You'll freeze,' she said. 'Don't you own slippers?'

'Yes.' His eyes lit up, and then, as if remembering. 'I'm not sure . . .' Instead he lit a fire. Wood and paper and kindling were mercifully heaped beside the guard. He formed them into a perfect pyramid, layer upon layer. 'Now,' he said, 'the matches,' but to Gertrude's relief he found them in the hearth. Thomas sat and watched the flames. The cuffs of his trousers sent out curls of steam.

'So,' he said eventually, 'what shall we do?' He gathered the vases together and shook up the flowers. He took the best from each bunch and rearranged them, trying to spring life back into them with his hands. A drooping chrysanthemum, its petals burnt, and a sprig of overgrown mint.

Gertrude hardly dared move. A pencil was placed in her hand, a sheet of paper on a board on her knee, and as she began to trace the forms she thought how definite each mark she made, how revealing each wrong stroke.

Thomas sat opposite and began to sketch. The sound of his pencil scratching soothed her ears. The fire spat, the rain hissed outside and she began to enjoy the nursery frill of each petal of her flower. She imagined the borders of a bedtime book, daisies and pansies holding hands, and soon she stopped looking altogether, lost in a memory of some other time.

'Well, then,' Thomas Everson said when she was still. He rose and stood beside her chair. 'Is there anything you want to ask?'

Gertrude blushed. Her sketch might have been done by a child. 'Until next week, then?' she offered, and, seeing the spiked lines of his own drawing, she leant forward to see what he had done. But he was already there. He gave it a quick look and, twisting it into a ball, he threw it into the fire.

'We need to find something that actually interests you,' he said before Gertrude could speak, and he walked to the door. 'Would a shilling be too much?'

'Of course.' Gertrude fumbled with her purse. 'Next Tuesday then, and I'll bring milk?'

Max watched the sky from the windows of the Sea House and wondered how he would finish his scroll. There were three small cottages on the Common, graded like steps into the slope, and he'd hoped to add them to the existing houses on one long ribbon of blue sky. He'd set a tent up, made with wind breaks and umbrellas, but water had fallen in a great loop from the roof and been blown in.

'It can wait.' Elsa stood beside him, holding his hand below the level of the sill. 'Tomorrow the rain might stop.'

They lay down on the bed, their bodies forced together by the weak mattress's dip. 'Tell me,' she said, 'where did they send you? Where were you interned?' For three days now they'd lived each other's lives, sharing each other's histories, making each other's pasts their own.

'Where? I was sent to Australia.' He was getting better at this. Talking. He could feel the words roll almost happily from his tongue. 'I was taking a course in book-keeping. Kaethe had arranged it, so that I would be able to get work with a law firm or a bank. I was sitting in a room with three other men, when a policeman came in and arrested me. "I am not a criminal," I told him, but he answered that during wartime there were worse criminals than murderers and thieves. First I was taken to a prison and held in a cell, then I was moved to a barracks, and then to the Isle of Man. After only a few days I was transported to Liverpool, and put on board a ship. There were about two thousand of us, all Austrian and German, emigrés and refugees. We were crammed into the hold, and had to sleep in layers, three-deep. Some were on the floor, others on wooden tables, and the luckier ones, in hammocks strung above.'

Would Elsa like to hear, he wondered, how soon the floor was awash with vomit, and how those more enterprising among them, in true Prussian style, set up the Toilet Police? There were ten toilets for two thousand, and so, it could be calculated, that each prisoner was allowed seven minutes a day. The Toilet Police set up a strict rota, calling up people as vacancies arose. 'Drei Männer rechts ran zum Pinkeln.' Three men to the right for peeing. It surprised Max that these words were still clearly etched into his brain.

'We did not know where we were going,' he told her. 'And the older the people were, the more they complained. One died, and then another, and I often lay awake at night and thought how much worse the conditions must have been for the slaves brought across from Africa. They died, a third at least, on each voyage. I was lucky. I had a hammock and almost no possessions. Some had managed to bring small treasures with them, and when they went missing it caused no end of sorrow. Three times we stopped. Once in Takoradi, which was a miserable shanty town as far as I could see, once in Cape Town, where I hungered to get off, and then in Fremantle in Western Australia, when I was too ill with an infection in my ear to go on deck and see it.

'Finally after nine weeks we arrived in Sydney. I see now that we were lucky to be sent away. In every respect our lives were better than they would have been if we'd stayed. The sun shone, the food was plentiful, and we were safe in our camp at Hay by the Murrumbidgee river. But we were allowed no news. No letters were written or received, and the silence was a torture.'

Max remembered the Australian newspapers and how flimsily they reported the war. They were full of the results of horse races and lurid descriptions of divorce. Sex in Australian newspapers was censored, but divorce came under Law. The editors made full use of this. Trousers, panties, doors opening unexpectedly and husbands coming home. The men would read aloud to each other and the thin canvas of their beds would groan. Sometimes in the back pages it was possible to glean a little information on the war. The bombing of London, the atrocities in France. But there was nothing that told him if Kaethe was still living, if his parents had managed to remain in their own home. And then the ban was lifted and they were allowed to write. Max's letter took three months to reach Kaethe, and hers another three months to reach him. She was alive, and the following week she wrote again, and the week after, again. She was his life line and his anchor, his mother, father, sister, his only link to himself.

'Say Hay for Happy,' he spoke the song they used to sing.

'And you feel snappy
And you don't want to die.
Even if you sell your overcoat,
for just the sight
of one more bite,
of tasty butterbrot . . .'

'So you were happy there,' Elsa interjected.

'Yes.' It hardly counted, but now he thought of it, he was.

'We set up a school,' he told Elsa, relief spreading through him, the memory of joy. 'It was possible to learn any language, and I worked every day on my English, promising myself I would not speak German again.' He looked up at Elsa and smiled. 'I took a course in higher mathematics. There were classes in Astronomy, Calligraphy, the Classics. Among the internees were several highly skilled doctors who all examined my ears. One suggested it was a build-up of wax that could be cured quite simply with a syringe, and another that it was a disease called Ménière's. Soon I would lose my balance, deteriorate, and die. Another doctor, who had also studied in Vienna, told me there was nothing wrong with me at all. A stubborn desire not to communicate, was his conclusion. And so stubbornly I ignored him from then on.

'It took a long time for the British to recognize that we were not enemies or spies, and when they did they sent a Major, an English-born Jew, to decide who should return. I was on that first ship with several dozen others, mostly married men. This time I had a cabin to myself and was waited upon by a host of Chinese stewards. They ran me baths and coaxed me with ice-cream, and when we arrived at Cristobal in the Caribbean I was given a pass by the ship's captain to go ashore.'

Max remembered how the whole town had become a brothel for the Americans, who were guarding the Panama Canal. In each shop window stood a woman, bare-breasted, her chest in sunlight, her face in shadow behind. Men strode up and down, deciding which bosom to choose, and when they'd made their choice, they disappeared inside.

'And did you have any money to spend?' Elsa asked him. 'In Cristobal? Did you make a choice?' She moved closer to him.

'I had enough to buy bananas.' Bananas, he had heard, were impossible to find in London and he wanted to surprise Kaethe with the gift. But the bananas ripened in his cabin, and as he sailed up the Mersey he ate the last one, brown and soggy, and threw the skin into the Liverpool docks.

Kaethe had been there to meet him, but at first it seemed the authorities would not let her take him home. The voyage had confused him, made him think he would be welcomed, offered an apology even, but this was not to be. Where were his papers? Why was he here at all? Was he fit to join the army? If not, he should once more be interned. It occurred to him then he should have stayed in Australia, joined the Hay Association, who vowed to meet up once a year, but Kaethe was trying hard to convince them.

'He's harmless,' she told them. 'Harmless!' she shouted into his ear and when he didn't flinch they relented and let him go.

That night Max lay desolate on his bed in the new house in Muswell Hill. While he'd been gone Kaethe had found the Renoir concealed in his drawer. She had taken it to a gallery in Cork Street and sold it for three hundred pounds. The dealer said it was a bread and butter Renoir, not worth very much at all. But it had been enough to buy a two bedroom terrace house, and proudly Kaethe had hung his own painting of her in the hall.

Elsa put her arms around him. 'Max . . .' She was breathing words to him he couldn't hear. 'Max.' He turned to find her laughing. 'Look.' She was pointing to the cupboard opposite, a label pasted to its door. *Spare sheets, blankets, pillowcases and life jackets.*

Max kissed her. 'Sing Hay for Happy . . .' He tried to lilt a tune. 'Did you never learn to make signs?'

'No.' He looked appalled. 'My father said that would be giving in.'

'Don't give in.' Elsa was teasing, her fingers sliding between

the buttons of his shirt. 'Never give in.' And she rolled into the
warm curve of his body so that with his hands he could listen to
her breath.

32

Elsa, I am ordering you back to London. I need you here and I don't see what can be keeping you so busy? Surely Kett doesn't need you every day to oversee the house. I have a note from him which says the work goes on, all is satisfactory, and he has been given the most detailed plans. Mendels are proving impossible over their loft, and Greenbergs – well, 'Greens' I should say – want to change almost everything that has been decided, the kitchen at the front, a living area upstairs . . . Mrs Benson at least is happy with her chairs and has asked if I would design a cabinet for the doctor. I thought I might make a stack of sliding drawers to keep the more grisly utensils out of sight, and with a shelf, wide and strong enough to pull out and examine babies on when they come in for their first checks. I enclose a rough sketch which you might comment on when you ARRIVE.

    Yours, without you, L.

Lily ran her fingers along the inside of the envelope, hoping to find the sketch welded to the seams, but there was nothing there.

Elsa, I am NOT trying to distress you. Surely I should be allowed to mention the word 'child' without an outcry, and I drew the infant bawling so that you could only be relieved that this was not your lot. So now I will have to come and comfort you, is that what you planned? You are cleverer and more deceitful than even I suspected, although of course my mother warned me all those years ago. 'A girl as beautiful as that . . .' So, I concede defeat. If you are too melancholy to travel, then I will come to you. Until Friday then, and just wait and see what I will do to cheer you up.

    Yours, in anticipation, L.

My dear, of course, I will be careful of the floods. Unless you are suggesting that I shouldn't come? I won't risk the train, but will leave here early on Saturday, so that at least I can see what is happening when the car is swept away by a typhoon. Then, as you say, I shall park up by the Ship and if you have to, you can row over to collect me. Is there a boat tied up under the house? Can it really be that wet? It has been nothing more than overcast here, and as we know our little strip of Ost sea always has better weather than anywhere else. I can hardly wait to see the Hut. Has there still been no news from Mrs Bugg about her husband? Do you intend to keep it on for the rest of the year? Kett should be finished by Christmas and then we can move back in to Hidden House. If the sea comes in over the river you could fish me some flounders from the bottom step. Or pull up a catch of tiddlers and fry them up with butter and flour. Take care and don't let yourself be so unhappy. I was thinking how recently you'd stopped dwelling on old sorrows and I was congratulating you in my heart. I should have spoken these thoughts out loud.

With love, as always, L.

Lily slid the letters back into their envelope, the envelope with her address in A. L. Lehmann's writing stamped neatly on the side. '*Sorry, sorry*', Nick had scrawled along one side, *I won't make it this weekend.* But today Nick was speeding his way towards her, would have crossed the border into Suffolk by now. He'd be flying up and over the hill of the Orwell Bridge, suspended for a moment, surrounded by nothing but sky. Would he notice that the bridge was like a dinosaur, its grey legs squat, its head so meek and narrow, the curve of its backbone ridged into a road?

Lily poured crumbs out of the bread bin, rinsed clean the sink. She opened the back door and looked out at the garden. Weeds were tangling through the flowerbeds and the grass was long. Was it her responsibility to tend it? she wondered, and she tugged at a trail of convolvulus, heard it rip as it clung on. She picked two yellow roses and put them in a bowl, and then, her stomach tightening, she went upstairs. There were the twin beds, modest and divided, and she placed the roses on the table in between. A lamp stood there already, its shade flounced with caramel-coloured flowers – the head of an aged aunt, still in her bath hat, intent on keeping the two beds apart. Lily plumped each pillow, straightened the sheets, and then as if she were simply tidying, she flung a dress over the wardrobe mirror, obscuring the glass.

When there was nothing more to do, she took her notes and letters out into the garden. She carried out a blanket and a heap of cushions, a cup of tea, so that when Nick arrived he could surprise her, studiously at work.

My dearest, yes, I think we should accept supper with Jilks. Is Meyer STILL there? And how very amusing that Gertrude has a friend. Is Meyer not offended? And has he finished his watercolour project? I shall arrive only hours after this letter and you can give me your answers then.

I have just looked at The Times and seen the obituary of Ronald Wilberforce (Sir!), who was my boss at the S.O.E. It made me think that it is eight years now and I'm still waiting to be debriefed. If anyone at all from the Special Forces had shown interest, what a difference that would have made. It may even have saved the life of our good friend Joseph Feuer. Never debriefed, never asked for his account after six months in solitary confinement, it still hurts me to know it, to feel him so unthanked. Could it have stopped him, do you think, from taking his own life? My girl, when you are a widow of eighty-five, I give you permission to accept a medal on my behalf. Not for my houses, all overrun and spoiled by those who took them as their own, but for the moment when my parachute opened and I floated down behind enemy lines.

My El, my sweet, sweet wife, wait for me, I will be with you soon. L x

Lily was startled by the hooting of a horn. She jumped up from her cushions and ran round to the gate.

'I can't park.' Nick was leaning from his open window, looking at the space she had left free for him. 'Whose car is this?'

Lily stared at the dust-black bonnet of Grae's Renault 5. The two Renaults were so close, parked so exactly at the same angle that they looked like twins.

'Your car has cloned,' Nick said drily and Lily glanced round wildly for another space.

'You could go down to the ferry,' she suggested. 'Drive past the pub and there's a car park straight ahead. I'm sorry,' she called after him as he began to turn. 'Just keep going straight.'

'Oh God, oh God, oh God,' she murmured, and she was almost knocked over by a family of cyclists freewheeling round the bend.

She waited for Nick on the Green, sitting on the bench, expecting him to appear at any moment. Where was he? She strained awkwardly round, and unable to sit still, she walked down to the harbour to meet him. She passed The Ship, scanning the wide stretch of the car park, irritation and anxiety beginning to mix. How could he be lost? And then she saw him standing at the Mr Whippy van, gazing at the illustrated lollies and cornets, oysters and 99s. Just before him in the queue were Em and Arrie. Lily stood in shadow by the wall, watching as the girls ordered, paid and turned away, licking the sticks of orange ice.

'Lily.' He was waving to her, a bottle of water in his hand. 'Two hours, twenty-seven minutes. Is that a record or what?' He strode over to her and kissed her. She couldn't help it, she looked round to check if they'd been seen. But Em and Arrie had their backs to her, were nothing more than two brightly coloured dashes climbing the white slope of the dunes.

Lily led Nick into the garden.

'This is nice.' He stood still, surprised, and she explained that now the other cottage was empty the shared garden was all hers.

'I expect it'll be rented out to someone else soon,' she said and to avoid drifting on to the subject of the 'wife-beater' she asked how his work was getting on.

'Not bad,' he sighed. 'But there are always so many things that can go wrong. All of a sudden it doesn't seem possible to get the beam flat against the ceiling, so now the clients . . .' He stopped and shook his head. 'You know what?' He sat down on her mound of cushions. 'It's fine. At least we've got the work.'

'And Holly?'

'Holly?' For a moment they both looked at each other, shocked. 'She's doing fine, Yes . . .' He was tugging and tearing at the grass. 'We're lucky to have her.' And when he looked up, his face was calm.

'So you're still working?' he asked, nodding towards her sheaf of papers. 'Wasn't this all meant to be handed in by now?'

'It was, but they said if I really needed an extension, I could give it in at the beginning of next term.'

Nick lay back, his head on a cushion, and examined his mobile phone. He moved it through the air, backward, and forwards. 'Isn't it possible to get a signal here?'

'I don't know. Maybe in the house?'

'Even less likely, I'd have thought.' Nick stood up and walked around the garden, into the kitchen and out into the lane.

'You could try using the phone box,' she said, following him, and she bit her lip to stop her smile.

Nick stood in the middle of the Green still scrutinizing his phone.

'Was it a very important call?'

Nick looked at her through narrowed eyes. 'All right, you win,' he said. 'I'll try the phone box. Do you have change?'

Lily ran into the house. She was grinning so hard it shocked her. She hadn't realized quite how frantically she'd been at war. She scooped up change, reaching into the lining of her bag, tipping up her purse, until her hands were jangling with tens and twenties, the weightless silver fish scales of fives. When she got back, Nick was already on the phone.

'Sure, sure.' He was drawing the real world towards him, 'Tell them we will.' She piled her change on to the ledge beside him, and as she did Nick's arm moved round her and he scooped up the phone box note. 'Yes, I know that, of course,' he said more softly, and she watched him as he read. *Call 999. Wait by the wall* . . . She stood beside him as he tried to decipher it, and then she saw that it had been altered, had been added to since she last looked. The cross she'd made was circled, the L, proceeded by an R. Lily took a pen out of her pocket and wrote 'Hello' along the top, and Nick, still talking, raised his eyebrows at her as she pinned it back down under its stone. 'Tell them that we have a contractual agreement.' Nick turned away. 'They should read it again if they're confused. Look, Tim, for God's sake' – the fivepences were being eaten as fast as he could pay – 'I'll be back in the office on Monday morning, and you can call me any time . . . Look, if I don't answer, leave a message and I'll drive out of the village and pick it up. Yes . . . There's some interference here, probably the power station . . . Yeah, Lily never mentions it, but there's a bloody great nuclear reactor just along the coast. . . . She's in denial, only sees areas of "outstanding natural beauty" everywhere she looks.' He began to laugh, his shoulders shaking with mirth, and she imagined the rest of the weekend spent driving up and down to the A12 to pick up messages from Tim.

'You know what I've been craving?' Nick curled one arm around her waist.

'What?' Lily swallowed as he whispered in her ear. 'My visit just wouldn't be complete without a pint at that fantastic pub.'

They took their drinks out into the garden where even the dogs were lolling in the last of the day's sun. There was some kind of game being played in a pebbled corner, men and women cheering and laughing, behind a square of fence.

'What are they doing?' Lily asked.

The landlord, in his corset, was leaning up against the fenced-off pitch, a row of dark brown pints of bitter lined up behind him on the wall.

'They're playing boules.'

There was a hush then as a tall man stooped to throw. He swung his arm low three times and then let the silver ball arc and land and roll. There was a low murmur of approval and shouts of 'Well done, Alf.'

'That's Alf.'

Lily craned to see. Without his hat, Alf looked strangely dashing, his hair shock-white and springy on his head.

'Who's Alf?' Nick asked, but the barman was wheezing out a taunt. 'Those balls look a bit rusty to me,' he said, and Alf caught at the words like a boy. 'Rusty balls?' He straightened up. 'Been a martyr to them all my life.' And the others gave a great cheer of a laugh.

Lily and Nick sat at a wooden table, the garden hedge cut back so that they could see the sea. They smiled at each other and touched glasses and then carried on watching the game. 'Can you shove that in a bit further?' Alf gave orders to adjust the marker, and right on cue another man turned to the woman beside him. 'I expect that's something you've had to say more than once, eh, Cassie?'

'You're too right there.' Cassie looked across at Alf, and there was a low groan and a whistle as they carried on with their game.

'You look well.' Nick reached for Lily's hand.

'Yes,' she said, 'it's probably the power station sending out those warming rays.' She gave him a small, cold smile and Nick held her gaze.

'Lily, honestly, is everything all right?'

'Yes,' she said, and to her surprise tears rose up hotly in her eyes. 'I'm fine.' But her whole being was bristling with anger, although she knew she had no right to feel anything but guilt. 'I'm fine, really.' It was as if all the hurts and grievances had sprung alive in her, the disappointments of the last three years. 'Why,' she said, her whole face flushing, 'do you never say you love me?'

Nick's hand startled in hers. 'I don't know what you mean?'

Lily looked down at the table. She wasn't going to ask him again.

'Look . . .' Nick was floundering. 'I thought it was obvious. When I begged you to be part of the company? When I asked you to move into my flat?'

Lily was battling with the corners of her mouth, wretched with the desire to cry.

'Wasn't it . . .' – he was angry himself now – 'wasn't it clear?'

'No. It wasn't clear. Since when has "You can put your clothes very neatly in this cupboard" meant . . . meant . . . anything more than that?'

'So is that what all this has been about? Going off. Holing up in the middle of nowhere. You've exiled yourself just to get away from me?'

'No,' she said, defensive. 'NO. I just feel tired out with waiting, that's all.'

'What?' It occurred to her he really didn't understand. 'Waiting for what??'

'To be allowed . . . I don't know . . .' She wiped away her tears. 'To be allowed . . .'

Nick reached across to her with both his hands. 'I don't know what you're talking about . . .' His voice had sunk to a whisper and his face was white. With a shock Lily remembered that she loved him.

'I'd like to be allowed . . .' – she swallowed – 'to dream a bit, to plan, to have some idea of the future. But that's never been allowed. I couldn't even mention Christmas until, well, virtually Christmas Eve.'

'OK.' Nick winced as if he was being forced to speak. 'When I think of romance . . . passion, I think about what's happening now. The present. I've been waiting for you to join me, Lily, to start living, to stop letting your life drift by.'

'But how could I?' She tried to pull her hand away. 'When I never knew if I'd be allowed to . . .' She didn't want to have to say it.

'To be allowed to what?'

'For thousands of years, I don't know, longer, women have been getting married, having babies, making a home. And now all of a sudden, me, I'm not supposed to want to do that. I'm meant to feel ashamed of even mentioning it. Supposed to pretend that it's the last thing on my mind.' Lily felt her face burning. She wrenched her hand away. She'd never wanted to have to say these things. 'Look, I don't even know if I want children, marriage, but I'd like to have a choice. Instead, what is there? Work hard, work harder, and maybe if you're lucky you'll get the chance to work so hard you can hardly breathe!'

Nick sat back and looked at her. 'You're only twenty-seven. Christ, what's the hurry? Women don't start having babies till they're at least forty-two.'

'I'm not talking about what's fashionable.' She glared at him. 'You're not the only one who's read *Hello*! I'm just trying to be honest. God' – she felt a wave of fury – 'I knew you'd make me feel ashamed.' She breathed out loudly. 'I just hate it, our life, it's all so cold. Not needing each other for anything.' A swell of laughter rose up from the game. Lily looked around, appalled to think that anyone might have heard.

'Well, if you hate it . . .' Nick was breathing hard and then, sighing, he slid along the bench to get another drink. A man was stooping, trying to control his shoulders as he aimed the ball.

'Good man.' The landlord leant over for the scores. 'What distance was that?' They all craned to see and Cassie held up her thumb and finger, a centimetre apart. 'Six inches,' she said, and the men all doubled over with their howls.

They were still laughing when Nick came back. 'What's the joke?' He had another pint of bitter, and a white wine for her.

'Nothing, it's too stupid, not even funny,' but she couldn't help smiling as she reached for her glass.

They drank in silence. The moon was full, cloud-white above them, and slowly as they sat there in the garden, the midges nibbling in swarms, the glasses gathering, the night closed in. No one arrived to clear their table and, each time one or other of them came back with a round, the empties were nudged and shunted into the middle of the table, until they were looking at each other across a sea of glassy rings. The game of boules went on, the pitch lit up by the windows of the pub, until eventually a winning team emerged and the players drifted off, slapping each other's backs companionably whether they had lost or won. Nick and Lily staggered up. Nick took her arm and gratefully she leant against him, drunk and hollow as if those few tears had ebbed out all her strength.

Along the lane, away from the lights of the pub, the dark was silken. The moon shone huge. 'What a night,' Nick said, and he held her hand tightly as they stumbled along the edge of the Green. They washed in silence, together in the bathroom, and climbed into their separate beds. 'Goodnight,' she said smiling at him across the bonnet of the lampshade and she sank into a swirling sleep. She woke in the early hours of the morning and gulped down a glass of water, and as she drank she heard the rain. It sounded cool and friendly, splattering on the panes and she drained the last drops and lay back down.

'Oh, Christ,' Nick woke her.

'What is it?' He was clutching his head.

'Tim,' he groaned. 'I forgot to check my mobile. It's all your fault,' he smiled weakly, 'with your revolutionary ideas. Disbanding feminism. Marching for the right to do the washing up . . .'

'Shut up, I didn't say that.' But she felt light-hearted as she drew the curtain on to a fine grey sheet of rain.

'You're leaking,' Nick said, still holding his head, and she twisted round to see her nightdress stained with blood. 'I was going to say come here . . .' – he lay back down – 'but maybe not.'

Lily ran herself a bath. She lay in it and pictured Grae, out in his beach hut, the girls flicking strands of wool, dangling them for Guinness to jump from one bunk to the next. She let her head sink under the water and felt her thoughts release. A new free month ahead of her. Relief. Disappointment, relief. She had a lifetime to be more careful. 'But they can't live there all winter . . .' She tried to work it out, and when she came up Nick was peering over her, naked, one leg raised as he tested the water for warmth. 'What were you saying?'

'Just talking to myself,' and she pulled her knees up to make room for him as he climbed in.

There was an umbrella in the cupboard. *Umbrella*. It had a label attached to it. *Do not use*. Lily was too superstitious to open it indoors. She pushed the head of it outside. 'It's better than nothing,' she called to Nick, looking up through the fraying holes, and they walked out into the rain. 'We could drive up to the main road in my car?' she said, noticing Grae's Renault had gone. 'We might even get a signal by the church.'

'It's all right.' Nick scrutinized the soft leather of his shoes. 'I can walk. Anyway, my bag's still in the boot.'

Even before they reached the car park they knew something was wrong. A crowd of men, the same crowd who were playing boules, were standing round Nick's car. It was the only car in the car park, and beside it, peering in through the window, was Grae. Lily felt the sight of him jolt through her.

'What's up?' Nick called and the men all turned.

'This your car?'

'Yes.' Nick strode ahead. 'Is something wrong?'

Lily caught Grae's eye and looked away.

'There was a high tide last night.' It was the champion of the boules game, Alf, standing out from the others. 'Came up past midnight. We went round everyone, got them to move their cars, but this one here, we didn't know whose it was.' He turned to Lily and smiled. 'We saw yours up on high ground, all safe and well, but we didn't know your friend here had brought his own.'

Nick peered into the car. There was seaweed clinging to the steering-wheel and grains of sand had collected in the pockets of each door. Water sat in muddy puddles in the crook of the seats.

'You won't be going anywhere in that,' Alf said, and the men all turned to each other and began to nod and talk.

Nick put his key in the lock of the boot and with a great creak wrenched it up. His leather bag sat in a swamp of water, a surf line already forming in a crust of white.

'It happens regular every few years,' Alf went on, 'the tide comes in, the river overflows. It's why we've got all the walls and the defences, to stop it coming up farther than it does.'

Lily felt a damp hand in her own. 'Hello.' It was Emerald in a bright blue mac.

'Are you all right?' Lily bent down to her. 'Were you flooded? How did you manage in the hut?'

'We're fine,' she said. 'And, anyway, Dad knew. He parked our car somewhere safe, and boarded up our door.'

Lily looked across at Grae who was standing watching Arrie as she waded through a puddle of mud.

'It only happens at full moon,' Em went on. 'Dad says if you're concentrating, if you keep an eye on the tides . . .' and she let go her hand and ran into the puddle, sending up a wave of water that washed over the top of her sister's boots.

Nick had his bag dripping at his side and he was locking up the car. 'I'd better call the AA,' he said, his face inscrutable, and he nodded to the men.

'You'll not be going anywhere in that,' one of them called over, 'not for a long while.' And cheerful almost with the knowledge of it, they all shook their heads.

'This blasted fucking god-forsaken place,' Nick cursed as soon as they were out of hearing.

'But you'll be covered by the insurance . . .' Lily tried. 'I mean, will you, for an act of God?'

'Fuck it, they'll have to tow me home.'

Lily stood outside the phone box while he called. The sky was

234

clearing, the rain had stopped. It was like a blanket lifting at the edges to let in a flood of blue.

'They'll be here,' Nick said, 'any time in the next two hours.'

They sat together on the bench. 'You could get the train home?' she ventured. 'Or take my car?' But he gave her such a withering look that she said nothing more.

They sat on the bench for an hour waiting for the recovery van. Lily brought out tea, water, paracetamol, a plate of toast. Nick sorted through the ruin of his bag.

'I almost forgot,' he said, slipping his hand into an inner pocket, 'I brought you this.' He handed her a folded sheet of paper. 'Someone emailed it to me and I thought it was something you should see.'

Lily unfolded the paper. *TIPS ON STAYING SAFE FOR WOMEN*. And as she read, the sun burst out from behind the cloud and turned the grass bright green. *IF YOU ARE EVER THROWN INTO THE BOOT OF A CAR, KICK OUT THE TAIL LIGHTS, STICK YOUR ARM THROUGH AND WAVE. THIS HAS SAVED MANY LIVES.*

Lily looked over at Nick.

'It's from America,' he said. He was watching the road.

THERE ARE THREE REASONS WHY WOMEN ARE ATTACKED.

1. *LACK OF AWARENESS. You must know where you are going and what is going on.*

2. *BODY LANGUAGE. Keep your head up. Swing your arms. Stand up straight.*

3. *WRONG PLACE. WRONG TIME. Don't walk alone at night.*

'Thanks.' She was incredulous. She didn't dare ask if it was a joke.

HOW TO AVOID BEING THE VICTIM OF A VIOLENT CRIME:

Always take the elevator instead of the stairs. Stairwells are the perfect crime spot. If the predator has a gun and you are not under his control,

235

always run. The predator will only hit you 4 in 100 times and even then it may not be a vital organ. RUN.

If you are parked next to a big van, enter your car from the passenger door. Most serial killers attack their victims by pulling them into their vans while the women are attempting to get into their cars.

Look at your parked car. If a male is sitting alone on the driver side, walk back into the mall.

I was going to send this to the ladies only: but guys, if you love your mothers, wives, sisters, daughters, you may want to pass this on to them. It is always better to be safe than sorry. BETTER PARANOID THAN DEAD.

Lily started to laugh. 'I can't believe . . .' and she began to read the email again.

'I printed it out' – Nick sounded hurt – 'especially for you.'

'Flowers might have been nicer . . .'

'Listen' – Nick turned to her – 'I didn't want to scare you, but that night when I came to surprise you, when you were camping . . . Or wherever you were . . . I saw . . .' Nick shivered. 'I saw a man walk across the Green. I think he came out of the phone box. At first I thought I was dreaming, but he stopped right by the car. He was a kind of tramp. His clothes were all rotten and moulded to his body, and he looked at me . . . I don't know, it scared me, and to think you hardly ever lock your door.'

'OK,' Lily nodded. 'OK.'

But just then the recovery van came round the corner and Nick sprang up and ran towards it, pointing and gesticulating, shouting to the driver to turn towards the sea.

'Is it, though?' she thought. 'Is it better to be paranoid than dead?' But all the same she folded the email carefully and pushed it into the pocket of her jeans.

33

Max stood on the Common in a downpour of rain. It was too wet even to make notes. He examined the low wall decorated with flints, pebbled in stripes of blue and brown, and thought how he must not forget the stones that were angled so neatly along the top. Behind the wall the houses looked ghostly, their windows dark and cold. He'd have to set them in sunlight, tie them to the others if they were to fit into his scroll. He took a shortcut back to Gertrude's, down a narrow, waterlogged lane, the reeds and grasses overhanging just at the height of his waist. He arrived, dripping, and was surprised to find Gertrude sitting at the table, making a drawing of her foot. She had her stocking off and one leg propped up on a chair.

'Hello,' she said, blushing, but she kept her foot where it was.

'Am I disturbing you?' Max unrolled his scroll.

'Not at all, I just don't usually see you here at this time of day.' She removed her other stocking and swapped feet.

Quickly, before the sight of her toes erased it, Max took up a pencil and sketched in the wall, the stacks of the chimneys, the row of attic windows and the path. He painted the sky, a light-filled wash of blue, ignoring his last glimpse of the cottages, cold and miserable against a streak of black.

'Will you be here on Saturday?' she asked. 'For dinner, I mean?'

'Yes,' he said. Did she know that he'd been using the racket of the weather to slip out of her house each night? 'Of course I will be here.'

'A warming meal . . .' she was talking to herself now. 'Soup, I think. Mushroom, or minestrone. And chicken pie. Some kind of crumble, perhaps . . . we could use up the last of the apples . . .'

Max nodded. He wanted to get back to mixing colours. Sunshine and the yellow-green of grass before the rain.

'You'll be able to meet Thomas Everson. It is ridiculous . . .'

But Max had begun to paint each pebble and although he could feel that she was talking, could hear the hum and echo of her voice, the inside of each word was lost to him as he worked on.

When eventually he looked up, her feet were done. She had replaced her stockings and was examining her sketch. The feet were a mirror image of each other, looming upright like boulders, the toes a mountain range. Max smoothed out the remainder of his scroll and found the creamy paper barely reached the end of the table.

'You're almost there.' Gertrude came round to face him. 'Only six or seven houses more?'

He looked at her. So she'd been counting, waiting for it to end, and he saw the colour on her face and neck of a whole summer of sun. 'I haven't forgotten our agreement . . .'

Gertrude shook her head. 'Don't worry about that.'

'But I did promise . . .'

'It's all right.' She put a hand out to him. 'It was I that promised. I promised Kaethe that I'd find something for you to do.'

'Yes.'

'And I have.' There was laughter in her eyes, and quickly he looked away.

'Thankyou,' he said, and for a moment there was silence.

'My young artist friend,' she went on. 'He's been giving me lessons in life drawing, and I . . .' She looked irrepressibly happy, happier than she'd looked since Kaethe first got ill. 'I've been helping him organize his things. Sorting, clearing, labelling. In fact I think he may be developing the village labelling mania. If it carries on, I'll have to find him help of quite a different kind.' Gertrude began to giggle like a girl. 'This morning, for the first time in a month, he was wearing socks that matched!'

*   *   *

The house was silent when Max stepped out into the night. The rain had lightened but the wind was wild, tearing at the branches, sending leaves and birds and tiny helpless insects gusting through the dark. He slipped out from the shelter of the porch and fought his way along the lane. The wind blew hard against him, trying with each roll to force him back. It took him twenty minutes to reach the harbour, clinging to walls and hedges, stepping side on into the gale, and then it turned and took him with it, rushing him down towards the sea. He felt he could have stretched his arms out and been billowed on, but instead he clung to the railings of the bridge. The houses all around were boarded up and empty. The Tea Room had closed for the winter, and the studios were shuttered up until the spring. A pale yellow beam flickered towards him from the Sea House, a candle stretching out an arm. Max began to run, lurching against the force of the gale, the earth oozing up water, puddles like lakes forming from below. 'Elsa!' he warned her as the screen door slammed.

Elsa was in bed. She was leafing through a book of photographs. *Israel: The Founding of a Nation*. Sent to her that morning by a friend. Max peeled off his coat and his jacket. He began to roll away the greased wool of his sweater, when he caught her watching him as if he were performing a striptease.

'Yes?' Self-consciously he removed his trousers and his socks, and, his hands still icy, he seized her sleepy form.

'In three days' time,' she said, 'he will be here.'

'In three days' time. Yes.' Max flung the covers off her and began to kiss each plane and crevice of her body, feeling the sweetness of his lust like honey, the blood in his ears like a storm. 'We must not waste a minute.'

'All right.' She was laughing, her face dissolving into crescents, her eyes, her eyelids and her mouth. Love, I love, ich liebe liebe love, he sang to her with his whole body, and it was only much later that he understood what she had said.

Three days, two nights, and one of them was gone. He got

up and dressed himself in the grey light of the morning. His clothes were damp and he felt shivery with grief. He bowed his head and marched back through the bitter weather, setting up his paints and his brushes, linking one cottage to another with a black swirl of sleet. Gertrude found him when she came down for breakfast, sketching the tall brick house that looked out over the river.

'Have you been out already?' she asked, noticing the dark ends of his trousers, and in answer he pulled his coat back on and slipped into the rain.

All day he hurried back and forth, memorizing small sections of the building. The two low windows on either side of the front door, the cacti lined along the sills. There was a model of a boat set on the doorstep and a necklace of dusty shells in the porch. Elsa found him by the fishermen's huts late in the afternoon. 'You agreed' – she stood before him – 'we wouldn't waste a moment.'

Max looked at her. Two days, he thought, in two days' time . . . He was weighted down by the burden of his stubbornness, but he could not shake it off. Instead he shrugged at the weather and made small measuring movements with his hands and eye in order that he might bring the proportions of each building home. Eventually Elsa walked away from him. Her narrow back was wrapped in black, her head bent to pick her way between the puddles. No. He watched her go. Please don't. Stay. But he made no move to follow her, and his voice stayed tight inside his head.

Max worked right into the evening, giving up on sunshine and painting in the storm. It was satisfying to mix the blacks and greys, to give the rain an angle as it came sleeting down.

'Did Elsa Lehmann have any advice for you?' Gertrude asked, laying out a game of patience on a small round table by the fire.

'Elsa . . .' Max caught at the name.

'Your letters. Did she mention to which publisher you might send them?'

'No.' It occurred to him that he had left Henry's letters on the

Sea House table, had painted the last stretch of his scroll without their help.

'No,' Max told her. 'She hasn't decided on the best place to send them yet.'

'I see,' Gertrude nodded and she continued with the cards.

Max lay in bed and watched the water spilling down the panes, his lip jutting miserably to think he need not be alone. He could be with Elsa, could have her body in the warm spoon of his own. Instead, an extra quilt pressed down on him, the blankets so dense and heavy he was unable to get warm. Inch by inch he dared his feet into the ice stretch of the sheet, and then he was asleep, dreaming, striking out through puddles, hoping to land on the shores of Hiddensee although each time the tide swept him away. Halt, halt. His drawer was floating by and he lunged after it, and there, undamaged, was the Renoir. He steered it home, dragged it up to the room which housed his table, and slotted it safely out of sight. His legs now were in a stew of heat. He tried to move them, throw off the quilt, but instead he had gone back to the art dealer in Cork Street, sweat pouring from his face as he listened to the man explain it was a buyer's market. He wouldn't get much for his second-rate Renoir, with so many orphaned paintings for sale. The man spoke as if it were a mystery, so many works of art suddenly unowned, carelessness perhaps, stupidity? And then Kaethe's face in oils was looking down at him from the landing of their home. 'I am alone,' he told her through the ceiling, and with a huge effort he forced himself awake.

Gertrude nudged pastry into the curve of the tin. It was strong and springy and gave her small quivers of delight. 'Alf?' She thought she heard the creak of the front door. 'Is that you?'

The boy was sitting on the bench pulling off his boots. His hair was plastered down, water dripping from his fringe. 'La, la la la la la la laaaaaaa.' He was singing. A perfect ripple of the scales.

Gertrude watched him as he tugged, the notes swelling with the effort of pulling off one boot. 'La la la la la la la laaaa.'

'How was Miss Cheese?' she asked, but his face when he looked up at her was mute.

Gertrude poured mashed apple into the pie dish and began to roll the crust. 'Would you set the table for me?'

Alf took napkins from the bureau drawer and teased the squares of cloth through wooden rings. He arranged the knives in diminishing sizes, the soup spoon to their right.

'Thankyou.' Gertrude lifted her sheet of pastry, floating it down over the apple like a quilt. She dented the sides, dusting them with milk, and slid it on to the larder shelf to wait. 'La la la la la la la laaaaa,' Gertrude sang as she boiled chicken and stirred flour into butter for a sauce. So many pies, she worried, but it was too late to start again. She had tried to get fish but, the weather being stormy, the men were unable to get out. 'Four dabs last week,' one fisherman told her, 'that was all the catch,' and he'd gone back to the Gannon Room to wait.

At seven-thirty exactly Thomas Everson arrived. He was carrying a black umbrella with a malacca handle, and his shirt had all its buttons in place. Gertrude, when she opened the door to him, saw that the weather had changed. The rain had stopped, the wind had calmed and the moon, visible for the first time in a week, was full. 'Max,' she called up the stairs, and, irritable suddenly with his inability to hear her, she strode up and knocked on his door. 'Our guests are arriving,' she shouted and, bracing herself for what she might see, she peered in.

Max was kneeling on the floor, hemmed in by his scroll. It started by the door – her own house, the walls a wash of raspberry – and ran up and down the village, over his bed, along the floor, crossing itself by the harbour, the gulls flocking by the river mouth. There was the Green, its triangle of grass, the pottery, the row of red-roofed cottages winding into Palmers Lane. There were blue roofs and orange walls, great bursts of foliage, and small spiked flowers.

Max had unrolled the last stretch under the window and was half-pinned behind the door.

'I am finished.' He looked up at her, and she put out a hand and helped him leap across.

'It's wonderful.' Gertrude stood and stared at it, the chimney pots, each one surprisingly different, the weathervanes, the intricate patterns of brick. There were swallows on the telegraph wires, the Dunnits' dog, its head on its paws, their chickens, scratching, white and grey. 'Can we exhibit it? Right now? Thomas is downstairs . . . We could . . .'

'NO!' Max reached for the door, but Gertrude had the handle.

'Let me have one more look.' There was the advert for the Natural History Exhibition pinned to the wall outside the shop, and another for the August bank holiday fête. Punch and Judy. Coconut shies. White Elephant and Games. There was the Gannon Room, its weathered boarding so badly in want of repair. But what surprised Gertrude were the people. A boy rolled a ball along Mill Lane, and two women, one pushing a baby, chatted as they ambled across the Green. Three men stood outside The Ship, reckless somehow in their summer clothes, leaning and talking, making jokes. 'Max.' she put an arm around him. She had expected his vision to be silent, flint and brick and stone. 'It's the most beautiful thing I've seen this year.'

'Thankyou.' He closed the door, and together they went downstairs.

Elsa was standing in the hall, smiling at Thomas, stretching out a hand. 'I see you two have met,' Gertrude broke in.

'Thomas Everson, Elsa Lehmann, and this' – she turned as if to introduce a minor Royal – 'is my guest of the summer, Max Meyer.'

'Hello, hello. Good evening.' Thomas blushed and Gertrude poured them all sherry.

'So what is it you do here in Steerborough?' Elsa turned back to Thomas, and he explained how he'd been left Fern Cottage by a godmother who had died earlier in the year.

'Your parents chose well for you,' she said.

'Yes. I lost my father when I was seven years old, and since then, it's true, people have been kind.' There was a moment's silence as respectfully they all took a sip of sherry.

'In the war?' Elsa asked, and Thomas said that no, his father had died of pneumonia a month before the start.

'Will we wait?' Gertrude looked towards the door. 'The pie might keep . . .' The pie in fact was already ruining, the pastry sinking into the sauce.

'Wait for Klaus?' Elsa looked as if she had entirely forgotten her husband. 'No, of course. He would insist we start. I've been expecting him since lunchtime. He must have been delayed on the road.'

Gertrude brought through a tureen of soup and started to ladle it out.

'Thankyou,' Max muttered, but he was lost to them tonight. His ears were full of noises. Crackling and whining, whistling. Am I losing my balance? he wondered as his spoon swayed before his face and, to steady himself, he repeated, 'I've finished my scroll, my scroll, my scroll.'

'A second helping?' Gertrude was leaning into him.

Yes, of course, but he didn't want to sit still. He wanted to race out into the night, drown his ears against the raging weather, watch for phosphorescence in the sea. Dutifully he ate. Spooning in the shards and shreds of pastry, sauce and chicken, custard, fruit. Eventually they were released from the table, and they stood uncomfortably before the unlit fire.

'It doesn't seem that Klaus will arrive tonight,' Gertrude said.

'No,' Elsa agreed.

'Leave the dishes.' Gertrude stretched, to show them that the evening was finished. 'Betty will be in in the morning.'

'So . . .' Elsa fetched her shawl and coat. 'I'd better get back, in case . . .'

Thomas stepped into place beside her. 'I could walk you home, I'm going that way myself.'

Max stumbled to her other side. 'No,' he said, exceedingly loudly. 'I shall walk you home.' There was a pause and everybody laughed.

'Perhaps I should come too?' Gertrude suggested, but all the same she hustled both men into the porch. 'If you're not back by midnight,' she called to Max as they started down the lane, 'I'll fetch the lifeboat men,' and Elsa turned and waved at her and thanked her for giving them all so much hot food.

'Hot food!' Gertrude shook her head, and she cleared the plates herself.

Max shook Thomas's hand on the corner of the Green.

'Goodnight,' he said to make it clear that they were parting, and he hurried on with Elsa. The moon was high and bright, but as soon as they had stepped down into the dip of the harbour they found themselves wading through water, ankle-deep. 'I am sorry.' Max tried to take her in his arms, but she pulled away, aiming for the skeleton of ridges between one stretch of sea water and the next. He followed awkwardly, trying to keep up, the wind whipping against him, flinging her shawl into his eyes. Eventually they climbed up on to the wooden veranda and were almost blown through the front door. 'I am so very sorry,' he tried again, and Elsa put a finger to her lips. She looked around. The room was empty. She ran to the ladder and began to climb. 'No,' she called, finally smiling at him, and idiotic with relief he followed her up.

The room was cold. The windows shivered in their panes. Max stoked the iron stove with logs, waiting for it to flame, and when he looked round Elsa had climbed, with all her clothes on, into bed. 'Come,' she said, and she held out an arm. Max pushed in beside her. He rubbed his woollen feet against her stockinged toes and slid one finger through the buttonhole of her blouse. She forced her hands into the lining of his sleeves and nuzzled her face against his shirt. 'I missed you.'

He held her so tight that steam began to rise from the checked

245

wool of her coat. The stove was roaring now, and Max felt his body melting under the bedclothes, Elsa burning into him as they lay wrapped together, their fingers enmeshed in seams and slits, fumbling with vests and suspenders, their blood about to burst. There were pearl drops of sweat on Elsa's forehead and the colours in her face were unbearably bright.

'What is that?' she asked when they lay cooling, the covers pushed off them, the fire almost burnt down. Max looked at her and saw that she was frightened.

'Surely it's not possible for him to arrive . . .'

'Shh.' Elsa gripped her arm. 'There it is again!' She got up and went to the trapdoor. 'My God.' She looked across at him and just then he felt it – the house shuddered as if it had been hit. Max hitched his trousers up with half a brace. He crouched beside her and looked down, and there below them, in three foot of water, the furniture was floating about in the room. The table, the bench, the high-backed chairs, knocking against one another in the flood. Max put his foot on the ladder, but Elsa caught his shirt. 'No,' she screamed, and just then the top half of the dresser toppled on to its back. The cups and plates and saucers lay in it like a boat and they watched as it steered itself towards the ladder and rammed against the wood.

Max and Elsa sprang back from the hole. 'God in heaven,' she said, and she ran to the window. They were in the middle of the sea. Water spread away from them on every side. 'HELP,' she called, and the room shivered with another crash. Max put his arm around her and pointed. The white hull of the Tea Room was moving. It had come free from its stilts and was sailing in to land. They watched it bobbing, elegant, the lace curtains at the window, a geranium in a patterned pot, close enough to see as it floated towards the black mouth of the estuary. 'HELP,' they both called together, and Max looked up at the roof above them to see where they might shelter next. Little Heaven was moving now, surging and rocking in against its neighbour, a low house, flimsy, taking it too as it swept towards the shore.

Elsa and Max ran to the far window and looked behind them at the sea. It was coming in, wave after wave, submerging the dunes, pouring into the marshes. Below them the water had risen. The chairs were on their backs, the table sunk, but the dresser was still there, rocking back and forth. Max stared down into it, wondering, could they use it as a raft, when he saw a bottle floating past. He lowered himself on to the stumps of the ladder and clinging with one hand to the boards above him, he hooked it up.

'Whisky!' He held it out to Elsa. She cracked open the top and took a long hot swallow. 'I won it in the raffle at the fête.' Max poured it into his mouth, and with each thud and shudder they swallowed a gulp more.

'Spare sheets, blankets, pillowcases, and life jackets!' Elsa remembered. They rushed to the cupboard at the end of the bed and found the mildewed jackets lying on a shelf. They put them on, almost incapable with laughter as they fiddled with buckles and straps, and when eventually they took up their lookout posts again they saw theirs was the only house left.

'Look at our view now.' There was nothing between them and dry land, just water, in a huge dark sweep. Max reached out for the bottle but Elsa held him still. 'I want you to know' – she pressed one hand to her stomach – 'I think . . . I am almost certain' – tears oozed up out of her eyes – 'that you've given me a child.'

Max held her. If the tide could only turn, take the house with it, drift them to a hidden slice of land. Take them to Holland, Belgium, take them to Australia, where they could start the second half of the century in peace.

34

A small crowd gathered to watch as Nick's car was attached to the back of the truck. 'You can sit in it,' the AA man told him, 'or come up front with me.' Nick swung his bag on to the high seat as if to claim a place, and Lily reached for his hand. 'Couldn't you stay?'

'Well . . . you can't ask for your vehicle to be towed a hundred miles, and then stay and have a picnic.'

'So it's you they're rescuing?' The certainty of his going had released her, and there, reflected in the tint of his glasses, was her smile. 'You'll miss the fête,' she said, 'and the Millennium exhibition.'

'I'll live.' He kissed her warmly. 'And, Lily, please, don't hate our life.' The van whirred into life, its black and yellow squares a hornets' nest of drama, Nick's car, low slung, almost sheepish as it trailed behind.

Very slowly Lily followed them up the hill. What will I do now? It struck her that from today she had only two weeks until her lease expired. 'Why,' she'd asked the lady at the estate agents, 'can't I take it on?' and the woman had looked at her, surprised. 'It's only available until the first of September,' she'd repeated, and Lily had been forced to go outside and stare into the shop window at the farms and cottages, beach huts and converted barns, all for sale at more than she could ever imagine being able to afford.

Two weeks, she told herself, and she tried to imagine going home. Heard the metal echo of the door as it clicked into its lock. There she was, dragging her bags along the corridor, anxious not to drop a sock, and she knew as she came into the bedroom, felt the bewilderment with which she viewed the wall of ordered clothes, that she couldn't go back. Maybe her old studio flat was empty. Could she risk the smirk of her landlord as she carried up her things? 'Still hanging on to those paintings?' he'd ask as she hauled them up the stairs. It would be cheaper and easier to stay in Suffolk. Find work, find somewhere else to rent. Grae's cottage was still empty . . . She glanced into its black windows. But she stopped herself, shaking out the thought.

Lily lay face down on Fern Cottage sofa, her legs trailing off over the arm. A chatter of birdsong trilled in through the open window and with half an eye she traced the rainbow edge of patterns trapped in the corners of each pane. What was she going to do? For a moment she was back home with her mother, kneeling beside her, stringing up bead necklaces, colouring and clipping, winding wool round discs of cardboard to make pompoms for which they never found a use. If only she still lived there, she could go home, and then a shadow fell across her from the open door. She roused herself numbly, gathering her strength to lift and turn, find out who it was, when a weight flung itself on top of her and pressed her down. Her chin knocked on the rough edge of the sofa, and her leg was twisted to one side. She struggled, her mouth pressed into the fluff and dust of brown, and then, finding herself pinned immovably, she screamed so loudly she thought her voice might tear. Run. Even if he has a gun, one in four, four in one, four in one hundred, and then she remembered her elbow and prised it free. She swung it down towards the floor and rammed it up with all her strength.

'Ahhhhhhhh.' Grae was lying on the carpet, holding his ribs where he'd been stabbed.

'My God.' She crawled towards him. 'Grae, my God, what are you doing?'

Grae doubled over in pain.

'Grae.' She sat beside him, stroking his head, breathing in the oil-damp tobacco scent of his hair.

'What am I doing??' He looked at her coldly. 'I was trying to give you a kiss.' He pulled away, wincing as he stood up. 'I don't half know how to choose them.' His mouth was thin with disappointment as he walked out of the room.

'Grae . . .' she called, but only softly. She stayed sitting on the floor. 'Oh God,' and she took Nick's gift from her back pocket, 'Tips on Staying Safe', and tore it up.

Lehmann's last letter lay in the heap of books by the door. The postmark was just visible. November 1953. *Elsa. You were right. The road is blocked, half sunk with water, earth from fields lying in the way. I have given up and returned home and tomorrow I shall try again. But I thought I would send this letter in case the postman has more luck in getting through than me, but more than anything I am sending it out of habit, so that you will know that whatever happens in this life, or in the next, I will always think of you. I want you to know that I am sorry for the things we couldn't do together, the places we didn't go, the people we had to leave behind, the little ones, invited, who chose not to come. But more than that, I'm grateful for the time we had. Don't ever be sad. You loved me, and that was all I asked.*

Lily read the letter again. Klaus Lehmann, 1900–1953. Did he know that he was going to die? She pushed her hand into the envelope, but there was nothing to give even the smallest clue. She went through to the bathroom and splashed water on her face. Her chin was grazed from her tussle on the sofa and her eyes were red. Very slowly she began to brush her hair. Lehmann, driving through the swollen roads of East Anglia, following his last letter, silt and earth from fields washing across his way. Was that how it happened? Or was he ill? And then she knew, and it shocked her that she'd never been quite sure. Grae wasn't the wife-beater. She thought she'd known it, but now she realized, she'd always had a doubt. 'I must apologize.' She was still brushing and her hair began to lift with static until she looked like a clown and she had to sprinkle it with water to smoothe it straight.

*   *   *

Lily walked the long way round to get to Grae. She needed time to calm herself and to stop her face from creasing into a mortified smile each time she thought of her elbow and its power. She crossed the bridge and walked along by the river, planning to cut back on to the ridge of sea defences, and step down to him across the sand. But once she was on the marshes, she couldn't stop. She was drawn on by a field of flowering thistle, its down white as a bed, and by the soft wood of the walkways, the wire mesh clinging to the planks like moss. Visions of Grae crowded in on her. His blue eyes squinting from the window of the waterlogged car, his mouth twisting away from a smile. She saw him working in Fern Cottage garden, sawing and hammering, his hat pulled over his ears, his plaid shirt jewelled with rain. And then his face so close to hers, laughing, the blue and sand colours of him, the smooth lobes of his ears. A sharp flick of desire licked through her, tingling in her knees, and then, remembering, she cupped her elbow in her hand and winced. She could feel the ache of it and, closing her eyes for a moment, she moaned with regret.

She was almost at the mill. She knew this ground now, in the same way she'd known each inch of pavement, each kerbstone of every corner of her walk to school. She knelt down to stroke the silver thread of grasses growing out of the river's edge, picking one to whisk away the swarms of midges hanging in the air.

The mill water was high, still swamped from last night's tides, and, as she stared down into it and then up through its cracked roof at the sky, she was gripped by the thought that she was not alone. Stop it, she ordered, the wretched 'Tips on Staying Safe' spelling itself in her mind, but her skin was cold with worry and her pulse was out of her control. Carefully, silently, she twisted in the doorway. There was nothing there but marsh and sea, a deep oblong of sky. She stepped out and turned, and then she saw them – the bog man, Bob, and A. L. Lehmann, tussling in a kind of dance. Their profiles were identical, their eyes over-shadowed by the same unruly brows. 'Take it,' Albert Lehmann hissed and, as they wrestled, Lily saw that he was forcing money into the other man's hand. Bob staggered back, the notes slotted into the black slashes of his arm, and then, standing very still, he let himself be hugged.

Lily crept round the side of the mill and ran. She streaked along the plank paths and hurtled through the avenue of grass, scrambling over the hillocks of mud until she was in the woods. More slowly she climbed the gate. There ahead of her was the lane that cut back up to the village hall and, as she expected, the grey Morris, parked half in the ditch. She stopped and caught her breath, and then, leaning on the faded bonnet, she decided she would wait.

'Excuse me.' At least an hour had passed, and Albert Lehmann was fumbling with a key, attempting to open his car door.

'What happened to him?' Lily asked, scrambling up from her seat against the tyre.

Lehmann slid in behind the wheel. 'It was an accident,' he muttered irritably. 'He didn't start the fire.'

'The fire?' Lily was bent over at the door, looking in at him through the car window.

'He wanted to preserve it. Our father's design. Lehmann's design, I mean. Through all those years, more than anything else that was what he wanted.' Albert started up his car. 'And then, when he discovered . . . well . . . it was hard for him. He'd been living in the house. But it was an accident.' He looked hard at Lily. 'He even called the fire brigade when it got out of control, but there'd been an arson attack on the Common, children setting fire to gorse, and by the time they got here the house was burning and he was just waiting by the wall.'

Lily was hardly following. 'When he discovered what?'

'Nothing, nothing.'

The car was nudging forward, roaring as it pulled out of the ditch. 'But I meant your father. What happened to him in 1953?'

'He never meant it to happen.' He shook his head, and sorrow-fully he drove off along the lane.

Lily bought four ice-creams from the Mr Whippy van and carried them down to the beach. She stepped over the sand, walking more quickly as they began to melt, arriving triumphant by the beach huts with all four ice-creams intact. But the beach hut was deserted, its window boarded up, and when she pulled at the handle she found a padlock on the door. Lily sat down at the table, still there with its three chairs and, slowly, in rotation, she began to lick the drips from each ice-cream.

'Our father,' she repeated, 'our father's design.' So A. L. Lehmann and the Bogman were brothers. Robert and Albert. Bob and Bert. And she remembered the photograph of the woman, haunted, holding those swaddled twins.

35

Gertrude was at the vicarage handing out blankets and warm drinks while Betty Wynwell stood by the window waiting for news of Alf. 'He'll be all right.' Gertrude pressed a cup of tea on her, whisky stirred in with the milk. 'He's out with Mabbs, he'll keep him safe.' But she felt a stab of worry as together they stared through the black glass.

It was Alf who had woken her. 'Miss Jilks!' His voice was familiar, although she couldn't remember ever having heard it before. 'There's a tempest blowing.' He was shaking her shoulder, 'Your friends are out.' It was only then she realized she was no longer dreaming. She rose and drew the curtain at the window. Water was lapping at the edges of the lawn.

'I'll wake Max.' But Alf said no, he was already up.

The boy waited while she dressed, pulling her clothes on over her nightgown, slipping her feet into wellington boots. Hand in hand they hurried towards the harbour. They stooped low, blinded by the wind, feeling for fallen wood, until they rounded the corner by The Ship. Gertrude had been expecting to battle down the hill, cross the bridge on to the mud flats, dash between the scaly stilts of houses until she reached the dunes. But here, a mile early, was the sea. A flat grey surge of water resting at their feet.

'Alf?' She turned to him, and he pointed towards the horizon to where there was a light. The Sea House – alone, without its neighbours, a square black shadow, its lower half submerged.

They stood and stared, and then a group of men appeared. Klaus Lehmann at the head of them, his clothes wringing, his face disfigured with alarm. The men were dragging a boat. They slid it into the water and before even one of them could stop him, Alf slipped out from her side and clambered in. Dick Mabbs took the oars, barking to Klaus to sit down, and although Gertrude called to Alf, shouted for him to climb out, he turned away from her and kept his eyes fixed on the light.

'Klaus,' she shouted, 'hand him out to me.' But Klaus's back was turned. The other men stood on the shore, shaking their heads, their eyes slanted as if they understood, and then one of them turned to Gertrude and said she'd be needed up at the vicarage to see to those that had been washed out of their homes.

'Yes, of course.' But she was afraid to leave. She watched the little boat plunge forward, lift and spin on the waves, until eventually, feeling the hard eyes of the men on her, she turned and made her way up the hill, where the vicarage was a blaze of candlelight and every member of the WI was rushing round with towels.

'He'll be back soon now, don't you worry.' She put an arm round Mrs Wynwell's shoulders, and felt the woman take a thorny breath in an effort not to cry.

Behind them the door opened and a family of five were ushered in. They'd been stranded in a holiday bungalow up by the Bailey bridge, and they'd stood on the roof with their baby wrapped in an eiderdown until two men from Eastonknoll had rowed across to them. The oldest boy was shivering and chattering as he told his tale, how they'd watched the river swell on either side, taking with it boats, the rails of jetties, and even a man hanging on to what looked like a door. He had shouted and called to them as he rushed past. Chickens, he'd seen, and the body of a cow, and all the time he talked, his mother stared from one to the other of her children, as if she couldn't believe that they'd survived.

Elsa and Max stood at the Sea House window waiting for the stilts to give way. There were no lights on land, the storm must have knocked out the electricity, and as far as they could tell the water reached beyond the Ship, trapping the inhabitants of Steerborough up above the Green.

'Max,' Elsa whispered, straining past the curve of his arm. 'Look.' She turned him around, and there, fighting its way towards them, was a boat. It was a tiny boat, just visible, its oars slashing the water, its prow slamming into hollows, as it fell from the top of each wave. There were three people in it, bent against the spray, and they were forcing their way towards the Sea House.

Elsa pulled Max down below the level of the window. 'The baby may be Klaus's.' She looked him in the eye and, taking one more swig of whisky, she leant out and screamed into the storm for help.

Elsa was the first to climb down. Max watched her as she stepped into the boat and fell into her husband's arms. He turned his back on them and climbed down too, and it was only when the fisherman turned the boat around that he saw the other figure in the boat was Alf. 'Are you all right?' he asked him, taking his wet hand in his, and Alf nodded, watching the disappearing mass of the Sea House as the tide swept them back in to land.

Lehmann was wet, shaking so violently that Elsa, even with both arms around him, couldn't hold him still. 'He tried to swim to you,' Mabbs told her. 'We had to fish him out with the promise of a boat.'

'Klaus' – her head rested on his arm – 'we agreed you would be careful.' She turned her eyes away from Max. 'Your mother was right not to trust me.'

'No.' Lehmann was stuttering with cold. 'You mustn't say that.' Max leant forward and offered him the whisky, and he took it, although without seeming to recognize that he was there. There were only a few drops left, wasting as his teeth rattled against the glass, and instinctively both Elsa and Max brought their hands up to hold the bottle still. How long was it going to take them? He peered into the dark, but there was no knowing any more where the water ended and the land began.

*   *   *

Gertrude and Betty Wynwell were folding blankets when the door burst open. 'We've saved them.' It was Alf. 'They won't be drowned.' His eyes and mouth, his teeth, even his hair glowed with pride. His mother dropped her blanket. She lifted him up, and for a moment Alf seemed to forget he was one of the lifeboat rescue men and buried his face in her neck.

Dick Mabbs, Max and Elsa struggled in with Klaus. He looked as if he had lost the power of his legs and his face was almond-white. They laid him out before the fire. His wet clothes were peeled away, dry clothes were brought for him and he was swaddled in blankets like a child. Gertrude pressed sweet tea to his lips but he coughed and choked and the liquid dribbled out.

'We need a doctor,' Elsa whispered, but the news came through that Eastonknoll was cut off by water on all sides. A woman and her little boy were drowned, and three old ladies were last seen trying to reach high ground.

'Take some tea yourself,' Gertrude told Elsa, who was crying without pause, but as she raised the cup to her mouth, she began to retch. Mortification flooded her face, and Max, who had been standing by like a sentry, turned away so suddenly that even Lehmann, prostrated between them, seemed to flinch.

'I'm sorry, I'm sorry.' Elsa laid her head on Klaus's chest, her tears, Gertrude imagined, seeping through into his waterlogged lungs. 'He's burning up,' she called, 'he's burning.'

Between them she and Gertrude moved him away from the fire. They laid cool flannels on his face and arms, dabbing at his neck and the inside of his elbows as he batted away their hands. 'What can we give him?' Elsa asked.

Gertrude looked around. There was no medicine here. Just scones and tea and blankets. If she had her book of cordials, she might find something in it to bring his fever down. 'Max?' She could remember only a recipe for cough mixture, vinegar and honey, and a cure for eczema: dock root mixed with lard. Gertrude squeezed herself between the people, eating, sleeping, chattering with high spirits or shock, and went to the door where she'd last seen him. 'Max?' she called into the dark, but he had gone.

'The tide has turned!' The news came in, and fresh tea was passed round in celebration, slabs of fruit cake and drop scones hot from the range.

36

Lily was still sitting outside the beach hut when she heard music drifting towards her from the Green. She stood up and stretched, and as she did so she kicked the uneaten cornets into the reeds. Where was Grae? She squinted at the horizon, Was he expecting another storm? And glancing up at the clear blue sky, she trudged off through the dunes.

The Green had transformed into a fair. Children, their faces painted – butterflies, leopards, cats and clowns, monsters, bumblebees and princesses – ran from game to game. Some tried their luck at bowling, throwing quoits, while others knocked coconuts from posts which actually fell when they were hit. The littlest ones dug for parcels in the lucky dip or bought tenpence tickets for the tombola. Behind a table two women and a man stood guarding a bowl of fruit. Lily watched as a boy paid his money and picked up a bell. As soon as it rang, the adults pulled blindfolds down over their eyes and began to spin their arms. They spun them fast until the bell rang again, and then they stopped and plunged their hands into the bowl.

'Bad luck.' The man smiled, pushing up his blindfold. 'Two bananas and a pear.' And as a consolation prize for failing to win on the human fruit machine the unlucky gambler was offered a boiled sweet.

There was a cake to guess the weight of. A doll that needed you to guess her name. And then the music that had led her here started up again. A band was playing right outside Lily's house. It was the girl from the ferry, singing into a microphone still in her rowing clothes, her heavy boots, her jeans, a short sleeved T-shirt showing the smooth brown ripple of her arms. There was a boy on

keyboards with bright white hair, and another, darker boy who
played the sax.

> 'Now you say you're sorry,
> Now I'm with someone new,
> But you can cry me a river . . .
> Cry me a river . . .
> Because I cried a river over you . . .'

The girl looked up on the word 'river' and smiled, and the whole
Green smiled with her.

Lily hummed along to the music as she sifted through a stall of
clothes. She pulled out polka-dot aprons, rose-patterned dresses in
size 20 and up, candy-striped shirts, their cuffs scorched by irons,
and a green velvet jacket with '70s lapels.

'One pound the lot,' Ethel called to her, hardly visible over the
mountain of remaining clothes, and Lily, rather than throw them
back, rummaged for her change.

A little further on, two tables had been pushed together. They
were piled with lampshades, napkin rings, dishcloths and bowls.
Scattered on the grass around were deckchairs and an old bicycle
with rusty wheels. Lily picked up a small tin saucepan with a
compartment inside dented like the petals of a flower. What it was
she didn't know, but it was irresistibly pretty. 35p the label said and
Lily held out her money.

'Oh,' the stall-holder protested. 'The egg poaching pan. That was
from a previous fête. It's 25p now.'

The window of Fern Cottage was latched open, and Lily pushed
her purchases through. What on earth am I going to do with them?
she wondered, but she couldn't help herself, she went out to search
for more.

At the far end of the Green the raffle was being drawn, the
numbers and prizes ringing out from a loudspeaker – a hamper
from Stoffer's, a bottle of whisky, dinner for two at The Ship! And

then a whistle blew and the children flew from every corner of the Green to where the Punch and Judy show had been set up. They arranged themselves in rows, cross-legged, gazing up, and then the Punch and Judy man appeared from behind his booth. He was tall and thin with a striped blazer, and his nose was miraculously hooked to fit his job. The children tensed towards him, their faces alight, and when he had them enchanted, he stepped back inside. Lily moved closer to watch. Bash went Punch. Waaa went Judy. Grrr went the dog. Hurrah shouted the children when the policeman appeared. Bash went Punch. Waa went the baby. Lily looked round for Em and Arrie, trying to identify them in the crowd, but if they were there, she couldn't tell through the disguise of so much face paint, however hard she stared at the straggled ends of hair.

The wind had calmed. It felt almost warm, and Max looked around him in amazement at the limbs of trees, the toppled chimneys, a beach hut lying on its side on the Green. He passed two fishermen carrying an old man in an armchair, and another guiding his blind wife. He expected to find the water receded, but the sea was still there, stretching out from the Wynwells' wooden cabin, a small wet stride away on its mound. Max raised his eyes to the sun, an angry orange in a slate-grey sky, and there, below it, rising from the water, was the Sea House, still intact.

Very slowly he walked along Mill Lane, round the curve of the drive to Gertrude's house. The front door was open, the rooms still dark, and he went upstairs and stepped across his scroll. He sat surrounded by it, gathering up his things – his clothes and boots, his paints, his hat. He looked round for the briefcase of his letters and remembered he could do without them now.

People passed him as he walked along the street, nodding as they hurried on their way. He walked past the vicarage, its chimneys pumping out smoke, its candles burning low, past the church, and on along the road until he'd missed the turning for the railway and left the village behind.

There was a banner outside the village hall advertising the Millennium exhibition. Lily paid her twenty pence and went in. A wall of screens had been set up, covered with large photos, and there she was, on the very first one, standing outside Fern Cottage with her key.

But the photograph wasn't of her. It was of the house. *A photographic record of Steerborough*, the caption read, and winding through the hall was every building in the village. Lily felt ridiculously happy, moving from one house to the next, allowed to stare quite openly at everybody's home. There was Marsh End, darkened and closed in, A. L. Lehmann's Morris parked in the long grass. Lily followed the curve of Mill Lane, looked through the wrought-iron railings at striped lawns, at a garden of statues, at a doorstep crowded with dogs. She inspected the first beginnings of the building emerging from its site. The photo had been taken from above, and beyond the four walls Lily saw the blackened tangle of a hedge. The branches were still there as if just in time it had been doused with water, but the leaves were gone, the undergrowth scorched flat. It occurred to her this might have been where Hidden House once stood. But how could it have been hidden if it was here? She stared at a wooden bungalow in Church Lane. The sky was turquoise above it and the owner, an old man, peered out from a garden of hollyhocks twelve foot high. Beside it was another garden, competing with next door, bursting with nasturtiums, Iceland poppies, dotted with forget-me-nots the same colour as the sky. If she could find a way to live here for another year . . . She could teach life drawing. Begin painting again. Maybe she could cut up her new material and make pillowcases, napkins, children's dresses, re-present them, revolutionized, at next year's fête. Or she could do all of these things, and take a job at the Eastonknoll hotel as well.

She was about to leave when she noticed a sign, and an arrow pointing to another room. *Special Exhibit*. She peered in, and there were a group of people hovering over a glass-topped table. A man was cranking a handle and with each turn they all crowded closer, smiling, shaking their heads, letting out small sighs. Lily stepped nearer and there, moving like the slowest film, was a painting of the village. She watched as the handle turned, its houses, lanes, gates and hedgerows hardly changed. There were animals and signposts, trees and flowers, some minutely drawn in pen and ink, others a blaze of abstract colour.

'Who painted this?' she asked.

'A visitor to the village. An artist. Max Joseph Meyer.' The man kept turning. 'One of the few lucky enough to have been taught by Cuthbert Henry. Meyer spent a summer here in 1953.' The man looked at her for a minute. 'As far as anyone knows, he never came back.' He wound the handle and there was Fern Cottage with Grae's abandoned house next door. 'There's been a recent exhibition of Meyer's in London. A resurgence of interest in him since his death.'

They were travelling along the street now, past the thatched cottage, moss-green even then, and then they turned the corner into Mill Lane. Lily held her breath. Hidden House, she would finally see it, in all its intricate detail, awash with colour, but there was nothing there. She looked up, about to ask, but the man was intently winding. There was the ferry man's hut, the jetty, the ferry man himself.

'Cuthbert Henry's son found a stack of drawings, and some rather good paintings too. He put on an exhibition at a gallery in London. Thomas Everson, you may know him? Lives in the village. He organized an outing. Yes and the Lehmann brothers, I've no idea why, but they were left land in Australia named in Meyer's will, although they didn't seem too happy about it! But it reminded me, all the fuss, about the scroll. I'm embarrassed to say it, but for years, really since the old Gannon Room was demolished, this scroll has been lying in a box under the stage. Here, if you look carefully, you can see where it's been joined.' Lily stared through the glass. The paper had been backed on to muslin, invisibly stitched. '123 foot long it is,' the man said proudly, and he continued to let it unroll.

There was The Ship, the wooden cabin below it, and, stretching out across what was now the car park, a group of white wooden houses on stilts. Lily watched them slowly cranking by, wondering what had become of them, wishing there was still a Tea Room, so inviting with its gingham curtains, and then she saw the Sea House, billowing out like a sail. It was so much bigger than the others, set forward, its weather-boarding silver, its plank steps grained with sand. There was a sign pinned to its porch. *To Let. Furnished*. Lily cupped a hand over her mouth. 'Thankyou,' she said to the man at the handle, and she ran from the hall.

Immediately she was caught up in a crowd of people, examining the plants and books on either side of the hall door. Frantic, she began to push, but people turned and looked at her with such bewilderment that she was forced to slow down. They're right, she told herself, there is no hurry, but then she found her way cordoned off by a game of tug of war. A rope was stretched across the Green and Alf was standing at its centre, blowing a whistle, rallying the children into teams. Trapped, she watched as they were counted, divided, allocated sides.

'PULL!' The whistle blew, and Alf strode up and down, roaring at each side in turn. Back and forth they slithered like one giant serpent until finally, dragging small bodies with it, the marker on the rope went over the chalk line. 'YES!!' A shout rang out from the victors and Alf flung a handful of sweets into the air. 'More,' the children screamed, leaping round him. 'More. More. More.'

Lily stepped over the abandoned rope. She picked up a stray sherbet lemon and, turning towards the harbour, she ran.

To Let, the sign still said. There was a London number printed below. 8306 2506. She didn't have a pen. 8306 2506, she repeated to herself, and for the first time in her life, she wished she had a mobile phone.

39

Dear Max, Gertrude wrote two days before the New Year of 1954. *I'm so sorry to have to give you the bad news, but Klaus Lehmann passed away this week, on Tuesday afternoon, at 4 p.m. He had been released from the hospital at Ipswich and was home at Hidden House, which he so loved, where we all thought he was bound to recover. But then his condition deteriorated, and his heart gave out. His heart. When all along we thought it was his lungs. I write to you because there will be a memorial here, and also because Elsa, in her dangerous condition – did you know that after all these years she is expecting a child? – needs support from all her friends. I have asked her to write, but she is laid low with grief. She says she does not want the baby, only wanted it for Klaus. I am sure once it is born that she will change her mind, but if this isn't so, if mother nature does not prove to be stronger than despair, then I have offered to take charge of it. I hope to prove, if I can, that it is possible for even the most unlucky infant to thrive.*

I wait to hear from you, and hope to see you next week, and thankyou again for leaving us the scroll.

Max had already packed. He had his ticket for Australia and the date of his boat, even a letter from the Hay Association welcoming him when he came.

> Say Hay for Happy,
> And you feel snappy,
> And you don't want to die . . .

No, he told himself, she doesn't love me. He would not change his mind.

40

8306 2506. Lily dialled for the fifteenth time that day and, as the numbers connected and the phone began to ring, she looked out over the Green. It was evening now and the stalls had gone, the games cleared away, the tables folded down. Either Em had been on litter-picking duty or someone very thorough had taken her place. There was nothing, not a sweet wrapper or a polystyrene cup to be seen, nothing in fact to show there'd been a fête. Just the grass which was no longer green but brown, trodden down by so many feet after a whole summer of sun. She felt inordinately fond of it, as if it were a friend, and she hoped for its sake that there might be a week of rain.

'Thomas Everson speaking.'

For a moment Lily couldn't think who she'd called. 'Oh yes. I was ringing about the Sea House.'

Thomas Everson sounded surprised. 'We don't usually get anyone wanting to rent it at this time of year.

'Yes . . .' he hesitated, when she asked if it was possible to take it on a long let. 'I'll have to think. If you want it for several months, then I'm sure we can work something out. It's better than having it empty. Do you know the house?'

'Yes, I'm in the village now.'

'Then you may know the water sometimes rises. Of course there are all sorts of sea defences now, weather warnings and such like, coastal patrols, but it does put some people off. Although of course there is a boat. How much can you afford?'

How much could she afford? Her mind was whirring.

'Could you manage £300 a month? That's what I usually charge out of season. And you leave money for the telephone.'

'Yes, of course.' She could make that much waitressing and still have at least four days to paint.

'Well, you can collect the key from a Mrs Cobbe on Church Lane. She'll have a dust round for you before you move in. There's just one thing . . .'

'Yes?'

'There's someone . . . How to put it? Someone, a family friend, who likes to sleep in the boat. Don't be alarmed, he won't harm you, and if it's not too much trouble and I hope you don't mind . . . but if you could offer him a cup of tea or a sandwich from time to time?'

'Yes.'

'We all try and keep an eye on him in the village, you see.'

'Yes.' Lily's throat tightened with tears. 'Of course. I didn't realize . . .'

Thomas Everson sighed. 'Well, that's settled then, and the main thing is the house, it won't be empty.'

'Thankyou so much.' Lily felt as if the keys were already in her hand. 'Thankyou again.'

The next morning, early, Lily walked down to look at her house. She climbed the steps and pressed her face against the glass. Inside it was extraordinarily neat. There was a tea cosy arranged around a pot, a spatula, a wooden spoon, even a washing-up brush, hanging from individually labelled hooks. There were labels everywhere, one stuck up beside the fridge. Lily squinted. *Fridge*, it said. But on the walls, leaping out against the wooden white, were paintings of flowers, bright bursts of colour against the tongue and groove. She pressed her face against the glass, straining to take every detail in, when something brushed against her leg. She started so violently she almost fell through the railings of the porch, and then she saw it was Grae's cat.

'Guinness.' She knelt down, nuzzling it behind the ears. 'Where are the others, eh?' Guinness mewed and purred, his white crown shivering with the pleasure of her strokes. 'Come on,' she said, and together they headed in the direction of the hut.

They took the sunken lane behind the beach, the cat, a little in front, its tail so straight, tipped with white like a third eye. They crossed the river, doubled back through the long reeds and came up below the dunes. Lily felt her stomach ripple and flip, but the hut was locked, the table bare, the ashes of the fire a grey smear against the sand. 'Where is he?' She felt aggrieved. 'Where has he been all night?' She rummaged in her pocket for a pen and, finding that she still didn't have one, she started, with the toe of her sandal, to write a message in the sand. *W h e r e t h e . . .* and then, sweeping the sand clean, she formed a giant question mark instead.

Guinness followed her home. He trotted into the kitchen and looked up at her beseechingly as she made tea. What did she have? She'd read somewhere that milk was bad for cats, so she opened a tin of tuna fish and scooped some on to a plate. The poor thing's starving, she thought, feeling doubly offended by Grae, and she heaped on the left-over pasta from last night. Guinness purred as he ate it up, licking up the tomato and cheese, and when it was gone he sauntered into the sitting-room and, seeing her pile of material, he curled himself into it and fell asleep.

Lily sat at the table with her tea. The house, the garden, the Green, all seemed unusually quiet. She hung her head. What must it have been like for Nick? Mortification flooded over her and she tried to imagine him waiting outside for her all night. There was a stack of paper on the table and she began to make a letterhead.

The Sea House
Steerborough
Suffolk.

She added a sketch of the house, its steps and stilts, and the terrace above, with a tiny figure, looking out.

Dear Nick,

I'm sorry about the weekend . . . going on like that. She looked out of the window. Was she sorry? She didn't know, but suddenly none of it seemed to be his fault. *I hope your journey home wasn't too bad, or is the AA man your new best friend? I've been thinking about what you said . . .* She began to chew the top of her pen. *Living in the present. Drifting around. Anyway, I don't know why, and I can't expect you to understand, but I thought I'd try living in the present. Here. I've rented another place, at least until Christmas. Somewhere fantastic –* she put an arrow shooting to the top – *with sea views and No Brown. I imagine you'll want me to come and get my things . . . I'm sorry. I promise I didn't plan this, but we need to sort things out.* Lily sat for a long time looking at the letter. She had an ache right in the centre of her chest. *I suppose we'll need to sort out money. I won't be able to keep paying two lots of rent.* She felt inexplicably tender towards him. She could almost feel the warmth of his shoulders as he'd pressed her against him that last time. Why had she resisted? Why had she let her mind chatter on so resentfully about what he'd said or not? Maybe she was better off on her own. *Thankyou for being so patient, Nick, and we'll talk very soon.* She added two seagulls to her drawing. Their wings like kisses, ticks against the sky. *You don't have to write. I'll ring. Love, L.*

On Tuesday morning she bicycled into Eastonknoll and walked through the town. There was an advertisement for a paper boy or girl, age 13 to 73. A full-time assistant was needed in the clothes shop, but the advert in the window of the hotel was gone. Lily pushed open the door. The hotel smell of the place, toast and chintz and carpet, hit her as she walked in. There was a sort of pulpit, low enough to lean on, behind which sat two girls. 'I was wondering,' she said, 'if there were any jobs available. There was a sign for a waitress . . . In the window.'

One of the girls smiled. 'There aren't any jobs right now. But after next week when a lot of the girls go back to college, there'll be plenty of work then.'

'Shall I come back, or could I fill in a form now?'

'All right.' She took up a pen. 'Have you had experience?'

'Yes.' Lily leant over the ledge. 'I worked in a restaurant in Covent Garden for four years.'

'London?' The girl was impressed and, although Lily knew it was ridiculous, she felt rather proud.

'Silver Service?'

'Yes.'

'Day or night?'

'Sorry?'

'Which shifts would you prefer?'

'I don't mind. No. Evening.' She imagined it might be wonderful to cycle home at midnight, to fly over the river bridge and wave at Bob the Bog as he swished past her in the dark.

'You can come back next Monday, and the manager will tell you anything you need to know.' The girl smiled at her, and then she turned to an ancient and extravagantly smart couple who were tottering down the stairs.

Lily cycled back to Steerborough, stopping for cat food at the shop, and then, unable to resist, she cycled down the track and over the river bridge until the beach huts came into view. She expected nothing, was certain the place would be deserted, but even before she saw them she heard Em and Arrie chattering.

'Hello.' She tried to keep her voice steady. They looked up at her and back down at a pile of string and sticks.

'We're making a kite,' Arrie said, and Em began to tape a plastic shape on to a frame of sticks. Lily crouched down beside them, her stomach jittery, terrified suddenly of seeing Grae, but when she looked up he was standing outside the beach hut, leaning against the door.

Shakily, she moved towards him. 'I wanted to say,' she said, 'about the other day. I'm really sorry, it's just you gave me a fright.'

'You're sorry?' His eyes were cold. 'I won't put up with it, being attacked.'

'Of course.' Lily swallowed. 'Why should you?'

He looked at her, a warning. 'I don't know what you mean.'

'Dad.' The children were around him. 'Show her what we found. Show her.' They were digging into his pocket, but Grae was first. He drew out his hand and opened it to reveal a small flat stone. There was a face drawn on it, in ink, and underneath, the four letters of her name.

'That's amazing.' Lily took the stone, her fingers just for a second grazing his palm. 'Of all the pebbles on the beach.' The face was not hers, though. Round with a feathery fringe, the eyes elaborately lashed.

'We found it at Minsfurd.' Em slipped a hand into hers. 'There was a washing-line exhibition, and somebody had a stall. We made Dad buy it.'

'It was brilliant,' Arrie said. 'And the washing-line that won, it was actually a horse, with reins made out of wire to hang the clothes on. Dad's going to enter something next year. Aren't you, Dad?'

Grae didn't answer.

'Mum says she'll help him. If we move back to the farm. She used to make loads of things before . . .' She looked up, hopeful. 'Before she had us, I mean.'

'Oh, go on, Dad,' Arrie chimed in. 'Mum did say she was sorry.' She'd tied a tail to the kite and now she ran with it along the beach. 'Uggleswade, Uggleswade. We can live at Uggleswade.'

'Uggleswade, Uggleswade . . .' Em followed her. 'Throw it up into the air, Arrie. Go on. Throw it.'

They stood and watched the children leap and shriek along the beach, chasing the kite as it arced and twirled and then dived down into the ground.

'So . . .' Lily said, 'you're trying again.' She remembered and handed the pebble back.

Grae took it. He nodded, his hat pulled half over his ears, his eyes turned away, and then at the last minute he caught her hand. 'Lily,' he whispered. 'I'm sorry.' There was a scream from the girls and the kite was up. 'I have to try with Sue, you see.'

'Yes,' she said. 'OK.'

He kissed her very lightly, and then, the kite above them, its tail fluttering, the girls came charging back.

Grae dropped her hand.

'Bye.' Lily bent down to embrace them. 'Bye,' she said more quietly to Grae. She walked past the hut and, glancing inside, she saw that their things were already packed.

Her bike was where she'd left it, stranded on the dune, the tin of Whiskas on its side in the basket. I forgot to tell them I've got Guinness. She stood there looking at the tin, knowing if she went back she'd cry, but when she arrived at Fern Cottage she found the cat so fast asleep in its mound of printed flowers that, even though she tried, it would not be moved.

41

Dear Max,

Thankyou so much for forwarding your address. I expect you will be interested to know that Elsa gave birth to twins! A little premature, but safely, on the 22nd May. Elsa has recovered quite incredibly and in order that she can get the help she needs (with no surviving family) she has come to live with me at Marsh End. The babies are thriving. She has called them Albert L. and Robert L., and they really are a delight. I would have written before but, with one thing and another, I haven't been able to find the time. Please do keep in touch with us and let us know about your new life.

With kind thoughts, Gertrude Jilks.

PS Alf is like a brother to both.

42

Lily was up early, adding the finishing touches to her first painting of the sky, when the postman knocked on the door.

'Good morning.' He handed her a parcel, and she thanked him with such feeling that he flushed and turned away.

My God, she thought, I must be lonely, and for a moment she stood shocked in the hall.

The parcel was from Nick. *Dear Lily* . . . Paint from her hands made thumb prints on the letter as she tipped the parcel's contents out on to the table. There were two packages, both wrapped round with thick layers of tissue, and Lily held them in her hand, feeling their irregular shapes as she continued to read. *Please, Lily, don't come and get your things. I've been thinking about what you said, and you're right, why shouldn't you make plans? Let's start with Christmas. We could go somewhere special with the profit from this job, or I could come to Suffolk. Anywhere, I mean it, as long as the sofa isn't brown. But before then I need to hear your voice. Open your present (it's already been charged), get in the car, and drive up the A12. When you find a signal, press 1, hold down for three seconds, listen, and then, please, call me back.*

Lily could feel her heart thumping as very slowly she unwrapped a mobile phone. It was small and silver. Very carefully she carried it to the car, laid it on the seat beside her, glancing at it almost constantly to see when the signal bars would appear. She stopped by the field of pigs. They had had babies again, or were they different pigs? But they lay outside their houses, squelched into the mud, while the tiny, sausage-pink animals squealed round them in a throng. Her fingers were trembling as she pressed the 1. She held it down as she put it to her ear.

'You have one new message,' she was informed and then Nick

was on the line. 'Lily it's me. There's something I've been wanting to say.' His voice went low and she felt cold, then hot. 'I love you, Lily. Did you hear that? I love you.' Nick started to laugh. 'It's not so hard, you're right. I love you, I love you. I've been wanting to say that since the first night we met.'

'You have no new messages.' The woman's voice cut in, but Lily kept the phone pressed to her ear.

For a long time she sat and looked at the pigs. They were smiling, she was sure of it, even when twelve small piglets all pushed and butted at their sides.

'Nick?' Her heart was thumping. 'I got your message. Thankyou. Thankyou so much. Ahh . . .' No, she couldn't say it to an answerphone. 'Let's meet up. I'll be expecting you at the Sea House, on Saturday night. Please come. It's my first night there. So . . . I'll make a special supper, and if it's high tide, park up by The Ship and I'll row over and get you in the boat.' She lowered her voice. She could see this was addictive. 'And Nick, thankyou. I can't say it now . . . But . . .' She took a deep breath. 'I'll see you then.'

Acknowledgements

I would like to thank Otto Samson and A.W. Freud for sending me their memoirs, 'Moorfred,' and 'Before the Anticlimax,' which proved to be a great help. I would also like to thank Sandra Heidecker and Katharina Bielenberg for translating so many of my grandfather Ernst Freud's letters. Many thanks are due to Wally Webb for telling me about the scroll, and to Richard Scott for showing it to me and alerting me to the correspondence between John Doman Turner and his mentor Spencer Gore. I am extremely grateful to Frederick Gore for letting me sit and read these letters, making it possible to create the 'great artist' Cuthbert Henry, and also to Karl Kolwitz, who, with no warning of my arrival, welcomed me to the island of Hiddensee and caught an eel for my lunch. Many thanks to Shawn Slovo for providing me with a silent room in which to work, and as always to David Morrissey for encouragement and support.

ESTHER FREUD

HIDEOUS KINKY

Two little girls are taken by their mother to Morocco on a 1960s pilgrimage of self-discovery. For Mum it is not just an escape from the grinding conventions of English life but a quest for personal fulfilment; her children, however, seek something more solid and stable amidst the shifting desert sands.

'Just open the book and begin, and instantly you will be first of all charmed, then intrigued and finally moved by this fascinating story' *Spectator*

'Delightful ... sparkles with allure' *The Times Literary Supplement*

PEERLESS FLATS

Sixteen-year-old Lisa moves to London at the close of the '70s, hoping to follow in her older sister Ruby's footsteps. Ruby has cropped hair, a drug habit and not one, but two unsuitable men. Enrolling on an acting course, Lisa decides that she too will enjoy living life to the full.

Yet Lisa finds herself burdened by responsibility. Whatever her own problems, those of her mother, her sister and even her small brother Max, always seem greater and more urgent. Striking out, she tracks her own path through the city, dabbling with drugs and romance, and refusing to lose faith in her belief that something fantastic is about to happen to mark the beginning of the rest of her life...

'Moving, compulsive and humane' *Spectator*

'Freud sounds out as a clear, attractive voice in the literary hubbub' *Observer*

'A delightful read' *The Times*

ESTHER FREUD

GAGLOW

Whilst posing for her father's latest painting, pregnant actress Sarah learns of the existence of Gaglow, the family's grand East German country estate seized before the war. With the fall of the Berlin Wall Gaglow is to be returned and Sarah finds herself compelled to discover the nature of her family's past.

Interweaving Sarah's pregnancy with her grandmother's childhood at Gaglow, Esther Freud brilliantly unites four generations of a family in a story marked by loss and time.

'Freud's prose is lyrical, her characters remarkable, and her story compelling' *Library Journal*

'A shrewd and absorbing novel, a near-seamless meshing of family feeling, history and imagination' *New York Times Book Review*

THE WILD

In the 1970s, in an old bakery converted into a home, two single-parent families have come together under one roof. For nine-year-old Tess it is a new start and she sees in William – the tall, blonde guitar-playing father of three – both the father she craves and a partner for her mother, Francine. Her brother Jake, however, feels nothing for William but contempt.

When Francine becomes involved with William, Tess – eager to share in their love – tries to please the adults as well as win Jake round. But Tess soon finds that good intentions don't always bring happiness and that adults are sometimes capable of making mistakes ...

'A beautiful book, savage and tender by turns. Nobody else can write this well about the bravery and the sad wisdom of children' Jonathan Coe

'It's wonderful... Tell every parent (and step-parent) you know to read *The Wild*' *The Times*